YELLOW LOCUST

JUSTIN JOSCHKO

Month9Books

Month9Books

For Lavender and Hannela:
May the world you inherit fare better than this one

AMERICA-THAT-WAS

Prairie
Republic

The Middle
Wastes

Republic of
California

Fallowfield

Visalia ★

Juarez

Far
Sea

Mejica

La Republique
Du Quebec

La Reine
Noyee ★

Jericho
★

Free State
of Niagara

Vineland
★

New
Canaan

Outer
Baronies

• K City

The New
New Confederacy
Atlanta
★

Delta
Sea

Galileian
Ocean

YELLOW LOCUST

Part I: Fallowfield

1: Praise New Canaan, Praise the Lord

Selena and Simon trudged west. Cracks snaked across crumbling asphalt, hemorrhaging weeds singed crisp by the sun. Neck-high stalks of yellow grass choked the once wide road into a claustrophobic pathway, its overgrown edges ragged and swaying in the frugal breeze. Selena pulled a small wagon behind her, which hopped and jerked over the cragged pavement. Its battered wheels whined for oil.

Simon wiped his forehead with one chapped palm, leaving a miasmic trail of mingled sweat and grime. Sunlight played off the rims of his glasses. His normally pale face flushed.

"Can we stop a minute?" he called.

Selena responded without slowing down. "Wait 'til we find some shade. You'll fry out here."

"I'm frying already."

"Then walk faster."

Groaning, Simon grabbed his sweater by its lower fringe and flapped. A pathetic wisp of stagnant air brushed against his belly. He longed to remove the sweater, but knew that his pasty skin, if exposed, would crackle and burn in minutes.

A frieze of buildings rose in the distance. Selena heaved an inward sigh of relief. They'd encountered such places before on their long trek through the great puckering abscess that was the center of this continent. Once great cities before the Last War a hundred years earlier, they stood now as ghosts of the endless plains, their crumbling buildings serving as nothing but a shell for some tiny, hardscrabble town carved into their bellies. The few citizens of these places—only K City boasted more than a hundred—seemed edgy and desperate and somehow misshapen, twisted by hardship into bent, gnome-like shapes. The vacant buildings of their dead cities held the ubiquitous yellow grass at bay, allowing them to scrape meagre livings from soil once entombed in asphalt and threaded with rotted power lines and gas pipes and the iron guts of an ancient sewage system. Such places saw few outside visitors, though so far, Selena had always found at least one farmer willing to trade good Standard for a few leeks or a head of cabbage. Selena hoped the trend would continue. It had been almost a week since they'd encountered another living soul, and their supplies were dwindling, especially their water.

By the time they reached the city's outskirts, it was dusk and they still hadn't encountered a soul. Buildings towered over them like the walls of a great grey canyon, channelling the wind into a steady gust that carried with it the stink of ancient sewage and rusting metal. Beads of glass from long-shattered windows littered the asphalt, jagged edges worn smooth by a century of wind and rain.

The grass followed the siblings into town, looming silently along the highway shoulders, lancing up through broken sidewalk slabs, squatting in the cavernous lobbies of derelict skyscrapers. It stalked them all the way to the city center, where a square kilometer of turf and asphalt had been pared away to uncover the silty soil beneath. Stakes with tips painted green, blue, and orange still jutted evenly along the field's southern edge, though whether the colors signified crop rotation or ownership, Selena couldn't say. Only one plant grew there now, and she was willing to bet it hadn't been deliberately planted. The yellow grass devoured every inch of naked soil, creating a neck-high carpet of brittle, oily stalks. *We aren't gonna find any food on offer here*, Selena thought, though she kept this opinion to herself—the last thing her brother needed was more bad news.

A fountain stood on a cobbled square beside the field, its ledge chipped and weathered. A bronze woman stood atop its stone platform, her face tarnished and scaly with grime. She held aloft a jug with a broken handle. Water dribbled from its spout. *No food, maybe, but water's more important anyway.*

Selena knelt to the water. A caustic stench of grease and bitter herbs rose from the pool. A skein of shimmery oil coated the water, stirred to a rainbow froth where the trickling spout spilled its endless contents. Selena rolled up her pant legs, removed her shoes, and waded into the fountain. The water's scummy skin clung to her leg hairs. She cupped her hands beneath the dribble.

Even before the water touched her lips, she knew it was bad. The stench of it lapped at her face like a hungry tongue. She sipped anyway, gagged, spat. Running or still, the water was hopelessly befouled. Its taste and smell lingered long enough for her to place it: the smell of the yellow grass, the few times she'd been forced to push her way directly through it. Not content with razing the town's crops, the vile stuff had also poisoned its water supply. *Whatever this shit is, it's thorough.*

Simon stared into the pool. The face it reflected was wan and distorted.

"This place is spooky," he said.

"It's not spooky. It's just abandoned."

"That's what makes it spooky. What do we do now?"

Selena rubbed her damp legs clean with a rag, wincing with distaste as the greasy water trickled over her fingers. "We move on, I guess. The water's foul, and I seriously doubt we're gonna find any food. But first, I want to check out some of the buildings near the field."

Simon chewed his lower lip. "You want to go in those things? Why?"

"Someone lived here once. They might've left things behind."

"Like food? In jars and stuff?"

If they were stupid or insane, maybe. "Could be. If nothing else, it'll let us sleep indoors for a change."

Though as run down and haggard as the rest of the city, the tenements next to the field at least showed signs of having supported life sometime this century. Windows bore bandages of plywood or ancient tarpaulin, and the litter of broken glass and other debris had been swept away. Tables stood beneath a jury-rigged awning, a couple of which even held ceramic mugs of stale or foetid water. Selena wondered if there might not be people left here after all, living off preserves or tending a rooftop garden. She knocked on the door of the nearest building.

"Hello? Hello? Is anyone here? My brother and I are travellers. We've come a long way and could use some food and water. We have Standard to trade."

Silently, Selena counted to thirty. When no one replied, she tried the door and found it opened freely.

The room was small, plain, and mostly bare. A steel drum punctured and bent into a makeshift stove stood in one corner, its roughly-hewn mouth blackened with soot. Above it, ductwork harvested from a neighboring tower hung from a hole in the ceiling, forming a crude chimney. A table sat in the far corner beside a ransacked cupboard, its surface dotted with scraps of inedible food—potato peels, corn husks, and shells from a nut Selena couldn't identify. The cupboard was empty save for a couple of spent matches and a cracked jar, its insides mouldering into grey-black goo.

Simon stood in the doorway, tugging nervously at the hem of his shirt.

"I don't like this place, Selena. It doesn't feel right in here."

"It's just a house, Simon."

"It's not a house. People live in houses."

"People lived here too."

"But not anymore."

Selena studied a bit of potato skin between thumb and forefinger. It felt slimy to the touch, its starches dissolved into pungent liquid. "No."

The second building they tried was much like the first, as was the third.

In the fourth building, they found bodies.

There were three of them—a child and two adults. The child was a girl; Selena could tell by the stringy blond hair sprawling down past her shoulders and the skirt draped over her matchstick thighs. The adults could have been anything. Their wrinkled skin clung to their bones like wet tissue paper, so thin it seemed the tiniest nudge would tear it wide open. Shadows pooled in the hollows of their cheeks, their sunken eyes, and in the valleys between each rib. They huddled together on a filthy mattress in the middle of the floor, their arms hooked around their vanished bellies, their hands atrophied into brittle, shovel-like appendages. Nearby stood a Lucite table with three place settings, each plate brimming with dried out clippings of yellow grass. In desperation, they'd tried to eat the only crop their town could grow. Selena recalled the sip of fountain water and shuddered. *Even starving, it must've tasted awful.*

"Stay outside, Simon. You don't need to see this."

A quiet moan told her she'd spoken too late. He bent forward, his glasses sliding down his nose, and gagged up a wad of stringy saliva. Selena stroked his back.

"Hey. Hey. It's alright. They're not gonna hurt you."

Simon's retching subsided. He swallowed with an audible *plunk* and rubbed his eyes. "I know."

"Let's go. If they didn't find anything to eat, neither will we."

They left town as the last of the sun's light drained from the sky. Selena would have welcomed a night on a mattress—even a saggy one with rust-eaten springs—but she knew without asking that Simon needed peace of mind more than a proper bed, and the ghosts in that place were still too fresh for him. She thought back on the villages she'd passed, each besieged by legions of yellow grass, cracking asphalt and shearing steel on its slow but inexorable journey to their arable hearts. How long until they ended up like this one?

The yellow grass was unknown in New Canaan—at least, she'd never heard it spoken of before—but beyond her country's borders it seemed to consume the world. The towns they'd passed through had different names for it: bitchweed, plague wheat, cropkiller. Words more spat than spoken, often punctuated by a solemn gesture, a cross or evil eye. The townsfolk knew little about where it came from, blaming gods or demons or the sins of some nefarious ancestor. Whatever its cause, it was everywhere, and seemed to grow thicker and taller the farther west they went.

It can't go on forever, she told herself. True enough, but it didn't have to. Another week was about all they could manage. After that they'd face two or maybe three days of staggering as dehydration closed its claws around their throats. A week of walking didn't buy you much in this monochromatic wasteland. And the grass gave no sign of abating. These thoughts piled onto Selena's shoulders. She shrugged them off as best she could, but they were barbed and sticky and clung to her skin like burrs of lead.

"Selena?" Simon's voice was parched and tired.

"Mmm?"

"Can we stop for the night?"

She glanced around as if this square mile of poison prairie might be different from the thousand that had preceded it. "Sure. We'll lose our light soon anyway."

They lifted the wagon and carried it into the grass. Sallow fronds licked and scratched at their faces, leaving an oily residue on their skin. They walked about fifteen feet, put the wagon down, and set about stomping flat a small circle. Stalks crunched beneath their feet, pulpy innards oozing bile. Selena continued stomping with a small smirk of pleasure. *Feel this, you bastards? I'm breaking you. Not the other way around.*

They supped on a can of kidney beans, passing the spoon back and forth after each bite. Simon stirred the dregs in an effort to scoop up the last bit of congealed bean juice. Selena offered Simon her canteen. He drank two deep glugs, raised the canteen to his lips for a third, and stopped himself. He handed it back to Selena, who took a swig of her own—really, more of a sip, but she mimed a bigger movement to put Simon's mind at ease—and, clasping the canteen between her knees, filled it with water from their last remaining jug. She hissed through her teeth as a few drops missed their mark. The parched earth drank them up greedily.

After supper, they rolled out their thin blankets and slept. Or tried to, anyhow. Heat groped Selena beneath the covers while the nubby remnants of the grass they'd trodden flat prodded her back—just one more reason to hate the beshitted stuff.

Selena's hand slipped inside her pants pocket and touched a corner of cool plastic. Her fingers curled around the object and squeezed until its edges bit into her palm. It weighed barely more than a pencil, but her father had handed it over as if tying a two-ton millstone around her neck. She recalled how he'd motioned her into the front hallway, his usually smooth face creased with worry. She'd studied that look and the object that had summoned it, and asked the first thing that came to her mind—a shallow question, maybe, but she sensed something dark in the deeper waters and hesitated to wade out too far.

"A data stick? What's this for?"

Her father glanced over his shoulder, the first rays of predawn light rolling like a fine mist through the kitchen window, while Selena's mother fussed over the buckles of a leather knapsack, which she'd filled to bursting with preserves and dried fruit and other essentials. Outside the Red Bell tolled its summons for the coming ceremony—the Salters were expected to file in early, but the Seraphim could arrive just as the spectacle began, their time being considered that much more important.

"Keep it with you." He spoke in a whisper over the drone of the washing machine, an ancient cube of white metal refurbished from the Last War. It did a lousy job with clothes, but was useful for drawing a curtain of sound between them and the angel ears imbedded in their bedroom and living room walls. "Wait for us at the cottage for two weeks. No longer. There should be food enough to support you both easily for at least that long. We'll be along before then and the four of us will arrange passage west. We have people looking out for us."

"Everything will be fine," added Selena's mother, still toying with the knapsack's buckles.

"And if two weeks is up and you haven't showed?"

"Then you go on without us. West. Over the mountains to the Republic. Don't stop until you're at the coast, in Visalia. Find a man named Hoster Telaine and give him that there." He pointed to the data stick.

"Why? I don't understand."

Selena's mother chewed her lower lip. Even in the hallway with the washing machine running, such loose talk was a terrible risk. There was no telling exactly where the angel ears stood or what they could hear.

"There's a war brewing, Selena. Between New Canaan and the Republic. A true war, not this cloak and dagger business we've been doing. New Canaan intends to march next year with its full strength."

Selena blinked once in surprise. For fifty years, New Canaan and The Republic of California had been bitter enemies, and in that time neither had fired a single direct shot at the other in anger. They were as two giants clinging to the edges of a dying continent, New Canaan on the east and the Republic on the west, glaring at one another balefully across its wild and empty expanse.

"They wouldn't dare," Selena said.

"In the past, no. But they're growing, and they're ready. The Republic ... isn't. They can't drive people the same way New Canaan can."

"Why not?" Selena was surprised to hear this, as in her parents' eyes, the Republic of California could do no wrong.

"Because they treat them like people," added her father. His voice was uncharacteristically harsh, its tone curdled and sour. "Not ..." he seemed unable to find a word for it.

"But still. How could they seriously manage an invasion? The Republic's on the other side of the continent. And Niagara could flank them if they tried."

Selena's mother shook her head. "Not anymore, it couldn't. Niagara has fallen."

Selena's mouth went dry. "I ... but how? When?"

"The Archbishop orchestrated a coup. Delduca and his men have been deposed."

Selena rubbed her eyes. Her entire life she'd grown up in a traitor's household, catching glimpses of her parents' silent war against the despotic state that housed them. But it seemed the war was silent no longer. The Republic was in New Canaan's crosshairs, its sole ally conquered. Though little more than a city state, Niagara was the only place besides The Republic of California to openly stand against New Canaan. Now, Selena supposed, The Republic stood alone.

"Okay, that's bad, but Niagara's just a tiny peninsula, right?"

"It was big enough to stand half a century. Now it belongs to the Archbishop, and so do its dams."

Selena hadn't considered this. Niagara's hydroelectric stations were the source of its power—literally and figuratively—and the chief reason the beleaguered city-state could hold its own against larger factions. With Niagara toppled and Delduca deposed, all that power flowed straight into New Canaan. Considering how electricity was rationed, even among the Seraphim, such a large influx meant big things for the state.

"It gets worse. We have an ear in the Diocese of Plague. Last week he slipped us that data stick." Selena's mother pointed to the device in Selena's hand. "On it are several hundred pages of notes and schematics for a new weapon. It's been in the works for a long time. Now it's done, and the Archbishop intends to use it."

"The attack's planned for the spring," her father added. "They're going to unleash the weapon somehow—it goes in the soil, I don't understand all the details. If the Republic get the files in time, they can prepare, find a way to protect themselves. If they don't, it's all over."

Selena hefted the data stick. It was a light thing, almost chintzy, its pale green carapace threatening to crack in her grasp. It was hard to imagine that the outcome of a war pivoted on its axis.

"We made ourselves a copy. You have the original. Whatever happens, you need to get that data to the Republic. By spring at the very latest."

"I won't do it," Selena said. The calmness in her voice shocked her.

"I can't just leave you."

"You will. The Republic needs us." Her mother blinked back tears. "All your life, you've lived in New Canaan. This is all you know. But there's better places than this, Selena, much, much better. It's our job to protect them."

"I know that."

"No, you don't. Not truly."

"Just come with us *now*, then." Selena's voice started to crack and anger seeped in through the fractures. "There's no sense in you staying here. Can't you see that?"

"There's still work to be done," her mother said. "We know the weapon and the timeline, but we still don't have the strategy. There's a source in the Templars we can leverage, but he needs more time. If we can get the attack plans from him, The Republic will have the tools to launch a counterattack."

"And if you shot the Archbishop, they'd be in even better shape. But you can't. If we're in danger, then we should leave. All of us."

Selena's father smiled. It made him look younger. "You don't have to worry about us, kid. We've kept ourselves hidden right under the Archbishop's nose for twenty years. We can manage another two weeks."

"Then why send me and Simon away?"

"It's just a precaution. In two weeks, we'll see you and we'll all go west together."

"That's bullshit," Selena growled. "Why would you say that when all three of us know that's total bullshit?"

"Selena—"

"Bullshit!"

Her father slapped her. He rubbed his hand, as if her cheek had struck his fingers and not the other way around.

"You'll go, Selena." he said. "With or without us, you'll go west."

"You're asking too much," Selena said, her voice watery. She sniffed. Her mother took her hands, turning them over, studying them.

"Nothing is too much for you, Selena. You can do this. You have to do this. I wish it weren't so, but it is. You need to be strong. For us, and for your brother." She let go of Selena's hands and fitted the knapsack onto her shoulders. "Does it feel okay?"

Selena nodded.

A knock sounded on the door, three strikes, quick and forceful. Selena's mother pulled the knapsack from Selena's shoulders and stuffed it behind a chair. Her father waited as long as he dared to answer the door—a couple of moments. A large man with a shaved head stood in the hallway. He wore a stormy grey uniform enlivened only by a pair of decorations pinned to his left breast. The first was a white cross encircled by a crown of green thorns, the New Canaan insignia. The second was a pair of silvery knights atop a red stallion. This, along with the pistol on his belt and the high calibre rifle slung over his shoulder, marked him as a Templar Knight, one of New Canaan's military and law enforcement officers.

"Mr. and Mrs. Flood?"

"Yes, that's us," said Selena's father.

"We're escorting your floor to the Red Theatre, sir. There's to be a large presentation today. Attendance is strongly encouraged. Would you come with me?"

"Of course." Selena's father was well aware of the sort of "encouragement" New Canaan favored. "Dear? Selena? Come along."

They joined a trickle of families led by Templar Knights to the elevator and crowded inside. In the lobby, the trickle became a stream, which became a river, which flowed toward the nearest mag train terminal, its track a silver ribbon stretching across the city. A train pulled up, a sleek-nosed serpent of glass and silvery metal, and the Templar ushered them inside.

"It's kind of you to watch out for us," said Selena's mother. "There's so much danger on the upper decks, after all."

If the Templar Knight noticed this slight, he gave no sign. "It never hurts to be cautious, ma'am."

"I'm sure the Archbishop couldn't agree more."

The pneumatic doors whooshed shut, cutting off the Templar Knight's reply. He stood on the platform, arms clasped behind his back, and watched the train glide out the terminal bay.

Most days the mag trains rode half-empty, ferrying the Seraphim to their destinations in roomy comfort, hundreds of feet above the rabble of Salters and Templar Knights. But when the Red Bell tolled, things got more crowded. Selena had to stand, the fingers of one hand knit tight around a polished steel railing, the other stuffed in her pocket, fidgeting with the data stick. Few people spoke, and those that did used soft, funereal voices. Rowdiness was a sin the Salters got away with, but Seraphim were held to a higher standard.

Jericho rushed by in a blur of chrome and stone and steel. Solar arrays topped each building, fanning outward like the wings of great silver birds. From this height, the city was almost beautiful, a silver-pronged crown adorning the nation state of New Canaan. The buildings glimmered in the hazy sunlight, casting long shadows that veiled the froth and clutter of the streets a hundred feet below, hiding the slums and shanty towns that clung like barnacles to the outer city, the Templar Knights with their loaded machine guns clutched to their chests, the toppled trash cans spewing sour gunk onto rubberized pavement, the addicts and beggars and whores with rotting faces, the oily stain of factory run-off that coated everything. It was easy not to see these things when you kept to the mag trains and office towers, easy to believe the skyline's pretty lies.

"What is this about?" Selena asked, leaning in toward her mother.

"I'm not sure," her mother replied, though the look on her face suggested she had a pretty good idea.

The train glided into Red Station, which, despite its name, bore hardly any color at all. Its floor was a piebald white stone made to simulate marble, its walls corrugated chrome. A clear glass ceiling hung overhead, suspended in a web of steel scaffolding. The passengers filed into its airy expanse, making their way along its inner corridors and over a covered pedestrian bridge.

The stream of people broke into numerous tributaries, each channeled into the balcony reserved for their Diocese. Selena's parents worked for the Diocese of Information, one of New Canaan's most prestigious branches. The seats were carved from oak and padded with cushions of plush red velvet. A graceful steel awning painted a flawless white protected them from sun and rain. Two Templars stood sentinel by the balcony's entrance, and a stooping man ushered Selena and her parents to their seats in the third row.

Beyond the golden railing lay the dirt floor of the Red Theatre. A vast oval of bleachers surrounded the stage, its wooden seats crowded with concentric rings of humanity stratified into New Canaan's rigid class structure. The lowest and largest ring held the Salters, a rowdy and soot-stained horde of factory workers and farmers, miners and longshoremen, loggers and janitors. Above them, prim and timid, were the Shepherds: clerks, shopkeepers, and factory foremen. At the top, ensconced in their gilded boxes, sat the Seraphim: families ordained by the Archbishop and his Cardinals as the state's overseeing elite. Selena's parents belonged to this group, the plushest and most pampered of New Canaan's citizens—and the most closely watched.

Salter, Shepherd, and Seraphim alike fixed their eyes on the center of the Red Theatre, where a strange device stood on enormous iron legs. A pill-shaped container the size of a small shipping freighter, it squatted in the dirt like a monstrous insect, its carapace shining sheets of segmented steel. Below, a great bonfire licked the container's belly. Even in her seat two hundred feet above the theatre floor, Selena could feel the heat of it. It crashed over the onlookers, drenching them with sweat and coating their nostrils with a strange slick odor.

"Andrew!"

The Caspians arrived, a young couple lower in the Diocese, their seats at the back of the balcony. Their son, Brian, was Simon's age, and the two were playing together when the Red Bell tolled.

"Hal, good to see you," said Selena's father. "Thanks for bringing Simon."

"My pleasure. Say, that's some contraption down there, huh?"

"Yeah, you could say that."

"Any idea what it's for?"

"I wish I knew."

Hal Caspian shuffled to his seat. As he found it, another man stepped inside. The aisle cleared in an instant, allowing him an unencumbered walk to the front row. He dressed in a style typical among the Seraphim—dark slacks and a single-breasted blazer fastened with brass buttons and embroidered with New Canaan's cross-in-thorns sigil—though the cocked beret and single epaulet over his left shoulder distinguished him as under-Cardinal. He paused at Selena's row and flicked a rogue lock of trim black hair from his forehead.

"Andrew, Emily! Always a pleasure."

"And for us, under-Cardinal Fontaine," replied Selena's mother, her words frostbitten and brittle. They bounced harmlessly off Fontaine, who wiped a thumbprint from a brass button and smoothed down the front of his blazer.

"Still the mouthpiece of the family, eh Emily?"

"She speaks when she has a mind to, Eric. As do I." Selena's father's tone was less icy, though a crisp formality hedged each syllable.

Fontaine snorted. "You two always were an odd pair. Still, it's good to see you attending. As I recall you've voiced some concern over our little shows here."

"We don't question their necessity, under-Cardinal," said Selena's mother. "Redemption is the lifeblood of our great state. But I confess it can be a little tough to watch at times."

"Yes, well some of us grasp the Archbishop's plans with more facility than others. Nonetheless, I'm glad you could join us. And your lovely children, of course."

"Of course, please pardon our rudeness. Selena, Simon, say hello to the under-Cardinal."

"Hello, under-Cardinal Fontaine," droned Simon in his best schoolboy voice. Selena nodded up at the man.

"Hello."

"Hello to the both of you. I hope you enjoy the show." With a wink and a nod, he descended the rest of the way to his seat, resting his feet on the balcony.

Selena returned her attention to the theatre floor. A scaffold of metal grating led from the top of the container to a gate in the outer theater, forming a stage. A microphone stood atop the scaffold, strafed by twin fifty-foot screens broadcasting a magnetized image of the container and the stage behind it. As Selena watched, a lone figure stepped through the gate and approached the microphone. The audience erupted in deafening cheers. The figure raised a hand and the cheers fell silent. Above him, the screens displayed close-ups of his face, with its sickle nose and pointed chin and probing eyes the color of glacial snow. It was a face everyone in the crowd knew well, for it hung above every altar and stared balefully down from every hall and school assembly and market square.

"Greetings to all of you, my noble flock!" crowed the Archbishop of New Canaan. A silken robe the color of the night sky masked his figure, though Selena noted the boniness of his fingers as he wiggled them in greeting. "I thank you for heeding the call of the Red Bell, and for joining us on this most momentous of days. For today marks a great victory for our Lord, as his wondrous salvation spreads to the darker corners of our continent. A contingent of the faithful, working against terrible odds, but for the flame of the Lord lighting their hearts, has successfully converted the heathenish state of Niagara to a pious dominion of New Canaan."

A collective gasp greeted this comment, followed by a thunder of applause and cheering. The Archbishop bathed in the adoring din, a beatific smile drifting across his face, before he silenced them once more with a soft calming gesture.

"Words cannot capture the noble sacrifice of our Templar Knights, nor the good and Lord-fearing citizens of New Canaan who worked with us to drive out the darkness from their blighted land. Bring him out, please!"

A procession of Templar Knights marched onto the stage, forming two neat rows. Between them walked a man with his hands bound behind his back. He wore a foreign military garb that had been through rough treatment in the past twenty-four hours; his pants were torn and muddy, his shirt stiff with blood. He stared defiantly at the

Archbishop, his hair dishevelled, his chin caked in coarse stubble, his grey moustache matted with dried spit.

"Who's he?" Selena whispered to her mother.

"Aldo Delduca. He's the President of the Free State of Niagara." Her tongue circled her lips. "Or he was, anyway."

The Archbishop held out his arms to Delduca as if in welcome. "This man ruled over a godless empire. He spread filth and corruption among his people, imprisoned those who stood with us, fired indiscriminately on our agents as they brought deliverance to his doorstep. Our blood paints his hands a deep crimson. Such sins require purging. And so we shall expunge them!"

Gears whirred and the container's segmented top opened, plates retracting to reveal a great pool of bubbling oil. The slick smell in the air grew stronger, its odor wet and palpable on Selena's cheeks. Delduca's face paled at the sight of the roiling liquid, though his jaw remained set. *A brave guy,* Selena thought. *For what little good it'll do him.*

"You soul belongs to our Lord, and you will answer his call. It comes for you now. And when you greet him, you shall be cleansed. For this, your body must bathe in our lake of fire. From the banks of hell may even the lowest demon ascend to heaven, once they have washed their sin from their hearts. The Lord is a being of infinite mercy, and I but his humble vessel." Reaching into the folds of his robe, the Archbishop drew a dagger. A single ruby glinted on the pommel like a winking bloodshot eye. The blade curved, fang-like, to a deadly tip. He raised the knife to the crowd, catching ribbons of firelight on its edge.

"So merciful is he, that he offers you a choice. Your body must be cleansed. However, if you wish, I will first anoint you myself, with blood and iron. This is the Lord's mercy, delivered through me. To seek it, you need only kneel before me and give voice your thanks."

Delduca spat at the Archbishop's feet. "Fuck your mercy, you tyrant. You think you've beaten us? You can't kill democracy." His voice was strong and deep and sonorous, loud enough to catch the Archbishop's microphone. He turned to the crowd, his chin thrusting outward defiantly, his eyes twin glints of steel. For a moment, he was a leader again, imperious and immovable as a statue of himself. "You fools are slaves. Every single one of you. Slaves with a lunatic for a master. My people will—"

A Templar Knight drove the butt of his rifle into Delduca's belly. Delduca doubled forward, spewing a thin mess of vomit onto the scaffold. The Templar grabbed him by the hair and yanked him upright, flecks of sick messing his silver moustache. The flash of fire was gone. Now he looked only old and weak ... and scared. The Archbishop's lip curled downward.

"As you wish."

The Templar grabbed Delduca by the arm and dragged him to the edge of the scaffold. A second Templar joined him as Delduca fought. The two Templars lifted him the last twenty yards, his toes scrabbling at the steel grating. He held his composure until the Templars dangled him over the precipice, where it broke with a high and hopeless wail.

"No, please! I'll take mercy! Mercy! *Mercy!*"

A splash, a scream, a hiss of hot oil on raw meat. Delduca writhed for a moment like a drowning man then laid still, his clothes flaking off to reveal blackening skin.

Selena's fingernails dug into her armrests. She clenched down on the sickness rising up inside her, aware she must, above all else, keep her composure. The Archbishop was having no such trouble. He preened along the stage like a strutting rooster.

"Niagara's sins are many. As you all know, absolution is not a bauble to be purchased at a market stall, nor a fruit to be plucked from a fecund tree. It must be bought and paid for in blood and in fire, earned through the righteous gauntlet of sacrifice. We shall save Niagara, as we shall one day save the heathens to the west, and the lands beyond the Galilean Ocean and the Far Sea. Now comes the first step on the path to global righteousness!"

With a flourish, the Archbishop stepped aside, deftly snatching the microphone from its stand. One of the Templars took the stand itself, leaving a clear path to the roiling cauldron. For a moment, the crowd stared as one into the dark mouth of the gate. The darkness shimmered, parted like a curtain, and a knot of people trudged onto the stage. They stared at the crowd with dumb livestock eyes. Men and women, young and old, dressed in soiled finery and dressed in rags, it didn't seem to matter. Selena saw a man whose left leg ended at the knee hobbling with a single crutch, his every step a gamble. She saw a woman clutching a toddler to her chest, silently stroking the child's downy hair. She saw beaten soldiers holding their wounded upright, their faces bronze masks bearing no emotion. Their footsteps rang out atop the scaffold as the Salters hooted and jeered. A wall of Templars marched behind them, jabbing the stragglers onward with polearms and clubbing those who tried to get away.

"Five hundred souls in need of salvation! Five hundred souls who took up arms against us, who hid their leader from our justice, who resisted us in their minds and hearts. Five hundred souls tainted by sin. We will cleanse them, my flock! Today marks Niagara's baptism, that it may be born in the eyes of our Lord!"

Selena had seen dozens of executions in the past, hundreds. But never one on this scale. The stream of people seemed to flow on forever, a slurry of broken humanity sludging into the roiling cauldron. Some wept, some pleaded, a few fought against the tide of pikes and halberds pushing them forward. But most simply marched, their faces bleary and distant, as hopelessly conquered as the land they'd come from.

"Praise New Canaan!" cried the Archbishop. "Praise the Lord!"

The oil's hissing intensified, the sound followed shortly by a chorus of screams, fresh shrieks erupting as the older ones dissolved into something wet and gurgling and less than human. The crowd took up the Archbishops words, stringing them into a chant. "Praise New Canaan! Praise the Lord! Praise New Canaan! Praise the Lord!"

Selena felt something sharp dig into her forearm. Simon's fingers grabbed her harder than she would have thought him capable. His face turned a noxious green. Selena took his hand in hers and squeezed. She caught his eye and with vast effort hoisted up a small, reassuring smile. *Have to be strong,* she thought desperately. Her free hand slipped into her pocket, where it cradled the data stick between sweaty figures. The

Archbishop's words rang in her head: *we shall save Niagara, as we shall one day save the heathens to the west, and the lands beyond the Galilean Ocean and the Far Sea.*

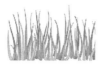

Lying on her bed of crushed grass, Selena put the data stick away, patting it to be sure it nestled cozily against her thigh. She listened to Simon's breathing. When she was convinced he was asleep, she slipped from beneath her covers and hunkered over him. They'd come a long way through a harsh and blighted landscape. The kid had done well, all things considered, but he was just about worn out. Sores clustered around the corners of his mouth, and baggy patches of purple-grey flesh frowned beneath his eyes. If he didn't get some proper rest soon, Selena wasn't sure he'd be able to go on. Even if they eked out a muddy stream or some wild onion, exhaustion alone would finish him. They needed real food, real shelter. People. And soon. Her mother's words echoed in her head as if carried to her on the breeze: *you need to be strong. For us, and for your brother.* All the strength in the world couldn't help her parents now. But she could still be strong for her brother.

She brushed a strand of hair from his forehead. His face softened at her touch, the knots of worry beneath his skin untying. He stirred. Selena scrambled back under her blanket and feigned sleep. Simon shifted position, muttered a mouthful of faint, garbled syllables, and lay still. Selena watched him for a moment before drawing her blanket up to her neck and rolling over. She touched the plastic rectangle a final time before allowing her hand to fall free. *Salvation's coming, California. It came for Niagara and now it's coming for you.*

You just better pray we get there first.

2: The Green

Leon felt the wall shift beneath his weight. Frank looked up from the stockpot as the shack tottered drunkenly to one side.

"Jesus Christ, you clumsy bastard! Be careful. You'll bring this whole place down on our heads."

"I'm sorry! I tripped."

"You tripped," Frank muttered. "Quit moving around so much then." He stirred with increased vigor.

Leon crossed his arms. "I wish we could get a bigger cookhouse."

"Yeah, well, what do you recommend? You wanna do this shit in town? Or out on the road, where the Shepherds could see us if they passed by?"

"No. I'm just sayin'."

"Yeah, well quit sayin' and start thinkin'."

Making small, deliberate movements, Leon crouched down to better see the pot's bubbling contents. Condensation from the steam mixed with the sweat on his forehead.

"Almost there," Leon said.

"A few minutes to go yet," replied Frank.

"Do you think—"

Frank's head jerked up, the motion sharp enough to cleave Leon's sentence in two.

"Do you hear that?"

"What," Leon asked, his voice a hoarse whisper.

"Listen," hissed Frank.

Leon listened. Footsteps. Two sets by the sound of it. And something else, too. A low rumble of wheels on pavement.

Frank tugged at his hair, his eyes bulging with fear. "Shit shit shit! I told you this place was no good!"

Leon strained his ears, groping for some other identifying sound. "I think it's coming from down the road."

Frank's tongue circled his lips. He got to his feet and peered through the rectangular slit in the wall that constituted the shack's lone window.

"Whoever it is, they're on foot."

Leon peered over Frank's shoulder. The window was only a few inches wide and he couldn't get much of a view. Still, he caught an eyeful of the field between them and the road, and could see nothing poking above the shitgrass.

"Maybe it isn't a person. Maybe it's just an animal or something," Leon suggested.

"What animal makes a noise like that? Someone's out there, looking for something."

Frank wrapped the handles of the stockpot in old rags and poured its contents into a small aluminum bowl. Splinters of crackling white mineral bounced over the rim and onto the dirt floor.

"Damn!"

Frank picked what splinters he could out of the dirt, dropped them in the bowl, and stashed the stockpot and hotplate in the corner.

"Alright, let's get out of here."

They crouched down among the shitgrass, peering at the road from between two large, greasy stalks.

"You don't gotta worry about getting busted," said Leon. "Look."

He pointed down the road. Two figures walked toward them. In the lead was a girl of maybe eighteen pulling a wagon. At least, Leon thought she was a girl. She wore her blond hair short, and her arms, though lean and hairless, were thick with cords of muscle. Her build was lithe and athletic, though partially hidden beneath a coarse poncho studded with patches. A bespectacled boy of maybe eleven shuffled several steps behind her, his shoulders slumped. He looked sort of like an albino, though there was a bit of color to his hair.

"Who the hell are they?" Frank whispered. "I've never seen either of 'em before."

"Maybe they're from K city, Frank! Or even farther!"

Frank's face broke into a wide, lupine smile. "What I really wanna know is, what's in that wagon?"

Frank tucked the bowl into a hollow between two tufts of shitgrass. He waited until the two kids were about ten feet away before stepping into view. The boy jumped, but the girl—she was definitely a girl; Leon noticed the slight curve of her hips and the swell of small breasts beneath her poncho—simply glanced up from the road. Leon followed him out a second later, his face flattening into a self-conscious frown.

"Hi there, folks," Frank said. He kept his tone as light and friendly as possible. "Hot day for travelling, wouldn't you say?"

The girl's grey eyes seemed to look both at and through Frank, as if he were nothing but a shadow discoloring a patch of the road ahead of her.

"Whatchya got there?"

Still the girl said nothing. The boy fidgeted behind her, more uncomfortable than frightened.

"I guess you're heading into Fallowfield. Well, we're what you'd call import inspectors. We make sure nothing nasty crosses town limits. And of course, we have to confiscate anything we think ain't appropriate."

Frank gave this comment a second to sink in. For all Leon could tell, the girl hadn't heard a thing. For a moment, the only sound was the wind through the grass. Leon shifted his weight from side to side. Refusing to be unnerved, Frank stepped forward, motioning Selena aside and bending down to look in the wagon.

"Let's see what we got he—"

The girl didn't seem to move so much as appear spontaneously in a new position. One moment her arms hung bored at her sides, the next they were extended, striking Frank's chest with a thump and sending him two tottering steps backward.

"Can we not do this, guys?" asked the boy. "Just let us go, okay?"

"Okay okay, let's make this clear," Frank said, rubbing his chest where the girl had shoved him. "We want the wagon. We're taking the wagon. That's happening no matter what goes on here. That's all that has to happen. But if you try to turn this into some kind of scene, a whole lot more can happen too. Now get out of the way."

The girl rolled her eyes. "Fuck off."

Frank's mouth shrank to a thin black line. His nostrils flared. He raised one hand and swished it forward, aiming to backhand this impertinent little bitch across the temple. His knuckles found only air. He raised his hand for another strike when a red geyser erupted from his nostrils and the ground rose to meet his back. He stared up at the sky, as if unsure what had happened. The girl stood above him, observing her bloody knuckles with distaste.

"Are we done?" the girl asked.

Frank snarled and leapt at her leg. His left hand clamped around her ankle, but before his right could find its mark, the girl seized it by the wrist. She kicked his broken nose with her free foot, dyeing Frank's world a screaming dizzy red. He watched through a shroud of pain as the girl twisted his arm, reared her leg back, and dealt a savage kick to his elbow.

Frank lay in a heap on the broken asphalt, howling. The girl looked at him, exhaled dismissively through her nose, and continued walking. The boy followed her.

Selena picked at a red speck beside her thumbnail. She'd washed her hands in a greasy puddle fifteen minutes after her encounter with her would-be robbers, but that one last fleck refused to come free. It was far from the first time another man's blood had sullied her hands, but something about the degenerate creep in the field made the thought particularly objectionable.

Still, despite their less than warm demeanor, Selena considered the thugs to be a good omen. They hadn't struck her as travellers, which suggested that some kind of homestead lay close by. A proper farming village would be just what she and Simon needed to rest and resupply, and maybe even learn a bit more about what to expect on the next leg of their journey. Of course, none of that seemed terribly likely among the wastes—the best she could hope for was another dusty hamlet entombed in the scabs of some metropolis past. One the ominous yellow grass had only besieged, not sacked.

A low ache crept into the soles of Selena's feet. When she slowed her pace, Simon went ahead of her. The two of them trudged up a seemingly endless hill, sunlight draped over them like vests of lead. Simon paused as he reached the crest, his hands frozen at his sides. As Selena approached, she could see the look of numb wonder on his face, his eyes so large they seemed to spill over onto his other features. Selena jogged to the crown of the hill to see what had struck him. The sight of it made her pause mid-step.

"Holy shit," she breathed.

Shortly beyond the crest of the hill, the yellow-grey grass that had subsumed Selena's world for over a month gave way in an instant to miles upon miles of verdant farmland, strips of amber wheat and rich mahogany soil and a green so fresh and fecund and bright it seemed almost to glow. *The green. My god, look at the green!*

Ensconced in the lush field, as if cradled in its arms, was a town. Or perhaps city was a better term, for it was a large and bustling place, with distinct districts and plazas radiating out from a central hub. A water tower and a sleek steel wind turbine stood side by side on a hillock to the north. Waterwheels spun languidly on the banks of a narrow river, and an arc of windmills—these ones stubby conical structures made of wood—twirled along the town's northwest corner.

Ramparts defined the town borders in streaks of brown and grey. The gates, however, stood open and inviting, and Selena could see processions of carts coming and going freely—mostly to the north and south, though there were steady trickles to the west as well. Only the east, where Selena and Simon stood, seemed free of traffic. Tiny figures filled the city streets, hauling carts, leading cattle or simply ambling. In a way, the people were a more shocking sight even than the farmland. There must have been thousands of them within the city walls, perhaps more than the sum total of those she'd encountered since first entering the yellow grass months before. They clustered with particular density at the central plaza and along the two wide, perpendicular roads that lay like crosshairs atop the city. One of those roads was the very path on which Selena and Simon stood, though it was in much better shape on the other side of the town, where the going smoothed out and cobblestones replaced crumbling pavement.

They walked briskly into town, wagon gliding serenely behind them. After untold miles of axle-snapping ridges and dips, the smoothness of the cobbles was heaven on Selena's wrist. Despite her overwhelming relief at finding a kernel of life within this vast and blighted landscape, Selena's survival instinct continued beeping its incessant cautions. She kept her eyes honed for hints of something amiss—serfs in chains, black-booted guards, market stages auctioning slaves to the highest bidder. Most of all, she kept stock of any flags she saw for fear of spotting New Canaan's sigil. If she saw it, she and Simon would have no choice but to run back the way they'd come and circle the town at a safe distance, to hell with their dwindling supply of food and water. There were worse ways to die than thirst and hunger—Aldo Delduca could tell you that much.

The buildings were mostly gabled roadhouses made from fresh— or at least freshly painted—lumber, their windows single-paned and rustic, the glass likely harvested from the dead cities to the east. A few brick buildings sprouted up between them. Selena noticed one marked

"Fallowfield Bank and Trust," its doors strafed by large men with clubs dangling from their wrists and tiny gold symbols pinned to their lapels, and a nondescript grey rectangle off a side street with a small sign: "Courthouse."

Simon's eyes roved over the scene, sweeping everything in with both arms.

"There's a tavern, Selena! I bet they do meals! And that vendor has fresh pears! And raspberries! Do you think they get fish out here? There's a stone well! Look!"

"We'll get to that, Simon."

They came upon a great cobbled plaza fringed by a wooden boardwalk. Vendors stood on upturned crates, cajoling passers-by to sample their berries, smell their fruit, or take an appraising look in the mouths of their sheep or cattle. The earthy smell of fresh produce covered the lower odors of sweat and horseshit, making them strangely palatable. The would-be buyers looked well fed and well attended, stalking the rows in fine synthetic silks, occasionally followed by horse-drawn carts or attended by burly men Selena took as hired guards. She saw one man hold a carrot up for inspection, his moustache curled and shimmery with resin. He took a bite, swallowed, and nodded.

"A fine crop. Four crates then. My man will load it up."

"Pleasure doing business," replied the farmer—though on a closer look, Selena wondered if he was a farmer at all. He dressed the part, decked out in a chambray shirt and dungarees, a Stetson hat balanced on his head. But his clothes were neatly pressed, his face pale and jowly, his fingers lineless and free of the stains of long-embedded dirt. If she shook his hand, Selena doubted she'd feel a single callus. Both buyer and seller looked healthy and prosperous beyond the wildest imaginings of this flat and blighted region. She felt as if she'd stepped into a mirage, and at the slightest jostling the whole town might crumble into dust.

Past the plaza, Selena found an inn. The innkeeper, a wispy figure with spidery hands and a shock of white hair, regarded her and Simon with a probing glance, as if they were a rare breed of insect crawling across his dinner plate.

"This place is for merchants and envoys, kids. Migrants get the tents and longhouses outside a town. You work the fields, you live in the fields."

"A tent's not gonna cut it. We've been on the road a long time." She withdrew a small stack of Standard notes. "We want a room."

A slippery grin filled the innkeeper's face. He plucked a few bills from the stack and folded it into his pocket. "Well hey, okay then. A guest's a guest, I say. Come on in. I'll show you to your room." He removed a ring full of fat iron keys from a peg on the wall. "Where you kids from, anyway?"

"K City," said Selena, the lie primed and ready.

"That so? Ain't had folks from the east come by in years. Last I'd heard that road was all shitgrass."

Shitgrass? That yellow weed had more names than it did square miles of prairie. "You're not far off. It's been rough going."

"I'll say. What brings you all the way out here, you don't mind me askin'?"

"Our parents passed last spring, and we lost claim to our freehold." More lies, each chambered and fired with an assassin's ease. "We've got an Uncle on the coast. He sent word saying he'd take us in."

"Well, you'll have a hell of a time getting' there this late in the season, sorry to say."

"Beg pardon?"

"It's coming on autumn. Mountain passes'll be snowed in by the time you reach 'em."

Selena bit her cheek, forcing her face to hold an even expression. "But it's boiling outside."

"Weather's funny in the mountains, kid. Trade from the Republic dried up weeks ago. Even the brass-balled caravans've already hauled ass back to Visalia. Only safe passage is way up near the Prairie Republic, and that's a long way to gamble on the weather. Right. Here's your room."

It wasn't much—two cots, a desk, a cast iron stove with a fitted exhaust pipe feeding into the ceiling, and a small wash basin and shower head offset by a slight depression in the floor and a curtain hanging from a tarnished aluminum rod—but it had a roof, and to Selena that was what counted. Simon played happily with the taps, delighted to see running water again after several months spent washing in and drinking from streams.

"Water comes from the tower. We pump it up there from a spring nearby. Nothing but wash water goes in the drains; for the resta your business, you go outside. If you plug up the drains we'll get word to the plumbing guys, but the cost is on you. Outhouse is around the way." He thrust a thumb vaguely over his shoulder.

Selena ran her finger along a crack in the plaster. The landlord clucked his tongue.

"Right. Enjoy your stay." He closed the door.

Selena took their remaining provisions from the wagon and lined them up along the counter beside the basin. They made a pathetic procession, barely enough to sustain them beyond end of day tomorrow. If Fallowfield had been another hundred miles farther west—perhaps as little as fifty—she wasn't sure they'd have lived to see it.

Locking the door behind him, the innkeeper walked down back alleys and side streets, whistling a meandering tune and nodding to the occasional passer-by. After ten minutes or so, he stepped from a dirt lane and into open pasture, waving to a few shepherds as he passed their flocks. He came to a longhouse made from interlocking logs, stretching beneath the shadow of a great clapboard manor house, which stood imposingly atop a hill. Casting a nervous glance at the manor, he rounded the log building and entered a door in its far end.

The shades were drawn and a satiny darkness covered the room, softening its corners. Two large men in faded jeans played cards around a battered Lucite table. Light filtered in between the slats in the blinds, and a bar of it gleamed off the tiny golden sigils in the shape of canes pinned to the men's lapels.

"I've got something your man might wanna hear."

One of the men tossed down an eight of clubs. "Spades," he said, then to the shopkeeper added, "that so? What you hear?"

"Nothing definite, but he may wanna take a peek. He's still into folks from out east, right?"

The man who'd spoken considered his cards. "Could be."

"Got a pair of 'em came into the inn. A girl of maybe eighteen, twenty, plus a boy, maybe ten or eleven. Claim they came from K City, but they don't sound like that lot, far as I remember. Sound to me like they come from a good deal farther east, if you get my drift. Don't know their plans, but they'll be staying a few nights at least."

The man grunted acknowledgement.

"That all you've got for me?" the innkeeper asked.

"Let's see how it plays out. We know where to find you."

The innkeeper left, the door swinging shut behind him. Once the sound of his footsteps disappeared, the two men laid their cards face down on the table.

3: An Invitation

Selena slumped into her apartment, tossed a burlap bag onto the counter, and collapsed onto her bed. She pressed the heels of her hands against her closed eyelids, igniting phantom fireworks that lingered after she sat up.

"Well?" Simon asked.

Selena sighed. "The landlord's story checks out. I talked to every merchant, coachman, and hired muscle I could find. They all said the same thing. Only passage through the mountains is up halfway to the Prairie Republic, and the snows'll close it weeks before we reach the foothills."

"So what do we do?"

Selena laughed sourly. "Wait until spring. That's what everyone says. Wagons'll start rolling again once the snow melts. We can buy passage on one. Or better yet, we can hitch a ride with the Templars on their way to burn down Visalia." She removed the data stick and twirled it between her fingers. *Six months, maybe less, to cross the second half of this hellish continent. And it turns out this one's the tough half. Nice joke.* "We keep asking questions, that's what we do. We rest a few days, buy supplies, and figure out the best way to go. Maybe the mountains are out, but it's a big continent, and this beshitted yellow grass can't stretch on forever."

Simon's eyes dropped to his lap, where a sheet of yellowing paper rest atop a scrap of balsa wood he'd found in an alley behind the inn. Graphite figures crowded the paper's surface, fillings its every corner with overlapping images, a cacophony of trees and towers and people and abstract shapes. Such were the remnants of the sketchbook he'd brought with him from New Canaan. Soon the paper would be too dark to hold any new shapes, and he'd be stuck scribbling pictures in the dirt. Selena wondered if they made paper out here. It couldn't hurt to get him a sheet or two, keep his spirits up.

Someone knocked on the door. Selena answered it, finding a man in his mid-twenties, tall, with thick forearms and a face shadowed with stubble. A golden pin in the shape of a cane glittered an inch or two above his heart. It stood out among the plain black cotton of his shirt, which he wore tucked into the waistband of jeans dyed a similar charcoal shade. A wooden club, hard and sleek and polished to shine, hung by a rawhide strap from his wrist.

"You the kids who came in from K City?"

Selena kept the door open only halfway. She watched the man's club hand closely. "Could be we are. Who are you?"

"I got a message for the two of you," he said, ignoring her question. "From the Mayor of Fallowfield." His eyes floated from Selena to Simon, who watched the exchange from his perch on the bed. A smile rose to the man's lips. "He'd like to invite you to dinner."

Selena blinked. She'd been prepared for an arrest warrant, an interrogation, maybe an ambush—but an invitation to dinner? Her imagination didn't stretch that far.

"Excuse me?"

"Pretty much how it sounds, I think. A dinner in The Mayor's company, hosted at his place on Shepherd's Hill. Tonight, ideally."

"Why?"

"He finds you interesting, I guess. Not too many people come in from the east. Mostly poison out that way, I hear."

"Who says we came from the east?"

"You did. This is a small town underneath all the hustle and bustle. Word gets around."

Selena didn't find this comforting. "And if we refuse?"

The man shrugged. "Someone else'll eat your share. No one's gonna come after you or run you outta town or nothing. This is a free city. What do you say?"

Selena rubbed the back of her head. "I dunno. I'll have to think about it."

"Suit yourself. You know where Shepherd's Hill is?"

"No," Selena admitted.

The man gave her directions. "Dinner's at six. There's a clock in Green Plaza that keeps time. Listen for the bells."

"Right."

The man left. Selena closed the door and stared for a moment at its coarse grain, her anger swept away. All she felt now was confusion and a creeping sense of unease.

"That was weird," said Simon.

"You've got that right."

"So are we gonna go?"

Selena ran her hands through her hair. "I dunno. If it's a set-up, it's the strangest set-up I've ever heard of. But I mean, what else could it be?"

"Maybe he's just being nice?"

Selena shook her head. "People aren't just nice, Simon. He wants something. The question is what?"

Simon's mouth grew small and pinched. "You don't think he … works for New Canaan, do you?"

"If he did, I can think of about fifty better ways to nab us. We're strangers here. He could say anything."

"So, we should go, then?"

"Yes. No. Shit, Simon. I don't have all the answers."

In the end, her stomach decided for her. It clenched painfully, a fist around a jagged stone. Sour bubbles grumbled their way up her esophagus.

"Well hell, I suppose we should at least wash up a little." She pulled at her grubby shirt with distaste.

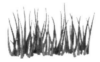

Frank stared at the fire. His injured arm hung in a sling. A fieldhand who'd done some sawbones work for the gangs in Juarez set his elbow for three pears and a hank of bone, but the nerves running from his forearm to his shoulder still thrummed with a low, constant ache. His nose had swollen to twice its normal size and its skin had taken on a shiny purple cast. The other men in the camp snickered every time they saw him. Except Leon, of course. He had adopted a solemn, almost pious manner in Frank's presence.

A cast iron cauldron hung over the flames, its contents bubbling. Leon scooped out two bowlfuls of thin broth. He kept one for himself and served the other to Frank, who nudged it aside with one foot.

"Not hungry," he mumbled.

"C'mon Frank," Leon said. "Broth'll help your arm heal up."

Frank's scowl deepened. Across the camp, the fieldhands laughed and chatted and sparred, honing their fists for the circle in hopes of victory and the riches it brought. A big win against one of the merchants' imported bruisers could mean a month's wages in a single stroke, enough to buy a weekend of whores or a bottle of cheap brandy or some other rough shard of happiness. Frank, small and spindly-armed, scoffed at this bravado. "Fists are for fools," he often snarled after bearing some slight or shove from a larger fieldhand. "There's other ways to get rich in this town." Leon, a large and looming figure, was much too timid to stand in the circle, and for that reason, he hoped Frank was right. Though so far, he hadn't seen much evidence of it.

The fire faded to embers. Leon sat in their somber glow, thinking of how lean the next couple of weeks were going to be. Frank couldn't do much of anything until his arm healed, and even with both their wages, broth, a few pears, and the odd heel of stale bread was about all they could manage. Hunger was a regular guest at the migrant camps, and it mingled effortlessly from group to group.

A skinny man with long, veiny forearms approached Frank and Leon from behind their tent. His eyes shifted conspicuously from side to side.

"Hey," he said.

"Hey yourself," said Frank, still staring at the fire.

"You got somethin' for me?" the man asked.

"Drop the cash in my lap," Frank said. "Then take a walk with my associate here."

The man took out an impressive stack of bills. Even without counting, Leon could tell it was more Standard than they made in two months of steady harvest work. The man placed it delicately on the ground between Frank's legs.

"You could be a little more subtle," Frank said. "And quit glancing around like that, for Chrissakes."

"Sorry," the man mumbled.

The man followed Leon away from the camp, keeping a good distance behind him. He found the spot Frank had showed him, a small clearing in the grass where a boulder lay half-buried in the dirt, and unearthed a parcel wrapped in the shredded remains of a plastic bag. He held it for a moment before handing it over, recounting in his head the steps Frank had explained to him. This was his first transaction, and the last thing he wanted was to screw it up.

The man took the package and held it reverently in his spindly fingers. Leon masked his fear with a veneer of contempt. He tried to think of something biting and dismissive to say.

"Now get outta here," he growled. The man looked at him strangely, but obeyed. Leon nodded to himself. *I guess Frank was right. There were other ways to get rich in this town.*

4: K City

The manor stood on the crest of a grassy hill. It was a building on a grand scale, three stories tall with clapboard siding and a steeply gabled roof. Giant windows gazed northward toward the town square. Columns of ivy wriggled up wrought iron trellises, giving the building a semi-herbaceous cast, as if it and the hill had merged into one entity. Still, it seemed somehow wrong amongst its bucolic surroundings, a stoic sojourner standing mutely outside of time.

"I guess this is the place," said Simon.

"You think?"

Selena shifted her gaze to the surrounding pasture. Young trees stretched their twining limbs toward the sun. Horses, sheep, and cattle grazed beneath their shade, tended by shepherds in chambray shirts or flowing brown robes. At the end of the field stood a long low building made of logs. A shepherds barracks, maybe? Whatever it was, it fit the landscape a lot more closely than the manor did.

"It's so green here," Simon said. "Look at all these cows."

"Let's hope this mayor guy serves up one of them. I haven't had a steak since we left Jericho."

Simon stopped walking. His hands hung loosely at his sides.

"We're never going back, are we?"

"Huh?"

"To Jericho. To New Canaan. We're never going back."

Selena looked at her brother. His face had grown set and stone-like. He stared forward, not daring to meet her eyes, as if even a glance from her would be enough to break his composure. Selena looked away, allowing him this small bit of privacy.

"No, Simon. I don't think we are."

"I miss it sometimes. I mean, it was awful and scary most of the time, but I still miss it. Is that weird?"

Selena gave it some thought. "I don't know."

They walked the rest of the way in silence. When they reached the door, they paused, Selena glancing over her shoulder at the shepherds, Simon scrutinizing the ornate design of the brass doorknocker.

"None of this makes any sense," grumbled Selena. She rapped her knuckles on the door.

A shadow smeared across the frosted glass panel to the left of the door. A man greeted them, his shoulders wider than the frame. His head was a cinder block, all blunted angles and grit, his features carved out crudely by blows from a ball-peen hammer, his eyes shards of busted jade. A deep, puckering scar curved upward from the corner of his mouth in a goblin's half-grin, giving his dour, thin-lipped face a strangely sardonic quality. A truncheon, black and polished to shine, hung from a rawhide strap over his wrist. Selena felt his gaze creep up and down her like a pair of roving centipedes.

"You kids here to see The Mayor?" he asked.

Selena nodded.

Inside, the manor was as palatial as Selena had expected, with high ceilings, ornate molding, and a spiral staircase. A chandelier hovered overhead like some celestial cephalopod, its glass baubles sparkling. Paintings crowded the walls, a motley jumble of portraits, landscapes, and still-lifes, each set in a gilded frame. Simon eyed them with a connoisseur's open-mouthed enthusiasm.

The servant—though Selena struggled to apply such a subservient term to such an imposing man—led Selena and Simon to the dining room, which was dominated by a huge mahogany table. At its far end sat a foppish man in a crushed velvet doublet. He was average-sized, with pale delicate fingers and a coif of blond hair. Yet there was a largeness to his presence, an intangible quality that fell across the table like a shadow. Selena found herself struggling to guess his age. Part of it was that she couldn't see his eyes; he wore a pair of aviator sunglasses with mirrored lenses. He spotted the two of them and raised a glass of red wine in greeting.

"Splendid! My guests have arrived. Come in!" He stood up and bowed, his lapels flapping. "On behalf of the town, allow me to extend to you our warmest welcome. Bernard, please fetch our guests some drinks."

Bernard disappeared, leaving Selena and Simon alone with The Mayor, the three of them around a table that could comfortably seat twenty. Despite its size, only three places were set, both to The Mayor's right. Simon sat down next to The Mayor, and Selena next to Simon. Bernard returned with a bottle of wine, undersized in his enormous hands. He filled Simon and Selena's glasses, twisting the bottle neatly so as not to spill a drop. The Mayor wafted the glass beneath his nose.

"It's an excellent vintage, or so I'm told. I'm not quite the sommelier I pretend to be. Wine is so hard to come by in these parts, after all. We have a brewery in town, and distilleries of varying qualities all over the region, but the climate simply refuses to support even a modest vineyard. Pity it's my drink of choice." The Mayor motioned with the glass for them to drink. "Please. Give me your honest opinion."

Simon took a tiny sip and pursed his lips. A tiny spasm rippled down his throat. "I-it's good," he said. Selena held the glass to the light, sniffed it, and gulped down a mouthful.

"I think it's good. I dunno, I don't really drink wine." She wiped her lips with the back of her hand, smearing red from wrist to knuckle.

"Few do, in this day and age." The Mayor took a long sip. "May I be so forward as to ask your names?"

"I'm Selena. This is my brother, Simon." Early on in their travels, Selena had considered adopting a fake first name, but had ultimately decided against it. It was too easy to slip up. And once someone realized you were using a fake name, they tended to find you a lot more interesting.

"A pleasure to meet you, Selena. And you as well, Simon. I am The Mayor of Fallowfield."

"I never would've guessed."

The Mayor gave a good-natured chuckle. "Fair enough, I'll answer that charge. Public service suits me, I suppose. And I can't say I don't enjoy its trappings. I'd like to thank the two of you for coming on such short notice."

"Sure," Selena said.

"I like your paintings," added Simon.

"Ah, kind of you to mention them. Art is somewhat of a passion of mine. Sadly, I lack the skill to paint myself."

"I love painting. I used to do it all the time back home."

Selena gave Simon a sharp kick under the table.

"Is that so? I must admit my ignorance. I didn't know K City had much in the way of culture."

"I don't know about culture," Selena said, spitballing. "But painting and drawing are both pretty common. It helps to pass the winters."

"Fascinating. Perhaps there is more to the place than I'd expected. Oh, splendid. The food's arrived."

Bernard entered holding a sterling silver tray. On it sat a roast chicken, a bowl of mashed potatoes, a gravy boat, and a heaping medley of steamed vegetables. He set the tray on the table and began portioning the food onto plates. The Mayor rubbed his hands together.

"Ah, thank you Bernard. It smells heavenly." He leaned in to Selena and Simon conspiratorially. "I normally do the cooking myself, but I haven't got much of a knack for it, so I enlisted the help of a few specialists for the occasion. Enjoy!"

Selena and Simon dug in without further prompting.

"I suppose you're both wondering why I invited you here this evening. I wish I could say that this dinner is no more than a courtesy extended to all visitors to our fair city on the green. Sadly, my intentions are entirely mercenary. But before I explain further, let me ask the two of you: how familiar are you with our region?"

"Not terribly," Selena said.

"Then it may be helpful if I give you some context."

Selena motioned for him to go on. A bit of context might be useful—though she thought it more likely that The Mayor simply liked to hear himself talk.

"Ours is a comfortable yet precarious existence—a strange juxtaposition, to be sure, but one to which the men and the women of Fallowfield have grown fairly accustomed. It may seem hard to believe, coming from a place like K City, but we too face the daily threat of yellow locust. Ugly, tenacious, awful stuff, as I'm sure the two of you are all too aware."

Selena nodded. She'd never heard the term yellow locust before in her life, but she'd become sufficiently well-acquainted with the region to guess its meaning. Not a bad name, though she still liked shitgrass better. "We mostly call it bitchweed back home."

"An evocative term. And tell me, where do they say the locust— bitchweed, as you so colorfully call it—comes from?"

"No one knows. Some folks say it was a devil that sowed the soil, turned it bad."

"Some people. But not you?"

"I don't believe in devils."

"Oh, devils certainly exist, but perhaps not in the way your kinfolk believe. In truth, yellow locust is not a naturally occurring plant. It is, to put it bluntly, a weapon. The most nefarious, diabolical, and brilliant piece of warfare ever designed. A country of five hundred million dropped to five in a generation a century ago, when the Last War sputtered to its ignominious halt, and the yellow locust killed more than all the guns and bombs and planes combined. One can dig shelters to escape the fiercest blasts, suits to deflect the strongest radiation, missile defense systems to repel the fastest airplanes, but no technology can battle starvation. So how do you truly fight dirty? Create a crop that grows everywhere, outcompetes even its best and genetically hardiest rivals, shrugs off the harshest poisons, ruins soil, and produces nothing but a bitter, toxic, brittle, utterly useless stalk of sickly grain. You can imagine what it did to the food supply of an unsuspecting nation. Armies march on their stomachs, after all. Why bother shooting them or dropping bombs when you can starve them out with a bit of botanical sabotage?"

The Mayor took a bite from his plate. He gestured to the window with his fork. "The Middle Wastes were once among the most fertile lands in the entire world. But now, places like Fallowfield exist as tiny islets peeking up from a vast and poisoned sea. Ours is the only arable land for a hundred miles in every direction. This is no accident. When I arrived on this spot fifteen years ago, it was as parched and barren as the thousand miles that preceded it. I came with a band of star-eyed migrants from the Confederacy, the outer baronies of New Canaan, the broken cities we passed on the road. Men and women of passion and conviction, keen to make a better life for themselves. They followed me into the desert, and were rewarded. For I came here equipped with a secret weapon."

Bernard circled the table, holding the bottle of wine by its neck as if it were the carcass of something he'd recently throttled. His demeanor was so unlike that of a servant that it made him seem faintly comic. Not that looking at him made Selena feel much like laughing. She refused his offer of a top-off with a wave of her hand. Simon was slower on the draw, and watched with clear concern as Bernard filled his glass to the brim. The Mayor took his own refill and waited until Bernard withdrew to continue speaking.

"You see, there is a special chemical agent that, when judiciously applied to a piece of land, can push back the locust, allowing the soil to once again sustain life-giving crops. It is expensive, of course, and the solution is only temporary, as the locust is too voracious and widespread to eradicate completely. Nevertheless, the agent allowed me to snatch back a few handfuls of Eden from this paradise lost, and breathe new life into the Middle Wastes.

"Our continued existence depends entirely on our ability to procure this agent, making trade the lifeblood of our city. This has made us the bread basket of the region, and hence quite wealthy, but it also makes us vulnerable. Trade must continue if we are to survive, and good trade comes from good information as much as good product. I make it my business to be informed of all the comings and goings within a thousand miles of Fallowfield, but my knowledge suffers an embarrassingly lull when it comes to the east. The roads are too poor, the population too sparse, and the yellow locust too relentless for any caravans or sojourners to make their way to us from that direction. When they do, I make it my business to inform myself to the best of my ability. Hence these dinners."

Selena scratched her cheek. "Well, I don't want to disappoint you or anything, but I don't really know how much we can tell you."

The Mayor waved her concern away. "No need to worry. I don't expect state secrets. Just tell me a little of life in the eastern outposts. Crop yields, any signs of unrest, things of that nature. For instance, do you ever hear from New Canaan?"

Simon made a choked, coughing sound. Strings of spittle tinted red from the wine clung to the corners of his mouth. He grabbed a napkin and dabbed his lips, shaking his head apologetically. "I'm sorry. Wrong pipe."

"New Canaan's never come out our way, as far as we know," said Selena. "Visitors mostly come from nearby, from Warrensburg and St. Joseph and Chillicothe." She plucked the names from the nooks and crevices of her memory. "I remember some voyageurs came once, down from *la Republique du Quebec*. But that was several years ago."

"But nothing from New Canaan? Curious."

Selena rolled her napkin into a tight tube, crimped its edges. "No, nothing from them. Is any of this news to you?"

"Bits and pieces. Every little bit helps. You've painted me quite a picture. Perhaps your brother can do the same, one day. Is the food to your liking, Simon?"

Simon looked down at his plate, empty save for a few scraps and a chicken bone. "Yeah. It's really great."

"Please have some more," The Mayor implored. He served Simon a thigh. "I cannot abide a hungry guest. More chicken, Selena?"

Selena's plate was only half finished, but her appetite was gone. "I'm fine."

His own plate cleared, The Mayor leaned back in his chair and nodded thoughtfully.

"There's one thing I have to ask, and I hope you don't find it too forward. Two youths out alone, trekking the wilds all the way from K City. It's quite extraordinary. What spurred you on to come so far?"

Selena told her story effortlessly, its delivery slick with hours of silent recitation on the road. Dead parents, lost freehold, a distant relative on the west coast. In a way, it wasn't far from the truth. The color was wrong, but they cut the same silhouette. The Mayor listened politely, only chiming in when she spoke of their destination.

"The west coast! Oh dear. That would certainly be a challenge."

"So we've heard. Folks say the mountains are impassable. Is that really true?"

"I'm afraid so. The only functional passage is many hundreds of miles to the north. By the time you reached it, the snows will have come."

Selena swallowed her frustration. "Fine. No mountains, then. But I've seen maps, and the mountains don't stretch on forever. What about to the south? Couldn't a caravan skirt under the mountains and sail back up the coast?"

"I'm afraid that would be more dangerous than braving the mountains themselves. Things in the south have become exceptionally ... *volatile* of late. If your hearts are set on heading west, the mountains are your best option. You'll be forced to wait out the winter, but should be able to secure passage next spring."

"Surely there's *someone* making trips to the south."

The Mayor stroked his chin. "A few caravans do brave the trip, hoping to secure lucrative trade with the *ciudades* beyond the southern wastes. But those that do are heavily fortified, and even then, they rarely make it back. If you want to make it in one piece, I would advise you to wait."

"Waiting's not an option. These caravans, where do I find them?"

"They come through town from time to time, seeking grain for their horses and food for their troops. I suspect you could negotiate passage, though such a journey would cost thousands of Standard."

Selena thought of her own dwindling pile of Standard. She had perhaps a hundred fifty left, probably less. *A problem. But a solvable one.*

"So you're saying one of these caravans'll eventually come through here?"

The Mayor tipped back his glass, finishing the last of its contents. Wine stained his lips a deep red, and when he smiled, his teeth looked bloody.

"My dear, everything comes through Fallowfield, so long as one has patience enough to wait for it."

They chatted amicably after dinner, but The Mayor could soon see Selena was eager to leave and he didn't keep her. He poured himself another glass of wine as Bernard showed them out. Bernard returned without a word and sat next to him, his large legs barely fitting beneath the table.

"So, Bernard? Little escapes your lawman's eye. What do you make of them?"

"Nice kid. The boy anyway."

"And the girl?"

"She's a tough nut."

The Mayor laughed. "Aptly put. Positively aglow with the surly arrogance of youth. And what of their story?"

"Didn't have much of one, if you ask me."

"On the contrary, I thought she performed quite admirably. A pity her accent gave her away. You can always tell a New Canaanite, it's something in the 'a's and 'r's."

"Does that mean she spotted you out, too?"

"I'm a special case, Bernard, you should know that by now. I'd go so far as to place her in Jericho, though I admit my ear might be a tad rusty. I've been away a long time. But she and the boy are both Seraphim, of that I'm sure. Some Bishop or Cardinal's whelps, no doubt. High up enough to have some value, if we're lucky. The question is why are they here? And why are they hiding?"

"Should we reach out to Eric?"

The Mayor dismissed this thought with a huff. "New Canaan can stay in the dark for the time being."

"They won't like that. You piss 'em off, you risk your Compound L goin' up in smoke."

"Perhaps. But I want to know what sort of hand I'm holding before I make my play."

Bernard nodded. "How do you want to handle it? Hard or soft touch?"

The Mayor considered his reflection in the wineglass, his face crimson and distorted. He scratched delicately at his lower eyelid, careful to keep from pushing his sunglasses up. "Soft touch, for now at least."

"You sure? Pull out a few fingernails, you can hear what you wanna hear pretty quick."

"I admire your artistry, Bernard. But this matter calls for pragmatism. Watch the girl, but at a distance. She strikes me as shrewd, and if she senses a net closing on her, she might bolt. The odd check-in will be plenty. I'll see what I can do with the boy. He seems more ... amenable."

"Very good."

"Keep it subtle, but not lax. Eventually Eric is going to want the brats, like it or not, and we'll need to be well positioned to give them to him. We don't want them to see the bars, but they should be there all the same. My little tale about the caravans likely bought us some time. If they look like they might go astray, we'll need to steer them back on course."

"And if steering doesn't work?"

"Then the hard touch it must be," The Mayor said, and finished his wine.

5: Rapeseed

Fallowfield was bustling but compact and the sun had only just risen when Selena reached the town's southern gate. Gilded wagons trundled past her, driven by coachmen and guarded by hawkish men with rifles. Plump merchants in clothes too fine for fieldwork rode inside them, their interiors gaudy with velvet and bulging with veins of precious metals. Selena stepped aside to let them pass; judging by the speed of the horses and the indifferent glance of the drivers, she suspected they'd simply run her down if she didn't.

A band of yellow-grey wasteland snared Fallowfield in place like a vast poison collar. If Selena was going to break out of it, she'd need help. The Mayor had given her a spark of hope with his talk of caravans, but a ride would mean little if she lacked the means to buy her and Simon passage. She needed Standard, and she could think of one way to make some.

Outside of its walls, Fallowfield changed. Its air of bucolic prosperity vanished, swept away by a derelict wind of dust and trash and rust-eaten machines abandoned on the roadside.

The picturesque rowhouses and orderly boardwalks gave way to rundown cottages and shacks with roofs of corrugated tin, the cheesemongers and bakeries to corn husks and smashed liquor bottles and cast iron cauldrons bubbling with soupy gruel. Half-naked children played in muddy pits while their parents toiled in the fields, their bare feet sleeved with pale calluses as thick as the soles of Selena's shoes.

From a distance, the land had seemed prosperous, but up close the crops looked ragged and nervous, their grip on the soil tenuous. Whole fields had fallen to the yellow locust, their neat rows choked by fronds of brittle grass. The cabins in those fields were particularly woebegone, their windows shattered, their roofs caved inward. They lay among the dead crops like skulls in a forgotten battlefield, their violent deaths eroded from memory.

At a bend in the road stood a tent city, ripped tarpaulins and toppled signs and shaggy strips of unearthed plastic tangled together into a sprawling and shifting metropolis. Muddy lanes, alleys, and cul-de-sacs wandered through the flimsy structures in odd and looping patterns that led nowhere. The place seemed less like something built than something grown, a vast fungus sprouting from the soggy earth. *So this is where the migrants live, for now at least. I wouldn't want to be out here come winter.*

Past the tent city rolled fields rife with migrants hoeing weeds, picking fruit, and harvesting rows of grain. Selena approached a woman kneeling bent-backed over a raspberry bush.

"Who's in charge here?"

The woman looked up, revealing wizened cheeks of tanned leather. Her hands continued plucking berries, her fingers deft as insects evolved to that purpose. She motioned with her head, not wanting to stall her labor for even the instant it would take to point.

"Thanks."

In a few steps, Selena realized she needn't have bothered the old woman. One glance at the man striding through the crops told her exactly who was in charge. Stooped and scraggly, he nevertheless moved with confidence through the rows of bushes, issuing clipped commands and reprobation and terse praise. His overalls were saggy and torn from years of work, and his fingernails were dark with soil.

He glanced up at Selena, his eyes beset by heavy bags and couched in a thicket of wrinkles. Red veins crisscrossed his bulbous nose.

"Yeah?"

"Are you in charge?" Selena asked.

"Yeah. Name's Magnus. What do you want?"

"My name's Selena. I'm looking for work, if you have any."

Magnus barked a single coarse laugh. "That so?"

"I can do whatever you need."

"You can't arrive on time, I can tell you that much. We start at dawn on this farm, girl. It look like dawn to you?"

Selena glanced around her. The fieldhands went about their tasks oblivious to her conversation, piling berries into baskets at their knees. Many of the baskets were already three quarters full, and she spotted one wiry young woman going for her second.

"I can pick up now with no trouble, and I'll be here before dawn tomorrow."

"You are, you're gonna be real disappointed."

"Can't you give me a chance?"

Magnus gave a snort of annoyance. "Listen, girl. I got all the hands I can manage and then some. I take you on, I gotta feed you, I gotta pay you. That's food and Standard outta my pile. And Fallowfield needs its cut. If it don't get it, I don't get Compound L."

"Compound L?" Selena asked. The name sounded familiar but she couldn't place it.

"It kills the shitgrass. You see that there?" Magnus pointed across the road to a field devoured by yellow locust. "That's what happens when we can't pay."

Selena regarded the blighted field. "They just let the grass take it back?"

"Shit, girl, all this is just borrowed, far as Fallowfield's concerned. If I don't deliver, they'll let me starve and give the next poor moke his own tract a land. Us field grunts ain't nothin' but a necessary evil to them." He spat in the direction of town. "They get the cake, we get the crumbs. And I don't got no crumbs to spare." Magnus motioned vaguely with his hand in a manner suggesting their conversation was done. Selena thanked him and moved on.

The other farmers were more polite than Magnus but no more helpful. A young man with flowing black hair and a birthmark over one eye named David Akros invited her back next season, but otherwise she received no offers. In a way, this didn't surprise her. The farmers seemed as weary and haggard as the migrants they employed, the sort of threadbare folks who really couldn't afford to feed an extra mouth. Selena didn't understand how such bounteous land could host such hungry people. She followed a wagon trail southwest until she came upon a field of gorgeous yellow flowers, their blooms so bright Selena nearly felt the need to shield her eyes.

"Rapeseed," explained a voice from behind her. "Makes good animal feed and cooking oil."

Selena turned. The man who'd spoken wore dungarees faded to the color of an overcast sky and a collared cotton shirt checkered white and red. On his head sat a wide-brimmed hat woven from straw. His skin was russet, wrinkled, and tough as leather. Tiny wrinkles encircled his brown eyes—a common trait among the men out here, Selena noticed.

"Couple of my people told me there's a young woman wandering about my fields. Not much to steal out here in the rapeseed, so I suspect she must be lookin' for me. Name's Harvey Freamon."

He extended a hand and Selena shook it. His fingers were callused and strong.

"Selena."

"How can I help you, Selena?"

"My brother and I just got into town. I was told you might be in need of more fieldhands."

Harvey sucked air through clenched teeth. "I'm sorry, girl, but I can barely feed the hands I got."

"Look, how about you give me the rest of the day. Whatever you need me to do, I'll do it. If you don't like my work, you don't have to pay me. Just give me a shot, okay?"

"You ain't gonna raise Cain if I say I ain't satisfied?"

"Not a word. I just want a chance."

Harvey scratched the back of his neck. "Guess I got that much to give."

He led her to a spot halfway down the field and handed her a scythe from a nearby wagon. Its blade was tarnished and rust-speckled but sharp as a razor.

"You ever use one of these?"

"No," Selena admitted.

"It takes some getting used to. Keep your grip light but firm. Swing through the crop, not into it."

Selena brought the scythe down in a smooth arc. It hewed through the field with ease.

Harvey's mouth hung open. He shut it with a toothy clack. "Do that again."

Selena did, several times. Each swing was neat and effortless, a swath of rapeseed tumbling in its wake. Harvey put his hands on his hips.

"Christ, girl, you sure you've never done this before?"

"I'd never even seen one of these things before today."

"Then you must've done it blindfolded, because you're an old hand at reaping. It normally takes months for my people to get a hang of the sickle."

"Thanks."

"You wanna thank me, keep at it."

"Does that mean I've got the job?"

"Hey now, as I recall I don't gotta make up my mind 'til I see what I got at the enda the day." Harvey winked. "But you keep up this pace, and I don't 'spect we're gonna have a problem."

The sun hoisted itself toward its zenith as Selena moved beneath it, a bronze-skinned speck in an ocean of shimmering yellow. Her scythe rose and fell, each neat arc matched by the crisp sigh of cut rapeseed. By noon she was covered in sweat, her palms were dotted with blisters, and her shoulders radiated a satisfying ache. She tucked her scythe beneath the wagon and followed the other fieldhands, half of whom chatted to one another in an unfamiliar tongue. They led her to a sloping hillock south of the fields, where a crescent of trees provided welcome respite from the midday sun. Selena found a shady spot to sit. She kicked off her shoes, kneaded her toes through the grass, and munched on an apple that, along with two plums and a small wedge of cheese, comprised her lunch. It wasn't much, but it seemed a good bit more decadent than what her fellow fieldhands enjoyed: mostly burdock roots and dandelion leaves and other bits of foraging, bolstered by a few spoonfuls of watery gruel. The gruel came from a cast iron cauldron some enterprising soul had set bubbling over a campfire. A bent old woman ladled the slop into lopsided clay bowls, which they traded for one half of a Standard note, torn in two. A pair of burly guards stood to her either side, looking stern. Selena wondered how one could do a full day's work fuelled by such meagre offerings.

As she bit into her apple, she noticed a girl of maybe fourteen sitting in the grass nearby. Her hair was stringy and matted, her arms so thin they seemed little more than bones clothed in olive fabric. Her eyes were rheumy and brown, and they regarded Selena's plums as if the tiny fruits were jewels stolen from some exotic kingdom. She looked from the plums to Selena and dropped her gaze, embarrassed. Selena felt a pang of pity, followed shortly by a pang of hunger. She weighed the two, found the former to be the stronger, and set one of the plums in the thin girl's lap.

The girl looked up, too stunned to speak. Selena nodded encouragingly. The girl prodded the plum as if afraid it might be booby-trapped, decided she didn't care if it was, and took a huge, sumptuous bite. Two more followed quickly and she was sucking the pit, tears welling in her watery eyes.

"*Gracias, senorita,*" she said, her voice shaky and awkward around the pit.

"It's okay."

Across the clearing, Selena spotted a pair of familiar faces: the two buffoons who'd accosted her on her way into town. The little one's arm hung in a sling patchy with food and sweat stains, but otherwise they seemed to be doing suspiciously well for themselves. While the other fieldhands subsisted on forage and gruel, they supped on sandwiches stuffed with dried meats and dripping with sauce. Strawberry stems and bits of cheese rind littered the ground at their feet. The fieldhands looked on with almost palpable longing, a few with strings of spittle hanging from their open mouths. *Something's off here.* She knew the merchants in town ate well, but how did these two idiots get so flush? And if they were so damn rich, what were they doing in these fields in the first place?

The smaller one noticed her. His face curdled. He nudged the big one, who regarded her with the face of a child who'd just heard something growling under his bed. Selena glanced away, hoping the little one would let it be and knowing he wouldn't. He stuffed the remains of his sandwich into his mouth, swallowed without enjoyment, and stalked over to her, the big one shuffling sheepishly behind him.

"You shouldn't need that anymore," Selena said, nodding to the sling. "It's only dislocated."

"You a doctor now?" the little one sneered.

"No, but I've broken a few bones in my day. Mostly other people's."

"Me and my pal here have a mind to break a few bones of our own. How's that sound?"

"Painful."

"You'd better watch your back, bitch. This ain't your town. You and your little boyfriend aren't welcome here."

"Huh. The mayor told us otherwise. Now I don't know who to believe."

"Believe this," the little one said, and spat. A gob of yellowish phlegm landed on Selena's knee. It trembled as she stood, wriggling like a piece of undercooked egg white.

Around them, the other fieldhands started taking real interest, rising on their haunches or whispering to friends or simply staring, eyes wide with excitement. A boy of fourteen with lean arms and olive skin thrust a jubilant fist in the air.

"Fight!"

More voices joined his, and soon half the crowd was chanting, voices pounding in the steady rhythm of war drums. Selena's fingers twitched, trembled, curled into fists. Her blood filled with salt and heat and iron, the pounding of her heart like fists on unprotected flesh. She saw uncertainly flicker across the little one's eyes, smelled the musk of his sudden wariness. He took a half-step back and she a half-step forward, hands rising to their natural place before her jaw, floating like buoys at the high water mark.

"Scuse me, am I interruptin' somethin'?"

The chanting ceased. Frank stepped back, his good arm raised in a conciliatory gesture. Harvey stepped between him and Selena.

"There a problem here?"

"No problem. Just a disagreement, is all."

"That so?" Harvey looked to Selena, who nodded. Harvey bobbed his head almost imperceptibly. "Ain't you folks got fields to tend to? I reckon lunch is over for today."

A chorus of grumblings and hoots and chatter filled the clearing as the fieldhands filed onto the path back to work. The big one seemed all too eager to join them. The little one hung back a second longer, setting Selena with a final sour sneer before shuffling off after his companion.

Harvey waited until the two thugs were out of earshot. "You okay?"

"Fine. Those guys don't scare me."

"They ain't exactly, what do they call 'em, *pandilleros,* I'll give you that. But that don't mean you shouldn't be careful. They got somethin' on the cook, throwin' that kind of money around. And Frank is one to bear a grudge. Though I don't doubt you can handle yourself." His gaze fell to her hands, which were still curled into fists. She forced them to loosen. They disobeyed for a moment, clenching still tighter, then relented. "But I don't want no violence in my fields. Understood?"

"Understood."

Harvey nodded. "Anyway, reason I came out here was I saw your work. You're a damn fine hand with a scythe, girl. I know you gave me the day to decide, but I can spot a good hand when I see it. I'm gonna pay you up for today in advance. There's more work tomorrow, if you want it." He handed her a one Standard note.

"That's it?" The words escaped before she knew she'd spoken them. She expected anger in response, or at least indignation at her ingratitude. Instead, Harvey looked more embarrassed then anything, his callused fingers scratching at the back of his head.

"I wish it was more, girl, but that's all I can afford. Once the Sheps collect it and the vendors sell it and The Mayor takes his cut, I got nothin' left. You can ask around all you want, but the goin' rate don't change."

Selena looked at the Standard note. *What did you expect, rich girl?* asked a mocking voice in Selena's head. It was her own, and it struck like a lash. *A handful of diamonds for every pound of flowers you hauled in?* At this rate, she could never earn enough to hire a caravan, especially not before spring. Hell, with her lodgings factored in, she was *losing* Standard. She could move to one of the camps once her two weeks' rent was up, but that would still put her too far behind to ever make it west. A tightness seized her chest, making every breath a struggle. *This place is a prison,* Selena realised. *Only instead of bars, its yellow locust. The biggest file in the world couldn't cut through all that.* The data stick burned her thigh like a lit torch, urging her westward in its silent, flame-tongued voice.

"Sorry. I don't want to sound ungrateful. It's just that my brother and I need to make our way west, and we're never gonna be able to afford it, at this rate. Isn't there some other way to earn a living around here?"

"Get a wagon and a silk suit," Harvey's voice was thorny with bitterness. "That'd serve you fine, believe you me."

"There's nothing else?" Selena asked. The pleading note in her voice sickened her, but there seemed little she could do to remove it.

"Only one way field grunts like you or me can make any real Standard in this town, and it ain't reapin' rapeseed."

"I'm listening."

Harvey sighed. "There's a regular fighting ring forms in Green Plaza most nights. Field hands go knuckle to knuckle while the merchants place bets. Winner gets a piece of the take. On a big night, that means a month's wages, maybe more. Sometimes the more flush traders'll find a guy they like and sponsor 'em, pay 'em a special wage to fight more guys at once, or take on one a their personal bodyguards. Most of 'em come back bruised and broke as ever, but a few a the good ones score big."

Selena thought of the town square as she'd first seen it, its air of quaint prosperity. It was tough to picture violence simmering beneath those market stalls.

"And this goes on every night?"

"Just about. There's a reason them field hands were so quick to sniff blood on you and Frank. Fightin's a way of life 'round these parts. Hell, even half of us landholders've taken a crack at the circle once or twice. Some years it's the only way to keep your head above water come winter." Harvey rubbed the side of his jaw as he spoke, his fingers tracing the winding path of an old and faded scar. "The merchants love watchin' the lower classes slug holy hell out of each other. Let's 'em feel tough. And they love throwin' their cash around while they do it."

"What about the field hands?"

Harvey shrugged. "Way life is 'round here, I 'spect fightin' is the only thing that makes 'em feel human."

Selena could relate.

6: Virgin Canvas

Simon sat on the edge of the bed, sketching to ignore the pain in his belly. He'd eaten the food Selena had left for him and lacked the courage to find more. He knew they only had a limited amount of Standard, and he didn't want to risk getting fleeced at one of the market stalls at the fringe of Green Plaza, where the traders and merchants bought their lunches.

The paper grew heavy and slick with graphite. Soon the whole thing would be one mass of black lines, and he'd be reduced to scribbling on the stained wooden board he used as a makeshift drafting table. For Simon, drawing had always been an act of almost sublime tranquility. It was the only time that the nerves in his belly ceased their constant sizzling, the only place where tremors never troubled his hands. He could do one thing truly well, and that was make pictures. At everything else, he faltered.

Unfortunately, New Canaan had little use for artists. His parents had enrolled him in St. Barbara's Architectural and Engineering Academy, hoping to leverage his creative skills into something more in line with New Canaan doctrine. He'd proven a capable enough student, but his heart lay in paints and charcoal and pencil sketching—activities his devout, toad-shaped headmaster viewed as grotesque and profane.

Only at home did he find an appreciative audience—in his parents, at least; Selena always considered his hobby a bit foolish. But now, his parents were gone. He began sketching them only to realise that he was already starting to forget what they looked like. The finer details of their faces evaded his grasp.

A knock on the door pulled him from his work. He dressed in a rush and eased the door open an inch.

Bernard's ruined cheek sneered down at him.

"Didn't wake you, did I?" he asked, in a voice that made it clear he didn't care one way or the other.

"No," Simon said, hoping the answer disappointed him.

"The Mayor has another invitation for you. Breakfast. Come with me."

"Just me? Not Selena?"

"She's working the field, isn't she?"

"Yeah. How do you know that?"

"Knowing what goes on in this town is my job, short stack. Now do you want to eat a hot meal or do you want to sit here and ask questions?"

"I'll come, I guess."

The walk was uncomfortable but mercifully short. Neither of them spoke a word on the half mile jaunt from the flophouse to The Mayor's manor. Bernard took Simon inside, upstairs, and down a hallway, where he opened a door and ushered Simon into a wide, spacious office. A great oaken battleship of a desk dominated the room, at which sat The Mayor.

"Simon my boy! I'm pleased you can make it. Have a seat. Thank you for fetching him Bernard, that will be all."

The Mayor wore a green knee-length jacket despite the heat, its bottom flaring like a cape, its lapels traced with whirling patterns of gold stitching. In front of him sat two plates piled high with fried potatoes, fresh bread, scrambled eggs, and strips of bacon. The rich, rustic smell of the dishes filled Simon's nostrils. Hunger burned his belly like a branding iron.

"Your timing is impeccable, I must say. I hope you haven't eaten already."

Simon shook his head. He didn't feel he could open his mouth unless it was to shovel a forkful of food into it. The Mayor didn't make him wait on ceremony. He cleared his plate before The Mayor had even halfway finished his. He felt a bit guilty for behaving so ravenously, and sat with conscious politeness as The Mayor picked at his plate, silently taking in the office.

Sunlight poured through great mullioned windows. The walls were clean, the furniture polished to shine. A Turkish rug, its surface alive with swirls and jags like creeping ivy, covered the bulk of the floor, leaving a thin perimeter of hardwood to trace the ornate molding. A shortwave radio sat atop a table by an inline bookshelf. Its steel body was tinted a military green, its analog dials and gauges contrasting with the sleek digital receiver connected to it by an umbilicus of sheathed wire. The radio's front panel hung open, revealing its electronic innards.

"What happened to your radio?"

"I wish I knew. It stopped working a few months ago and I cannot figure out why. Its value was mostly aesthetic to begin with, but it still irks me to have it non-functioning. I had one of the Shepherds look at it, but sadly he couldn't solve the problem. Fallowfield is a veritable library of knowledge on crops and livestock, but sadly lacking in technical expertise. We rely on neighboring towns for such things, but even they do little but tinker crudely with the fossils of the Last War. True innovation lies on the coasts, in the Republic of California and New Canaan. But I'm afraid both regions have their own affairs to consider, and pay proverbial backwaters like us little mind."

"What about the windmills?" Simon asked. He'd noticed several of them towering over the shops to the north of town, their blades spinning languidly.

"All assembled by visiting electricians and builders. We are growers, not makers here in Fallowfield. But such is the benefit of a region built on trade. One can afford to lack a few skills."

"May I take a look?"

The Mayor motioned to the radio, palm up. "Be my guest."

Simon peeked inside. It was old technology, definitely pre-Last War, though it had been modified since then. The additions were strange, leading to an auxiliary switch on the chassis, but the core components were simple enough. Simon turned the radio's body to better capture the light streaming through the window.

"A lot of these wires are corroded pretty bad, but the real problem is a blown capacitor. Right here." Simon pointed to a small nodule rising from a circuit board. "You'll need a new part."

"And that's all that's wrong with it?"

"I couldn't say for sure until we tried it, but it might be."

"Interesting. I had no idea you had such facility with machines."

"That's what I went to school for."

"My ignorance abounds. I didn't know K City had any proper institutes of learning, let alone ones focused on pre-War technology."

Simon's cheeks grew hot. *Stupid!* Two minutes into the conversation and he was already screwing up their cover! He wanted to trust The Mayor, but New Canaan was never as far away as it seemed. Aldo Delduca floated up from the murky depths of his memory, his blackened corpse still screaming. Simon plunged the poor man back down where he wouldn't have to see him.

"Well, uh, it wasn't really a school like how you're thinking. But there are some technicians and mechanics who came from New Canaan. They train some of us to take over when they're gone. We call it school."

"Fascinating. I would very much like to set up such a program, but expatriates from the coasts are rare creatures in the Wastes. However, I didn't invite you here simply to have you fix my radio. There's something I'd like to show you. Please follow me."

The Mayor walked around his desk and opened a narrow door tucked between two bookshelves. Through the door was a room little wider than a hallway, its outer wall lined with double-paned windows. A rumpled blue tarpaulin covered the floor. On the tarp sat an easel. Painting supplies formed an orderly procession along the inside wall: oil paints in yellowing plastic bottles; brushes, both salvaged synthetics and newer ones made from tree branches and horse hair; various cups and beakers; and a painter's palette.

"Wow, you paint?" asked Simon.

The Mayor laughed. "No, I'm afraid not. But I was hoping that you did."

"Me?"

The Mayor picked up a paintbrush and ran his thumb across its bristles. "To my great dismay, I was not imbued with an artist's talents, though I like to believe I possess an artist's soul. I do at least love fine things. Music, literature, wine. But paintings most of all. Would that I could put brush to canvas and conjure worlds with a twitch of my fingers, but try as I might, I produce nothing but vulgar smudges.

"You mentioned at our dinner that you've tried your hand at painting in the past, and I suspect you might have had a good deal more success than I. I'd like to do what I can to nurture that talent, give it the light and nourishment it needs to grow."

Simon bit his lip. "Gee, that's really nice of you, Mr. Mayor. I really appreciate it. But I don't know what Selena would think of me spending my time painting. She's not big into that stuff. I'm supposed to be helping around the house."

"Surely your flat isn't big enough to need twenty-four-hour maintenance? You must have some spare time. I wouldn't ask you to keep to any sort of schedule. And if supporting your household is a matter of concern, I'd be happy to compensate you for your time."

"You'd pay me to paint?"

"Money is not a problem for me, Simon. I don't want for much in that regard. But out here, art has become a far rarer commodity. I seek it, but most of what I find is musty and faded and old. What I truly want is something fresh and young and new, and if I have to pay to make it, well, in my eyes that is Standard well spent."

Simon approached the easel, his fingers rasping over the virgin canvas, wondering how best to fill its vast and vacant surface. His mind's eye filled it with phantom brushstrokes, whirling and slashing with impossible speed, retrieving misplaced pigment and fixing lines and tweaking color. He grabbed the palette and began dotting it with small blobs of paint. "It'll probably take me a while," he said.

"Not to worry," The Mayor said. "I can wait."

7: Gristle and Thew

Selena's body spent the afternoon in the fields, dutifully harvesting row upon row of rapeseed. But her mind drifted back through the years and miles, to a time that felt at once several months and several lifetimes ago.

The air in the Salters' circle was fetid and heavy. The stink of a hundred soiled bodies dribbled from the concrete ceiling and soaked into the dirt floor, a mingled stench of piss and sweat and blood and bile. Selena forced it down by the lungful, inoculating herself. She would not reveal her disgust to the leering eyes that surrounded her, that named her rich girl, Seraphim spawn, pampered and soft-skinned. The first two might have been true, but her skin was anything but soft.

The first time she'd descended into the subterranean ring, no one would touch her. She heard the rabble of the crowd echoing off the concrete ceiling, noted the moment it dropped off like a duck shot dead by a hunter mid-flight. A chorus of faces saw her and fell silent, leaving a vacuum of sound that sucked at her flesh. She strode through the masses, leaving footprints in the sloppy earth, tasting the air in a sour cloud on the back of her tongue. The two fighters at the center of the ring—shirtless, arms and chests and legs bulging with twists of muscle—stared with the outsized eyes of frightened children. She stood between them, fists raised in a fighting stance.

"Who's first?" she asked.

They dropped their arms and their eyes, kicked imaginary stones. "We won't fight you, miss. Please leave us alone."

"What do you mean? I asked you to fight."

"Go home, deacon's blood!" cried a voice, safely anonymous within the crowd. "This ain't your place!"

"Yeah! Go fuck a Templar, you want the piss beaten outta you so bad!"

Selena glances around at the lowly faces surrounding her, each filled with impotent hostility. *They could rush down and kill me,* she thought. *There's hundreds of them. They could bash my skull to bits in less than a minute. But they won't.* One of the fighters—a boy of maybe eighteen, his chin dotted with tufts of downy stubble—gave her a pleading look.

"We mustn't touch Seraphim," he whispered. "It's the Red Theatre if we do."

"I knew a boy who bumped one of your lot on the Galilean beaches," said the other. "They put him against two lions with naught but a stick. I saw them cats pull his guts out with their teeth."

"Look, I don't want your damn genuflections, and I don't want to punish you for touching me. I want a fight."

"Respect, miss, but I reckon you'd be best off fightin' your own kind."

Her own kind. Selena couldn't comprehend of a more pathetic bunch. Prissy, preening, their knuckles padded and their every blow dictated by coaches and tallied by referees. That wasn't fighting. It was ballet. Selena wanted a real fight with real people, craved the unleavened crunch of knuckle on bone, the savage grace of true combat. It would occur to her later that she'd used the Salters much as the Cardinals and Bishops did, and she would feel ashamed at the memory of it. But in the moment, she wanted only to be one of them, to cast off the shackles of privilege.

"One of you grow a pair of balls and hit me, already."

The two fighters just stood there, chewing their lips, shuffling from foot to foot. Selena exhaled sharply through her nostrils.

"Fine." She threw a cross. It struck the younger Salter in the jaw and sent him staggering backward. He cupped his face, instinctively catching the blood that dribbled from the side of his mouth. She hit the other fighter with an uppercut, knocking him onto his back. The first fighter had found his footing by then and Selena was on him, hurling jabs and crosses. He blocked this time but wouldn't strike out at her. Selena's fists flew harder, occasionally making their target on his face or chest or abdomen. His cheek started to swell. Bruises erupted over his body like the marks of a hemorrhagic plague. In desperation, he snapped out a right hook, catching Selena beneath the left ear. She staggered back, one hand raised to her bludgeoned head. The crowd gasped as one. The fighter stared down at his fist as if it were a murderer and he its unwitting accomplice. Selena spat onto the muddy ground and smiled.

"It's about fucking time. Come on."

She had three fights that day and won them all. The next day came four, one of which she lost—though her opponent came out of it little better than she did, his broad face shell-shocked and pale. Slowly, she transitioned in their eyes from spy to sideshow novelty—eccentric, amusing, but not respected. Respect came after a dozen fights and as many victories, when one hulking fighter after another hobbled clear of the mocking eyes that surrounded them, bodies and egos equally bruised. At this point, the men knew she was no dilettante, slumming for stories to share over high tea with her filigreed friends. This strange girl was a fighter, and no mistake. Yet they still delighted in every slip that betrayed her gilded heritage—the way her nose wrinkled at the scabrous offerings of the food vendors, at the prissy way she flicked effluvium from her fingers after breaking an opponent's nose (a habit she'd curtailed with reasonable success). She was still the rich girl, but she was also the champ. She would keep fighting until the latter role eclipsed the former—and love every second of it. This was true combat, stripped of padded gloves and gum shields, of bells and rules and "gentleman's tactics," of a scoring system that reduced the struggle to a mere dog show, where form outweighed fury. This was raw. This was real. This was thunder in her heart and lightning in her veins. It was this that dragged her through the mud and trash of the lower city, this that made her risk her safety and her family's good standing—an item all the more precious for them being traitors, for they hid behind it like a shroud.

On a chilly morning three weeks before Niagara fell, a coil of gristle and thew stepped from the crowd and regarded Selena with a weasel's cunning eyes. The men in the Salters' circle lacked the sculpted physiques common to boxers in the Templar Officers' gyms, who built their muscles with sophisticated machines, tallying reps and counting calories. The Salters drew their strength from raw labor, driving plows, hauling heavy burdens and bullying temperamental factory equipment into something approaching proper function. Their bodies were ugly, thorny and relentlessly tough. They fought without technique but with unparalleled guile, punches slick with atavistic speed, ruthless, unpredictable. The man approaching her now was no exception. He came in without warning, his hand more claw than fist, and struck for her temple. Selena threw her head forward, catching the blow at the wrist and stealing its power. Her fists rocketed forward, pummeling the man's unprotected face. He grinned as his lips split and his nose cracked, hurling out a low cross that took Selena in the gut and bent her forward. They grappled for a moment before Selena shoved him back. The man laughed through ruined teeth. Selena allowed herself to smile back. Her eyes settled on the droplet of blood hanging from his chin. He wiped it away with his forearm, swallowed.

The man learned his lesson, and his next attack was more measured. He came in, feinted, and threw a quick volley of jabs that ricocheted harmlessly off Selena's raised forearms. She shot back and found no more success than he had. They circled, locked in a fragile pause that either party could shatter with a single twitch of the shoulder. Selena let the man break it. He came in snarling with a right hook. Selena ducked it and punished his ribcage, forcing the man backward. His feet slid through the dirt, scrambling for purchase. He was nearly down. Selena reared back for a final blow.

A comet of crackling white matter struck the ground to Selena's left and exploded, flooding the room with a blinding flash of light. A concussive boom followed, rattling Selena's teeth in her jaw and setting her ears to ringing. Figures swathed in grey broke through the crowd, punching and stomping any unfortunate lump of flesh that stood in their way. The Salters scattered, stumbling into walls and clutching their ringing heads. Selena blinked her way through the glittering orbs of overexposure that blocked her vision. She turned to run but a firm hand snared her bicep, joined in short order by another.

The lights in her eyes began to fade, allowing her a better view of the men who'd grabbed her. Templars. She should've known.

The Templars dragged her from the ring and marched her into a building and down a long corridor lit with flickering fluorescent tubes. Near the end of the hallway, they shoved her into a cramped cube of space—it felt too cold and naked to be called a room—lit by a lone forty-watt bulb. The walls, floor, and ceiling were all concrete painted a uniform shade of pea green. A steel table stood in the center of the room, its legs bolted to the floor. There were no chairs, so the man standing opposite her merely leaned on the table, his arms great pillars of muscle supporting his considerable weight.

He was not fat, simply large, his shoulders the breadth of two men side by side, his waist comparatively trim but still gargantuan, his face long and rough and angular. He wore a Templar uniform decorated with silver epaulettes and a series of chevrons cascading up his right arm. *A Paladin,* noted Selena. *So this is big, then.* The fabric of his uniform stretched taut across his broad shoulders, pristine and almost supernaturally free of wrinkles. A sword hung from a strap at the small of his back, its handle pointing improbably downward towards his right hip while the blade crested upwards like the prow of a ship in choppy waters. Selena wondered absently how it stayed in its hilt.

The door shut behind her. The light over the man's head carved great valleys of shadow into his cheeks and beneath his chin.

"Miss Flood," he said, eyeing her up and down. It was a lustless appraisal, as if she were a malfunctioning piece of machinery. "You've caused a great deal of inconvenience for the Templars today. If your father were not in so key a position with his Diocese, you'd be facing severe punishment. Lashes and stockading are still not out of the question."

"I didn't inconvenience anyone."

"Ten men went into the Salters' circle to collect you, putting themselves at a modest but tangible risk. There's a reason we don't go down there. The control we exact on the streets loosens in those caverns. This is as it should be. They are a safety valve and should not be tampered with."

"You're the ones tampering with them," sulked Selena. "I didn't go bust up their fight. All I did was join in. How is that any business of yours?"

"The circle of blood is a Salter's pastime. It belongs to them. Your participation in it is unbefitting your station. It embarrasses you, it embarrasses your family, and it embarrasses our entire class. You're among the Seraphim—not to mention a young woman. Fighting of any sort is distasteful enough from you. Fighting with Salters is borderline miscegenation. It sends the wrong message."

The man rounded the table and stood in front of Selena, his chest inches from her face.

"I do not often waste my time lecturing little girls on their manners. For the sake of your father's station, I have made an exception. I do not intend to make another. You will by no means join, attend, or witness another circle of blood. You will not associate with Salters in any way, and will cut any ties you might have with them immediately. If I hear otherwise, you and your family will suffer for it."

His black eyes dared Selena to reply. She bit her tongue hard enough to leave teeth marks and said nothing. The man took a single step backward and motioned to the door.

"Your parents have been alerted to your impropriety. They may have their own punishment for you. If they have any sense, it will be severe. But as for me, our conversation is done. By the grace of God and the Archbishop, you've been given one reprieve. Do not expect a second."

As if to demonstrate his commitment to this claim, the Paladin twitched a finger and half a dozen Templars entered the room. Each pair dragged between them a Salter from the circle of blood. Selena recognized two of them: the wiry man she'd fought that day, smiling through broken teeth and a nose swollen to the size and colour of an aubergine; and the boy who'd punched her on her very first day in the circle, his split lips quivering behind a peach fuzz beard. The third man was a stranger to her, some poor fool seized from the crowd at random. The wiry man stared impassively at the Templars, his eyes sparkling with wry amusement. The boy whimpered senselessly, eyes saucer-big and pleading. The stranger stared, too bludgeoned to do otherwise.

"There are consequences to every action, girl. And Salters must pay a blood price for mingling with their betters."

Moving with savage speed, the Paladin unsheathed his sword and plunged it into the stranger's belly. A froth of blood and saliva gurgled from his mouth. He toppled backward, ribbons of sliced intestine tumbling over his lap. The Templars who had held him let him drop.

The boy let out a thin scream until the Templar to his right elbowed the wind from his gut. The wiry man kept smiling, almost beatifically. The Paladin flicked a spray of gore from his blade and raised it for a second strike.

"This isn't fair!" Selena cried, stepping forward. The Templars who had held the dead man seized her by the arms and dragged her back. "They didn't do anything! That one didn't even want to fight me! I made him."

"Nevertheless," said the Paladin.

They made her watch until it was finished .

Selena found her own way back to her family's apartment, where her parents were waiting for her. Selena and her mother stood in the hallway while her father put a load of laundry through the washing machine.

"What the hell were you thinking?" Selena's mother spat. "You could've been hurt."

If only. "It's a fight, mom," replied Selena. "You can always get hurt. Besides, you didn't care when you thought I was training at Samson's gym."

"That's completely different. Samson's gym is one of the best facilities in Jericho. Half the men there are Templar officers. They know how to fight civilly, to make sure everything stays sporting."

"That's why they're so useless! A real fight isn't sporting. And it sure as hell isn't civil. You wouldn't understand."

"I understand that my daughter can't be seen getting in bare knuckle brawls with Salters."

"I thought we were all equal inside. That all this Seraphim bullshit was just a New Canaan ruse."

Her mother bristled. "It's not about that and you know it. It just raises too many questions. And we can't afford to draw any extra attention to ourselves."

"This has nothing to do with the Republic!"

"That doesn't matter. Attention is attention. There are eyes everywhere, Selena, and we don't want any more of them turned our way."

"Look, I don't want to talk about this right now." She stared at her hands. They were cleaned by all accounts, but they felt filthy, as if she'd stuck them wrist deep into the bodies of the Salters the Paladin had killed. That *she* had killed. *We're supposed to be the heroes. But the people who touch us die just the same.*

Selena's father put a hand on her shoulder. "We've never understood your … inclination for fighting, but we've tried to support you. We've given you the best trainers, the nicest gyms. Can't that be enough?"

As it turned out, it couldn't, but Selena behaved as if it was. She knew the pressure her parents were under, the extent to which New Canaan's leaden glare bore down upon even its most privileged citizens, how a word misspoken could mean public torture and death in a week's time. But more than that, she remembered the look on the boy's face as the Paladin's blade bit into his neck. When they'd first met, he'd told her that she'd get him killed, and in her arrogance, she'd assumed that she knew better.

So, she made the most of the Templar gyms, suffered the upturned noses and posh sneers as she studied her Salter strategies, and tried her best to ignore the embers burning hotly beneath the cool ash.

But Jericho was far away, and propriety wasn't a watchword in Fallowfield. It was time to unearth the embers, to fan the flames. Selena expected they'd burn all the hotter for their waiting.

Lanterns suffused the bar with greasy light. They hung from the walls and the pillars bisecting the long, low-ceilinged room, and squatted in the centers of wooden tables around which shaggy men grumbled and played cards and drank. Their dim glow draped a flattering veil of shadows over the stained floors and scarred faces and nicked furniture. The bar smelled of beer, whiskey, and tobacco. Sawdust covered the floor, soaking up the pools of spilled liquor and masking scabs of old vomit.

Selena sat at the bar. She massaged her forehead with one hand and glanced surreptitiously around the room, wondering who to approach. The bartender caught her eye and came over, polishing a stout glass. She was a small woman with a complexion cured by years of tobacco smoke.

"Can I get for ya?" she asked.

"Pint, please," Selena said, sliding two Standard notes across the bar. She didn't particularly want one, but if she bought a drink she figured she might get a little information in the bargain. "I here there's a lot of street fighting around these parts."

"Fair bit, I suppose." The bartender worked as she spoke, mopping a glass with a damp rag and filling it with sudsy blond liquid drawn from a wooden barrel. "You lookin' to make a wager?"

"No. I'm looking to join."

The bartender gave Selena a skeptical glance. Selena met it evenly. "Fraid I don't know much about that. Tony'd be the guy to talk to. I ain't seen him around today." She plopped Selena's pint down in front of her. A bit of beer slopped over the edge. Selena took a sip, careful to avoid the bits of chipped glass marring the rim.

"You know how I can get in touch with him?"

"Wait around here long enough and he'll show up."

"How long, thereabouts?"

"Could be a couple hours. Could be a couple weeks. Tony comes and goes as he pleases."

Selena chewed her lip. Two weeks was a lot longer than she was willing to sit on her heels. The data stick seemed to grow heavier every instant, tossing its swelling wait impatiently westward. "And no one else sets up fights around here?"

"He's the only one has permission, far as I know. You could try to get one going yourself, but the Shepherds'll throw you in jail like as not. The Mayor likes to keep that stuff controlled."

A man dressed in filthy overalls and a rumpled straw hat ran into the tavern, kicking up clouds of sawdust.

"Street fight!" he yelled, and disappeared as quickly as he'd come. Conversation ceased. For a moment, the only sound was the guttering of the lanterns' greasy flames. Then chairs scraped hardpan, glasses clunked on tabletops, and a murmur of excitement roiled the crowd. A plague of barflies swarmed into the street.

The bartender gave Selena a sly wink.

"Looks like you're in luck, honey."

Selena left her beer on the counter and went to find the crowd.

She heard them before she saw them, the scuff of boots on cobblestones and the murmur of overlapping voices. A ring of onlookers formed in the southeast corner of the city's central square, merchants in the middle, migrants orbiting the edges and straining for a proper view. *These people* do *like fighting. Half the city must be out here.* Selena nudged her way inside, earning herself a few sour glances from beruffled traders annoyed that some dirty upstart would deign to rub shoulders with them.

Two men stood in the center of the ring. The one nearest to Selena was well over six feet tall, and must have weighed two hundred and fifty pounds. His lower half bulged in a distended pear shape, but his arms were thick and muscular. He held a large wooden maul in one meaty fist. Across from him stood his opponent. The afternoon sun was at his back, and to Selena he appeared as little more than a silhouette. He was a thin man, only a few inches shorter than his opponent, but likely half the weight. He wore loose and flowing clothes beneath a black and red serape. His face was long, with pronounced cheekbones and a tapering, feminine chin, and encircled by a corona of curly black hair. In his hand was a knife, its blade barely six inches long. Next to the big man's maul, it seemed almost comically undersized.

"Look at that guy," said a young merchant standing next to Selena. "The big fella could use him for a toothpick."

"He's lucky we're standing here," added another man, fingers skating over his carefully oiled goatee. "Otherwise the wind'd blow him away!"

The thin man casually cleaned his fingernails on his serape. His opponent hefted his maul, patting the weighted end against his palm.

A stocky, baldheaded man muscled his way into the ring. He held a brass bowl out in front of him. His arms were hairy and covered in crude tattoos depicting what Selena guessed were supposed to be flames, although they were poorly rendered in a single swampy shade of green.

"Place your bets! The big fella's black, the beanpole's white. Two to one on black." The tattooed man lowered the bowl and held it to his body with one arm, using the other to take cash from the spectators and hand out tiny objects from the bowl. As he came closer, Selena saw they were small stones, polished smooth and sanded into a distinct button shape. They came in two colors, white and black. Most people who bet took black stones, though Selena spotted a few clutching white ones to their chests.

The tattooed man made his way briskly around the circle. Beside Selena, a merchant with a large ruffled collar held out a small handful of bills and took in return three black stones. On her other side, an old man in a tradesman's scruffy garb paid the tattooed man a smaller sum and took two white stones.

"Whoa, I'd just as soon take your money, grey, if you're gonna give it away," the young merchant said. The older man said nothing in return.

Having made his rounds, the tattooed man slipped into a crevice on the edge of the crowd. He blew a small whistle. The thin man slid forward, closing the distance between himself and the giant, and the fight began.

The giant had seen combat before, and the thin man's charge didn't startle him. He was ready with a swift and immensely powerful swing of his maul. It was well-timed, but the thin man knew his trade well too, and he stopped just short of the maul's furious arc. He closed the rest of the distance and swept his knife upward. The giant dodged with some success; the blade missed his jaw but nicked his nose and drew a few droplets of blood.

Smiling, the thin man slipped back to his side of the ring. The giant, incensed by his trivial but embarrassing injury, pursued. The maul swung with devastating force, the sound of it like a mag train barrelling by, but the thin man seemed entirely unafraid. He flirted with its deadly weight, letting it pass mere inches from his face, dodging back just enough to keep from having his brains dashed clear out of his skull. The giant swung faster and harder, grunting with exertion. The crowd backed away nervously every time he got too close, afraid a rogue blow might collapse a ribcage or render a skull into splinters.

The giant brought his maul round low, aiming for the thin man's knees. It was a shrewd blow, and surprisingly fast for such a big weapon, but the thin man dodged it almost casually, raising first one leg and then the other as if skipping rope. He struck out with his knife again, but this time he wasn't being playful. The blade sunk in just above the giant's left hip, twisted, and slashed its way free.

The thin man advanced, keeping pace with the giant, walking him slowly and deliberately around the perimeter of the crowd. The giant, aware that he was growing weaker, stood his ground. His only chance was to end the fight quickly, before he bled out. He raised the maul, arms tucked against his sides, breath coming in labored gasps. The thin man stopped just out of reach and watched the giant, his head cocked curiously to one side.

The ring grew still. The air pressure seemed to drop, sucking the crowd closer to the action. Only the thin man seemed calm. He paused to nibble on the cuticle of his middle finger, checked his fingernail, and took a single step forward, bringing him within range of the giant's maul. The giant struck. It was a backhanded swing, the fastest strike the giant had thrown, delivered beautifully and without any warning. By the time most of the onlookers even saw it coming it had already failed.

An incredulous gasp rose from the crowd. For a moment, they weren't sure if the thin man had been hit or not. The blunted tip of the maul seemed almost to have passed through him. Only Selena noticed how he'd leaned back, allowing just enough room for the weapon to pass by him.

Closing the gap before the swing had even reached its terminus, the thin man slipped his knife deftly between the giant's ribs. The blade slid along, tracing the contours of the giant's ribcage, and popped free with an ugly liquid smack. The giant dropped his maul. He staggered back several paces, hands pressed to his chest. The thin man removed a stained rag from his pocket and wiped his blade clean. The giant staggered, fell. Blood pooled in the cracks between the cobblestones.

Gradually, the crowd realized the fight was over. There was no elation and little chatter. Those who'd bet on the giant seemed too stunned to grumble or cry foul, and the fortunate few who'd placed wagers on the thin man seemed unsurprised by the outcome. They collected their winnings silently, forcing back smiles. The losers queued sulkily behind them, keen to return their black chips and get back their small deposits.

Selena watched the thin man polish his knife with a linen handkerchief, inspect it closely, and fold the blade into the handle. A switchblade. Selena couldn't recall seeing one before, though she knew of a few hardened Salters in the slums of West Jericho who favored them. The thin man pocketed the blade and turned to leave, but spotted Selena staring at him. He tilted his head to one side.

The plaza filled back in. Vendors wheeled their carts into position, eager to occupy the now vacant swath of prime real estate. The migrants slinked off, their free entertainment over. The merchants, sated by their bloody distraction, returned to business.

Pushing the strange knife fighter from her mind, Selena muscled her way through the crowd until she reached the tattooed man. He stood at the end of a long snaking line. Selena came up beside him.

"You Tony?"

"Who's asking?"

"Names Selena. You the one who arranges the fights here?"

"You guessed it. You wanna cash in your chit you get in line like everyone else." He continued collecting stones and passing out winnings and deposits as he spoke. The stones made a plinking sound as they rained into the bowl. Selena saw a small symbol scribbled on each of them in silver ink. An anti-counterfeit measure, she figured.

"I don't have a chit, and it's not a bet I'm after. It's a fight."

Tony grinned. His smile resembled the desolate skyline of a city bombed to rubble.

"Throw a punch at one of these mooks in line here. You'll get your wish."

"I want an organized fight. In Green Plaza."

"You ever seen my fights? There not something you wanna step into lightly."

Selena recalled the way the thin man's blade had gutted the giant, the spurt-gush-trickle of blood on the dusty cobbles, the callus way they dragged his corpse aside. *This isn't playtime, Selena. Be careful.* "I'm aware."

"Most of the men I get are twice your size, and none of them got any qualms about crushing your pretty little head between their fists. Them field grunts are animals. All they got is fightin' and to them it's all they need."

"Are your fights always to the death?" The thought gave Selena pause. The Salter's circle was rough, but at least both parties who walked in always walked out again.

Tony drummed his fingers on the belly of his bowl. Smudgy green flames danced and flickered along his forearm. "They aren't *always* anything. That's the whole point. The fight's over when the winner calls it and the loser ain't in a spot to disagree. Sometimes they finish with a beating. Sometimes they take it further. You want a bit of gentle sparring, you take yourself elsewhere."

Selena considered her options. If she went west without supplies or a caravan, she was dead meat. If she grubbed it in the fields, she'd like as not still be here years after New Canaan had already crossed the mountains—and probably have starved or frozen to death in the bargain. That left the fights. They were a risk not just for her, but for the Republic. If she died in the ring, the data stick would most likely rot with her.

"What's the take?" she asked.

"Winner gets fifty percent of the pot once all bets are paid out. Loser gets jack."

"What's a typical pot?"

"Varies from crowd to crowd. Three hundred Standard most days. With a good draw, four."

A hundred and fifty Standard. Harvey was right. That beats the hell out of reaping. Even without a caravan, a few winning fights could buy a lot of food, fresh clothes, maybe even a rifle. "Fifty percent's a pretty stiff fee for a promoter."

"What can I say, kid? I'm the only game in town. Give me a couple days to sort something out. I'll get in touch with my guys, see if any of 'em are okay with hitting ladies."

"Even if they're not, I'm game. Make things a lot simpler on my end."

Tony flashed a smile. Selena regretted her witticism. "It ain't gonna be that easy on you. Still interested?"

"Book it."

"You got balls, kid," Tony said, looking her up and down. "In a manner of speaking, of course. Come by here at six-after-midday two days from today. I'll see who I got. But I'm warning you, kid. In my circle, fat drunks and glass-jawed braggarts don't cut it. My guys are fighters."

"Good," Selena said. "Then me and them will have something in common."

8: The Red Dragon

Simon bounded up the staircase and into the office where The Mayor sat at his giant desk, leafing through a leather-bound ledger and scrawling notes.

"Ah! Simon my boy. The muse calls, does she? I won't keep her waiting."

Simon dotted his palette with fresh blobs of paint, scooted his stool close to his easel, and set to work. The brush made tiny, furtive strokes against the canvas. Most of the work was already done. All that Simon had left to do was touch up some details. Within an hour, he was holding his canvas aloft, checking it against the afternoon light.

"I'm finished," he said.

The Mayor rubbed his hands together. "Aha! The long-awaited moment has arrived! Shall we do a formal unveiling, or may I see it unframed?"

"You can see it."

The Mayor stepped into the narrow room. Simon held the canvas with its painted side facing his chest, making sure to keep clear of the parts still tacky with drying paint.

"Are you ready?" he asked.

"I quiver with anticipation."

"Okay." Simon turned the canvas.

Selena stood before a backdrop of stormy greys, her eyes staring determinedly at some point in the far distance. Her skin bore a healthy glow not quite matched by her corporeal counterpart, and the dirt beneath her nails and matted in her callused fingertips was gone. Otherwise, it was her. Her bronze skin glistened, gentle brushstrokes delicately implying the downy hairs on her forearms, and subtle shading suggested the cords of muscle taut within. The Mayor looked it over, his eyes enigmas behind opaque glass.

"An incredible likeness," he said. "Your sister will surely be pleased."

"You think so?"

"I don't doubt it. Though I must admit, Simon, I'd rather hoped you were making something for my collection."

"Oh! I'm sorry, I didn't, I just thought I could use some practice—"

The Mayor raised a hand. "A simple miscommunication. Nothing to apologize for."

"You can keep it, if you want to. I mean, it's your canvas and paints and stuff."

"No, no. It's not my intention to make you my personal artistic servant. If I wanted you to paint something specific, I should have commissioned it. Take this one with you, by all means."

"You really think Selena'll like it?" Simon asked.

"Certainly. Who wouldn't?"

Unfortunately, Simon thought he had a pretty good idea.

Frank ran his thumbs over the Standard notes, leaving a sweaty trail. Leon reached out, not quite daring to touch them. Frank would hand him his share eventually, but first he needed to complete his tiny sacrament to their good fortune.

Things really were looking up. Their side business brought in Standard on a scale Leon could scarcely fathom. He no longer had to stretch a handful of currants or a lone pear into lunch, but filled his belly on salami and cheese wedges and sandwiches made on fresh bread. Dinners of bone broth vanished in favor of rich chili and sausages and roasted legs of lamb. Fallowfield's inner market, all but closed to them in the past—by its prohibitive prices and whiffs of elitism, if not by actual law—spread its arms widely in welcome. Leon found himself frequenting shops he'd never even known existed—cheesemongers, butchers, and traders of spice, ale, and garnishes.

Leon preferred eating these heady repasts in secret, but Frank felt a need to flaunt their fortune over the other fieldhands, smacking his lips as he tucked into succulent chicken breasts or a spoonful of hearty beef stew. Such antagonism invited a brawl, at the very least, but so far the other fieldhands hadn't raised so much as a finger to them. Perhaps their business suggested dangerous connections. In any case, Leon hoped this strange protection held out, since Frank wasn't about to change his ways anytime soon.

They sat in the Rye and Sickle, one of the few establishments in Fallowfield that catered largely to fieldhands. Even Frank knew better than to set foot in one of the upscale merchant taverns on the northern road. Money or not, such a move would be noticed by the wrong people. People who weren't intimidated by assumed connections with the *pandilleros* down south. Frank held a jug of ale in one fist, slurping down mouthfuls straight from the neck. The greasy remnants of fried potatoes and bacon littered the table in front of him. He gave the Standard a final appreciative sniff then counted out Leon's half, which Leon promptly tucked into a pouch he'd had sewn into the inside of his pants.

"This is the way it's supposed to be, eh Leon?" Frank licked a crumb of bacon from the corner of his mouth. His ire at the blond girl and her brother had faded over the last couple days, soothed by the comforts of his sudden affluence. "Meals cooked for ya, beer by the jug-full. Proper beer, too, not the watered-down crap they pull from the kegs in this joint." Frank rubbed the jug with a fondness that was almost sensual. It held a rich pale ale crafted by Izzy Bauer, a seasoned brewer on the north end of the city. Tonya, the barmaid, kept them on hand for slumming merchants or their bodyguards, who sometimes favored the Sickle's looser atmosphere. Fieldhands and farmers stuck by necessity to hooch or the thin and piss-warm house brew. A few sitting nearby studied Frank's jug with undisguised resentment. Frank met their eyes and chugged down gulletfuls of amber liquid. He finished the bottle and the two of them left the bar.

Leon didn't like dealing in the city itself—there were more Shepherds, for one thing, and overdoses or other mishaps among merchants were actually investigated—but Frank insisted this was where the money was, and in that he was inarguably correct. Selling to fieldhands was carrion eating, picking scraps of meat from rotting bones; selling to merchants was big game hunting—the take was rich and juicy, but the prey could bite you right back if you weren't careful. And the merchants were thick on the ground today—plump, gloating, resplendent in synthetic Jericho silks and ancient jewels and ruffs of fine lace—though at the moment they weren't doing much trading. They gathered in Green Plaza in a loose circle, at the nucleus of which a man stood between two Shepherds. His soiled chambray shirt and ratty overalls hung loose as a jacket on a scarecrow, the bony wrists peeking from torn shirt cuffs the only sign of his painful thinness—apart from his hollow cheeks and parchment skin. The merchants observed the man with contempt and a little wry amusement.

At the fringe of the crowd stood a small group of farmers, their clothes filthy and ill-fitting, their faces sombre. They seemed out of place in the city, peasants swept by circumstance into the hallway of a palace. Leon spotted Harvey among them, heavy bags weighing down his eyelids. Frank glanced his way and sneered.

"Look at those assholes. They act like bigshots when they're bossin' us around, but what've they got? I bet none of 'em could even afford half the meal we just had." He puffed out his chest. "The fields are for suckers, pal. Slingin' rock in the city, that's where it's at. I'm done bein' used." He approached a burly carriage guard and made a small rubbing gesture with his thumb and fingers. The guard licked the corner of his mouth and extended three fingers in a sideways W shape. Frank flashed back all five fingers splayed, clenched, and repeated two more times. The guard nodded.

Frank nudged Leon, who fished a package out of a hand-sewn pocket concealed inside his shirt. He let the package slip between his fingers. The guard sniffed dismissively, probed his tongue into the folds of his cheek one last time, and in a single fluid motion grabbed the package and stuffed a wad of bills into Leon's hand. Leon clutched the bills instinctively, hiding them in his large, meaty fist. As he did with every sale, he felt a moment of dislocated panic, sure a gang of Shepherds would leap from the shadows and drag him off to the courthouse for sentencing.

"Do we have to do this here?" he asked. "It's so crowded."

"That's what makes it safe, stupid! Ain't you never heard of hiding in plain sight?"

Leon bit his lip. "No."

Frank gave a grunt of disgust. "It means that if there's lots of people around, they're all too busy lookin' at each other to be lookin' at you."

"Oh."

Gradually, Leon's anxiety abated, though he knew it would return with the next sale, and the next. The fact he was witnessing his own possible future certainly didn't help. For this was no regular fighting circle, but a court-mandated punishment. Only three crimes in Fallowfield merited such a treatment: murder, narcotics sales, and withholding of city-state resources. Frank and Leon were guilty of the second, the woebegone farmer of the third.

The crowd parted to admit two men. The first was an enormous Shepherd, his left cheek twisted by a hook-shaped scar running from mouth to ear. He was dressed in plain black garb, his pistol and truncheon nowhere in evidence. The second man was The Mayor, resplendent in a red velvet coat and breeches. The farmer paid them no attention. He stared impassively into the crowd, ignoring every jeer and catcall lobbed his way by the merchants.

The Mayor's hands spread and the crowd fell silent. Sunlight set his reflective lenses aflame with a piercing white glow.

"My fellow townsfolk and esteemed traders. It is never a happy occasion, my standing in this circle before you. As a city and a country in one, we exist as a single organism, one that has acclimatised itself to the harsh conditions the Middle Wastes imposes upon us. Ours is a hard existence, and every cell must function optimally if we are to survive. It is this fact that makes the crime of which James Crawley is guilty all the more egregious, for he took from us that which we need most: our food."

Crawley barked a bitter laugh. "I look like I've been eatin' well at your expense, Mayor?"

One of the Shepherds struck Crawley in the back of the head. He fought to stand and only just managed it. The Shepherd grabbed him by the collar and yanked him back into position. The Mayor continued as if uninterrupted.

"The fecund lands surrounding Fallowfield belong to all of us, not simply those privileged few entrusted with their stewardship. We sow, grow, reap, and gain as one, which is why our noble Shepherds collect and distribute our produce. These are sold to the benefit of all Fallowfield residents. But sadly, some see fit to exploit the sumptuous bounty under their charge, and withhold from our Shepherds more than is their right. In this, they rob from the very folks who have bestowed their trust upon them, and bring us all a step closer to the ruin and starvation camped forever outside our gates. Therefore, they must face a hard but necessary punishment.

"But ours is also a merciful society, and James Crawley may yet earn his life, guilty though he is. For the men of the field live by their own code, and each may be granted reprieve through combat. The captain of the Shepherds, Bernard Templeton, will stand as Fallowfield's champion. Should Crawley best him, he will have proven his worth and face only exile, his claims to his land and holdings forfeit."

"Feh. They ain't worth shit anyhow." Crawley's voice came out cracked and raw. "You people are nothin' but vultures. We work our fingers to the bone every summer, drought or flood, good crop or bad, and every winter we eat scraps and pray for an early thaw. I seen too many friends a mine not make it to springtime cause your precious Mayor took everything they had and called it a tithe. I looked in my cellar and I knew it would happen to me. So I kept what I needed to feed me and mine. I don't see none a you starvin' for it. Piss on your justice. One day you'll see where it gets you. We'll—"

Bernard glided over the cobbles like some giant bird of prey. His fist caught Crawley square in the stomach, doubling him forward. Green sputum flecked with dots of blood sprayed from his mouth. The Shepherds to his either side let go of his arms, spilling him onto the cobblestones. Bernard grabbed him by the hair and dragged him to his feet, wrenching a yelp of pain from his throat. The Mayor gave an indulgent grin.

"May the trial by combat begin."

It wasn't a fight, not really. Crawley made an effort, his resignation devoured by his instincts for survival, but the so-called trial by combat was nothing but a grisly form of execution.

The fieldhands saw the fighting circle as their sole chance for salvation, a spark of hope in an otherwise dank and barren field. Inevitably, the younger farmers would also try their hands at the circle, hoping to eke out enough winnings to sustain them through another lean winter. They scrabbled and growled while the merchants dangled scraps of Standard over their heads, laughing at the spectacle. Only the older ones resisted—not for lack of want or hunger, but because they knew they'd lose, and their weathered bodies could not afford the time away from their fields necessary to recuperate. The system was debasing and cruel, but it hardened the fieldhands' fists and honed their instincts.

Yet their skill, their ferocity, their desperation, whatever elements of advantage they'd gathered through their many brawls with one another, all of it broke against Bernard like waves against a granite shore. No one ever beat him. So far as Leon knew, no defendant had even so much as given him a black eye.

The big man moved with studied efficiency, a smile playing on his lips. Crawley floundered like a drowning man, limbs flailing fruitlessly, his face a patchwork of bruised and ruptured flesh. At one point, he tried to claw his way through the crowd, but the merchants shoved him back, hooting laughter. The farmers clenched their fists at the spectacle. Some turned away, others watched with grim determination, their presence a kind of vigil.

Eventually Bernard grew bored, or perhaps sensed the waning interest of the crowd. He threw a cross that landed squarely on Crawley's chin. Crawley flew back half a dozen feet and landed on his back with an anguished gasp. Bernard strolled over to him, set his boot on the side of Crawley's head, and stomped down. Leon's stomach shrivelled at the wet cracking sound.

The merchants cheered. The farmers didn't share their enthusiasm. A few wept, others stared at The Mayor with undisguised hatred. Leon simply felt sick. It was too easy to imagine his own head beneath that boot, the moment of unbearable pressure before his skull burst like a spoiled egg, spilling its runny contents onto the cobbles for crows to pick clean.

Gradually the crowd dispersed. Frank managed another couple quick deals, each one culminating with a single icy squeeze of Leon's heart. When the last safe customers trickled away, Frank and Leon returned to the fields, their pockets heavy with Standard.

"We got this town by the balls, pal," Frank said, his voice buoyant. Leon nodded, though he shared none of his friend's jubilation. The sound of Crawley's fracturing skull rang in his ears like an undying echo. Even worse, in a way, was the emerald fire that had burned in Bernard's eyes as he'd delivered the killing blow. It was the triumphant gaze of a man who loved his work and wanted to do a lot more of it.

Leon had no interest in keeping him in business.

The Rye and Sickle was surprisingly quiet. Some sort of public forum was happening outside in Green Plaza, but Selena's mind was too focused on her upcoming fight to pay it any attention. A fiddler girl tuned her instrument in the corner—her labors partially hidden by a curtain of wavy red hair—and a loose assortment of early drinkers slumped across a few tables, but the place was otherwise empty. Selena ordered a beer, found a place near the door, and sat, waiting for Tony. The fiddler rosined her bow and began to play. Her strokes were light and her voice soft; she was clearly practicing for a later set, not performing. But the bar was quiet enough for Selena to catch the tune anyway, a ballad from before the Last War, preserved over the intervening century by oral tradition.

"Ooh, the storm is threatening, my very life today. If I can't find some shelter, oh Lord, I'm gonna fade away."

Selena listened, enjoying herself, and soon Tony slid in opposite her. He helped himself to a sip of her beer.

"Surprised to find you here," Tony said.

"You thought I was a liar?"

"I thought you might have some sense."

"'Fraid not. You find me an opponent?"

"I did. Hey Kaeric!"

The man who appeared behind Tony was young, well-muscled, and dressed in a Shepherd's pin. A red beard resplendently braided with silver ribbons hung down past his collarbone, a lean and hungry smile shining through its curly red foliage. His fingers toyed with the rawhide strap connecting a sleek hardwood truncheon to his wrist.

"Selena, this is Kaeric. Round the circle, they call him The Red Dragon. Kaeric, meet Selena."

"Pleasure," Kaeric said, eyeing her up and down.

"This is all you have for me?" Selena asked.

"Everyone else was either bruised, busy, or didn't take to fightin' a girl."

"Don't bother me none," grinned Kaeric. "Meat is meat."

Spoken like a man who's never had a decent steak in his life, thought

Selena. In truth, she didn't believe Tony for a second. There had to be dozens of fieldhands out there spoiling for a fight. This was a test. They were trying to bluff her out, to scare her into quitting. But Selena had fought hard men before. Next to some of the Salters she'd toe-to-toed with, Kaeric was a lump of jelly.

"Fine. Let's do it."

In Green Plaza, a fresh circle formed naturally and without any noticeable prompting around the combatants. It was as if the magnetic tension between Selena and Kaeric drew them forward, pulling at the metal in their blood. Tony raised his tattooed arms in an unsuccessful attempt to quell the swelling chatter.

"Shut up!" barked Kaeric, his voice a gunshot. The talkers fell silent.

"The girl and the dragon," bellowed Tony. "A fable in the making! White for the girl, black for the dragon! Girl pays out six to one!" Tony jingled his brass bowl. The merchants chatted among themselves, placing bets and elbowing one another in the ribs. A clutch of farmers stood slightly back from the crowd, watching with a collective gaze of inscrutable intensity. They placed no bets, but Selena sensed that they felt a great deal riding on this fight all the same. She pushed them from her mind, focussing her attention squarely on her opponent.

Tony signalled for the fight to begin. As the two fighters came together, Selena felt something brusk and potent rush into her, a gust of wind that stirred cooling ashes into flame. The taste of blood and salt and copper soaked her tongue, the hothouse stink of bodies pricked her nostrils. Her senses flared, her sinews thrummed, her muscles coiled like hungry serpents. Half a continent away, beyond the parched soil and ruined cities of the Middle Wastes, she'd found her way back to the circle of blood. This was home, in a way New Canaan could never be. Nebulous, transient, vicious, but unquestionably home.

Kaeric slinked along the arc of the circle, eyeteeth long and flashing. Selena kept pace, her arms raised in a boxer's stance, matching the bigger man step for step. Kaeric brought his fists up in parody of Selena's posture. Selena stared back, expressionless. A good guard protected more than your head and chest—it protected your mind, too. Selena had seen many fights where the winner wielded weaker fists but a stronger psyche.

Kaeric threw a cross and Selena stepped aside. His fist whistled past her head. He had power, but his technique was crude, and what punches he landed merely grazed Selena's forearms or punished her biceps. Her vulnerable spots, her face and neck and belly, eluded him. She chanced a jab to his ribs—drawing a quick grunt and a poorly suppressed grimace of pain—stepped back, and parried his next few punches. Kaeric grew annoyed and came at her harder, but his fists found nothing but air. Selena jumped in with a right hook. It was a knock-out swing, a steel piston driving from her calves on up, but it landed poorly. She overextended, upsetting her balance and opening a narrow window where her dukes were down. Kaeric leapt deftly through it. He launched a jab that split Selena's lip and sent a thin jet of blood spurting onto the dusty cobblestones.

Selena took several shuffling steps back, turtling behind her folded arms. In the Salter's circle that would've ended it, but Fallowfield fights had no such safety valves. Kaeric pursued, his face stretched into a slick grin. *Maybe this wasn't so smart after all.*

He pounded her mercilessly, but Selena's guard held fast. She needed it to. Jab or not, his punch had been *strong*. Selena could still feel it rattling about her skull. A few more like that and her fighting days might well be over.

Selena doled out punches frugally. Kaeric was more aggressive, but couldn't slalom his way through Selena's guard. The two soon fell into a pattern of parries and fakes, neither making any ground. It became a cautious fight, devoid of much of the usual blood and thunder, and the crowd grew restless. Onlookers jeered. A few threw pebbles and peanut shells. These taunts bounced harmlessly off of Selena. The same could not be said of Kaeric. He swore back at the crowd, beating his chest and making feints as if to attack them. Behind the parapets of her composure, Selena saw an opportunity. She slipped through the cracks of his fractured concentration and landed a few deft jabs, including one that broke his nose. Cartilage crackled with a sound like fat spitting from a cooking fire. Blood dribbled down his chin. The crowd resumed its cheering, but it took on a mocking edge, the crust of their fear flensed away to reveal a churning, bilious contempt. The farmers cheered with savage glee, howling with delight at the Shepherd's cracked visage.

"Hey Kaeric! If you survive this one, you wanna go at my grandma next?"

"She snip your balls off before the fight, Kaeric?"

Kaeric's patience broke. He charged at Selena, fist flying in a savage haymaker. Selena stepped forward and let the blow pass behind her. She locked Kaeric's arm beneath her elbow, dropped her shoulder, and threw a fierce uppercut. Kaeric's head snapped back. His braided beard traced his fall like the tail of a comet.

She was on him before he landed, clamping one arm around his neck and pinning his forearm tight against his spine. Selena was no wrestler, but she'd learned a few holds in Jericho's Templar gyms and she dredged them up from the depths of her memory now, limbs moving instinctively and without pause. She dug her knee into the small of his back and held on as hard as she could. Kaeric bucked and writhed. In response, Selena slid his forearm farther up his back. His shoulder bulged. It looked ready to burst out of its skin.

Kaeric held out as best he could, but his best was no more than a few seconds. His free hand tapped the ground frantically. Selena let him go. The crowd's stunned silence gave way to cheers. Kaeric stumbled to his feet. Blood matted his beard. He swayed like a drunkard, massaging his injured shoulder.

Selena took half a step back from him, her hands raised above her waist, not quite in a fighting stance but ready to take one if the need arose.

Kaeric spat a bloody glob of phlegm onto the cobbles and smiled humorlessly.

"Luck," he said, and walked off, head held aloft with purposeful dignity.

No, not luck, Selena silently corrected. *Technique.*

Limping slightly, Selena slumped her way to back to the Rye and

Sickle. She ordered a drink, sought the shadiest corner she could find, and slouched against the bench seat, a pint of watery lager pressed to her split lip. The beer was lukewarm, but the residual coolness of the glass felt soothing. When the pain withdrew to a dull throb, she set the glass down and began unwrapping the strip of cotton stretched around her knuckles. Her fingers gasped relief. She linked them into a single blunt instrument and probed her neck, her jaw, her sides, feeling for the sharp icepick of pain that would indicate a break or rupture. Tony sat down opposite her and watched without comment.

"That was some takedown, kid," he said.

"Yeah, well, they can't all be knucklebusters." Selena knew the crowd came to see knockouts, not pins. She expected Tony to offer her a reduced cut, or to threaten to withhold her take altogether. Instead, he counted out his earnings into two equal piles, peeled a twenty Standard note off of one, placed it on the other, and slid Selena the heavier stack. Selena looked at the money curiously and, tucking it into her pants pocket, asked "what's the extra twenty for?"

"For a damn fine show."

"What're you talking about? That fight was lousy. We barely landed a punch."

"Maybe not, but you kept it interesting to the last. Just where the hell'd you learn to fight like that?"

"East," Selena said.

"Well then remind me never to piss a lady off I'm ever out that way. Let me tell you something, kid: not one man in that crowd expected you to come out on top, and sure as hell not to do it so damn fast, with a pin. You know how many people bet on you? Three. In a crowd of over fifty. Even with the long odds I took damn near twice as much as I regularly do. And the fools cheered as you flushed their money away! That's pure spectacle, kid. That's theatre."

"Glad to hear it. Give me a day to get the swelling down and put me in again."

Tony inhaled through his ruined teeth. "Fraid it ain't that simple."

"Why not? You said yourself I'm theatre."

"Sure, but who pays to see the same show twice?"

"It won't be the same show if you put me up against someone else."

"I'm not sure I got someone else. Kaeric was one of our toughest guys. People see you put him down, they're gonna start placin' bets on your side. The long odds won't be so long, and the take ain't gonna be a third of what it was. What's more, I get a face out there too often it's gonna go stale on me. It's a problem of what you call diminishing returns. I could get you out again this week, take the pittance, then put you on the rotation, but you ain't gonna make any real money that way."

"You seem to do okay."

Tony shrugged. "Only one a me, darling, I got damn near a hundred of you bruisers at any one time. Shit, half the field grunts tug my sleeves every chance they get, dreamin' a riches and glory. Can only cut a pie so many ways 'fore all anyone gets is crumbs."

"Great. So where does that leave me?"

"Two hundred Standard ahead for the moment. Best count your blessings and learn another trade." He rapped his knuckles on the counter and left, flashing Selena a final hideous smile.

Well, shit, thought Selena. *That was a good twenty minutes.* Now what was she supposed to do? Two hundred Standard was quite a boon, but it wouldn't go far when it came to stocking up for a journey through the Wastes. Even if she worked her way into Tony's rotation, it would still mean scrimping her way through a months-long stay in Fallowfield, and Selena didn't like the thought of staying for even another two weeks. The data stick was a lit coal in her pocket, burning its urgent way through the meat of her thigh. *How many months until spring? Six? Five?* She could feel New Canaan gearing up across the wasteland, the first pistons firing in its great engine of war. *Too slow. Every turn I take, the path is still too damn slow.*

Distracted by her sombre frame of mind, Selena didn't notice the man had sat down beside her until he scraped the bottom of his glass on the table. It took a second longer to place him—the knife fighter, the one who'd killed the giant in Green Plaza. He leaned forward, his checkered serape billowing out in front of him, his narrow cheeks dark with stubble. When he smiled, his teeth seemed almost to flash, as if lit from within.

"May I have this seat?" he asked, having already taken it.

"I guess." Selena sipped her beer. The suds stung her split lip.

"My name is Marcus," the man said. "I believe you know my work?"

"I saw your fight, yeah."

"And I saw yours. It was, how you say, quite the spectacle. Most in the crowd thought you would fail."

"But not you," Selena said, her voice parched with cynicism.

Eyeteeth flashed in the gloom. "No, I thought the same. But I saw my mistake before the others did. You are a true *luchadora,* yes? A woman of the warrior arts?"

"I wouldn't put it that way. I'm a street fighter."

"Ah, I see. You claim to be a wild woman, a scrapper from the streets. But in your fists, your form, I see training."

"Yeah, so what?"

Marcus shifted back in his chair, studying his hands. "I heard you speak to Tony. You will fight for him again soon?"

"As soon as he'll put me back on."

"The fight will be easier. But the pay will also be small."

"So he said."

"Fallowfield fights can be good fights. But they are only one tree in a forest. You shake and you shake, but once the easy acorns fall you will starve before they grow back again. Better to walk the woods with a fellow forager, one who knows the best trees, the ripest fruits, the most bountiful bushes."

"What are you proposing?"

Marcus held his glass to the light. It contained two fingers of smoky liquid. "You wish to go west, yes?"

"Yeah."

"I can get you there."

Selena perked up an eyebrow. "And what do you want in return?"

"Fight for me. In the rings throughout the Middle Wastes. Fallowfield is not the only city with violence in its blood. There is much desperation in the locust, and to fight is to survive. I will show you the richest trees and you will shake the branches. We will both grow fat on the fruits. And when our bellies are full, we will ride through the southern wastes."

"How many fights are we talking?"

Marcus tallied figures with his hands. "Not many. Perhaps one dozen, perhaps two. This depends on the crowds. And whether you win or lose."

"I don't have that kind of time. My brother and I need to make it to the west coast by winter."

"And you will accomplish this by staying in Fallowfield?"

"I'm going to hire a caravan," Selena said, shifting in her seat. Saying it aloud, it seemed a flimsy plan.

"And what if one does not come?"

"The Mayor told me they pass by often enough." Selena cringed as she said it. The truth was, she didn't put much trust in what The Mayor told her. She'd asked a few questions about him around town, and while the answers were flattering enough, they seemed always tainted by a faint anxiety, a subtle nervous flicking of the eyes from side to side.

"Often enough for who? Him, or you? This is not much of a promise. And if they do pass through, can you trust you will find them? Do you know the drivers? The routes?"

Selena said nothing.

"You have a gift, girl, but these lands are not yours. I have walked these wastes for many years. I know the paths, and I know the people."

"And you call The Mayor vague," drawled Selena. "I can't afford to spend the winter following you over these shithole fields."

"Very well. Come with me for two weeks. When the fighting is done, we will split what we earn. In that time you make enough easily for supplies, horses, everything you need. I will help you get it, and we will ride south together. Do we have a deal?"

Selena looked Marcus up and down. His serape hid his narrow shoulders, masking his true dimensions. She figured it must make him more difficult to stab.

"Why do you need me? You seem to be doing well enough on your own."

"A fighter must drift to make his money, yes? But no matter how far you go, your name always travels farther. Sometimes, it overstays its welcome. Not so many bets, not so many fights. But a fresh face from the east, a girl no less, who is ten times as tough as she looks? This is fortune waiting to be made. This is opportunity. And I am not a man to pass up such opportunities."

Selena studied her reflection in the contents of her glass. Trusting this man felt weird, but sooner or later she was going to have to trust *someone*. She and Simon couldn't cross the wastelands to the south unaided. Every single merchant she'd spoken to had told her that much. They needed help, and so far, Marcus was the only one to provide an even remotely tangible offer.

But was it one worth taking?

Two weeks of solid fighting. It was a risk, and not a small one. She could be badly injured, crippled, even killed. Then the data stick would fall to Simon. And if he failed to reach the west coast? New Canaan would devour the continent, drown the Republic in blood and venom and boiling oil. Her life, her brother's life, the lives of her parents, all of them will have been spent for nothing. For an idea torn from the pages of history and tossed into the fire.

She'd never been to the Republic of California, never walked its roads or met its people. But her parents had died because they believed it should live. Now Selena needed to face the same stakes, and she would stand until death brought her down and not a moment before. If that stand meant fighting for this strange man in his even stranger country, then so be it.

"My brother would have to come with us. I don't want to leave him on his own."

Marcus arched an eyebrow. "So you agree?"

"I didn't say that. I'm still deciding. But if I go, he goes, too."

"Family first," Marcus smiled. "I have no trouble with this. I am in the city for four days. If you wish, come to me before that time and we will go together."

"Two weeks."

"Two weeks," Marcus agreed.

"And you'll get me to the west coast."

"Until your toes touch the Far Ocean."

Marcus downed his drink in a single rolling swig.

"I will see you soon, Selena," he said, and left, passing through the barroom crowd like a shadow. Selena saw a flicker of his serape, then nothing. She finished her drink, annoyed by his presumption. See you soon, he'd said, no trace of a question in his voice. As if he knew her decision before she did.

And the most annoying part was, he did.

9: Compound L

Simon sat at the foot of his bed and chewed nervously at his thumbnail. Out the window the moon was bloated and full, its edges dissolving into darkness.

The door opened and Selena stepped inside. She took of her poncho and draped it over the kitchen counter.

"Where were you?" asked Simon.

"Down at the Rye and Sickle."

"Why?"

"I had a street fight."

Simon's eyes dropped to the nappy carpet. He balled the loose fabric of his t-shirt in his hands. "Oh."

"And I won, in case you were wondering."

"Oh. Good."

"You don't have to give me that face, Simon. I used to have fights all the time, back in Jericho."

"I know."

"It's what I'm good at."

"I know." His eyes still downcast, his hands still worrying his shirt hem.

Selena's fingers traced the tiny rectangular bulge pressing against her hipbone. Her eyes wandered from Simon's face and settled on the painting leaning against the wall. She held it up to the moonlight, observing the delicate brushstrokes that comprised her oil and canvas doppelganger.

"What is this?"

"A painting."

Selena held the painting up for inspection. "You painted this?"

"I did."

"Looks just like me. Where did you get paints?"

"The Mayor has them. He set up a studio in his house where I can paint stuff some afternoons."

Selena cupped her face with one hand. She held Simon's painting in the other, her thumb dimpling the canvas.

"You're supposed to be preparing for our trip, Simon. Not painting pretty pictures in some mansion."

"He pays me," Simon sulked. "He probably pays me more than that farmer pays you."

"What do you mean he pays you? He pays you to *paint?*"

Simon held out a fan of ten Standard notes, their rumpled edges flapping slightly. Selena examined the painting again, though this time she seemed to really look at it.

"How much is he willing to pay?"

"I dunno. It depends on how long I'm there and what I paint, I guess."

"Well paint whatever he wants you to paint, then. Will he buy them off you?"

"I think so."

"Do you think he'd buy this one?"

"You … you don't want it?"

Selena bit her lip. *Jesus. Smooth move, you asshole. Why don't you just spit on the thing and be done with it?* "It's not that, Simon. It's just, I don't own a house. What am I supposed to do with a painting? Besides, there's something I need to talk to you about. We're not going to be here for much longer."

"What do you mean?"

"There's a man I met at the Rye and Sickle. I guess you'd call him a promoter. He's going to take us west."

"I thought we were going to get a caravan, like The Mayor said."

"With this guy's offer, we can be on the road in three weeks. If we try to get a caravan, we could wait around town for months. By the time one shows up, we'll be flat broke."

"You don't know that for sure. We could talk to The Mayor about it. He could help us."

"Are you not listening to me? That's the last thing we should do."

"He's a nice guy, Selena. I bet if we just told him we were in trouble, he'd give us all the help we need."

Selena rubbed her temples. "You can't know that, Simon."

"Oh, but you know this promoter guy is out to help us? You trust him, but not The Mayor?"

"It's two different things."

"How?"

"I'm not telling him about our past, for one."

"At least The Mayor took us in and offered us food and a safe place to stay."

"There. There's the problem, Simon. Why'd he do those things? I know what Marcus wants out of this deal. I don't know why The Mayor does anything. I don't know why he's in charge, I don't know what sort of power his Shepherds have, and I don't know what he's capable of. Most of all, I don't know if he works for New Canaan."

"Maybe he's just nice!" Selena took a step backward, as surprised at Simon's sudden anger as he seemed to be. "Is that so hard to believe? That people could be nice to us? Be nice to me? How can you be so … so ungrateful?"

Selena pressed the heels of her hands against her eyelids. "I swear to god, Simon. Sometimes it feels like I picked you up in some bumpkin town on the outskirts of New Canaan. Have you forgotten where we came from? Have you forgotten what they did to mom and dad?"

"What's that got to do with anything?"

Selena walked toward Simon until their faces were nearly touching. "Everything, Simon. It's got everything to do with our situation, with where we're going, with how we need to carry ourselves. I know this guy's given you a few attaboys and it feels good, but we don't know anything about him." She reached out and grabbed his collar. "You should see that. I need you to see that because I can't be the one looking over our shoulders all the time. That has to be both of us."

Simon thrust his chin out. He forced himself to meet Selena's eyes. "You're just doing this to punish me. You know I'm happy here and that's why you don't want to stay. It always has to be your way, your idea."

"It has nothing to do with that."

"Then why?"

"*This* is why," she hissed, shoving the data stick into Simon's face. He recoiled as if it were a blade or hot poker, something cruel and barbed and built to cause immeasurable harm. A worm of guilt wriggled through Selena's belly but she kept her hand firm. She needed to be strong. For her parents, for the Republic, for Simon most of all. But she didn't feel strong. She felt like a bully, and she spoke as if trudging barefoot over a field of broken glass. "Mom and dad died for this, Simon. They died screaming on crosses—"

"—Stop it—"

"—with nails in their hands—"

"—*Stop it!*—"

"—so that we could bring this data stick to the Republic. If we fail, the Republic falls, New Canaan gets the whole continent to itself, and mom and dad'll have died or nothing. Remember Aldo Delduca?"

"Of course I remember Aldo Delduca! How am I ever supposed to forget him when you keep bringing him up?"

Selena's voice feinted beneath Simon's shout, dropping to a deadly near-whisper. *This has to hurt. There's no other way.* It was hard to say who felt it more. "Niagara was a small place and a small enemy. When the Archbishop conquered it, he boiled five hundred people alive. And that's just what he *showed* us. He hates the Republic way more. How many people will he kill if it falls to him? How many people will he burn to death, disembowel, or crucify? Is that what you want?"

"No." Simon's voice was tiny, petulant, defeated.

"We're the only ones that can stop it, Simon. If we fuck up, our deaths will be the first of *thousands*. Remember that." She turned away and massaged her aching knuckles. *We just need to reach Visalia.* Once they did that she could unshoulder that damned data stick, relinquish the strength she wore like a truss, the resolve that felt so much like cruelty. "We have a little under a week to get ready. Do all the painting you want until then, but keep your mouth shut. Got it?"

Simon didn't answer. His eyes fixed on the Selena he'd painted, her stern face frozen, unrelenting, staring with fierce determination at some point beyond the horizon.

Simon slumped into The Mayor's office, the painting of Selena in his arms. The Mayor sat at his desk scribbling figures in a leather-bound ledger.

"Simon, my boy. What are you doing with that painting? Didn't you give it to your sister?"

"I did. She said we didn't have anywhere to hang it."

"Your apartment has walls, surely."

"Yeah, it's just ... can I leave this here?"

The Mayor took the painting and studied it.

"Of course. I'd be honored to house your earliest masterpiece."

Simon slouched into his annex and set a fresh canvas on his easel. He sat in front of it for an hour, willing an image to break through its eggshell-blank surface, but nothing would come. He fidgeted with a paintbrush, running his thumb over its dry bristles and slapping out a dirge into his cupped palm. He was still fidgeting an hour later when Bernard stepped into The Mayor's office.

"Some of the farmers are outside, sir. They wanna speak to you."

Sighing, the Mayor rubbed his forehead.

"Heavy is the head, Bernard. You carve out paradise from perdition, and still the masses quibble at every turn."

"You want me to tell 'em to get lost?"

"No, no. Let them have their say."

Three men entered a few minutes later. Dirt fell in clumps from the sides of their boots, littering The Mayor's fine Turkish rug. Simon expected them to be a little thinner and less clean than the merchants, given their jobs, but the disparity shocked him. Their faces were sallow and weathered, and soiled clothes hung loosely on their scrawny frames. Each favored Bernard and The Mayor with looks of almost overwhelming repugnance. It was the kind of gaze that suggested they'd caught the two of them jointly deflowering a close relative. The Mayor, ignoring this sour greeting, met them with a magnanimous wave.

"Gentlemen. Always a pleasure to hear notes from the trenches. How can I help you?"

"You know damn well how you can help us," grunted the oldest of the bunch. His blue eyes peered through a thicket of wrinkles. A bulbous nose sat between them, red-veined and lumpy, with tufts of hair descending from each nostril. "Your goons are askin' for more a my crops than I can even grow. You take it all and leave us with scraps."

"It takes a great deal of resources to run a successful city, Magnus. You forget about the myriad amenities your patronage buys you each day."

"You mean your damn water tower and cobbled streets and 'lectric lights? We don't see any a that south of the wall. We wade in the filth and the dark while you and your fat merchant buddies suck up cigars in your damn parlors."

"I don't smoke. And I was referring to much deeper amenities. Protection from outside hostility. A free and prosperous trading network, with roads from Juarez to the Prairie Republic. And let's not forget Compound L. Without it, your freehold would be so much poison grass."

The dark-skinned farmer tugged at the straps of his overalls. "We don't object to payin' our fair share, but we've had a dry year. If I give you everything you're askin' for, me an' my family ain't gonna have enough food to last the winter."

"You exaggerate, Harvey. If you have any trouble, Fallowfield will assist you."

"Right," growled Magnus, his eyes drifting over to Bernard. "Just like you assisted Crawley."

The Mayor's face clamped down into a stern frown. "Jack Crawley was a thief. He kept what wasn't his to keep, and suffered the consequences." Bernard punctuated this remark with a crack of his knuckles. His ruined cheek gave its perpetual sinister grin.

"Jack Crawley was starving and desperate. The drought this spring hit his fields hard. He coulda given you every last spud and stalk and he'd still be in the hole to you a hundred pounds. What the hell was he supposed to eat come winter?"

"Nevertheless. Withholding goods from Fallowfield is a crime against the city and all of its people. It's a crime against you. You should be pleased that I root out such deviousness before it can bear fruit."

"Starve it out, more like."

"Please, Magnus. Such histrionics only serve to discredit you."

"Histrionics? My cellar's bare. This is harvest season, and even now, my family's down to turnips and carrot greens. If you don't ease up your take, I'll be chewin' the leather from our shoes come January."

"Lean times come and go. It's the nature of your trade."

"When's the last lean time that hit you and yours, huh? How many farmers we lose last winter? Quentin Brown. Jackie Taylor. Quinn Rourke."

"Old men die, Magnus. I would have thought you'd be coming around to that reality by now."

Magnus gave a look that reached well past anger. It was something approaching hate. "Brown was sixty-one. And he was the oldest of 'em.

They starved, plain and simple."

"You're forgetting that it is by my hand that you have anything to eat at all. I provide you people with Compound L, which is single-handedly responsible for your continued existence, as well as mine. As such, it's a very expensive chemical. I need everything I can get from you to afford it."

"So you say. We still haven't so much as seen the guy you get it from."

"My supplier guards his trade secrets closely. His is a dangerous business. Therefore, he is comfortable dealing with me and me alone."

"That's awful convenient, ain't it?"

"Its convenience or lack thereof is not my concern. The tithe remains as it is, as it must be. If you cannot meet it, I'm sure there are a few upwardly mobile fieldhands who would welcome the chance. We are not short on land in these parts, gentleman. Only Compound L."

The other two farmers stormed off, leaving Harvey behind. He dug his toe into the carpet, swiveling his foot like a scolded child.

"It's my daughter, Mr. Mayor. Emily. She's pregnant, you see, and I ain't got enough to feed her even with the harvest comin' in. Come winter I'm afraid she'll lose the baby."

"As I said, Harvey, there are certain economic realities we must abide by. But Fallowfield is a prosperous place. I'm sure you'll be fine."

Harvey studied the carpet. "Right. Economic realities."

"Hey, Harv," called Bernard. "You need the Standard that bad? Why don't you send that daughter a yours down to my cabin one night? I got a couple ... chores she could take care of."

Harvey's fingers balled into fists. He stared at Bernard's golem-like face, at the jagged concrete angles of his body, at the slate-hard muscle covering his arms and chest. His hands loosened. He left the office without another word.

"Crude, Bernard, most crude," said The Mayor, hiding a smile with little success.

Bernard shrugged. "I like 'em pregnant."

The Mayor spotted Simon watching. His smile smoothed into a

prim line. "Power comes with its own headaches, my boy. It gives me no pleasure to take more than they want to give, but such folk always underestimate the true costs of good governance."

"Mmm," Simon replied.

"However, perhaps there is a way I can leaven their spirits." The Mayor snapped his fingers. "I have an idea. Simon my boy, you're a deft hand with machines, are you not? You certainly gave my radio an apt diagnosis."

"Uh, I guess so."

"I wonder if you would consider lending your talents around the farms, to assist them in some small repairs. You would be compensated for your time, of course."

"Okay."

The Mayor walked over, spotted the blank canvas.

"Inspiration is fleeting today, I gather?"

"Mmm."

The Mayor turned to Simon, concern showing through his mirrored lenses. "If you don't mind me saying so, Simon, you don't quite seem yourself this morning. Is something the matter?"

Simon felt the words rising up through him, heaving to his lips like so much bile. He remembered what Selena had said about secrecy, about protecting themselves, about being careful. But she wasn't being careful. She was being reckless. Even if she would hate him for it, Simon knew they needed help. And The Mayor could help them.

"Yeah," Simon said. "Something's the matter."

And he told him.

10: The Floods

The cabin cowered in the woods like a frightened mollusk, low walls tucked beneath the protective shell of its sloping roof. Trees shrouded it on every side, broad branches intertwined in the warp and weft of a huge knit blanket, allowing only the thinnest needles of light to stab through.

As members of the Seraphim, the Floods could own a small slice of property in the Outer Baronies—segments of nationalized land with no current strategic or material use—and were allowed to spend two weeks there free of their duties. These short weeks counted among Simon's fondest memories. He recalled long summer days on the veranda, sunlight lancing through the trees, his mother and father speaking with an easy looseness they could never allow themselves at home.

This cabin seemed entirely different—darker, somehow—though it was the same one he'd always come to as a child. It was as if the cottage were a pet gone rabid, its glazed eyes feral and half-starved.

They set their bags down as soon as they entered. Simon opened his mouth to speak but Selena silenced him with a single raised finger. She'd been tight-lipped since they boarded the mag train at Lazarus Station, cutting off each and every question he posed with a slash of her index finger. Now they were finally in their safe place and she still wouldn't talk to him. Simon wasn't sure how much more silence he could stand.

Selena pulled a small metal device from her bag and began running it along the walls in slow, measured circles. A low hissing sound dribbled from the machine's innards. Checking for angel ears was common practice whenever they arrived at the cabin, but the search had always been nominal. The devices had short ranges and gobbled power, necessitating regular battery changes or a direct line into a building's power grid. The cottage, miles from anywhere and completely without electricity, thwarted them on both fronts. But Selena scanned the walls with a methodical drive that bordered on the obsessive, hovering the detector over every square inch of ceiling, wall, and floor.

When she'd finally finished, she closed all the blinds, lit a pair of candles, and motioned to Simon that he may speak.

"Can you please tell me what's going on?"

"We're spending our summer holiday at the cabin, like we always do."

"Yeah, but when are mom and dad going to get here?"

"Soon."

"How soon?"

"I don't know, Simon. I don't think they know either."

"Why didn't they come with us?"

"They had important business to take care of."

"But it takes days to get here. If they don't come soon they're gonna show up just as we need to pack up and go back to Jericho."

Selena rubbed her temples. "We're not going back to Jericho, Simon. None of us are."

"What do you mean? We're moving?"

"Yes."

"Where? To Levant? One of the Baronies?"

"No, Simon. We're leaving New Canaan. Forever."

The declaration hit Simon like a hammer to the chest. Leave New Canaan? *Forever?* He knew it was a cruel and dangerous place, full of secrets and backstabbing. He hated the Templars, and the terrible televisions and radio programs his parents called propaganda, and the gruesome executions—Aldo Delduca still writhed before him every time he shut his eyelids, blackened skin crackling with each twitch of crispy muscle. But Jericho was the only place he'd ever lived, and New Canaan marked the boundaries of the known world. There were monsters, cannibals, and bloodthirsty rapist bandits beyond its borders, or so his teachers had always told him. How were the four of them supposed to survive out there, alone and unprotected?

"I don't understand. Why do we have to leave?"

"Mom and dad didn't tell me everything, Simon. I just know that things are changing. It has to do with New Canaan taking over Niagara. They're stronger now, and they're moving west. The Republic of California is in trouble. There's some information they need and mom and dad are trying to get it. And if the Archbishop ever finds out they took it, we'll all be in serious trouble. That's why we can't go back."

"Is that where we're going? The Republic?"

Selena nodded.

A spark of excitement lit within the gloomy depths of Simon's fear. He'd grown up hearing about the Republic of California. His parents spoke of it in words of quiet reverence—in the hallway with the washer on, which was one of the only times the angel ears couldn't hear them. They told him it was a good and just place, where people said what they wanted and could have any sort of job they were good at. Where prayer wasn't mandatory and no one got their heads chopped off or boiled alive in oil. The last true stronghold of America-That-Was, and the only place tough enough to scare the Archbishop.

He'd even seen footage of it, though the action on screen was fake. Half a dozen video discs, smuggled in by their parents and stored beneath the floorboards beside their fireplace. The disc player alone was contraband, illicit enough to bring about ten years in the purgatorial mines. The videos, if discovered, meant death—and an ugly, protracted one at that. Selena and Simon could watch them only at night with headphones on, the radio tuned to a pious station near the angel ears. They showed a world of justice and freedom, where rugged heroes struck back against tyrants—many of which bore more than a passing resemblance to the Archbishop. Where intrepid Salters (though the Republic had no such word) worked their way from poverty to power, bolstered only by their ingenuity and grit. These were dangerous, thrilling ideas, and Simon was proud to know his parents secretly worked for such a place. But he never thought he'd actually see it in person.

Simon spent the first few days thinking about their new life in the Republic. He drew pictures of it in his sketchpad until half the pages were sooty with graphite, elaborate cityscapes cobbled together from videos and the caprices of his imagination. Selena had no such outlet. She stalked about the room, peering out at the woods from between the blinds. Each afternoon she disappeared for hours. She often returned with food or other essentials, claiming this was the purpose of her journey. But she could easily have brought home four days' worth of supplies in a single trip, suggesting she had other errands as well.

After four days, Simon's excitement started to corrode at the edges, sizzling away beneath a caustic tide of anxiety. Selena did her best to calm him, repeating a litany of all the things they had to look forward to in the Republic.

"No angel ears, no Templar Knights, no watching every word we say, no putting the radio on whenever we want to watch a video. It's going to be great, Simon. We just need to hold tight and keep quiet and everything'll be fine."

On the second week, Selena started spending her mornings at the kitchen table, poring over maps. She marked up the earth with lines and arrows, measured distances with her thumb and pinky as impromptu calipers, jotted notes in the margins.

"What are you doing?"

"You're the artist. You tell me."

"Is this the way we're going?"

"I haven't decided."

"Mom and dad will know the way, won't they?"

"Better than me, but they've never been either. And we need to be prepared, just in case."

"In case of what?"

"Leave it, Simon."

"In case of what?"

Selena slammed her fist on the table hard enough to rattle the kitchen drawers. "I said leave it!"

Simon slept poorly that night. The trees seemed to claw at the windows, knotted fingers probing for the slightest opening, and the wind filled the cottage with a high lupine howl. He found Selena at the table the next morning, still puzzling over her maps.

"I want to go into town with you today."

"Who says I'm going?"

"You go every day."

"It's a lot safer for me to go alone. Two of us will just draw more attention."

"I don't want to be here by myself."

"Tough."

"You can't lock me in here. And if you leave without me I'm going to follow you."

"Simon, for Christ's sake."

"Please, Selena."

Sighing, Selena tucked herself back into her maps. "Fine. But bring a pack with some food and water."

They left shortly after noon. The sky was cloudless, and blades of sunlight pierced the canopy of foliage. After a mile or so on a thin path spongy with dead leaves and pine needles, they left the woods and joined a small road winding its way through wheat fields bustling with laborers. The followed the road past farms, ponds, and brooks and into a rustic village. A stone church marked the town center, its steeple looming over the small wooden buildings like a stern schoolmarm. A few Templars stood amongst the crowd, their red and silver emblems gleaming atop their stark grey uniforms. Carbine rifles hung from straps over their shoulders.

Selena crossed the town square and entered the general store, its screen door propped open to admit a frugal breeze. Light filtered through windows translucent with street dust, giving everything inside a yellowish cast. She gave the clerk a Standard note and took a copy of Gabriel's Horn. The articles in new Canaan newspapers where hopelessly censored, if not outright fabricated, but they were the only publications you could legally sell. Simon guessed that Selena didn't have the connections way out here to get a Silent Frontier or Setting Star or any other pamphlets from the underground press their parents would read, discuss in hushed voices, and burn.

Tucking the newspaper under one arm, Selena left the store and sat beneath an oak tree on the edge of town. Simon read over her shoulder, though she flipped pages too quickly and he couldn't catch more than snippets. The front page lauded the recent "liberation" of Niagara. Subsequent articles profiled the grateful population (all quotations spoken in flawless Jericho Salter dialect, strangely), titillated readers with the wretched conditions under which they supposedly lived, and iterated the cruelties, vices, and sins of the late republic's former president, Aldo Delduca, whose charred remains now decorated a cross jutting from the mouth of his waterfall.

Selena reached the end of the paper and stuffed it in her bag. She walked back to the market square, her stride less tense than it had been.

"What do you want to eat?" Selena said.

"Roast beef?"

"We had beef two days ago. Only Seraphim have meat more than once a week. We don't want to draw any attention to ourselves. I can get us some field mushrooms and bacon drippings."

"Ugh."

"Well what do you suggest? We could—"

A cloud of dust hovered over the road north of town. From it emerged a young boy astride a large and powerful palfrey. He held on his back a canvas bag stuffed with papers, a few of which he pulled out and waved through the air as he reached the center of town.

"Breaking News! Treason plot foiled! Traitors put on crosses in Red Theatre! Read on for one Standard!"

Selena snatched a copy from the messenger's bag. Her eyes raced over the text. Simon came up beside her, terrified of what he'd see but helpless to keep from looking, dragged forward the way one is in nightmares, when you know the monster is behind you but you swivel your head all the same. Selena shoved him away. Behind her, the messenger extended a hand.

"Hey, lady, you gotta pay for that. It's one Standard. Lady!"

"I don't want it," she said, and threw the paper back at him. He caught it and smoothed out the wrinkles with a palm, muttering under his breath.

Simon didn't see the picture. But he didn't need to. He'd been to enough executions in his short life to imagine this one clearly. The act itself wasn't as bad as some of the others, though it was unquestionably awful. The truly awful part was how they wriggled after. Humanity drained away from you on the cross, pumped out by the force of your suffering, your convulsions and ravings descending the evolutionary ladder—simian, mammalian, reptilian—until you were something that should never have been alive in the first place. Then, if you were fortunate, you died.

The next part Simon had trouble remembering. He recalled screaming, the hot sting of tears, Selena's arms rough beneath his armpits, hauling him upright and away. Faces in the crowd smearing past him, distorted features mocking, curious, or concerned. A nail of ice in his belly, and an invisible mallet pounding it ever deeper, its blows continuing long after the nail head had found home and the point could drive no further.

His memories coalesced, and he recalled himself and Selena trudging through an unfamiliar wood. For two hours, Selena walked in total stone-faced silence. Nothing Simon said or did could provoke even the smallest response. When he collapsed, weeping, she yanked him up by the collar and dragged him along, and when he ran off she adjusted course to find him, her pace brisk and relentless, but otherwise she moved with all the subtlety and emotion of a mag train gliding down its tracks. Simon was starting to worry that something inside her had broken when she veered suddenly off course and disappeared into a grove of trees. Simon scrambled after her.

She stood before a large maple tree, her face a foot from its trunk. Simon could hear her whispering something, though the words were too soft to make out. When she finished, she pummeled the tree, sending chips of shattered bark flying in every direction. She kept going until her fists were raw and bloody, tatters of skin hanging from her knuckles, then lowered her arms and continued on the way she'd been going.

They spent the night in a small clearing, their only bed a sparse field of grass. Simon was surprised to find he slept, and more surprised still when he awoke in the night to Selena crying. She stood in the shadows beyond the treeline, her face muffled by hands still bloody from her assault on the maple, but there was no mistaking the sound. He'd never heard nor seen her cry before in his life. It scared him in a way nothing on their journey had—not even the news about his parents. He wanted nothing more than to burrow in his blanket and wait until morning. Instead, he crawled across the forest floor and took his sister in his arms.

Her body was taut as a coiled spring, her eyes as vacant as the starless sky. She could've struck him, choked him, killed him for all he knew. There seemed nothing of the old Selena left on her face, as if her mind were a city that the ages had swept away, leaving a barren patch of sand and rubble. He squeezed anyway, and soon he felt her squeeze him back. Drops of warm liquid dampened his collar. Neither sibling spoke.

They stayed that way for a long while, and then they slept.

The next morning, as they resumed their journey, Simon realized they should have reached the cottage hours ago. He asked Selena about it.

"We're not going back," she replied.

Simon, surprised he'd gotten an answer, prodded further. "Why not?"

"Too risky. If mom and dad …" She paused, swallowed, tried again. "New Canaan knows. That means they're probably looking for us, and the cottage is registered."

"But my sketchbook is there!"

"And our cookware. And our extra blankets and survival gear. And most of our food. But we have enough to last us until we're out of the Barony, and I kept all our Standard with me."

Simon's face went pale. "The maps! They're on the kitchen table! They'll know exactly where we're going!"

"No, they won't. They'll see the arrows I drew, which have us going north to *la Republique du Quebec* and cutting over from there. We're going southwest." She pulled one of the maps from her bag and slapped it with the back of her hand.

Simon's jaw went slack. "You made phoney maps?"

Selena shrugged. "We need to be careful."

"But how did you know they were coming?"

"I don't know anything, Simon. I don't know if they'll look for us at the cottage and I don't know if they'll buy what they find. But I wanted to prepare for the worst."

"But you knew to bring the real map, and our food and things."

"Preparing for the worst."

"Oh."

"Listen," Selena stopped walking. She tilted Simon's chin up until his eyes met hers. The tumult of rage and sadness had been swept aside, leaving a driven, intense clarity that he found no less frightening. "You were right."

Simon blinked. "Huh?"

"About coming with me into town. You should've come every time. It seemed simpler to leave you back at the cottage, and ... and I liked having a few hours to myself. But if you hadn't come with me then you would've been back at the cabin by yourself when I got the news, and for all I know the Templars would've gotten you."

"But we don't even know if the Templars have come."

"It doesn't matter. The point is you're my brother, and I shouldn'tve left you behind." Selena set her hands on Simon's shoulders, her fingers strong but gentle. "I'm sorry."

Simon had to force himself to meet Selena's eyes. Contrition sounded strange from her lips. Probably he had heard his sister apologize at some point in the past, but it still felt as alien as her crying had. "It's okay."

"I need to tell you something else. Mom and dad knew they might not make it to the cottage. They were trying to get something from Jericho before they left, something really risky. It had to do with the Republic, the Templar's plans for an attack. Something big. The plan was to get the data and give it to their contact on the west coast. His name is Hoster Telaine, and he lives in the capital, Visalia. That's the man we need to talk to. That's where we need to go."

"But mom and dad can't get the data now," Simon said. "We can't help them."

"They never got the last bit, true. But they've been working at this for a long time. Half the story they couldn't get. The other half they did. That's the bit they gave to me."

Selena slipped a hand into her pocket and pulled out a slender data stick. It was encased in a green chassis, its end marked with the crest of New Canaan, a white cross encircled by a crown of thorns.

"What's on it?"

Selena bit her lip. "I don't know, exactly. It's a weapon of some kind. Mom and dad were very clear. If they don't make it to us, we have to get this stick to Hoster Telaine in Visalia. He can use it to stop New Canaan before they launch their invasion in the spring."

Simon stared at the stick. It seemed such a small thing. "And what if he doesn't get it in time?"

Selena's eyes followed Simon's to the data stick. "Then the Republic will fall. It'll be New Canaan coast to coast in a few years' time. And we'll be out of places to run to."

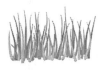

Simon wiped his face on his sleeve, leaving a translucent trail of snot from wrist to elbow. He smudged it away with a thumb, embarrassed. "That's pretty much it. We hiked to the Shawnee Free Zone and spent most of our Standard on supplies for the trip west. From there we went into the yellow locust and then we made it here."

"My word, Simon. I don't know what to say. I'm deeply sorry for your loss. New Canaan has a long reach and a black heart. It can be hard to feel safe anywhere."

"But what should I do? I wasn't supposed to tell you any of this. If Selena finds out I did, she'll kill me."

The Mayor touched an index finger to his lips. "Perhaps we should keep this our secret, for the time being. I don't like the thought of lying to your sister. She obvious cares about you very much, and wants only her best for you. But I think a direct approach will only galvanize her further. Do I read the situation correctly?"

Simon swallowed. "Yeah, I think so."

"Very well. I'll see what I can do. In the meantime, we'll keep this conversation between ourselves. Does that sound good?"

"Yeah." Simon wrapped his arms around The Mayor's waist. "Thank you. Thank you for everything."

"It's my pleasure, child. You deserve better than life has given you, and if I can do a small part to right that wrong, I consider it a more than fair reward for my efforts."

Simon took a honking sniff and wiped his nose on his forearm. "I'd better get home. Selena'll wonder where I am."

"Certainly. It won't do to worry her. Oh, one last thing. This data stick, you said it was green?"

"Yeah," Simon said, surprised by the triviality of the question. "Why?"

"Simple curiosity. Knowledge has long been my vice. I'm sorry if it seemed a flippant question."

"That's okay." Simon pulled on the hem of his shirt. "Will we be okay?"

"You're going to be just fine, Simon," said The Mayor, his arms extended. "I'm going to see to it."

11: A Crossfire Hurricane

The merchant pulled at his collar. A waddle of flesh jiggled beneath his chin, freeing an odor of rancid sweat made somehow more odious by a liberal application of perfume. It felt as if someone were trying to cram an entire garden up Leon's nose. He breathed through pursed lips while Frank dickered.

"We want fifty Standard."

"I've got no assurance of quality. If I'm gonna buy from some runty field picker, I expect the price to match."

"You think this is one of your fuckin' auction blocks, chief? You want the high, you gotta pay. I ain't runnin' a cheese shop here."

They stood at the center of Green Plaza in broad daylight, bickering over the price of a substance that, if found in their possession, could earn the merchant a lifetime banishment from Fallowfield's walls, and Leon and Frank a lethal bout with the captain of the Shepherds. Frank seemed indifferent to the risk. His hubris had grown so big it bordered on the delusional. He acted as if he were just another merchant strutting Green Plaza in his silks and baubles, swapping more Standard in an afternoon than men of his former ilk made in their whole lives.

"You could show me the merchandise, at least," complained the merchant. "Fifty Standard should buy that much."

"Come on, Frank," Leon whispered. "Let's do this and get outta here."

"Will you relax?" Frank hissed, his face inches from Leon's ear. "You're making us look like chumps." He turned to the merchant. "Show me the Standard, I'll show you the goods."

Rolling his eyes, the merchant withdrew a fifty Standard note from a small leather purse. He snapped it taut between chubby thumb and forefinger. "Satisfied?"

Frank snatched the note and tossed the merchant a small baggy of whitish powder. "Thanks, bud."

"No, thank you." The merchant cocked his head to the side. "Alright, it's done."

A trio of Shepherds materialized from the crowd. One seized Leon by the elbow, the second dropped a weighty hand on Frank's shoulder. Frank tried to bolt, but the third Shepherd smashed his face in with a truncheon. Blood and bits of teeth splattered the cobbles. The Shepherd took the fifty Standard note, folded a second note inside it, and handed the pair back to the merchant. "Thanks for your help, sir."

The merchant gave a small bow, palm pressed to palm. "I'm always happy to help your esteemed town, gentlemen. These field scum so often forget their place, it's up to us to teach it to them."

A clutch of amused onlookers gathered around the fringes of the scene. Leon thought of all the execution fights he'd attended over the years, and realised with a stab of remorse that most of those people had felt much like he felt now. Naked and flayed, their guts exposed to the gawking masses.

The Shepherds led them from Green Plaza and down the eastern street. After escaping the larger crowds, they snuck down a back alley and into a narrow side street. Cobblestones replaced hardpan, and the eaves of the houses loomed overhead.

"Hey, this isn't the way to the courthouse," said Leon.

By way of reply, the Shepherd drove his knee into Leon's gut and pulled a burlap sack over his head. After that, they marched to some spot on the outskirts of town.

The ground rolled softly up and down, its gentle hills furred with shin-high grass. Sheep bleated in the distance. A large hand fell firmly on Leon's shoulder.

"Steps. Five of 'em."

Leon took the stairs slowly, not trusting the voice's count. After the fifth step Leon's foot found a wide, wooden surface, his footsteps resonating in the hollow space underneath. A veranda. The hand returned to his shoulder, guiding his progress.

Carpet dampened Leon's footfalls in places. Elsewhere the soles of his shoes clacked against hardwood. He stepped, turned, stepped, veered right, stepped some more, turned, and paused. Knuckles rapped against a solid door. A muffled voice bid them enter, the door opened, and the hand guided Leon inside.

The hand moved from Leon's shoulder to his head, where it pulled his hood free. The darkness vanished. In its place appeared The Mayor, his elbows resting on a giant oaken desk, his index fingers pressing gently against his lips. Leon's face, small, scared, and bulging in the middle, stared back at him from each mirrored lens.

"Gentlemen," The Mayor said. "We have much to discuss."

The door closed with a soft click. The Shepherds were gone. The Mayor upended a fibrous burlap bag over his desk, spilling twists of ragged plastic wrapped around lumps of crystalline matter. He lifted one of the packets and tore it open. Shards of crystal the color of sour milk littered his desk, their powdery residue clinging to his fingers.

Leon swallowed. Frank aped confusion, his brow overly furrowed and his tongue circling his lips.

"What are those?" he asked. "I've never seen nothin' like that before."

The Mayor gave an almost imperceptible shake of the head. "Spare me. We've got word from half a dozen sources about your little side business, and Shepherds saw you sell this very product to a paid informant," he motioned to the packets of white crystal on the table. "You are, of course, aware of the penalty for selling narcotic substances to Fallowfield residents?"

Leon nodded. He thought of Crawley's puffy, bulge-eyed face as Bernard's foot came down on his temple.

The Mayor dangled one of the plastic packets by its tattered fringe. "I consider myself to be a reasonably permissive man. I allow you your distilleries and tobacconists, your taverns and parlors, your love shacks and gambling houses. I permit your street fights, even those to the death, so long as only those who agree to the fight's terms are harmed. I abide the whores and brothels, and would even go so far as to cautiously endorse the better strains of cannabis the traders bring up from Juarez. I tolerate these things because they will exist in Fallowfield regardless, and because they can be enjoyed, mostly, without lasting harm.

"This, however, cannot. It corrupts my workforce and undermines the quality of my city, and I will not tolerate its use or sale." The Mayor threw the packet onto the desk. "The path forward seems clear. We have laws, and the entire community suffers when I fail to enforce them. You were both caught red-handed in a capital offence, and a number of residents can attribute similar illicit dealings to your characters."

Frank's tongue made a frantic circle around his lips. His fingers drummed against his thighs, his eyes roving the room like frightened rodents scrambling to escape their cage. Leon knew Frank well enough to sense the violence festering beneath the surface of his thoughts. *He's gonna try something.*

The Mayor's mirrored gaze missed none of this. He motioned to a shelf on the left wall. "There is a statuette next to the bookends there. Pre-War, marble with a pewter base. It would make an excellent bludgeon, particularly if swung bottom out. You may or may not have spotted it, though I'm sure you've seen the antique bayonet hanging above the mantle. Stupid ideas, both, though possessed of a certain base cunning. I would expect no less—and no more—from creatures such as you. You are two against one, after all, and one of you is quite large. But I would not still be Mayor of Fallowfield if I could be so easily outwitted by a pair of boorish field scum." He reached in his jacket and removed a sleek metal device festooned with a single red button. "New Canaan technology. I had it installed shortly after my arrival in these blighted wastes. The red button triggers a piercing siren that will summon every Shepherd within a dozen miles to my aid, the closest of which stand but a few feet outside this door. No, your path from this office is set, and I'm afraid it leads straight to Green Plaza— and not as merchants."

Leon made a whimpering sound in the back of his throat.

The Mayor slipped the device into his coat pocket and leaned back in his chair, hands folded at his waist. "However, perhaps the three of us can reach an arrangement that we all find a little less … *distasteful.*"

Frank began nodding so fast his head almost appeared to be vibrating. "Yeah, sure. I mean, we're, like, open to negotiation."

The Mayor buffed his fingernails on his frock coat. "No, I can assure you, you're not. Negotiation implies that you have some sort of leverage. What you have are options. Two of them, to be precise. The first, we've already mentioned: face due punishment for your crimes. The second, I suspect you may find preferable.

"Should you choose option two, you will return to the fields tomorrow morning and go about your work—your legal work. From there, you will follow these directions to the letter."

The Mayor laid out the plan step by step. By the time he'd finished, Frank was bobbing his head enthusiastically. Leon felt like he was going to be sick.

"Yeah, sure," said Frank. "We can do that for you, no problem."

"Good. Should you succeed in this endeavour, you will still be expected to leave Fallowfield permanently, but your lives will remain intact. Am I making myself clear?"

"Definitely, definitely," said Frank.

"Good. Tomorrow evening. Until then, keep your noses—and your lungs—clean."

"Who is it?" blurted Leon. He felt The Mayor's silver gaze boring into him. "I mean, who's the … the target? What's his name?"

"*Her* name is unimportant," said The Mayor. "You'll know her when you see her. Though actually, I suppose I can show you." The Mayor grabbed a painting leaned against the side of his desk and presented it to Frank and Leon.

Frank's face bloated with a big toothy grin.

As he walked the city streets, Leon realized how rarely he'd seen Fallowfield after dark. It was a cold, quiet, forlorn place, full of barred doors and shuttered windows and the faint, endless hiss of wind through the eaves. Shadows dripped from awnings and pooled in alleys like puddles of fetid rainwater.

Things livened up once he reached Green Plaza. Tradesmen and off duty bodyguards speckled the cobbled square, throwing dice and smoking hand-rolled cigarettes and trading swigs from glass bottles. Women in ersatz silk and lace and wisps of sheer fabric trawled the boardwalks, painted faces wreathed with perfume. Shepherds walked among them, their golden pins gleaming in the dark.

Leon stepped into the Rye and Sickle. Music cartwheeled through the room. A pigtailed girl of maybe fourteen slashed blistering melodies from a battered fiddle while a balding man strummed accompanying chords on a nylon string guitar. Their voices entwined in sumptuous harmony, hollering out an old standard.

"I was born, in a crossfire hurricane!"

A few patrons, giddy with liquor, danced and stomped about the grimy floor, but most of the barflies sat at the tavern's roughly-hewn tables, a mismatched motley of pint glasses and wooden cups and metal steins clutched in their hands or raised to their lips. Corn oil lanterns flickered at the center of every table, their flames made amber and otherworldly by spiky carapaces of stained glass.

Leon nudged and sidled his way through the thicket of bodies and chairs, murmuring apologies, until he reached a small, oblong table at the far corner of the tavern. A lean figure slumped against the wall, the gaslight above him casting a veil of shadows over his face. His was a body of long limbs and sharp angles, narrow shoulders shrouded in a serape checkered black and red. Eyes like flecks of copper glimmered beneath a spill of curly black hair.

Leon sat down. The man balanced his chair on its back two legs and clasped his hands behind his head.

"Tony says you wanted to talk."

Leon nodded. "I've got this job. It's sort of a job, more like a ... an assignment. I'm not getting paid for it. Anyway, it's a thing we gotta do. And the trouble is, I dunno if we can do it. It's not, uh, not our specialty."

"I understand. You seek, how you say, a sub-contractor, yes?"

"No, no not quite." In truth, it was exactly what he wanted, but Frank wouldn't hear of it.

"My partner, he wants to do this personally. I guess you could say he's not good at accepting help. I can't stop him, but I thought I could take out, I guess you could call it an insurance policy. Someone to watch out for us, you know, in case things don't work out so well."

The thin man set his chair's front legs down with a small thud. "So I take it your business partner is unaware of this ... insurance policy, yes?"

"I think it's better if he doesn't know. That way if things work out, you can just sort of slip away, and Frank—" Leon clacked his teeth, as if hoping to catch the name before it escaped his lips. "Uh, my business partner can assume he took care of things all on his own."

"But if things do not 'work out', as you say, then ..." The thin man let the sentence hang unfinished between them.

"Then I'd like you to step in and, uh, finish things up for us. Real quick, you know."

The thin man's smile grew teeth. "I am in the business of quick."

"So we have a deal?"

The thin man shrugged. From beneath his serape, he withdrew a small strip of black metal. He thumbed an invisible trigger and a sharp *schwick* sliced the air in two. A silver blade glittered in the shadows. The thin man studied his face in its reflection. Leon slid a stack of bills across the table. The thin man took the money, counted it, and nodded. He tucked the bills away beneath his serape and twirled the switchblade. It glided effortlessly between his fingers.

"When and where?" the thin man asked.

Leon told him. "Do you know the spot?"

"I will find it."

"Okay. Good." Leon traced his finger over the table's rough, fibrous grain. The thin man put away his switchblade.

"We are done here," he said.

"Oh. Uh, okay. Great. Thanks. Good, uh, good doing business with you."

"Of course." The thin man darted forward. He seemed to lengthen as he moved, his body projecting over the table like the neck of a striking cobra. Leon flinched, shoulders folded inward, arms drawn to his chest. The thin man held out his hand.

Leon shook it.

"Until we meet again. Leon, yes?"

"Yeah, Leon. Right. Until then …"

"Marcus," the thin man said. "You may say it. I do not hide from my name."

Leon stood up. Marcus folded his hands behind his head and closed his eyes. He hummed softly to himself as Leon wove his way back through the chairs and tables and drunkards, his large stomach sucked in, mumbling apologies.

12: Plans

After flirting with autumn, Fallowfield flung itself back into summer's scalding arms. Rivers of sweat cascaded down Selena's neck, forming great inland lakes at the small of her back and the hollow between her breasts. By ten-after-midday she felt like a wrung-out sponge, her parched pores gasping for moisture. She knew that night she'd be burnt red from shoulder to wrist despite her bronze skin and best efforts to cover herself from the sun.

It's weird, but I'm going to miss this. Selena ran her fingers through her hair and flicked away droplets of sweat. Reaping was hard work, but it was a pure sort of labor. A simple twist of the shoulders, that's all anyone asked of you, and at the day's end you stood at the edge of a great swath of mown rapeseed, the stalks collected in a wagon behind you, and felt as if you'd accomplished something. If it paid enough to buy actual food, it would be an okay job. But it didn't, so she worked only to fritter away the three days before Marcus would take her on the road.

Behind her someone coughed. Selena whirled round, brandishing her scythe. A man in overalls and a straw hat backed away, arms raised. He was fiftyish, pale, with a paunchy belly and a patchwork of grey and black stubble that made him look slightly ill.

"Easy, easy! I ain't here to do no harm."

Selena lowered her scythe. The man swallowed a collection of spit.

"You Selena?"

"Yeah."

The man glanced around nervously, his hand twining through a sprig of rapeseed.

"Heard you've been askin' some questions 'bout The Mayor."

"So what if I have?"

The man stopped his constant roving gaze to focus on Selena. "It's just, some folks from away can be curious 'bout where a man like him gets all that Compound L. Stuff like that, only a couple a places got the means to make it."

Selena's hands tightened around the scythe's handle. "Wait, you mean New Cana—"

"Can't talk here. You wanna know more, meet me at my barn at ten-after-midnight. I'm at Bull's Field. You can ask in town if you don't know the way, but do it early and say it's for fieldwork."

"Who are you?"

"No names. They'll be time for that later."

"You know mine. I want to know yours."

The man's eyes rolled in their sockets. "John," he whispered. "John McCulloch. Ten-after-midnight tonight." As he spoke the man was already receding through the rapeseed. Selena heard the rustle of his body through the rows, then nothing.

The rest of the morning passed in a haze of questions, asked to the wind between swings of her sickle. Who was this McCulloch? Why had he sought her out of all people? And what did he have to say about The Mayor? And New Canaan? The wind offered no answers, only a long and lonely sigh through the rapeseed.

At noon, Selena left her scythe and her questions at the edge of the field and staked out a shady spot beneath a crooked poplar tree. She mulled over McCulloch's offer between bites of her apple. Was he saying that The Mayor had dealings with New Canaan? If so, what did that mean for her and Simon? Communication between the two states couldn't be very direct, given that the Middle Wastes lay between them. All the same, it would make skipping town that much more pressing. She wasn't sure how much she could trust this McCulloch. He seemed a shifty sort. *You'd be shifty too, wouldn't you, if you were from this town and stepping on The Mayor's toes?* Selena didn't understand all the angles, but she could tell that there was certainly no love lost between the farmers and merchants—and it was clear on whose side The Mayor stood.

Her lunch finished, Selena grabbed her scythe and hacked at the rapeseed until the sun kissed the horizon, then returned to her tiny apartment to wait. Simon was nowhere to be found, most likely spending the evening with his beloved Mayor. Distrust wriggled like a worm in Selena's brain. She longed to pluck it free and examine it, but it was imbedded much too deep. She supped without enthusiasm on a hank of cheese and another two apples. Her stomach rumbled when she was done, annoyed and unsated.

Just forget it. You're leaving town in a few days anyway. Keep your mouth shut and slip away without fanfare. None of this is any of your business.

But if New Canaan was a player out here, it very much *was* her business.

These days, New Canaan's plans were the only business that mattered.

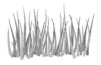

The barn was old and saggy, its red paint peeling, its shattered windows covered with strips of milky plastic. An ancient barn elevator stood next to it like the reassembled remains of some improbable dinosaur, its ossified neck stretching to the loft door, which hung open and swung stiffly in the breeze.

Selena approached the barn and slipped inside. Straw several days past changing coated the floor, the smell of rancid animal piss rising from matted clumps. Many of the stalls were empty. Slightly less than half held livestock: mostly cattle, mostly sleeping. She took a quick tour of the barn and found nothing of interest. There were no conspirators, no notes, no sign the barn was used for anything but its intended purpose. She wondered if the whole thing had been a joke.

Something above her creaked. It could have been the wind striking the outer wall, or a loose beam buckling as the air cooled, or one of the million other sounds endemic to aged wooden buildings, but an instinct buried deep in Selena's gut told her it was something else: the groan of floorboards beneath someone's shifting weight. Suddenly being the butt of a farmer's half-witted prank seemed too optimistic a scenario. Her thoughts treaded darker ground, and found it fertile.

Who was up there?

Selena found a wooden ladder that led up to the hayloft. She gripped a rung, paused. She wasn't an easily intimidated person, but nor was she foolhardy. So, long as she was on the ladder, she would be absolutely defenseless. Whoever was up there—if there was anyone up there—would know that too.

"McCulloch?" she called up the ladder. "John? Is that you?"

The darkness gave no reply.

Selena looked over her shoulder. If there was to be an ambush, now would be the time to strike. She counted to five in her head and no one came. Not an ambush, then. But what? Currents of coppery rage washed through her blood. Someone was fucking with her, and they were going to pay for it.

But first, she needed another way up.

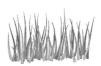

Leon hoisted himself up the ladder into a long low room with a sloping ceiling. Clumps of soiled hay grouted the cracks between the floorboards. The air was dry and itchy with particles of straw. Tonight was the night. Tonight, he would either become a murderer or a corpse.

He rubbed his eyes and, holding back a sneeze, peered out the loft's wide double doors. The night sky had grown a bruised shade of purple-black. Wind rustled the wheat, whistled through the trees, tugged at the roots of his hair. Something small and metal flashed in the muted moonlight. Barely visible amongst the silhouette of rye, Leon saw a lean figure in a checkered serape, head haloed by a ring of wild black hair. It disappeared as quickly as it came. Leon felt dizzy with relief. Marcus had held up his side of the bargain. He retreated into the loft and took his place next to the ladder, shoulders nestled into the cruxes between the exposed support beams. Frank stood on the ladder's other side. With their backs pressed flat to the wall they were all but invisible to anyone climbing up from below, yet a mere half step put them within striking distance of the porthole.

Frank drew a long hunting knife. Leon took out his own weapon: a mattock filched from John McCulloch's storage shed. Its adze was worn to a shapeless nub and the prongs of its forked end were rust-flecked and dull, but Leon didn't much care. He didn't intend to use it. He could hold the girl down, punch or kick her if necessary, but he didn't think he could deliver the killing blow. It was just as well, since Frank seemed all too eager to do it himself. That was, of course, if he got the opportunity. Leon wasn't sure how realistic this plan really was, but Frank had reached a point where arguing simply ceased to work. Questions or dissent of any kind were met with rage and scorn. His tracks were set, and they carried him recklessly forward. Leon only hoped they wouldn't lead him off a cliff.

Across the field came the susurrus of footsteps muted by the ankle-high grass. They picked up as they hit the gravel surrounding the barn, making a sultry sound like a shaken maraca. The barn door squeaked open, its hinges moaning feebly.

The ladder creaked. Leon tightened his grip on the mattock,

squeezing the handle until his palm began to ache. He waited for the telltale groan of the ladder but heard nothing. Seconds passed. Surely she couldn't be climbing? Even with inhuman stealth, one could not possibly ascend a ladder as old as this one without making a sound.

Frank leaned out from the shadows and peered over the edge of the porthole. His face betrayed shock, confusion, anger.

"Where the fuck'd she go?" he mouthed. In answer, the rustle of straw called softly from the barn floor. Footsteps shimmied like a snake through long grass, leading back the way they had come. The barn door creaked. Leon stared at his mattock as if hoping it would tell him something he didn't know.

"Hey Frank," whispered Leon. "Listen, I think maybe we should—"

The night exploded with metallic rattling. Frank and Leon exchanged a bemused look. Was she climbing the barn elevator? The damn thing looked ready to fall over. They shuffled toward the loft door and took positions on its either side, bodies tucked against the narrow lip of the doorframe. As an ambush, it wasn't quite as ideal as the ladder, but it still gave them the upper hand. Frank held his knife at the ready.

A column of moonlight poured through the door and drizzled over the floorboards, tinting them a pale and unearthly shade of blue. A drop of shadowy ink darkened the moonlight's ethereal puddle. It flowed outward, taking a human shape. Leon adjusted his grip on the mattock.

The shadow froze. Leon stared into its silhouetted shape as if it had eyes he could meet, a face he could read, a soul he could implore to turn back before it was too late and this whole dirty business got well and truly rolling. The shadow kept its poise. For a moment, Leon thought he'd somehow reached it, held it at bay with his psychic plea. Then the shadow became a blur and the blur became a girl and the world took on a ruthless speed.

She landed with a thud, rolled, and leapt to her feet. Frank thrust his knife at her as she flew, throwing his whole weight into the jab. He hit only air. His momentum sent him lurching forward toward the ledge. The girl chambered her foot, readying a savage kick aimed square at Frank's midriff. The fight could have easily been over there. The kick would've been more than enough to send Frank hurtling out the loft door, head ricocheting off the jagged spine of the barn elevator before landing with a sickening thud on the gravel thirty feet below. Leon would've given up, even if it meant his death. He had no fight without Frank. But Frank wasn't dead yet.

So he leapt.

Leon was a big man. Six foot four and an easy two hundred and ninety pounds. Much of that weight was flesh, not muscle, but there was a lot of it, and Leon hurled it at the girl with all the force he could muster. He took her around the waist, his beefy arms encircling her as they fell. The girl managed to twist, cat-like, in his grasp, so that they each hit the ground on their sides instead of Leon landing square on top of her. Still, she was pinned, and all her struggling could not break Leon's grip.

The girl bucked and fought and Leon squeezed. She was strong— uncannily, impossibly strong—but Leon was much, much bigger and had her arms trapped, robbing her punches of their power. The two of them writhed and twisted, the girl's elbows digging into Leon's ribs, her heels smashing his shins. Leon could only squeeze tighter. He struggled to one knee.

"Frank," he wheezed. "Frank, for God's sake."

Frank slouched forward with knife in hand, a hungry smile oozing across his face. The girl threw her head back, mashing Leon's nose. Blood flowed from his nostrils, soaking her hair and running down his chest. Leon held on, but the pain loosened his grip enough for her to get an arm free. She pried up the middle finger of his left hand and folded it back until its nail lay flush with Leon's wrist. There was a brittle snap as the bone gave way. Leon screamed. The girl slipped her other arm free but still Leon held on, consolidating his grip around her waist.

She caught Frank's wrist just as the blade was closing in on her face. Its tip dimpled her cheek. She torqued his arm and struck his wrist with her free hand. The knife clattered to the floor. Frank grabbed it and ran headlong into the girl, knocking her and Leon backwards. He stood over them, knife raised. Here Leon's bulk worked against him; there was much more of him to hit than there was of her. Frank slashed out, grunting savagely. His knife nicked the girl's forearm. His second swing caught Leon in the elbow. Leon yowled. His finger throbbed. Blood filled his mouth, its coppery taste making him retch.

"Hold still, bitch!" Frank cried. He straddled the writhing pile of flesh and blood and tangled limbs, pushing the girl's arms aside to get a clear shot. He brought the knife down slowly, trading speed for force. The girl tried to shove him aside, but gravity was to Frank's advantage, and with every parry he would right himself, square his balance, and keep coming.

"Pull her head back!" Frank screamed. Leon thrust his good hand into the girl's hair and yanked, drawing her chin upward.

"Oh, here it comes, baby," Frank muttered, unable to spare enough breath to shout. "You're gonna fucking get it."

The blade inched closer. The girl somehow mustered even more strength. She held Frank's wrist, her tendons taut and thrumming. Leon closed his eyes. A hot jet of blood soaked his already blood-slickened face, dampened his hair, stung his eyes. The girl's struggling slowed. Her body grew still. Leon opened his eyes.

Frank hung over him, a pale wraith staring dumbly at nothing. A crimson rictus split his neck, drooling thick red globs of blood and bile. His arms hung limp. Marcus stood behind him, his grin as sharp and bright as his switchblade.

Marcus let Frank's body fall to the floor, where it landed in an undignified heap, a bundle of flesh stained with blood and piss. He'd wet himself as his throat opened. The girl scrambled to her feet. Leon remained where he was, his eyes fixed on Marcus, who returned his incredulous stare with a small, apologetic smile. He crouched down beside Leon.

"You—"

"Ssshhhhh," Marcus held an index finger to his lips. "I know."

"I trusted you," Leon whined.

He shrugged apologetically. "Yes, I am sorry about that."

"But why?"

"I have plans," Marcus replied, and plunged his switchblade into Leon's heart. "And I am afraid you do not fit into them."

Leon bucked. His hands hung in the air, palms out, beseeching. Marcus offered them nothing. Rebuffed, they fell to the floor, twitched once, and lay still.

13: A Prisoner in a Pretty Cage

Marcus's serape fluttered. Beneath him, the dead men lay in congealing puddles of blood and effluvia, their coppery, electric, and buzzingly alive smell already morphing into something fouler. He stepped over the bodies, cleaning his switchblade with a ratty cloth.

"That was not bad," he said. "But I expected better."

"What—"

"I will explain, but first we must go. We are, how you say, in the eye of the hurricane."

Marcus stepped onto the grain elevator and descended effortlessly. Selena, too dumbstruck to do otherwise, followed. Marcus waited at the bottom, tapping his foot impatiently. The elevator moaned and flexed beneath her feet, a mechanical serpent desperate to shake her loose. She had always prided herself on having excellent balance, but compared to Marcus she moved with all the grace of an arthritic eighty-year-old. She landed with a stumble but kept her footing. Before she was fully upright, Marcus was already on the move.

"Would you wait a second? Just what is all this?"

"As I said, I will explain. But we are in danger. Come." He grabbed her hand and half pulled, half led her into the tall grass. Rustling shafts of wheat marked their every step.

"How did you know what they were planning?"

"They hired me."

Selena yanked her arm free and stepped back, raising her fists in a fighting stance. "They *hired* you?"

Marcus rolled his eyes. "If I wished you dead, Lena, then I am going about it most strangely, yes? The big man approached me last night. He feared you—as he should—and wished to, how you say, tip the odds in his favour. I did not know his target, but when I saw you approach, I understood. And I made a choice. They have no value to me. You do."

"How flattering. So those thugs wanted to off me and you offed them instead. Thanks. But if that's the case then I don't see what the worry is."

"They are not the source of danger," Marcus said. "He is."

Marcus swept his hands outward, parting the grass and revealing a body lying at their feet. Flies buzzed around its cut throat. Selena's eyes dropped from the wound to the man's lapel, where a small gold pin in the shape of a shepherd's cane glittered in the dark.

"A Shepherd? What the hell was he doing out here?"

"Waiting to clean up the mess. You think those buffoons planned all this themselves? Who told you to come here?"

"The farmer. McCulloch."

"And he takes orders from two fieldhands? You are a clever girl, Lena. You must see the truth. They were being good boys, all of them. Doing as father tells them. This one was too." Marcus kicked the body. "And whoever killed who, this one was told to finish the job. It would look like a robbery gone wrong. Cattle thieves. McCulloch would say you agreed to muck out his barn for extra cash. You were so eager for Standard, after all. You caught these men in the act, and desperate men are dangerous men, yes?"

Selena stared down at the body, visually tracing the sweep of his ruined neck. A fly landed on its bloody ridge, proboscis snuffling greedily at the gore. Her stomach somersaulted. "How do you know all this?"

Marcus' grin cut through the gloom. "All men are singers with a blade to their throats. This one sang many pretty songs."

"What else did he say?"

"That he was to dress the scene to tell a story, and to search your body for a small plastic stick."

Selena's hand fell reflexively to her hip, cradling the bulge of plastic tucked into her pants pocket. *He knows!* The thought tore through her mind like a shriek. *The Mayor knows about me and Simon! About New Canaan!! About the data stick!!!* Her stomach performed a few more feats of acrobatics. She understood now McCulloch's veiled comment about New Canaan. It wasn't intel. It was bait.

"This is insane. How could The Mayor even know ..." but before the question was even spoken, she knew; *Simon. Fucking Simon. Fucking scared, weak, reckless,* infuriating *Simon.* She could kill him.

And she wasn't the only one.

The thought plunged her heart into a bucket of ice water. She bolted through the grass, oblivious to the nicks and scratches the stalks left on her skin, and to Marcus calling after her in a hoarse whisper-shout.

"Lena! Wait!"

She ran with only the faintest sense of direction, scrambling toward where she thought town must be. Once she broke clear of the grass, she could get her bearings. Fallowfield was an hour away by foot, but at a steady run, she could make it in twenty minutes, maybe less. She and Simon could be miles away before sun up. They would move south, rob a merchant for supplies if they needed to, and drag themselves west by tooth and claw. They'd lingered much too long already. Fallowfield had sucked her in, lulled her with its bucolic charm only to close around her like a Venus fly trap. But Selena was no fly, and it would take more than some poisonous grass to hold her in place.

The wheat fell away and Selena found herself on a moonlit path. A quick glance around revealed it as the southern road. She legged it north toward town, urging her overcharged thighs to pump faster, hurling herself down the straightaway and around a bend.

By the time she saw the horseman, his rifle was already trained on her chest. His massive frame hulked over the saddle, rifle butt dwarfed by a gargantuan shoulder. He regarded her with eyes like twin discs of green-grey tundra, his face humorless save for the scar curling up one cheek like a lunatic's lopsided smile.

Hands seized Selena's collar and dragged her into the wheat. Tatters of displaced air scratched her cheek as the bullet whizzed by, piercing the place she'd been a half-second before. She scrambled deeper into the grass, zigzagging behind Marcus, who held her wrist like a leash. In any other situation, she'd resent being led like piece of livestock, but too much was happening too fast and she clung to any suggested action as if it were flotsam in a storm-ravaged sea. Behind her came the clatter of approaching hooves, a manic rhythm beneath the crisp snapping of a rifle being cocked. Marcus snaked right and the sounds trampled past them, streaking through the wheat before rounding back for another pass. Gunfire bellowed over the field, bullet after bullet streaking through the grass and into the dirt. Marcus breached the edge of the grass and slid into a culvert, nestling into the thicket of reeds sprouting from the mud. Selena followed.

Three times the shooter circled toward them, once coming close enough for Selena to hear the horse's heavy breathing and the soft curses of its rider. When it left for the last time, the final hoofbeats disappearing with distance, Marcus rose from the culvert.

"I have seen this Shepherd before. He is The Mayor's right-hand man. You are in worse trouble than I guessed." His eyes fell to her hip pocket, where Selena's fingers unconsciously traced along the edges of the data stick. "Come, there is a safe place a few miles from town. We must be there before sun-up."

"Hold on. We need to get my brother first."

Marcus frowned. "I'm sorry, Lena. This is impossible."

"What do you mean it's impossible? He's my brother. I can't just leave him."

"Do you think you can ride up to your house and take him? The commander of the Shepherds hunts you, and he is not foolish. Your brother is being watched. Go for him and you will be shot before you reach town."

"I don't care. I don't have a choice."

"There are always choices. You may choose life, or death. I do not call this a hard decision, but my mind is not clouded with foolish hero's thoughts."

"It's not between life and death. It's between my life and my brother's."

"Your brother is only in danger if the Shepherds take you. If you should die, he would lose his value. So long as you are free, he lives. To kill him would give you no cause to return, yes? If you care for him, you will keep yourself alive and free."

"While he lives a prisoner."

"Perhaps. But a prisoner in a pretty cage."

Selena ground her teeth together. "Great. What's not to like about that?"

"Even a man like The Mayor must watch his reputation. The farmers are filth to him, but the merchants? There he must seem just, fair, not the sort of man who tortures young boys. This is why he did not simply shoot you in daylight. He must cover his tracks. So long as the boy suspects nothing, The Mayor will treat him kindly. This is the simplest way to handle him. Think as The Mayor does. Better the puppy than the wolf, yes?"

Selena massaged her temples. Her head ached. "You're asking me to abandon my brother. I can't do that."

"Abandon? No. We will come for him in time."

"When?"

Marcus buffed his fingernails on his serape. "I made an offer to you in the Rye and Sickle. Do you still wish to take it?"

"Things have changed."

"This is true. So has my offer. Come with me. I will show you the fiercest rings, the greatest fights. You will fight and you will win, and when the debt is paid, I will help you free your brother *and* I will get you west."

"You expect me to leave Simon in this hellhole for two whole weeks?"

"You misunderstand, Lena. Two weeks was our first deal. Things have changed much since this time. Now you will ride with me until I say the debt is paid. Only then will we collect your brother."

Selena glared at Marcus, anger a metallic sting at the back of her throat. "You said two weeks."

"Two weeks to take you south, yes. But to rescue a brother in the bargain? This will cost much. I may never be able to return to Fallowfield. For this, I must be, how you say, sufficiently compensated."

Selena closed her eyes, exhaled. "Okay, fine. I'll fight every asshole east of the mountains if I have to. Just help me get my brother out of here."

"Now is not the time. The Mayor's guard must be down. It is better, safer, to fight while he stays here."

"Bullshit. You don't care about his safety. You just want to keep a hold on me."

In response, Marcus only smiled.

"Look, here's a deal for you. Help me get Simon and the three of us will go south together. There must be fighting circles near Juarez. I'll fight for you for as long as it takes to pay you, whatever the cost, okay?"

"A pretty picture. But what would stop you from considering the debt paid before I do? How can I be sure you will stay?"

"I'll stay. I promise."

"Promises are fine things. But a trapped brother is better, yes?"

Selena grabbed Marcus by his serape. He was a good six inches taller than she was, but he stooped readily to her level, making no effort to evade her grasp. Her frustration seemed to amuse him.

"This isn't a game."

"No? Then why do you play so foolishly?"

An itch worked its way up Selena's fingers, an impulse to slap the pretentious smirk from this absurd man's face, maybe even to throw a left hook and make kindling of his jawbone. But a faint voice inside her told her that would be a bad idea. This thin, swarthy, almost dainty man was not yet her enemy, but should he become as much, she would regret it. Lord knows she didn't need any more than she had already. Her hands loosened, the coarse threads of the serape whispering against her fingers.

"The night vanishes, Lena. You must make a choice. Come with me and live. Go to your brother and die. Choose."

Selena's fingers knitted through her hair. She tugged at the roots. The pain helped her focus. The moment hung distended in time, a water droplet on a bent frond. Stay or go, she needed to act. Behind her, the grass stirred, though whether by wind or approaching Shepherd she had no idea. *You have to be strong.* She'd always considered herself to be strong, but this was a different sort of strength: making ugly decisions and living with the scars they left.

God, a voice inside her moaned. *What kind of choices are these?*

She made one, all the same.

Part II: Shitgrass

14: Luchadora

The Mayor leaned forward on his desk, chin cradled in his hands. Light from the mullioned windows played off the surface of his sunglasses. Across from him stood a pudgy farmer in dirt-smeared overalls. His hands twitched like frightened mice, scurrying within the safety of his front pocket. Bernard sat on a bench in the far corner of the room, silently observing the meeting.

"Can't we meet somewhere else?" the farmer pleaded. "I don't like the other guys seein' me come here."

The Mayor touched a hand to his heart. "John, are you ashamed of our friendship?"

John McCulloch tugged at the straps of his overalls. "You know them other farmers don't trust you." *Something of an understatement,* The Mayor thought. *One might just as easily say the Archbishop of New Canaan has a tiff with The Republic of California.*

"Magnus and his maladjusted ilk only just came here pleading poverty, begging for forgiveness of their tithes. If they see you they'll assume you're doing the same."

"Things are different now, after that business with my barn. The other farmers have questions."

"And I've supplied you with answers. The girl was at your barn to complete some after-hours repairs. It's no secret that she was trying to scrape together some extra money. While working in the loft, she overheard a couple of ne'er-do-well fieldhands with a known history for illegal activity trying to steal your livestock. She intervened, and in the ensuing struggle two of the would-be robbers died and the rest fled the scene, removing the girl either as a hostage or to hide her body. She's now missing and—though you can keep this much from the boy—presumed dead."

McCulloch sucked on his gums, drawing patterns with his foot in the warp and weft of The Mayor's carpet. "That's all fine until the girl shows up sayin' otherwise."

"The girl is being taken care of as we speak. You have nothing to worry about, save for continuing to convince me of your usefulness."

"Hey, I done plenty for you!"

"And I for you." The Mayor reached out and stroked a finger along the waddle of flesh beneath McCulloch's neck. "Did you not have beef for dinner twice these past weeks? Do you not enjoy fat cellars while your compatriots pluck dandelion roots from the parched earth? Ours is an ongoing exchange, John. The past has little to do with it, and what has been given can easily be taken away. What do you have for me?"

McCulloch swallowed. "I seen Magnus and them spending a lot of time at the back end of his property. There's an old grain silo there, one a them Pre-War jobs, and I seen 'em comin' and goin' from those parts an awful lot."

"I suspect wheat gets quite lonely in those stacks. Perhaps they're simply keeping it company."

"I don't think they got wheat in there … " McCulloch said, his voice earnest but slightly patronizing. The Mayor rolled his eyes, a gesture he telegraphed despite his mirrored sunglasses.

"Yes, thank you for clarifying. Could you enlighten me as to what purpose they've put it toward?"

"No way to tell. They've got the door locked tight, tumblers and padlock both, and there ain't no windows to speak of. The old roof entrance is still open, but they put bars across it. You'd need a hacksaw and all night to get through 'em."

The Mayor touched a finger to his own chin. "How far apart are these bars?"

"About yea big." MCulloch set his hands at his mid-chest and belly button, as if holding an invisible box. "I tried fittin' through, but I couldn't make it. And I ain't that big."

"Interesting."

"I'll keep lookin', but like I say, they ain't gonna let me just wander about. That land means an awful lot to them."

A wrinkle appeared in the space between The Mayor's eyebrows. "That land is only livable because of my efforts. Do not let them instruct you otherwise. You may go now."

Once they were alone, The Mayor turned to Bernard. "Name me a man who built a better city out of such shoddy materials. It's a wonder this place hasn't fallen apart already. And they act as if *I'm* the problem!"

"The peons gotta grumble. It's part of their job."

The Mayor steepled his fingers. "Quite. And the silo? What do we make of that?"

"Only way we'll find out is if I get a few of my boys to smash down that door with an axe."

"I admire your enthusiasm, Bernard, as always. But I can think of a subtler approach. Leave the silo to me. Your job is the girl. Has there been any word?"

"I've got my best men on it. If she's anywhere in a hundred miles, they'll find her soon enough."

The Mayor shifted back in his chair. "Yesterday wouldn't be soon enough. Send out another five Shepherds. I want her in my possession by the end of the week."

"Still dead or alive?"

"Quite frankly, dead might be easier to deal with. But hold on to her body and all her effects. She can still be of use to me as a corpse."

This was only partially true. The Mayor needed Selena, but it wasn't her body that held any value to him, whether the heart was still beating or not.

It was the contents of her pockets.

Green. The boy had said green. The Mayor had been a long time away from New Canaan bureaucracy, but he knew they loved their symbols. Color choices were never made lightly. Each Diocese had its own proprietary shade. White for the Templars. Grey for knowledge. Red for commerce.

And green for biochemical warfare.

The wagon lurched down the road. Every dip, bump, crag, crease, clump, and pebble strewn along the worn and undulating trail reverberated up its rickety wooden frame and broadcast its vibrations into the small of Selena's back. The sky was dark and she was tired, but the constant jerk and thud of the wagon's clumsy flatbed made sleep more or less impossible.

Seven people rode along with her: the driver up front on his perch and the remaining six crammed together in the back, half buried in drifts of straw. The wagon was big enough to seat ten comfortably, but bushels full of autumnal produce took up the entire front half, leaving the travellers pressed tight together to avoid tumbling over the tailgate, which was nothing more than a few stiff lengths of wire wrapped around a bent nail. Selena wasn't sure exactly what kind of produce the wagon was carrying; the driver had nailed canvas over the bushels to keep hungry riders from pilfering his goods.

The countryside was as tedious as the road was long, and the road was long indeed. It ran north from Fallowfield in a meandering line, cutting first through verdant farmland, then the marshy banks of a reservoir, then a vast and vacant desert of shitgrass. Tumbledown farmhouses in various states of collapse dotted the landscape. Many had been ransacked for building materials, leaving only their naked frames to moulder like skeletons picked clean by carrion.

Marcus sat opposite Selena, his legs entwined uncomfortably with hers. He appeared to be sleeping. Selena watched him for a moment. His grin flashed in the dark. Selena quickly looked away. His teeth disappeared behind his lips, which curled upward in a small, satisfied smile.

Selena shifted in her cramped seat and wondered for the fiftieth time what she was doing, where she was going, and why she'd left her brother behind. The decision sizzled like a hot coal in her belly, searing her guts with guilt and second-guessing. She hated to think what he must be feeling, alone in a city he barely knew. He would have to assume she'd either been killed or had abandoned him, and she didn't know which assumption pained her more. Twice she leaned forward, ready to wake Marcus and demand he bring her back to Fallowfield and to hell with the risk, yet both times she relented. She told herself it was to keep her and Simon safe, to stay strong until they could resume their journey west—the only thing that really mattered. But beneath that thought slinked something dank and grim and shy of daylight, a sensation she wasn't willing to own up to. A sense, almost, of relief.

As dawn approached, the landscape changed. The shitgrass ocean grew shallower, its surface dotted with islets of lumber and concrete and steel. Shoals of broken tarmac carved the field into uneven strips. Gutted houses stood on naked beams or lay broken in a stew of tar and rainwater, mouldering in the cookpots of their concrete foundations. Here and there rose street signs, obelisks marking the passage of the long since dead, their names—syrupy things like Walnut Court and Daisy Avenue and Parkside Lane—brief and enigmatic epitaphs.

A short while later the ruins gave way to great grey pillars of glass and concrete and steel. Selena stared up at them, unimpressed. She'd seen much the same in K City and half a dozen other Middle Waste cities. The buildings were giants aged beyond their prime, wheezy, stoop-shouldered, and grey, their windows dulled with cataracts of grime or else shattered entirely. A few leaned drunkenly, supported by the shoulders of their sturdier brethren. But unlike in K City and the rest, many of these buildings seemed to be inhabited. Selena spotted more than a few men and women in the windows, and many rooms sported lanterns or makeshift blinds. Solar panels festooned the upper floors, and a few windmills sprouted from rooftops like enormous mechanical flowers.

The streets churned with life. Silk-swaddled merchants led wagons full of potash or scrap metal or grain down crowded streets, shouting abuse at laggards, gawkers, and greedy vendors setting up ramshackle tables on the already over-clogged thoroughfare. Waves of people crashed against buildings, cresting over medians laid down ages before. As with Fallowfield, the merchants appeared to make up a well-fed minority distinct from the peons in their sooty, soiled garb. The harsh, industrial smell of smoke and metal lingered in the air, rising like a ghost from the pores of the city and drifting beneath the more familiar odors of sweat and horseshit and rusting metal.

Marcus stretched in long, lazy motions before rising to his feet and stepping lightly over the side of the wagon. Selena grabbed her rucksack and leapt out after him. The driver shot them a distrustful glance and tugged at the protective canvas that covered his produce, making sure a flap had not been peeled back and a few precious apples palmed.

Marcus led Selena against the current of the crowd, slipping neat as a shadow through throngs of pack mules and merchants haggling over the price of flour and salt and twine. Selena bumped and shoved and jostled behind him, swearing beneath her breath at Marcus' impossible agility.

"What do all these people even do in this city?" she asked. "The locust is as thick as I've ever seen it. There's no farmland."

"Denver is not a town for farmers, Lena. It is for builders. The men here make many things. Tools, weapons, gun powder, medicines. They look to Fallowfield for their food, and Fallowfield looks to them for such goods. The merchants sell each to the other and grow fat on the profits. The workers eat the scraps."

"Yeah? So what does that leave for us?"

Marcus smiled. "You would be surprised."

They turned down an alley and the crowds fell away. Marcus stopped before a utility door pressed his thumb against a small buzzer. After a minute or so, the door squealed open, shedding slivers of green paint. A man stepped forward. His face parted the darkness in which he stood as if rising to the surface of a murky lake. His nose came first, upturned and bulbous, the prow of a fleshy ship. His chin was next, lumpy and bejowled, followed in short order by a large and bony forehead. Thin lips lay half-buried in an overgrowth of black stubble. His eyes were last, deep green orbs that never fully surfaced. A scum of shadow covered them, trapped in the tidal pools of large and deep-set sockets.

The man slapped Marcus on the shoulder with affectionate vigor. His belly shook.

"It is good to see you again, Marc. How is Juarez?"

"As hellish as when you left, I am sure," replied Marcus. "Though I have not been in years. Work has a carried me elsewhere. It has been a long ride."

The man looked at Selena then back at Marcus. *"Su senora?"* he asked.

Marcus shook his head. *"Una luchadora."*

The man arched his eyebrows. "That shall be something to see." He turned to Selena and gave a deep bow.

"Saludos, luchadora. I am called Gustavo. Your friend is a killer and a scoundrel, but he is good company. Come." He beckoned them inside. "You have found us at a good time."

Gustavo led them down a stairwell and through a narrow hall lined floor to ceiling with grime-slickened tile. The air had the damp and mossy feel of an underground cavern. The only light came from a doorway at the end of the hall, as did the fusillade of voices hurling insults and praise.

Through the doorway was a large concrete floor ringed with bleachers. Men sat on splintery wooden benches, bouncing with almost childish excitement and pumping their fists in the air. A few rocked silently back and forth, their faces pale and clammy. On the ground, two men circled each other. Both were shirtless and well-muscled, their bodies slick with perspiration. Selena's mind snapped instantly to the slums of Jericho, her days throwing punches in the circle of blood. The room heaved with the same low stink, a musk of sweat and blood and dirt atop something more nameless and primal, a livewire buzz of strength and cunning.

The men's fists hovered at chin level, occasionally darting forward in quick jabs that invariably fell short. Selena sized up both men and found them wanting. They were clumsy and slow, lacking both the technical proficiency of the Templars and the animal grace of the Salters. *These fools wouldn't last five seconds in a Jericho ring.*

The thinner man lunged and the fight took on a different flavor. The two bodies collided in a flurry of limbs and snarls and thumps. Arms slapped and scrabbled and jabbed, legs stomped on feet and struck blindly at shins. The bigger man landed a lucky punch, striking his opponent on the ridge of his jaw. It was a strong blow but a clumsy one. The other man tottered on his feet and the aggressor, though half blind with pain from the haymaker, still managed to bring him down. Their groundwork was even worse than their boxing, a drunken flurry of aimless holds and rabbit punches against a backdrop of labored grunting.

"These guys don't know how to fight at all," Selena muttered.

"These are not trained fighters, Lena. Most of the men you see are day laborers and tradesmen. They are big and muscled and dumb. They fight for the same reason the field hands of Fallowfield do. Because all other doors are closed to them."

Two men stepped briskly into the ring and pulled the fighters apart. They separated easily, one with arms raised in triumph and the other slump-shouldered and dejected.

"Then why are we here?"

"Because we are businesspeople, yes? And businesspeople can spot an untapped market."

146

Selena watched more fights. They soon ran together into one sloshing mess of blood and bruises and bludgeoned heads. Everyone was terrible. Marcus passed the time speaking with the man sitting next to him, who was older and better dressed than anyone else in the room. He wore a neatly-pressed brown suit that would have fit him beautifully if he were ten pounds lighter. Rings encircled his chubby fingers, their golden bands studded with glittering stones. Selena couldn't hear them over the noise of the crowd.

Marcus motioned to Selena. The bejewelled man regarded her without expression. He said something to Marcus, who arched his eyebrows and said something else in reply. The bejewelled man appeared to think for a moment, rubbed his hands together, and spoke to one of the men sitting in front of him. The other man—a subordinate, clearly—jumped up from his seat and clambered awkwardly down the bleachers. The bejewelled man signaled to Gustavo, pointed to Selena, and made an incomprehensible gesture. Gustavo grunted his way up the bleachers to where Selena and Marcus sat. He placed a meaty hand on Selena's shoulder.

"Do you want a fight, *luchadora?*"

Selena nodded. She took two strips of cloth from her knapsack and, following Gustavo to the centre of the ring, wrapped her hands tight. The crowd's collective gaze swarmed her, crawling over her skin like a swath of flies. The bleachers hummed and rattled. Gustavo raised a hand and the thrum receded.

"We have a new fighter," he said. "Does anyone volunteer to be her match?"

The bejewelled man cleared his throat. His subordinate clambered back to his seat, giving an OK sign.

"I believe Roger might be interested," said the bejewelled man. "Ain't that right, Roger?"

"You know it, Mr. Robson." A tall, shirtless figure rose from the crowd and stepped lithely into the ring. His face was pockmarked and round, a fleshy globe perched atop broad shoulders and fringed with tufts of thinning black hair. He was an oddly-proportioned man, with a simian slouch and a thin waist that terminated in stumpy legs while his upper body bulged with toned, twitching muscle.

Gustavo stepped from between the fighters, took his place in the crux between two sets of bleachers, and crossed his arms. This, as far as Selena could tell, was the signal that the fight had started.

Roger raised his fists and set them orbiting one another in small circles. It was an awkward, ungainly fighting stance, but at least he had one. Selena bobbed in, ducked a cross, and delivered a flurry of punches to Roger's abdomen. The first one landed, but he tucked in with a grunt and the rest glanced off his elbows. Selena deked back as he threw a hook. She heard the hiss of his knuckles slashing by and felt the wake of air they displaced. It figured that, after the procession of abysmal performances she'd seen, the man she was up against would be the one who could actually fight.

Selena fought with feigned aggression, making calculated advances that looked wild but really served to test Roger's limits. Range was his biggest asset. He was a tall man to begin with, maybe six-foot-four, but his arms were even longer than they should have been. And though lanky, he was strong. The few punches he landed had hurt like hell.

But for all his advantages, he was slow and ungainly and untrained. His technique was self-conscious and unnatural. He checked his form constantly as if muddling through the steps of a dance half-remembered. Selena's technique, meanwhile, was second nature, an intricate pattern of feints and sidesteps and parries chiselled into her by years of training.

Selena pummelled Roger's abdomen. The blows took their toll. Roger's stance grew hunched and pained. The soles of his feet scraped across the concrete, exhausted and clumsy. A well-placed hook or two to the jaw could have ended things, but Selena wasn't tall enough to get a good shot unless Roger left himself open, and he was far too cautious a fighter for that. Worse still, he began to discover his reach. Fists flew like artillery from a distant hill, caroming into Selena's wrists and biceps and sides. They lacked the full brunt of his strength, but they hurt, and as long as they were flying, it was almost impossible to slide in close.

The crowd cheered, jeered, stomped, and slapped their hands against the bleachers. Only Marcus and Mr. Robson seemed immune to the fervor. Marcus picked his teeth with his thumbnail while Mr. Robson sat beside him, one chubby leg crossed casually over the other.

Revelling in his reach, Roger grew giddy and aggressive. He smiled crazily, his long arms pistoning and pinwheeling while Selena dodged, strafed, and manoeuvred. She let him come at her, parrying blows with sharp, economic twitches of the wrist and staying just close enough for him to keep punching. She marked the timbre of his breath, the speed and depth of each rise and fall, waiting for shallow, raspy notes to sound among the deeper, more urgent chorus.

Eventually they came. His feet, already scraping the concrete, began to catch and stumble. His swings grew wider. Selena dodged them and watched, dodged them and watched, until his arm kinked awkwardly and an ill-aimed haymaker soared half a foot above her head, his body trailing on tiptoe in its wake. As he came in toward her, Selena stepped in to meet him, coiled, and struck.

The blow began at her heels and rippled upward, gaining strength like a tidal wave rushing toward the shore until it crashed against his chin. A flurry of punches followed, quick strikes whipping from the shoulder that broke his nose and burst his lip and pummeled his unprotected stomach. Roger staggered beneath the assault, falling first to one knee then onto his back. Gustavo called an end to it. The crowd cheered, a great roaring jubilation peppered with moans of incredulous shock.

Selena left the ring and sat down on the first row of benches. She unwrapped her aching knuckles. Behind her, Mr. Robson reached into the folds of his jacket and pulled out a small paper bag, which he tossed lightly into Marcus' lap. Marcus peered inside, folded it shut, and whispered something to Robson. Robson laughed, though his eyes retained a coldness that Selena didn't like. Marcus gave him a quick pat on the shoulder, stood, and with his usual grace strode down the benches two at a time. He landed with a small flourish in front of Selena and flicked the paper bag with his middle finger.

"We should go," he said.

"You aren't fighting?"

"In good time. This is not my sort of arena. Come."

They spent the night in a flophouse on the outer edge of town. The room was cramped, dirty, and bare save for two cots pushed chastely to opposite walls, but it afforded an impressive view of the countryside. Not that there was much to look at. Yellow locust swallowed everything, its jaundiced stalks stretching well beyond the horizon. Selena put a hand to the glass, soothing her chafed knuckles on its cool surface. Marcus sat on the end of his cot, counting the money.

"There is much night left, and Denver is ours. We should celebrate your victory. Come."

"I think I'll just stay here."

Marcus tsked. "It is a precious life, Lena. Do not spend too much of it in such depressing places."

"We shouldn't draw too much attention to ourselves. I'm a wanted woman, remember?"

"Suit yourself. I will return."

After Marcus had left, Selena moved his cot in front of the door. It wouldn't stop anyone determined to enter, but it would at least alert her to their presence. She returned to the window, watching the autumn wind trace patterns in the yellow locust. Somewhere beyond those desolate leagues, her brother slept soundly. Or didn't. She couldn't venture to guess how he was doing.

She climbed into bed without undressing. The cot sagged beneath her weight, its springs whining. She tossed this way and that, finding comfort in no position. However she lay, the data stick seemed to always dig its corners into her hip, fate's bony finger prodding her forward.

But which way was forward?

15: Fists

A sunbeam diffused across the ripples and folds of Simon's sheets, leaving shadowy spots like flies caught in a web of honeyed yellow. The web's bright tendrils crept upward until they strung across Simon's face. Simon scrunched his eyes against the brightness. Sunlight pierced the membrane of his desultory interior universe and spilled him into the waking world. Shards of his dream lay around him, dissolving. He fumbled through them, wanting to observe a few fragments before the dream disintegrated altogether. He recalled a sea of yellowing grass, the clatter of hooves, the reflective sheen of glass or metal, but that was all. The pieces wouldn't fit together and the more he tried to connect them the quicker they broke apart.

Simon sat up. His toes kneaded the Turkish rug that covered the floor. He fumbled for his glasses and put them on. The world became crisp, its blurry edges shorn.

He opened his closet and rifled through an assortment of velvet, suede, and cotton garments. After months spent in the same ragged jeans and hoodie, the scope and volume of selection still astounded him. He slipped on a paisley shirt and buttoned a pair of home-stitched khakis. His new wardrobe had come with his room, a small, bright, cheerful chamber off the eastern annex of The Mayor's mansion. He'd moved in at The Mayor's suggestion four days after Selena disappeared. At first, he'd refused the offer; it felt wrong somehow, as if by moving he were cutting free his hope of her returning. But three nights spent alone in his apartment had made the room unbearable, its silence thrumming with a cold electricity that buzzed through his bones and rattled his teeth.

The days were better, since Simon had plenty to keep him busy. He spent mornings and evenings with The Mayor, filling canvas after canvas with the pigments spilling from his overcrowded imagination. The afternoons he walked or rode to the outlying farms, where he would lend a hand fixing bits of broken farming equipment or wiring run-down cottages with a few dim lightbulbs. Simon was no Bishop of Light, but he understood the basics and the farmers, many of whom lived in tumbledown shacks and struggled with anything more sophisticated than an on-off switch, seemed sincerely grateful for his help. It felt good working, made his time in Fallowfield feel like something more than simple charity. There were moments, lost in the gentle fog of his duties, where he felt sort of happy. But inevitably the fog would clear, revealing a cold mirthless light that brought the ugly, blemished truth into cruel clarity. Selena was gone, his parents were gone, and he was alone in the middle of a great poisoned veldt.

After getting dressed, Simon walked a familiar path to the Mayor's office—which was now his office, too. *There won't be any news,* he thought. *Don't get your stupid hopes up because nothing happened and there won't be any news. If they found something they would've woken you up, but they didn't so there won't be any news.* He repeated this silently to himself, reciting it with every step, but it didn't do any good. A bright cruel cord of hope cinched his stomach tighter and tighter.

The Mayor clapped his hands together in a kind of prim jubilation. "Ah Simon, how are you this morning?"

"Did they find anything?"

The Mayor sighed. "Simon, I assure you if I learned anything definitive of your sister's whereabouts, you would be the first to know.

The men I sent to look for her are among my best. They know the region down to the smallest detail. If she can be found, they will find her."

The cord gave a final tug and snapped. Simon's insides deflated like a popped balloon.

"I don't understand what happened," he said, his voice cracking. "Why'd she run away? It doesn't make any sense."

The Mayor set a hand on Simon's shoulder. "It's a mystery, Simon. But I'm sure behind that mystery lies a good reason for your sister's actions. She would not simply abandon you, of that I'm sure."

Simon looked up at The Mayor. "You ... you think so?"

"Certainly."

"Is she hurt, do you think?" He'd asked these questions before, of course, but asking them had become a kind of ritual, as if his incantations fueled a lantern that might, if left burning long enough, lead her home.

"I don't dare speculate, my boy. I know how much it hurts not knowing, but my best guesses would be just that, guesses."

Simon nodded glumly.

"I have something to show you." The Mayor slid from his seat and rounded the desk. He guided Simon to the window-lined annex of his studio. Inside, three paintings leaned against the wall in a neat row, their edges adorned with rippling slats of gilded pine. The paintings were all plays on a similar theme: dramatic landscapes viewed from a great height by a solitary figure. Mountains fringed the horizon in every scene. Simon ran his finger over one of the frames. The wood was warm and rich, the gilding that swirled in arabesques atop it cold and slick with polish.

"You framed them," Simon said, his voice soft with wonder. The Mayor laughed.

"Would that I could lay claim to such skill, child. No, I merely had them framed. Terrence Saunders is Fallowfield's most talented carpenter. He did the work. It lends a certain grandeur to the pieces, wouldn't you say?"

Simon's fingers continued to trace the paths of gold that wound up and down the frame.

"However, Simon, there's also a more … unpleasant matter I need to discuss with you."

"Is it Selena?"

"It concerns her; yes."

The cord lassoed Simon's guts once again. "But—"

"I told you we're looking but have no answers yet? That's the absolute truth, Simon. I wouldn't keep anything from you on that score. All I have are suspicions. I don't know what happened to your sister, but I have a guess as to who's behind it, and why."

"Who?"

"Magnus. David Akros. Harvey Freamon."

"You mean those farmers?" Simon's world seemed to slip an axle. "But why? What do they have against Selena?"

The Mayor reached thumb and forefinger behind his sunglasses and massaged his eyelids, careful to leave the reflective lenses in place. "Here is where I'm afraid I may have played a role in this tragedy, however unwittingly. To explain how, I should tell you a little about how I came to be Mayor of this place.

"I am not from the Middle Wastes, Simon, as you have probably guessed. In fact, the place where I was born might be familiar to you. Do you recall the tenements on Barnabas Street? The pre-War buildings, made from red brick?"

Simon stared at The Mayor, open-mouthed. "You're from New Canaan? From *Jericho?*"

"I am indeed. In fact, I even knew your parents. Or rather, knew of them. I suspect they would have trouble picking me out from a field of farmers, but we met on a few occasions. People in their position have little cause to remember the likes of people in mine."

"What position?"

The Mayor smiled. "A Shepherd. A very different sort of thing there than here, I'm sure you'll agree. I've given the name a bit more … *clout* in this part of the world. I was a glorified clerk, living in southend tenements raised a few meagre stories above the rabble, subject to electricity rations, subsisting on alley meats on lean weeks when the price of beef spiked. It's a world you could scarcely contemplate.

"I climbed my way out of those tenements and onto the lower rungs of the Seraphim. A shepherd is never welcome in the inner ranks—they spend too much time watching over the Salters, and the stink never fully washes off—but a few of us do manage to feast on the scraps from your table. I was one of those. I'm no soldier, as you can well see, but I have a keen strategic mind, and the Templars have much use for strategy. I staked out a post on their bureaucratic fringes and set about making a name for myself.

"Still, I wish I'd known your parents better. For it appears we shared a common purpose in opposing New Canaan. They tried espionage. I tried a coup."

Simon blinked, still reeling from the unexpected discovery of a fellow New Canaanite out here in the Middle Wastes. To say Simon hated New Canaan would be an understatement, but it still felt to him, however perversely, as home. Meeting a countryman in this strange land comforted him—particularly since said countryman was apparently as much of an outcast as he and Selena were. "I never heard of any coup."

"I wouldn't expect you to have. The winners write the headlines, after all, and it would serve New Canaan poorly to report on internal dissent, even if that dissent was successfully quashed. Much better to project an image of peace and plenty than a jackboot stomping out rebellions. I tried to seize some land in the outer baronies and was driven out. So I rounded up some dissatisfied peasants and the remnants of my loyal men and struck out west, in search of my destiny. I found it here, in Fallowfield.

"As our little town has grown, so too have the ambitions of its inhabitants. The farmers and I often butt heads over decisions of governance and trade, as you saw the other day. I'm now afraid those scuffles have turned to something darker. My Shepherds, with Bernard at the helm, have unearthed the first rumblings of a conspiracy against me.

"According to him, the farmers take umbrage with my leadership, and rather than face me on a political level, see fit to use coarser methods. Fortunately, I'm well protected. Magnus and his ilk lack the strength to take me on directly. So they have reached out to a place that might view me as a common enemy."

"New Canaan," Simon said. His hands trembled.

"That is Bernard's suspicion. I sincerely doubt I mean much of anything to the Archbishop. After all, I'm naught but a would-be rebel quietly serving a life of exile in the western wilds. But you and your sister are a very different story. If Magnus knew about, or even suspected, the existence of your data stick, he would have a powerful bargaining chip. The Templars would do anything to keep sensitive data from falling into the hands of the Republic of California. Sending a few Templars to wipe me out would be, to their eyes, Standard well spent."

Simon's insides felt like the trodden remains of winter slush, cold and dirty and kicked about some ghetto gutter. If what The Mayor said was right, then he and Selena were in much greater danger than they'd realized. Or he was, at any rate. Selena might be well past danger by now, lying gutted in some barren field. Simon blinked back tears, as if keeping them in could drown the image before it surfaced again.

"What do we do?"

"At the moment, there is frustratingly little I can do. I may be fencing with shadows on this whole thing, and to strike out based on a few unfounded whispers would be unlawful and immoral. What I need is proof, at least enough to satisfy my own mind."

"How can we get it?"

The Mayor scratched beneath his ear. "There is one way. But it carries with it a degree of risk. I'm afraid it would fall on your shoulders."

"Me?"

The Mayor turned to the window. "You're right. I shouldn't have even suggested it. You're a boy, it would be wrong to put you in any sort of danger."

"But I'm already in danger, right?"

"Not of the same immediacy."

Simon inhaled. He thought of Selena, how she would act if he was missing. "What would you need me to do?"

The Mayor gave Simon a long, pensive look. "Let me preface by saying you don't need to do this. I can find another solution, I'm sure of it. It'll only take me some time."

"I understand. So what would you need me to do?"

The Mayor told him.

The grass whispered to Selena. She could hear its hushed chatter, malicious and mirthful, as the stalks crowded in on all sides. Fronds licked her face, leaving a pins and needles tingling on her cheeks, her arms, her chest. Walking through it was like wading waist deep through swampy water, each step deliberate and slow. She had no idea how long she'd been walking or where she was going. She knew only that she needed to get there, and that she was terribly late.

She clawed her way forward, repulsed by the touch of the grass but helpless to avoid it. Occasionally she found a sign to guide her or a path to ease her progress, but the signs were all senseless—words dribbling from their faces like ink in the rain—and the paths were soon swallowed by the endless, hungry field. Overhead the sky was a bruised and brooding purple-black, its clouds whirling in a great gyre. The wind clawed the tips of the yellow locust. Simon's voice carried on its vicious currents, high and desperate, calling her name.

"Simon!" she cried back, but Simon didn't seem to hear. He repeated her name over and over. No matter how fast Selena ran, he grew no closer, and his voice seemed always to be coming from a new direction.

"Simon! Where are you?! Stay still!"

She kept running, and gradually she realized that she wasn't running to her brother, but *from* something else altogether. It stalked her through the grass, loud, awful and formless as the rumble of distant thunder. Selena caught glimpses of it through the stalks. She couldn't make out its shape, but its flesh was luminous and mirrored, as if scaled with steel polished to impossible brightness. She knew without seeing that it was hungry, and though it had no eyes, it could detect her with some primordial sense outside of her comprehension, could taste her heartbeat, hear her terror, and smell the Morse code panic of her thumping arteries.

The beast pounced and she woke, biting back a scream. The fields dissolved into yellow mist, and the sound of her brother merged into a murmured argument between unfamiliar voices. Feigning sleep, she rolled on her side and peered through her eyelashes. Two women stood in their underwear, clothes cradled in their arms. Between them stood Marcus, his shirt undone, a curlicue of black pubic hair periscoping up from the top of his pants. He muttered something to the girls, which only one of them seemed to understand. The other, fairer-skinned girl looked in puzzlement at Marcus and the dark-haired woman.

"What's he saying? What are you guys talking about?"

The girl who spoke Marcus' mother tongue shouted something with venom, to which Marcus replied by counting out a few bills and tossing them at her with a kind of forced indifference. The girl made a show of being insulted while gathering up the bills alongside her fair-skinned partner. The two women left in a huff, pointedly slamming the door behind them. Marcus ran his hands through his hair, sighed, and looked at Selena. His face split in a sly grin.

"Up with the dawn, girl." He buttoned his shirt, wrapped his serape around his shoulders, and gave his switchblade an experimental flick. The blade whizzed cleanly from its handle. He clicked it home, slipped the knife into its tiny sheath, and put on his boots.

"We must eat. We will fight this morning before we ride. Morning fights are not good fights—most men are still sober, yes? And sober men bet less. But there is money here still, and I wish to ride by noon."

"You go ahead," Selena said. "I'm sitting this one out."

"Sitting out? Are you a golden-ringed *jugador* who can afford to watch others at their labors?"

"You've sat plenty out since we started this. My ribs are still sore from yesterday. I need to pace myself." This was partly true, for her opponent the day before—a wiry man with a golden earring and scar tissue tears carved into his cheeks—had given her a fierce kick to the sternum that still ached. But she was more concerned about the way her dream hovered at the edge of her senses, the unease it had conjured bleeding into her waking mind.

"Ah, but you and me, we have different obligations, yes?"

"And I won't be able to meet those obligations if I get beaten to a pulp, will I?"

The smile that hung endlessly about Marcus' lips vanished, leaving in its place a cold and mirthless line that hardened his face, making it rough and haggard. In that instant, Selena saw behind the clownish façade that billowed around Marcus like his serape, hiding his true contours. This was the Marcus people saw before they died on the tip of his knife.

"A street fighter gets no rest, Lena. There are debts to pay and days to ride. You will fight."

Selena opened her mouth to protest, weighed the expression on Marcus' face, closed it. *I've sold myself into slavery,* she thought darkly. *And for what? A crappy bed in a dozen nothing towns and a few hollow promises?*

The town—Selena had stopped bothering to learn their names—was little more than an inn and a crossroads, the main square a patch of bare earth soupy with mud and rainwater. It dimpled slightly beneath her feet, leaving ghostly footprints that echoed her every step. The sky was murky and overcast, reminding her unpleasantly of her dream. She suppressed the thought of it, her brother, and anything to do with Fallowfield, and shouldered her way into the fighter's circle, where a barrel-shaped man with simian arms and a beard of grey gristle leered at her, his tongue probing towards her grotesquely.

"Pink meat," he cooed. "Gonna get some pink meat. So sweet. Gonna pound it tender."

The fight was fast, ugly, and brutal. Selena's circumspection fell away like shed skin, revealing a creature that was all thorns and talons and teeth. And fists—fists most of all. They broke the fat man's jaw and sank wrist-deep into his flabby stomach. They rained like meteors on his kidneys and liver, loosening his bowels and bloodying the piss that trickled down his leg. They yanked him up by his greasy hair and slammed him down, striking like piledrivers at his prostrate torso.

Two men grabbed Selena around the armpits and dragged her away. Selena fought their grasp, her mouth nearly dislocating to accommodate the width and fury of her scream. Her vision pared to a razor's keenness, and she saw herself reflected in one of the men's eyes: incisors bared, muscles taut as steel cables, grey eyes like thunderclouds bearing down on a stranded schooner, promising oblivion. She let herself go limp and, when her acquiescence was clear, shrugged the men away. Her opponent lay in a broken heap, the muddy earth hiding the worst of his wounds. She rubbed her face and felt streaks of oily blood and matted hair trace her touch. Of all the men and women in the crowd, only Marcus eyed her without fear.

"Very good. That was not so hard, yes?"

Selena cleaned her hands on the fringe of Marcus' serape. He looked down, amusement crackling across his lips.

"Next time I say I'm sitting one out," Selena whispered. "I'm sitting one out."

Marcus didn't object. She chose to take this as a victory. *This has to end soon. I'm going to make a mistake or the winter is going to slip away from me. In either case, I'll be fucked, and so will Simon. And so will the Republic.*

She stormed off in search of a stream to wash her hands, her fingers picking compulsively at the shape the data stick raised in her jeans.

The crowd scattered before her.

16: Silo

The fields looked different at night. Moonlight painted them black and silver, flattening trees, corn stalks, and barns into stark silhouettes. The daytime sounds of birdsong and trundling wagons and the jocular back-and-forth of fieldhands were gone, replaced by a sparser, mournful score of owl hoots and wind-rustled branches. Simon's heartbeat pounded in his ears like some deafening piece of machinery, overclocked and approaching malfunction. He forced himself to take deep, measured breaths until the beating slowed.

The farms were hard to tell apart in the dark, but Simon's target was fairly easy to spot. The silo thrust skyward like some colossus' skeletal finger, admonishing the gods for its premature burial. Its metal skin shone bone pale in the moonlight, the patches of rust like blood stains indifferently rinsed away. Simon gripped the ladder.

The wind grew sharper as he climbed, turning his sweaty skin to ice. He wanted nothing more than to freeze, lock his arms through the bars, and wait for morning. But the longer he stayed on that ladder the more likely it was he'd be spotted, and he feared discovery by the farmers almost as much as he feared falling.

A railed balcony encircled the silo's domed top. Simon clambered onto it, absurdly grateful to be back on a horizontal surface, He knitted his fingers through its steel grate flooring. Eventually the waves of nausea roiling his stomach subsided and he was able to stand. He scuttled to the silo's entrance, one hand constantly clutching the railing.

Steel bars crisscrossed the doorway, haphazardly spaced and listing slightly to one side or the other. Their tapering left a gap to the right of the doorframe, around knee-height, that Simon thought he might be able to fit through. He removed his backpack and stuffed it through the opening. Light filtered through the gaps for a few feet before the darkness swallowed them. He pushed the pack to the side, ensuring it remained within the lighted alcove. The last thing he wanted was to inadvertently fling his pack off a high ledge. He knelt and wriggled his way into the gap. His head slid through easily, his shoulders with only a bit of wriggling. He crawled forward. The cold bar slid along his ribcage, compressed his stomach, and snagged around his hips. He tilted to either side but his lower half wouldn't slip through.

Panic set him flailing, fingernails scrabbling at the dusty floor. He took a few more deep breaths, downshifting his heartbeat to a lower gear. *Relax, dummy. You think Selena would freak out over something like this? If your shoulders fit, your hips will fit too.* He crab-walked and found he was right. His waist had slipped toward the center of the doorway, where the gap between bars narrowed. Pressed against the right jamb, he fit through easily.

The dome of the silo was cool and musty, filled with the smell of fermenting grain and corroded metal. Simon reached in his bag and removed a small electric torch The Mayor had lent him. He flicked the switch and cast a cone of light around the room. A hole described its center. Simon approached it cautiously. It was three feet or so in diameter and smoothly cut, its gaping maw blocked by a piece of steel grating. Simon feared this too might be bolted down—the bars were much too narrow to pass through—but a quick tug revealed that nothing but gravity held it in place. He dragged the grate partway aside, grunting with exertion.

As he stood over the partially exposed hole, Simon noticed another smell beyond the mildew and metal. Something caustic and industrial, the sort of fumes that reddened eyes and ate through lungs. Simon wished he'd brought a mask, or at least a bandanna to tie around his face. He shone his torch into the opening, but the distance to the floor was too great, and the light dissolved before it touched ground.

From his pack, Simon removed a fat spool of entwined ropes. He found the looped ends and tied them around the grate, triple-checking each knot and doing his best to get them near the grate's center. When he was sure the knots were true, he let the spool drop. It uncoiled as it fell, revealing a rope ladder seventy-five feet long. The rope was distressingly thin, about the thickness of his pinky finger, and Simon tugged on it aggressively for a full minute before he was willing to give the ladder his weight—a more complex undertaking than he'd first figured. He could reach the ladder easily enough with his arm, but when he sat and extended his feet, it put him at a strange angle, his shoulders too far back to reach beneath the grate and grab hold.

Simon perched on the lip of the hole, his legs dangling down into darkness. He hooked the ladder over with one foot and pulled it up until he had a few feet of slack. He set his feet firmly on one of the lower rungs. The rope nestled against the heel of his shoe. He put the backpack on and dropped the torch inside—he didn't relish the thought of descending into darkness, but knew he'd want both hands free for this job. He grabbed an upper rung and sat there for a moment, steeling himself for what he needed to do next. When he felt somewhat calm—somewhat being the best he could hope for—he took a deep breath, scooted forward, and allowed himself to swing into the dark.

He didn't scream. Later this fact would give him more than a touch of pride, but at that instant making sound seemed vastly beyond his capabilities. He could only grip and pray as the rope pendulumed forward and back, its momentum seeming to grow with each cycle, as if propelled by some malignant force. Eventually, mercifully, the force relinquished its grip, and the rope came to something approaching a halt. Only then could Simon unclench his hand long enough to drop his grip a single rung.

The first ten feet took ages. After that, things got easier. The blackness around him, so ominous to descend into at first, became something of a comfort. It was easy to convince himself he was only a few feet off the ground, even as he climbed lower and lower.

Just as he began to worry that the ladder would end before the drop did, his shoe touched concrete. He pulled the electric torch from his backpack and cradled it to his chest. Part of him wanted nothing more than to climb back up the ladder and go home. But if the key to finding Selena was in this place and he let his fear keep him from finding her, he wouldn't be able to live with himself. Holding the torch aloft with feigned confidence, Simon flicked it on and swept the beam around him in a slow circle.

A procession of ramshackle industrial equipment ran the whole length of the circular room, pausing only long enough to allow space for the silo's door, a roughly retrofitted portal blocked with segmented sheets of iron. Great steel vats, their bellies rusty and distended, stood beside tables overflowing with salvage from some pre-Last War laboratory: ancient beakers and rubber gloves and reams of paper full of scribbled notes. Diagrams plastered the wall above one of the workstations, depicting a typhoon of arrows and hieroglyphs all crashing atop one another.

The center of the room was empty, but for one large item: a decrepit truck, jury-rigged with a hodgepodge of old parts. In New Canaan, wheeled vehicles were rarities reserved solely for the Templars, the Archbishop, and a scant few other Seraphim. Seeing one out here, even one in such poor shape, was a dislocating experience. He ran a finger over its piebald surface, dislodging flecks of old paint and eroding metal. The truck was a two-seater with a tiny cab, its windows empty frames, its seats long since rotted away and replaced with a bench carved from wood. Behind the cab ran a flatbed, onto which had been grafted a huge sideways drum. A spigot extended from the back of the drum, its tip fitted with a wide-mouthed nozzle. Pulleys ran the underside of the chassis, where they connected to a crank inside the cab, allowing the driver to wag the spigot like an outsized tail. A few valves sprouted up like steel mushrooms alongside the crank.

Simon didn't know what to make of any of this. From The Mayor's description, he'd expected torture devices or stockpiled munitions. Maybe even a few dead bodies. He was relieved to find none of this, but mystified by the silo's actual contents. The chemicals they were brewing could've been explosives, he supposed, but who sprayed explosives from the back of a rinky-dink truck?

Swinging the pack from his shoulders, Simon removed the last item it contained: a case, the size of a large book, made from sleek black metal. The Mayor's instructions in how to use it were brief, but intoned gravely.

"Find a discreet place and attach it there. It should be difficult to spot, but not too far from where people may congregate. If there's some sort of siting area or work surface, put it nearby. Its range is fairly poor, and I don't want to miss anything."

Simon recalled handling it in The Mayor's lighted office, studying its rounded corners and ominous black shell. "What is it?"

"You're familiar, I trust, with angel ears? This is a more primitive member of the same family. It's much bigger and bulkier than the sort New Canaan uses, but I don't have access to their level of technology, and moreover mine has no electric line to tap into and must provide its own power. It should broadcast for two weeks, at least."

"You think they'll talk about Selena?"

"If they have anything to say, they'll say it in that silo. I'll have myself or a Shepherd listen around the clock."

"And what if they admit to taking her?"

"In that case, we'll do everything in our power to get her back, Simon. This I swear to you."

"And if she's … " He couldn't bring himself to say it. The Mayor put a hand on his shoulder.

"Then justice will be done, my boy."

Simon crawled under a metal folding table next to one of the vats. The back of the device had been fitted with magnets, and it stuck to the underside of the table with ease. He grabbed his bag and began climbing back up the ladder.

It was hard going. The ladder bucked and twisted in his grasp. The rungs chafed his palms, leaving them red and raw. Above him, the grate made ominous moaning sounds, as if preparing to come clattering down on top of him.

Red-faced and huffing, Simon pulled himself through the hole and dragged the grate back into position. He untied the rope ladder and began feeding it through the bars, gathering its slack in a loose pile behind him. He'd pulled it up about halfway when the silo door opened with a clatter. Moonlight misted through the opening.

"Can't we do this at a decent hour?" A man's voice, middle-aged, its tone froggy and brambled with sleep.

"We don't want anyone seein' us." Another voice, older and sharper. Simon recognized it as belonging to the old farmer who'd met The Mayor in his office. He fumbled for the name, found it: Magnus. "Now get in already so I can close the door."

Simon's arms worked beyond their known capabilities, hoisting in a manic cycle of pull-release-grab. The ladder seemed to stretch on forever. He heard the silo door clatter shut, draping the room in resumed darkness.

"It's your silo. Who's gonna say boo if you got a couple fellas using it? Tell the fieldhands we're painting."

"With the door shut? Don't be daft. Now get the light so we can get started," the old farmer said.

Light?! Simon tugged still harder. The final feet of the rope ladder whipped up and smacked him in the face, rough fibres scratching his cheek. He suppressed a cry.

A piston of smoky light fired upward from the hole. Simon recoiled as if it might burn him, rolling backward into a pile of scratchy rope.

"I don't see why Harvey and David never have to do this," the unknown voice grumbled.

"Because they don't know boo about this business. You're the only one who's got the background. Plus, I need your help with the truck."

"They should be in here pickin' it up, then."

"Four farmers at night're more suspicious than two. Now quit bellyachin' and get to work."

Simon groaned. Most likely, they were going to be here for hours. He could be stuck here all night. Then he'd have to climb down the ladder in daylight, with fieldhands coming and going on the path. There's no way he could do it without being seen. And what if they discovered the box? The first thing they'd do would be search the silo top to bottom. And what would they do with him when they found him?

Working as quietly as possible, Simon coiled the ladder into a crude cylinder and stuffed it in his pack. There was more room with the angel ear gone, but he couldn't roll the ladder half as tight as Bernard had managed and bits of it jutted out awkwardly from the pack's mouth. Simon wedged the electric torch into a pocket and crept to the doorway.

Going out was easier than going in, perhaps because he knew he could fit. The night air had grown even more frigid, icy fingers raking his ears and pinching the back of his neck. He secured the backpack and began the long climb down, each movement calculated and slow, slow, slow.

His feet touched ground an eternity later. He took a few rubbery steps away from the ladder, found his balance, and scurried down the path. He didn't slow down until he was well out of sight from the silo door.

17: All but Princes and Politicians

Bernard stepped onto the grass, his latest bit of intel still tingling pleasantly in his ears.

As Commander of the Shepherds—and a Templar Knight before that—Bernard had built his reputation on always getting whatever or whomever he sought. When the Flood girl eluded him, he'd felt a blemish erupt on the face of that reputation, an unsightly boil that upset him far more than his disfigured cheek ever could. It was thus with a rare and genuine smile that he'd greeted his Denver informant, a musteline teamster with wiry arms and a wispy moustache scabbed with the crumbs of meals long since eaten. His name was Carter, and he was not the sort of man Bernard normally liked dealing with. But the story he'd brought with him went a long way in sweetening that otherwise bitter pill. He'd shown up on Bernard's doorstep, picking at a flaky zit on his chin and grinning like a cat that had eaten the canary and the cream in one greedy gulp.

"Heard you Sheps have an ear out 'bout a blond girl 'bout eighteen or so, okay to look at but kicks like a rabid mule."

"Say we do. What of it?"

He peeled a layer of skin from the pimple, examined it, flicked it aside. "Seen her in Gustavo's pit not three nights ago, poundin' Roger Furlong's bean head stupid—or stupider, guess I should say." His smile brought to mind a set of chipped and yellowing china, some bits missing, others cracked beyond possible use.

"That so?" Bernard's face was a stone parapet, behind which his excitement hid. The Denver fighting pit? It was so obvious he'd seen right past it.

"It's so, alright. Came up in the company of Marcus Ramirez, one a them knife boys from down Juarez way."

Bernard tittered silently behind his granite façade. This just got better and better. No wonder she'd been able to best one of his own boys and two fieldhands besides—*all dead from knife wounds*, his lawman's mind added. Friendless Selena wasn't quite so friendless after all. That made her marginally more dangerous.

But also a whole lot easier to track.

Keeping his expression underwhelmed, Bernard dipped into his informant coffer and paid Carter generously. A good ear was a good ear, regardless of the face that wore it.

"We never spoke," Bernard instructed.

He gave Carter five minutes to scuttle off to his bar or brothel of choice, then left his cottage. The night air felt good on his face. He walked across the field to the Shepherd barracks, a long, low-roofed building built at the foot of Shepherd's Hill. More dormitory than barracks, the building contained a series of small rooms with two to four beds each, flanked by a common living area and kitchen. Its accommodations were Spartan but well-built, warm in the winter and cool in the summer, with clean running water and electricity—far more than the farmers beyond the city ramparts enjoyed.

The Shepherds grew quiet as Bernard walked past. Their backs straightened, their hands fell to their sides. The younger ones bowed their heads respectfully or simply stared forward. The older ones saluted, a reflex held over from their Templar days that Bernard made no effort to snuff out; obedience was a valuable trait, whatever its origins.

Kaeric lay on the floor of his room, shirtless, doing push-ups. His shoulder muscles rippled beneath his skin. A pneumatic hiss escaped from between his teeth with each push. He looked up, his braided beard flopping like a dead fish, and with a final shove leaped upright. It was a show-off move, but fairly impressive. He cocked a saucy salute in the New Canaan style that was just on the safe side of insubordinate. Bernard frowned. Kaeric was one of his best recruits outside of the ex-Templars who'd defected alongside him, a good marksman and a better brawler, but his discipline was lacking. Bernard would have to beat some more sense into the boy, teach him a healthy respect for the rank and file.

But now wasn't the time.

"You have a job. You want it?"

"Sure."

"Good. Cause you get no say in the matter." Bernard closed the door. "You know the girl who kicked your ass?"

"You gotta be more specific than that."

Bernard saw through the flimsy joke to the wall of ice brooding behind it. It looked cold and jagged and hard. "You want another go at her? This time you'll have better odds."

"Of course. But I thought you sent Branson, Kryzyrski, and McCoy out already."

"I did. They're out there still. Which means I can't tell 'em that we got an eye witness who puts her in the company of one Marcus Ramirez."

"That mejjy knife fighter?"

"The very same. He's not the sort of guy to have a fixed address, but he does have profile. He should be a lot easier to find than some girl no one's heard of."

"You want me to take care of him?"

"Here's how you'll do it."

They spoke for several minutes, Bernard explaining the mission, Kaeric asking a few clarifying questions and repeating the steps back to him.

"You got it?" Bernard asked.

"I got it, sir. I won't let you down."

"If I thought you would, I'dve picked someone else."

Kaeric kept his face composed. Bernard left, shaking his head. The boy was quick enough, but cocky. Bernard's thoughts turned to the girl, wondering just how the hell a woman had beaten one of his best Shepherds in single combat. True, she wasn't much of a woman in the sense Bernard saw them—a ropey, lean, athletic type, with barely an ounce of T or A on her. He preferred curves and soft, yielding flesh. Still, he'd had his share of wiry types, willing and not, and none of them had ever shown anything like enough strength and cunning to take down someone like the Dragon. Hell, if a girl could take on a young buck like Kaeric, who's to say she couldn't—

No. Foolish thought. Bernard brushed it away as if flicking a spider from his arm but its uneasy, tainted feeling left footprints on his mind. He'd visit one of Fallowfield's brothels tonight, he decided. Only warm, soft skin could scrub the feeling away.

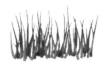

The room was dingy and caked with grime, but crowded despite its shabbiness. Men laughed, bickered, and slammed their steins together, slopping watery yellow beer onto the cracked and buckled floorboards. A few women sat among them, some playing cards and trading jeers with equal vulgarity, though more served drinks, flashed cleavage, or gyrated on tables. It was more or less the same room they invariably ended up in after a fight, Marcus with his booze and cards and women, Selena slumped in the corner, itemizing the various aches and cuts and bruises that maligned her body. There were more than a few of these, the latest being the cramp in her ass wrought by the knobby and unyielding surface of the metal stool on which she sat.

"You should not be so uptight," said Marcus. He sat at a nearby table with a group of revellers in various states of drunkenness. He had matched the heaviest drinkers among them glass for glass, yet his fingers were steady as they twined through the hair of the whore perched on his lap. "You are tonight an exulted warrior. Celebrate your victory. Drink wine. Have a woman or a man. There is a fellow in a back room with hashish from the northwest. Partake. Celebrate."

"I'm fine with this," Selena grunted, motioning to her beer.

"It is unhealthy always to be so grim. Celebration refreshes the soul. Sit as you do and you will sour by twenty."

"Keep drinking that scotch and you'll pickle by thirty."

Marcus laughed. "Pickles can be sweet. Sour is sour."

"I'm sour, all right. It's been two weeks and you're still dragging me from one shitty town to the next. I don't have time for much more of this."

"You must learn patience, Lena."

Tell that to the Republic of California. The heat of summer was slipping away, leaving in its absence an autumnal chill like some filthy rime on Selena's guts. The fights were coming up fast enough—she sometimes had three or four in a single day—but the conclusion of her service seemed to creep no closer. And more fights meant more opportunities to screw up. Selena knew she was good, but being good wasn't always enough. You needed to be lucky, too, and no one's luck lasted forever. She'd had a few close calls already, times where only a twitch of reflex or an opponent's poor footing had kept her from a cracked skull or worse.

In these moments, her mind flew to the data stick in her pocket. She pictured its plastic chassis wilting and cracking against her rotting thigh, the two unceremoniously buried together in some pauper's grave. The last hope of the Republic rendered so much useless meat and silicon thanks to a backwater bruiser and a fifty-Standard brawl. It was madness bringing the thing into the circles with her—what if someone booted her in the hip and broke it?—but she couldn't think of any better options. She sure as hell didn't trust Marcus enough to let him hold it, and stashing it under a rock or under some flophouse bed would only drive her crazy. No, it needed to stay on her person—and her person needed to get back to her brother and away to the west.

"You don't make any sense at all, you know that?" complained Selena. "It's always more fights, more money, press on and on and on, then we wind up in some hole and you blow half of it."

Marcus shrugged. "This is, how you say, a matter of opinion, yes?"

"If you're not going to make good on our deal, just tell me and I'll go get my brother myself."

"Go, then. Your wrists wear no shackles."

Selena sulked into her beer. *Right. And how far into town would I get before Bernard and his goons lynched me?* "There's different sorts of shackles, asshole, and you know it."

"Too true, girl. We drink so that we do not feel their sting."

Marcus raised a finger, signalling for another round. But the man who came to his table carried no tray. He wore dungaree overalls faded at the knees and a checkered chambray shirt. A black bandanna covered the lower half of his face. He tugged at the straps of his overalls.

"You Marcus Ramirez?"

"I am indeed."

"Can we talk? In private?"

"Of course. You and I. And her."

The masked man looked at Selena, seeming to notice her for the first time. His eyebrows arched quizzically, wrinkling a birthmark that blotted the left side of his forehead. Selena was no less surprised by the announcement—when Marcus had said "her," she'd thought it just as likely that he was referring to one of the whores on his lap.

"I said alone."

"And I will shake off this chaff gladly. But Lena and I are confederates. My business is her business."

First I've heard of that.

The masked man shrugged to mask his annoyance and followed Marcus to one of the back rooms.

Privacy was a relative thing in a brothel. Rooms—if you could even call them rooms—lined a narrow hallway, each divided by little more than a plank of salvaged plywood or scrap metal. When these were unavailable, the builder opted for slats of mismatched hardwood caulked with scabrous and yellowing globs of plaster. Marcus chose a room in a relatively quiet corner and motioned Selena and the man into a space little larger than a stable stall, almost all of it taken up by a saggy bed. Stains of spurious origin covered the sheets, which had turned the colour of rancid teeth. A sickly alkaline smell filled Selena's nostrils.

Marcus sat on the bed, his bony ass sinking nearly to the floor. Selena and the man both chose to stand. The masked man drew a curtain—the only separation between the room and the hall—and scratched at a spot beneath his bandanna.

"I'm told you do jobs," he said, speaking in a hushed tone.

"As do all but princes and politicians. What is your point?"

The man tossed a piece of paper toward the bed. It fluttered into Marcus' lap.

"We have one for you. The pay is ten thousand Standard."

Selena's breath caught at the mention of such a sum. *Here's something.*

Marcus perked up an eyebrow. "You have ten thousand Standard?"

The man shifted. "Five hundred up front. We'll have the rest for you once the job is done. More, even."

"Five hundred? How generous." Marcus lifted the sheet of paper. He laughed, folded the paper neatly, and set it aside. "Lunacy. I did not take you for a joker."

"Wait, what?" Selena interjected. The masked man ignored her, addressing Marcus.

"This is no joke. We'll pay ten thousand Standard upon completion."

"Of course. Tell me, how much of this money do have on hand? If I took your deal, could you even pay me the five hundred you promise?"

The man's cheeks grew red. Beads of sweat collected along his hairline. "It would be delivered to you promptly."

"Ah, of course."

"We can go as high as twenty thousand if you act within the next month."

"Why not offer me a million? No, I am sorry. I am not in this business any longer."

Selena and the masked man united in shock. The man was the first to speak, though he managed only a single word.

"But—"

"Please," Marcus said, and raised a hand. The man stormed out, swatting the curtain aside and stomping his way into the crowd. Selena turned to Marcus, her jaw clenched so tight it felt as if her teeth might shatter.

"Tell me you didn't just turn down ten thousand Standard."

"I turned down pretty words. These things smell sweet, but they cannot be spent."

"Well what about five hundred? That's still nothing to piss on."

"Not every job is worth taking, Lena. If you do not know this already, you will learn it one day to your sorrow." Placing hands on knees, Marcus rose. "I return to my revelry. Enjoy the room, if you wish. I suspect you could find a willing companion."

Selena retched. Marcus, chuckling, disappeared through the curtain, his movement so sleek he parted it with barely a ripple. Selena glowered at the space where he'd been. All this big talk about earning money, and the man wouldn't even pursue a job with a potential payout of ten thousand Standard. Fighting paid better than farm work, but she still hadn't yet come close to earning that much on the circuit. Moving delicately so as not to brush her fingers against the filthy mattress, Selena picked up the piece of paper. She'd expected a map or detailed instructions, but all she found were four words printed in neat script: The Mayor of Fallowfield.

18: Pillar of Smoke

Simon sat in the grass, his shirt rolled up to his forearms, exposing downy hairs clotted with dirt and grease. The assemblage of a broken generator lay strewn across a blanket at his feet, its parts arranged neatly to facilitate reconstruction. Holding the rotor in his lap, he looped row after meticulous row of copper wire along its length. He was hot, his fingers stiff, his nose itchy with pollen, yet he felt strangely content.

At Saint Barbara Academy—where children of the Seraphim trained for careers as architects and engineers at the Diocese of Genesis—he'd always hated the hands-on repair lessons the most. They were hard and boring and often served to emphasize his weakness, as he struggled to lift equipment or guide power tools or loosen bolts the larger students handled with ease. He'd much preferred the drafting courses, with their sketching and elegant linework, but Saint Barbara children were expected to develop both practical and theoretical engineering skills. Now, marooned in the Wastes a thousand miles from the nearest drafting table, Simon was grateful for the breadth of his enforced tutelage.

When he had wrapped the rotor to his satisfaction, Simon reassembled the generator, replacing stripped screws and corroded bolts with new or refurbished parts from his growing store. He'd given The Mayor a list of necessary supplies, and The Mayor had delivered. Magnus came by once Simon had put the generator back together, his perpetual scowl replaced by a look of subdued satisfaction.

"She looks good," he said. "Will she run?"

Simon kept his gaze locked on the generator. He couldn't look at Magnus without revealing his uncertainty about the man, and that could be dangerous. Could this grumpy old farmer really be responsible for chasing Selena away? Maybe even killing her? It seemed impossible to believe, but there was so much about this place he didn't know, the faces all masks behind which anything might be hiding.

"Let's see," he said.

He filled the reservoir with rendered rapeseed oil, flipped a switch, and pulled the ripcord. The generator purred to life, its rumblings carrying up through Simon's shoes.

"You done a good job, kid. This'll run a heater?"

"Anything electric."

"Beautiful. This'll be a real—"

An explosion incinerated the rest of his sentence. A wave of heat crashed over Simon, followed by a behemoth roar that overwhelmed the generator's docile purring. A pillar of smoke propped up the sky before listing sideways with the prevailing wind. Magnus ran toward the source of the blast. Simon followed, a terrible certainty solidifying in his belly.

The silo slumped in ruins. Shards of aluminum lacerated the scorched grass, protruding ends bent and blackened. The domed top lay capsized a hundred feet away. Fieldhands choked on smoke or clutched limbs ravaged by shrapnel or just stared in awe at the destruction. Simon saw at least three dead bodies lying in static orbit around the ruined silo.

Magnus rushed headlong into the field, lifting debris off of bodies and making tourniquets with sticks and shredded strips of clothing.

"Grady! Go to the camps and get every set of hands out here. De Fleur! Ride into town and get the docs. Take a horse from my barn.

Polly's the fastest, use her. The rest of you, start dressing wounds!" He worked briskly and with unfailing courage, though his eyes kept drifting to the smoking remnants of the silo, rheumy with anguish and fury.

Simon ran without conscious purpose, his legs pumping simply because they refused to do otherwise. He cut through a narrow cornfield, a move which took him away from town but toward The Mayor's manor. Simon seized onto this objective, grateful for a place to run that wasn't simply "away." *Good. That's good. I'll tell The Mayor. It's his town, he should know something's gone wrong. And if anyone knows what to do in this kind of situation, it'll be him.* Heart racing, breath heaving, legs sizzling with lactic acid, Simon crested a small hill.

He might as well have struck a brick wall. He froze, his mouth filling with sour fluid.

Bernard stood beneath the shade of a bent and wizened oak tree. He held a portable transceiver in his incomplete hand. Binoculars dangled from a strap around his neck, which he used to study the wreckage before stalking off into a clutch of nearby elms.

He's responding to the fire, Simon told himself. *He's the boss of the Shepherds, after all. They probably deal with this sort of thing all the time. He's probably rushing off to get help right now.*

Only Bernard didn't look like a man rushing anywhere. His steps were furtive, his observation of the carnage cold-blooded and calm. People were dying amongst the flames and yet he moved without urgency. If he wasn't going for help, where was he going?

And why had he been there in the first place?

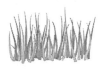

Marcus moved with feline grace, his head thrust forward, his face a dead-eyed mask revealing nothing. His opponent—broad-chested, lean, a cartography of tattoos scrawled up his arms—ran his tongue across his matted moustache and sneered. Both men held knives: the opponent's over a foot from end to end, its blade a hook of polished steel honed to an absurd sharpness; Marcus's thin, light, and damp with the blood of the man it had killed ten minutes earlier.

The first fighter's body lay at the edge of the ring, bent slightly to accommodate the contours of the crowd. A few onlookers were wary of its presence, but those standing next to it acted as if it were a tree stump or some other impediment of no real consequence. One man, burly and bearded, rested a boot-clad foot on the dead man's abdomen. Violence really was in the bloodstream of this region. Not even the Salters took this kind of brutality as a matter of course.

Selena watched as Marcus punctured the other man's lung. The opponent dropped his knife, clutched his aerated chest, took two shambling steps, and collapsed. His body hit the mud with a flatulent splat. Marcus soaked the bloodied tip of his switchblade in puddle water, cleaned it on the dead man's shirt, and grabbed the bowie knife. Two large men took the dead man by the arms and dragged his body next to the first one, leaving them in a pile like so much cordwood. The bookies added up their earnings and Marcus took his cut. He put the stack of bills away without counting it and handed the bowie knife to Selena.

"What's this?"

"There are times when a knife is a good thing to have. These roads can be dangerous."

Selena wrapped the knife in a hank of loose cloth she kept on hand to bandage wounds and stuck it in her waistband.

"You wear it well," Marcus said, smiling. "Now come. I found us a ride."

A wagon waited up the sodden dirt road, its wooden wheels sinking in the muck. The horse to which it was tethered whinnied impatiently, ignoring the driver's feeble pleas to calm down.

"Easy girl," he said, his voice trembling.

Unsure how long the driver would be able to keep his horse

stationary, Marcus and Selena wasted no time in hopping onto the uncovered wagon. Selena had only just staked out a seat amongst the carpet of straw when the horse took off, yanking the mired wheels free from the swampy ground.

The road grew drier and the going grew quicker as the wagon rolled its way uphill. Selena watched the sepulchral remains of the outer city pass by through the gap between the wagon's wooden slats.

"Hey, driver." said Marcus. "You missed the road."

"Meant to. This here's a shortcut."

Selena peered over the railing. The path diverged to the right while the wagon rolled straight on, brittle stalks crunching beneath its wheels.

"I did not ask you to take a shortcut, and you did not mention one to me when I hired you."

The driver sniffed. "Didn't see no point in it. Who doesn't like a shortcut? Get you to Woodsend two hours quicker. Maybe three. What's not to like, huh?"

Marcus shrugged his shoulders and slouched against the railing, his eyes closed. Selena was sure he could sense her watching him; there was something telling in the arch of his eyebrows and the upturned corners of his mouth.

"What's your deal, anyway?" she asked.

Marcus opened one eye. "My deal?"

"Yeah. You say you're after some big score, but I can't figure out why."

"Fighters must think of the future, Lena. I will not always be fast. When you live by your speed, you must get rich before you get slow, yes?"

"I've heard the bets you've placed, and seen the kind of Standard you've raked in. You've already earned enough to live comfortably for another twenty years. How much do you really need?"

"Fifty thousand Standard," Marcus said. Selena thought he was joking, but the words had come out in a sigh.

"Fifty thousand?! What, are you planning to buy, a Barony?"

"Money is like water, girl. Always flowing from my fingers."

"Maybe it wouldn't if you didn't turn it all into booze."

Marcus laughed. "Yes, but then I would spend much time thinking, and too much thinking is dangerous in the circle. There is poetry in my soul, and I must drown it in wine or it will never stop singing. Poets make poor fighters. They are much too in love with death."

Selena listened to the clack of the wheels on the dirt, the sound mirroring the turning of her thoughts. "Fifty thousand Standard is a very specific number."

"So earn me another thousand, I will not begrudge you."

"You'll take more, but not less. Why?"

"I have debts. Men own these debts, and so own me. They pull my strings and I dance prettily."

Selena considered the lanky, jagged man opposite her. The thought of anyone owning him seemed ludicrous. He was far too sharp a blade to hold.

"Debts from what?"

"From the arrogance of youth." His tone made it clear that he would offer no further details.

"Okay, fine. Come west with us. Help me get Simon and the three of us will go to the Republic together. Surely we can scrape together enough supplies to manage it by now."

"This is true. But as I told you in the barn, our deal has changed. We have enough Standard for your purposes perhaps, but not yet for mine. When my debts are paid, we will free your brother, not before."

"Why bother paying them at all? Take the money and run with us. No debt collector is gonna follow you all the way to Visalia."

"It is not my life I fear for. Would you leave Simon in the hands of vengeful debtors?"

Selena, thinking of her brother back in Fallowfield, said nothing.

"I made mistakes, and I am not the only one who has paid for them. You have never been to Juarez, yes?"

Selena shook her head.

"It is not a city. It is a war zone. There are no Shepherds, no lawmen. The only protection comes from gangs, who squabble like children and die like animals. These men make your Mayor look like a kitten. They are the men I owe. And if I do not pay them, they will not forgive me."

"Do you have children?" Selena asked. The thought plunked like a cold stone in her belly.

"No children. But a mother. Aunts, uncles, cousins. Friends. The *pandilleros* will fall on them like a plague. Only one man will be spared." Marcus pointed to himself.

"How long do you have to pay?" Selena asked.

"Enough. Always enough for the interest to grow. I bring them all the Standard I can and they give me letters. All is well until the day I cannot pay."

"It might help if you stopped blowing so much money on your little nights out, you know."

Hands in his lap, Marcus gazed up at the haze-heavy sky. "It is, some nights, much easier to forget than to remember, yes?"

The wagon slowed. The road in front of them had shrunk to little more than twin scars, each the width of a wagon wheel. The driver prodded ineffectually at his horse with a riding crop.

"I was told this was a shortcut," Marcus said, frowning. "A shorter distance means little if we spend the whole time standing around."

"She's tired, is all," the driver said. His eyes drifted across the field then darted back to the horse. He reached forward and fiddled with the harness.

"I am not sure how familiar you are with horses, but they are not so much for being side-eyed. You have a leather strap. Perhaps you should use it."

"Hey, I know how to drive a horse." The driver's eyes wandered afield once more, searching through the tall grass. They jumped back to the horse. "He just needs a quick rest, is all. Give him a minute and we'll be on our way lickety split. You're still hours ahead a schedule, fella. You should be thanking me."

Marcus let out an exasperated breath. "Look at you. You are pulling on the bridle. Here. Let me teach you something about animals." Marcus reached over the driver's shoulder. The driver recoiled. His gaze returned to the grass, and this time Selena managed to follow it to a spot a dozen feet out where the stalks stirred independent of the wind. Time stretched like toffee, each moment long and slow and thickly fluid. She opened her mouth to scream Marcus' name, to tell him to duck, but before she could get the words out a figure emerged from the grass. His green eyes were shards of broken glass atop a sickle grin. His beard, ornately braided, hung down to his belly. It swung to the side as he raised a rifle to his shoulder and fired.

Selena felt her head jerk back. Impossible heat enveloped the right side of her face. Her ear was on fire, her eye melting, her skin a molten slurry. She felt the sun touch down from forehead to jaw and force her backward with its inexorable mass, shoving her over the wagon's railing and into the grass where she sank through the darkness, swallowed like a penny tossed down a bottomless well.

19: A Roadmap of Hell

Marcus had always been fast. Even as a young child barely out of diapers, he could snatch an apple, a toffee, or a rubber ball from an older child and toddle gleefully away, outpacing those who should, by rights, have caught him easily. Through the years, he grew taller, leaner, and quicker still, and hard candy from grubby hands became gold rings and coin purses and wallets. He could snatch a fly from the air as easily as plucking a stone from the floor of a cobbled plaza, cut cards with such skill that even the seasoned *jugadores* with their steel wool stubble and sun-cracked faces could never match him. The brawny footballers and hard-stomached *luchadores* could take his punches, but they couldn't avoid them. And when a skinny fist sprouts a six inch steel blade, the power of its punch loses all importance. The only factor is speed, and in speed, Marcus had the world beat.

But not even he could outrun bullets.

Marcus saw the gunman rise from the grass, instantly pegging him as Kaeric, the Shepherd thug who fought in Fallowfield's circle. By the time the first shot had struck Selena in the head, Marcus had already triggered his switchblade and folded himself around the driver, making him into a wriggling and uncooperative shield.

The horse, startled by the gunshot, bolted forward. Marcus reached for the reins, but they slipped through his fingers. He stared with disbelief as the horse left the wagon behind it, the harness that had held it to the shafts of the wagon flapping freely as it ran.

Kaeric cocked his rifle and turned his attention to Marcus, who slipped back behind his unwilling aegis. The driver struggled to free himself, but Marcus was strong for his size and the old man couldn't break his grip. Kaeric fired. Marcus could feel the impact as three slugs struck the driver in quick succession, sending spasms through his brittle body.

"Said I was safe," the old man wheezed, indignant. Marcus smiled as the old man died, though his smile was bitter. He should have seen this coming the moment his fidgety guide had led him off the path. He should have smelled the treachery. Kaeric paused, his aim confounded by the old man's lolling corpse and Marcus' figure-masking serape. Still, things did not look good. The ambush had been well-planned. The ground on which they rode was rough and gravelly, the shitgrass omnipresent but stunted, barely waist-high—deep enough to provide cover when motionless, but far too shallow to slither through undetected.

Moving the dead man's body the barest fragment of an inch, Marcus chanced a glance at Kaeric. He stood twenty feet back, his feet planted shoulder-width apart, sighting down the rifle's barrel. If he had a clear shot, he wouldn't miss. That meant Marcus couldn't afford to miss either.

Marcus threw the driver's body forward while letting himself roll back and to the side. As he fell, he snapped out with his right arm, sending his switchblade lancing through the air at Kaeric's neck. His aim was true, but the gunman, jerking in pure reflex, torqued his body to the right. The blade sank deep into the meat of his shoulder. Its hilt trembled like the tail of an arrow. Kaeric cried out and sank to one knee. Marcus completed his roll and landed in a crouch behind the wagon.

Shit, his mind screamed. *Shit shit shit!* Kaeric was hurt, but not dead. Not even incapacitated. And Marcus was unarmed. His position was untenable without a gun and an armed assassin was ten strides away from a clear shot.

Marcus heard Kaeric grunt as he pulled the knife free. There was a faint *whoosh* as he tossed it aside and a soft thump as it landed. Marcus felt a flash of anger at his knife's callous mistreatment. He scrambled through the dirt, searching for a rock large enough to serve as a weapon. The biggest he could find was the size of a sparrow's egg.

Kaeric approached the wagon. He made no effort to mask his footsteps or to lure Marcus from his cover. There was no point. Marcus kept digging, hunting madly for a fist-sized stone or a chunk of concrete or an abandoned railroad spike. He found nothing but dirt and roots and gravel. Kaeric stepped into view. He raised his rifle, taking careful aim. Marcus stood, arms slightly spread. He would not let himself die on his knees.

Something fast and silver scraped across Kaeric's throat. A jet of blood soaked his beard and dyed the yellow grass red. He fell to the ground. Behind him stood Selena, bloodied bowie knife in hand. The right side of her head was a roadmap of hell. Blood caked to her cheek and soaked her poncho and dripped from the end of her chin. The knife dropped from her fingers. She swayed on her feet, took two steps, and fell forward.

Marcus rushed over to Selena. He grabbed the rifle from Kaeric's twitching hands and spent its last rounds petulantly in his already-dying head. Guns gave ignoble deaths, and Marcus shot the dying man for no other reason than to deny him the purity of a death by blade. His petty revenge accomplished, he tossed the gun away with a shiver of distaste, lifted Selena in a fireman's carry, and laid her gently on the floor of the wagon. Using her bowie knife, he cut strips from her poncho and wrapped them tightly around her jaw.

He found his switchblade after five minutes of furious searching. He polished the blade with the silken cloth he kept for that purpose, flipped it into its hilt, kissed it, and tucked it away in its tiny scabbard. His hand returned to the pocket several times as he walked, unconsciously checking to make sure the knife was still there.

The horse took a little longer to track down. He found it at a dried-up stream, drinking brown water from a puddle. It seemed confused and wary of its sudden freedom, and came to Marcus willingly enough. He reassured it with soft words and a gentle stroking of its mane, then climbed on and rode it bareback to the wagon.

Selena lay semi-conscious in a puddle of tacky half-dried blood, squeezing a pear into a wad of mealy pulp. Marcus checked her bandages, tucked a folded strip of poncho beneath her head for a pillow, and snapped his fingers in front of her eyes. She moaned and raised a hand to her injured ear. Marcus grabbed her wrist and gently lowered her arm.

"Better not, Lena," he said. "Just lay still, okay? I am going to get you help."

Marcus led the horse into position and hitched it to the wagon. As he worked, it occurred to him again how strange it was that the horse had gotten loose in the first place. After a moment of fiddling with the straps, he saw exactly how it had happened. The hitch was rigged with a kill switch. By simply pulling a small peg free from its socket, the entire harness detached, severing every tie between horse and wagon. Such a design was more than unusual—it was, as far as Marcus knew, entirely original. There was no need for something like that in normal practice, and the setup cost the wagon considerable speed. After securing the hitch and tying the pin in place with another strip of Selena's tattered poncho, Marcus settled into the driver's perch and spurred the horse on.

They rode for a long time. Marcus looked back on several occasions, each time expecting to see Selena's lifeless body sprawled on the wagon floor, and each time noticing with increasing astonishment—and eventually a grain of bemused admiration—an anguished shift of an elbow or the dogged rise and fall of her chest.

Marcus found the main road and followed it. He soon saw a small collection of buildings in the distance beyond a sign reading *South Sturgis*. A sigh of relief rose to his lips. South Sturgis was little more than a strip of squat wooden buildings with gardens on their roofs—

the only way to keep their crops free of yellow locust—but it had a sawbones and that was all he needed at the moment. He urged the horse onward. The wagon's wheels juddered over rutted ground. He pulled up in front of the clinic and whistled for the hostler, who stood up begrudgingly from his shady stool. Marcus threw twenty Standard in his direction, quickening his pace considerably. He vaulted into the wagon bed, grabbed Selena under her arms, and carried her to the clinic door, where a harried looking woman was already lathering her hands with antiseptic foam.

"You are quick," Marcus said, impressed.

"Quick pays in this business. Bring her inside."

Marcus puffed out his cheeks. "There are orderlies for this, yes?"

"Yeah, you're looking at 'em. Grab an arm."

"This seems unwise. I am no doctor. I will only get in the way."

"Look, your friend is in a delicate condition, and I won't be doing her any favors by dragging her around on my own. I need help to get her into the clinic."

Marcus glanced past the doctor into the hallway. He didn't like hospitals. Dread filled him with its frigid vapor, pushing at his lungs until there seemed to be no room for air. *Foolishness. It is a building like any other, nothing more.* With a tug at his collar, Marcus helped carry Selena inside.

They set her down on a cot and the doctor set to dressing her head. Marcus counted out a stack of Standard.

"This should cover any expenses in her care, yes?"

"We can deal with that later. I want to get her sorted first."

"I am afraid I must go," Marcus said, his fingers twitching against his thighs. "When she wakes, tell her that she can reach me through Gustavo. She will know of whom I speak."

"Wait, don't you want—"

But Marcus was already gone, shame burning his cheeks. He needed to get away, not just from the hospital but the town. It stank of death, a charnel house odor pouring from the hospital like soot from a coal furnace, clouds of it settling on his skin and drowning the road.

He needed a new city, a new circle, a new enemy. In combat, death could be outpaced, outfought, outrun. It charged you head on, came in the swing of sword or mace or mallet, in the slash of a blade, not in withered organs or jaundiced flesh or bilious, rancid blood.

The buildings fell away and Marcus slowed, hands braced against his thighs, breath damp and heavy. He mopped his forehead with the hem of his serape, grateful that he was alone. He smoothed his hair against his head, fumbled through his rucksack, and took a long swig of whiskey from a brushed metal flask. The cheap liquor burned on its way down, but it calmed him all the same. He was alone again, and he couldn't afford to wait on Selena's recovery. It felt callous, but his was a callous business. There was no room for sentiment in the circle. You either pared it away or it weighed you down, left you vulnerable.

Be well, Lena, he thought, sorry he hadn't said as much in person. *Perhaps I will have another chance.*

But he doubted it.

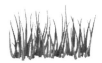

The Mayor opened his desk drawer and removed his revolver, savoring its weight in his hand. He checked the cylinder to make sure all six chambers were loaded, snapped it back in place, and spun it with the heel of his hand. The *clikita-clakata* it made as it revolved reminded him of the roller coaster at Gilead Park. Job's Trial, it had been called—a touch didactically, but what in New Canaan wasn't? The Mayor remembered it well, a smooth band of shiny steel winding and arching along the coast. The park had been built for children of the Seraphim, but on certain occasions, the Shepherds' whelps were allowed a few hours' diversion. He wondered if Job's Trial was still running, or if the salty air had finally eaten through it.

The Mayor set the gun back in the drawer and reached for a far more potent weapon. On the desk stood a black briefcase with bronze clasps, inside of which rested a sleek slab of brushed metal. The Mayor removed the slab, set it on the desktop, and thumbed a tiny latch. The slab creaked open, revealing a thin glass screen on one side, and on the other a matrix of buttons, each marked with a different character. The Mayor traced his finger over the recessed letters, which elicited a faint clack at his touch.

Computers had little use in the Middle Wastes. Electricity was scarce and unreliable, the populace barely capable of wielding pen and paper, let alone a keyboard. But it seemed this one would serve a much more practical purpose—though he needed Selena's data stick first.

The stick was the axel on which his whole plan turned, but it seemed he might have to get the wheel spinning without it. A wheel with no axel must be carefully balanced lest it topple, but The Mayor had little choice but to trust his reflexes. The situation was simply growing too volatile.

He'd known in his heart what the silo contained before Simon gave his breathless report of the vats and vials and the jury-rigged truck, but hearing it spoken brought the urgency of matters into stark relief. Those filthy ingrate farmers had figured out the formula for Compound L. The Mayor wasn't sure where or how, but they were making it—he'd had Bernard siphon a sample from the silo ruins just to be sure.

Until now, The Mayor had always held the balance of power. He controlled Compound L, and if the farmers balked at his price and refused to pay, there was always more land, and other pliable rubes willing to rise from field grunt to sharecropper. Over the years, this power had allowed The Mayor to extort absurd sums from the farmers under the guise of buying Compound L—a substance that, in truth, cost him nothing more than a bit of information and token fealty. His gouging grew bolder each year. He knew it rankled the farmers and had ruined more than a few of them, but it amused him to see how willingly they would roll over for him, whimpering like dogs before their master's shaken fist.

He didn't even have any concrete plans for the money. Certainly he didn't need all of it. He'd toyed with expanding his borders, purchasing consideration among the Ministers of the Prairie Republic to *la Republique du Quebec,* or maybe funding a coup in one of the semi-anarchic city-states of Mejica. Any one of those things could pay dividends down the road, if he orchestrated them carefully.

But now, Magnus and his crew had their own supply of Compound L, and that made them dangerous. Bombing the silo had slowed them down, but it wouldn't stop them. The knowledge was out there, and he could do nothing about it. Such a crisis would lead lesser leaders to defection or self-imposed exile. But The Mayor was no lesser leader, and he saw a way to turn his negative into a positive.

It was time to call in New Canaan.

20: The Diocese of Plague

Simon awoke with a shroud on his senses and a sour taste on his tongue. Shards of sunlight pierced his aching red eyes. The night before was a scrambled mess of images. He reassembled the pieces slowly, placing tiny tiles of sight and sound and smell in sequence until a memory took shape.

He recalled the coldness of the glass in his hands, and the odd, sweetly antiseptic smell of the liquid inside it. He'd found the bottle in The Mayor's pantry. It was squat and ornate, with diamond-shaped facets texturing its neck. He'd smuggled it upstairs, pulled out the cork stopper, and taken a tiny sip, stifling a shudder.

A formless sort of guilt had wrung his belly at first, but Simon had grown accustomed to such queasy feelings and could ignore them long enough to get a few swallows down. It had been weeks since he'd seen Selena. People said that time made things easier, but Simon found each day a little more tiresome than the last, a little more pointless. He got himself up, ate his meals, even painted when the mood struck him—though it struck him less and less, and the results grew duller and less inspired with every twitch of his brush. His appetite followed, withering in his belly until a few crackers or a single apricot seemed to fill him up, and soon the impulse to just lie in bed became all but impossible to ignore. Every morning set another five pounds upon his chest, and his muscles were increasingly unable to shrug off the burden.

He'd grabbed his first bottle two days after the incident at the silo, when the guttural rending of steel had rumbled unabated in his ears for forty-eight consecutive hours, and the image of body parts strewn about the grass painted itself onto the undersides of his eyelids.

"It's tragic," The Mayor had said that first afternoon, hands clasped behind his back. He stared out the window of his office toward Fallowfield's southern holdings, where hands of smoke still reached up angrily from the silo's blackened ruins. Simon retreated to The Mayor's desk, where the accusing fingers of soot and ash couldn't point him out.

"What a terrible, terrible waste," The Mayor went on. "Five fieldhands died in that blast, five good men and women. And poor Otto Hellmich, trapped inside that conflagration. Regardless of what he might've been up to in there, it's a terrible shame. I wish it had been otherwise."

Simon held his glasses in his lap, compulsively folding and unfolding the stiff metal arms. The rubber tips were worn and warped in places, he noticed, the steel within bulging out like bone shards in a compound fracture. He'd need new ones one day. And where in this hateful wasteland could he expect to find them? He couldn't ask this question, so he'd asked another.

"What happened?"

The Mayor touched his fingers to the glass. "You mentioned that they'd set up a laboratory of sorts. I can only assume that something went terribly wrong in the manufacturing. It's a dreadful thought, to what purpose such volatile materials might have been put."

"Like what?"

"Given what happened, an explosive seems most likely."

"It didn't look like they were making a bomb."

The Mayor returned to his desk. "Even though Fallowfield's laws protected them, they would have still known to be cautious, Simon. I suspect the truck you saw was merely a front. I have no proof, of course, but what agent would one willingly spray on one's crops that had such monstrous destructive power? No, the evidence points squarely at high explosives."

It seemed the most rational explanation to Simon, too, but that did nothing to mute the screams or strip away the images that vandalized his sleep. The bottle had been an off the cuff choice, a desperate fumbling he didn't even remember making. But it had worked. His recollections of the evening that followed—abstract, warped, and cubist in their rendering—were tinted with relief. So at some point—and again, he had trouble pinpointing the wheres and whens—he grabbed another, hiding it each morning beneath his mattress, agog at how much of its contents had evaporated in the night. Soon both bottles were empty. Simon snuck them into the cellar where the other empties were kept for refilling.

The first two bottles had been plain and anonymous, smoky green cylinders tapering to a needle neck and filled with flavourless clear hooch. The rum was different, a rich and cloudy spirit in a fine fluted glass body. Simon thought The Mayor might actually miss this one, and committed himself to returning it early the next morning.

But first, another drink. After two the taste wasn't so bad. A sense of buoyancy filled him. His head was a balloon wafting side to side in a soft and changing breeze. He took another swallow and chuckled at nothing. Anxiety sloughed from his shoulders like so much dead skin, leaving a plush pink nakedness thrumming with heat. Who needed a home? Who needed a sister? Why worry about any of that stuff? What was worry after all but a ruse, a foist, a cruel joke one played on oneself? It was so clear to see once you wiped away the grimy thoughts that collected during the day, the greasy film of guilt and hurt—and booze made a pretty good solvent. He clutched the bottle of rum to his chest, listening to the liquid slosh in its belly and relishing the texture of its neck on his fingers. God, he felt good.

The memory dissolved. Simon lay back in bed, the heels of his palms pressed to his eye sockets. His eyes were red and puffy, his nose plugged. A wheezy whistle marked each exhaled breath. Eventually the pressure in his skull abated and he was able to stand. He wanted to remain in bed but his belly felt like a clay pot in a kiln, hollow and scorching, and he needed something to fill and cool it. He scooped up the bottle with clumsy fingers, nearly dropped it, and tiptoed to the kitchen. The bottle was noticeably lighter than when he'd taken it, so he topped it off with a bit of water from the kitchen tap before stashing it back on the shelf. He filled two glasses of water and downed them both. The water seemed barely to reach his belly; his mouth and tongue soaked it up like desert soil. His stomach gurgling with acid and his head run through with pins, Simon prepared his usual breakfast: eggs, thick-cut rashers of bacon, and bread all fried together in the same cast iron pan. He worked bent double, trying to move as little as possible. Miraculously, he managed to pull it together. The sizzle in his belly receded, only to be replaced by an icy cramp as Bernard crooked his mangled hand at him.

"Mayor wants to see you. Finish your breakfast and come with me."

Simon let his fork clatter onto the plate. He no longer felt like eating anyway.

Bernard showed him into The Mayor's office.

"You sent for me?" Simon asked.

"Simon my boy! Yes, I did indeed. Please, have a seat."

Simon sank into a chair, his head supported by the heel of his hand. He spotted a familiar shape on The Mayor's desk and ran a hand along its metal edges.

"Is that a lightbook?"

"Quite so. Perhaps the only one in a thousand miles. It hasn't much purpose around these parts, of course, but I find simply looking at it sometimes helps to quell a bit of homesickness. But I must confess, I didn't call you in here to discuss lightbooks. I have another a favor to ask."

Simon's face blanched. The Mayor chuckled disarmingly.

"Fear not, my boy. This is no cloak and dagger operation. You've performed admirably and with bravery, and I wouldn't in good conscious ask more of you. This is a far more mundane matter."

The Mayor reached into his desk drawer and pulled out a handful of capacitors, salvaged from scraps of old machinery throughout the region.

"Do you recall when you mentioned you could fix my radio?"

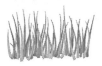

The world was a vista of featureless grey. It permeated everything, saturating her until she couldn't distinguish herself from the nothingness around her. She was a space so vast she was meaningless, a size so large she was invisible, a signal so intense and all-encompassing, she may as well not exist, for she drowned out the universe.

After a length of time both instant and eternal, she became aware of things beyond the all-pervasive greyness. Smell came first. Sharp odors of bleach and blood and urine atop the softer smell of grass and flowers. Taste, a sister sense, followed quickly, a tang of bitter breaths congealed after a week of missed brushings. Next came texture, the rustle of starched fabric and the yield of quilted springs and the tackiness of wet gauze. Sound followed, a symphony of squeaks and drips and rustles, of footsteps and poured liquids and metal implements clinking together. Sight came last, begrudgingly, evident only in an asymmetry of grey, whirls of light and blotches of dark, shades shifting and bleeding into one another until suddenly cohering into a single form.

Selena blinked. She was in a clinic of some kind, steel counters scrubbed clean and lined with metal implements polished to shine. Something soft and sticky was affixed to the side of her head. She touched it and a sharp pain needled through her skull.

At the far end of the room, a thin, middle-aged woman in a white smock washed her hands in a porcelain basin. Her brown hair was tied back in a ponytail. She walked over and jotted something on a slate hanging from Selena's bedpost by a string.

"I was wondering when you'd wake up," she said. "Things were looking grim there for a little while."

"Where am I?"

The woman raised her hand. "Please, no need to thank me."

Selena rubbed her finger along the outer ridge of her bandage. The skin there was tender, but the pain didn't return. "I thought doctors were above that stuff. Didn't you take an oath?"

The woman pulled Selena's hand away from her bandaged head and set it firmly in her lap. "Maybe where you're from, but in the Middle Wastes, we're a little less formal. You're in a place called South Sturgis. There's no North Sturgis, in case you were wondering. Maybe there was once, who knows? Local quirk. What's your name?"

"Selena."

"Well Selena, I'm Molly. Molly Stewart. You try to rob somebody or something?"

"Huh?"

"Nothing personal. It's just that round these parts, most people who come in with your troubles tried to roll a merchant wagon and came off the worse for it. Most of those guys ride with armed guards, you know."

"What are you talking about?"

"Somebody blew half your ear off, that's what I'm talking about."

Selena stared at the woman. "Is that your official diagnosis?"

Molly laughed. She took a bottle of clear gel from a nearby table, rubbed a large dollop of it between her hands, and began undressing Selena's wound. "Yeah, you got it. A textbook case of bullet ear. The damage was significant. It didn't just take off the ear. It grazed your skull. The good news, though, is that it missed your ear canal. An inch or so farther down and you'd be deaf on that side. I managed to save the lower half, too, so your directional hearing shouldn't be too affected.

"The blood loss was more or less controlled when you got here. The real danger's the infection. Tried three different kinds of antibiotics before we finally got it under control. It was touch and go for a while. You even dropped into something I don't quite dare call a coma at the end."

Selena winced. Molly's slightly rambling account had been muffled by the bandage and the tearing sounds it made as it pulled free. Selena reached up reflexively to touch the exposed skin. Molly slapped her hand away.

"Point is, you were lights out for almost a day. I was starting to wonder if you were gonna snap out of it or slip away altogether, but it looks like you went for option one."

Molly dabbed ointment on a cotton ball and touched it to Selena's ear. Selena hissed through gritted teeth. "Jesus!"

"Yeah, it's no picnic. But neither's a brain infection. Hold still." Molly applied another drop of ointment, tossed the wad of cotton into a plastic bin at the foot of the bed, and re-wrapped Selena's head with fresh gauze. Selena grimaced but let the doctor do her work.

"How long have I been here?"

"Three days. Your friend brought you in. Skinny guy, from one of the *Mejise* provinces by the sound of him. He paid for your care in Standard and took off. Even left his horse and wagon behind." Molly gave Selena a steady, arch-browed look that said she knew better than to ask.

Selena settled her head back against her pillow, tilting it to the left to keep the bulging fabric from touching her injured ear. It was comfy, for all its thin frugality, and the pillow was the nicest she'd set her head on in some time. She wasn't sure whether to be grateful that Marcus got her medical care or pissed off that he bailed right after. *Why choose? I've got room in me for both.*

"Did he leave a message for me or anything?"

"As a matter of fact, he did. Told me to tell you that once you're up and able, you should find Gustavo. That make any sense?"

Selena nodded. Denver was a slog from here no doubt, but at least it gave her a destination. She felt a little better.

"Is it alright if I rest up for a few hours before I go?"

Molly barked an incredulous laugh. "Few hours? Try a few weeks, honey."

Selena blinked. "Excuse me?"

"Did you maybe forget the part where I told you that you got shot in the head?"

"You said the bullet grazed me."

"Graze was putting it delicately. That bullet dug a damn culvert in your skull. Had the angle changed by an inch it'dve bored a hole right through to your brain. Plus, your infection's down, but not out. You need to finish up your antibiotics, and I don't like the idea of you riding through shitgrass until you've properly healed. That stuff's not just ugly. It's poison."

It wasn't so much Molly's insistence that kept Selena in bed as it was the tidal wave of nausea that washed over her when she tried to stand. An intense pressure, not quite pain but certainly unpleasant, pulsed on the injured side of her head, its throbbing rhythm abating only when she set her head back against the pillow, hurt-side-up. And even then, it didn't disappear completely, only receded partway behind the curtain of her consciousness. A weeks-long hiatus was out of the question, but Selena knew she wasn't going anywhere for at least a few days.

Unless, of course, the Shepherds found her first.

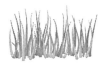

The Mayor settled into his finest wingback chair, a glass of brandy balanced on one leather armrest. The fingers of his right hand circled the rim, while the left held the microphone of his now functional radio transceiver. He had to give New Canaan credit. It was a hellish, soul-grinding place that trod with spiked soles on the backs of its people, but if Simon was anything short of exceptional, it had some fine schools—

for its Seraphim children, at least. The transceiver scanned the selected band of frequencies. When it stopped, he depressed the microphone trigger.

"Under-Cardinal Fontaine? This is Fallowfield. Repeat, Fallowfield. Do you copy?"

Static answered him, crystallizing into a voice. "Ross. Haven't heard your voice in a while. Can't say I missed it."

"Whereas I dreamed of your mellifluous intonations every night. Fortunately, my fair city has finally acquired someone with discretion and a measure of technical competence. We will no longer have to rely on intermediaries." The Mayor was rather disappointed at this, as he'd enjoyed his break from Eric Fontaine's hostile barbs and conceited babble. When the radio broke, he considered it more blessing than curse—but of course some matters were much too delicate to trust to messengers.

"Thank god for that," Fontaine drawled. "They were even duller than you were."

The Mayor rolled his eyes at Fontaine's supposed wit. *About as sharp as a damp dishrag. Does it do your ego good, Eric, to belittle the provincials? I suspect you're a fun man to have at a party.* "You wound me, under-Cardinal."

"It's Cardinal now, as a matter of fact. I rooted out a couple of traitors and was rewarded for my efforts—justly, if I may say so myself."

You would, wouldn't you? "As a former traitor, I'm not sure how I feel about that."

"No need to get uptight, Ross. As far as the Archbishop's concerned, your past is all water under the bridge."

"I'm pleased to know the man keeps room in his heart for forgiveness, even for sinners like me."

"I wouldn't call it forgiveness. He just doesn't care. You and your little uprising were only so much shit wiped off the Archbishop's nethers. The folks I nabbed actually mattered. Important difference. But enough chitchat. What do you have for me?"

"The Republic remains quiet. Trade from beyond the mountains was unusually sparse this summer. Now that the snows are less than two months off, it will cease altogether until next spring."

"So, nothing. You've got nothing. It's been the same your past half dozen reports. I'm starting to think this isn't worth ten barrels of defoliant a shot."

"Don't blame the sentinel because the borders are quiet. You need me for the instant when they're not. Ten barrels of Compound L cost you a bit of Salter sweat. Knowledge is priceless."

"Depends on the sort of knowledge you mean. 'Nothing happened' doesn't tell me much."

It would if you weren't an imbecile. The Mayor poured extra honey over his next words to mask their bitterness. "There has been one other small occurrence of note. Strictly speaking, it falls outside the purview of New Republic activity, but what's a bent rule between friends?"

"Get on with it."

"Two young migrants have recently come to Fallowfield from the east. They are of most interesting parentage. Perhaps you've heard of them. Selena and Simon Flood."

Fontaine's voice revealed nothing but disinterest—but a calculated sort of disinterest, to The Mayor's ear. "Traitors' whelps. What of it?"

"Not the same traitors responsible for your ever-so-deserved promotion, I trust? That would be quite the coincidence, wouldn't you say?"

"I don't particularly care whose kids they are. They're still just kids."

"Seraphim kids, though, are they not? I thought that New Canaan frowned on emigration, particularly among its elites. They tend to carry off too much valuable state property. In their pockets, in their luggage, but mostly in the space between their ears."

"Nice try. The Floods told us that their children knew nothing of their treason, that they just thought they had to run away for political reasons."

"And you trust their word in this matter implicitly, of course."

"They were under significant pressure to tell the truth. We figure they lied about where their children were exactly, probably out of fear.

But they didn't have the strength to lie about much else, in the end."

"Is that so? I venture a parent's love is stronger than you give it credit for. I'm quite aware of your ... *powers of persuasion*. And yet they kept from you not only young Selena and Simon's knowledge of their plot, but their possession of a data stick full of documents you'd just as soon keep quiet."

The Mayor could hear Fontaine's smile. "Bluffs aren't going to work on me, Ross."

"Certainly not. You're much too clever a man for that. But you're also clever enough to understand the balance of risk and reward. If I'm lying, you'll find out soon enough, and I'll pay dearly for it. And what will this cost you? A hundred Templars' time, and a trifling inconvenience. Hardly the stuff to bankrupt an empire. But if I'm telling the truth, and you do nothing? Well, I can't guarantee that the Floods won't wriggle out of my grasp and scurry over the mountains. Think of what the Republic of California would make of it, two defectors carrying a complete breakdown on Blue Vole."

The Mayor wielded the last two words like an assassin's dagger, sliding it deftly into Fontaine's heart. That the stick contained Blue Vole was a guess, albeit an educated one—the Diocese of Plague had spent its time on little else. It was his only weapon, and he had to trust it. If the blade was faulty, he was doomed. But even as the last syllable struck home, he knew it wasn't.

When Fontaine next spoke, the words were stiff and bloodless. All the color had drained from his voice. "Okay, assume there is a stick. How could you know what's on it?"

Skepticism. You are *clever.* "The lightbook you gave me for my reports. A fine thing, in much better shape than this old radio. And quite compatible with New Canaan's data sticks, even five years on. So many things it can do. Read. Write. Copy."

"What are you asking?"

"Nothing you should fear. I'm merely proposing a partnership between our states. Something that benefits both of us. I've heard of your recent conquest of Niagara. Congratulations. It warms my heart to hear that such a vile regime has been toppled. Why, I'm told the former governors even forced their citizens to vote; I shudder at the thought."

"You're pretty well informed, for someone stuck on the far side of the Middle Wastes."

"I'm your eyes in the west, am I not? Eyes can glance in more than one direction."

"Do you have a point?"

"My words always have a destination. But I like to take my time on the way and enjoy the view. My point is this. Blue Vole has only one ultimate target, you know that as well as I. Niagara has fallen, the Republic is next, and from there the continent is yours. Such weighty acquisitions will require the expansion of your government. You'll need local overseers, friendly faces with an ear cocked to the locals, competent men to rule beneath your banner. I wish to nominate myself."

The smile was back, though not so loud as before. "Quite a promotion, isn't that Ross? From mayor of some two-bit backwater to governor of New Canaan's western coast?"

"I need not take every acre you conquer, Fontaine. I ask only for stewardship of the land already under my possession."

"I seem to recall you having some problems with our oversight, in the past."

"Time and circumstance can make allies of the fiercest enemies. We already enjoy a successful trading partnership, bartering Compound L for intelligence."

"Limited, in your case," drawled Fontaine. Whipped or not, the man couldn't resist a barbed comment.

"I'm no fool, Eric, regardless of what you might think of me. I know which way the wind is blowing. New Canaan's star is rising, and I wish to hitch my wagon to it. What does that really cost you? A smattering of shepherd clerks and migrant workers from the more crowded baronies, a few Templars to help me keep order, some extra Compound L."

"And in exchange—"

"The data stick and all its contents back in your hands. My copies will remain with me—simply to guarantee my safety, you understand."

"And the kids?"

"Returned to New Canaan, if that is what you wish." *One of them as a corpse, most likely.* But The Mayor would cross that bridge when he came to it.

"I'll run it up the chain."

A big Cardinal like you, asking permission like a schoolboy begging teacher for a hall pass? That must rankle, Eric. "That's all I ask. Though I do suggest you act quickly. The situation here has grown ever so slightly ... volatile."

"How volatile?"

"Nothing a hundred or so Templars couldn't mitigate. All the same, I wouldn't want the Flood children to slip away in the ensuing chaos."

A few seconds of silence crackled over the airwaves. The Mayor allowed Fontaine to break them. "Okay. I'll be there in ten days, less if the roads are clear. We'll sort out your little problem and then talk this matter through in person."

"I'm delighted to hear it. Be sure to bring some men with experience tending land, as well. Fallowfield is rife with sin, I'm sad to say. The farmers here need a little salvation, and we all know how effective the Archbishop's methods are at scouring souls clean."

"Quite," replied Fontaine, his voice curt. The Mayor could tell he didn't like taking orders—especially not from a lowly shepherd—but he didn't openly buck them. A good sign. "Until I see you then."

"Always good speaking with you, Eric."

A click signaled that Eric had signed off. The Mayor set the microphone back in its cradle. He allowed himself a few moments of private celebration, then called Bernard into the room.

"The conversation go well?"

"As well as expected. They curse me, but they'll come. And they'll expect two Floods when they get there."

"You've got the boy wrapped around your finger. That should count for something."

Not nearly enough, The Mayor thought, but held his tongue. He'd kept the existence of the data stick from everyone, including Bernard. It was rare for him to conceal anything from his chief enforcer, but the stick was too important to speak of unless absolutely necessary. If anyone else knew about it, they could easily find a way to twist that knowledge to their own advantage, and The Mayor hated competition.

"Don't take the boy's loyalty as a foregone conclusion. He's frightened and sheltered and more than a little gullible, but he's not stupid. You should never have let him see you on that hill. That was sloppy."

"I needed to be in range with the switch. And we wanted to make sure at least one of 'em was inside when it happened, and that means a clear sightline. Who knew the kid would bolt for your place? Anyway, you smoothed it over, didn't you?"

"I'd just as soon not have to smooth over matters in the first place. We need the boy, and keeping him is a lot easier if he stays amenable. Locking him away leads to a lot of annoying complications. Much better to keep him scared of everyone but us."

"Understood."

"Good. We've pulled the pin on this grenade—in more ways than one—and now we need to throw it before it blows up in our faces. If Fontaine gets here and we have no data stick to show him, he won't respond kindly. The search for the Flood girl has become an even higher priority. I want you to helm it yourself. She must, absolutely must, be in our custody by the end of the week. If for some reason it looks as if she cannot be apprehended in that time, I want you to see to it that she receives an important message."

Nodding, Bernard listened.

21: Ultimatum

Marcus watched the flame of his corn-oil lantern gutter. Part of him wanted to let it die. He was tired, and sleep seemed like a fine idea. But another part of him—the atavistic lizard mind that he had fed and tamed and trained—knew there was still work to be done. A sickening red rictus split his arm from wrist to elbow. The skin around its edges had already taken on an ugly, swollen look.

A bottle cast a translucent green shadow on the wall. Marcus wrapped his fingers around its neck, savoring the chill of the glass, and drank deeply. A caustic grain alcohol of indeterminate origin burned him throat to navel. The booze was rotgut, and he'd paid far too much for it. It did, however, have one thing going for it: it was extremely, *extremely* alcoholic. Marcus was a little afraid to keep it too close to an open flame, lest the fumes catch fire, and so set it as far from the lantern as possible while still having it within easy reach.

Marcus reached into his rucksack and removed a needle and a spool of black thread. He threaded the needle, his fingers steady as stone, and sank it into the bottle of alcohol until it touched bottom. He reeled the needle in, dried it off, and poured the bottle over his injured arm. A terrible cleansing fire burned him to the bone. Marcus bit back a scream. He took a few measured breaths, gripped the needle, and began working it through his skin, tugging the string taut with each loop. Once he had started, he did not allow himself to stop.

In less than two minutes it was done. Marcus twiddled his fingers experimentally. The lean, ropey muscles in his forearm bulged and twitched but the stitches held fast. He drained the rest of the grain alcohol less a few swallows over his newly sutured arm, noting with pleasure that the wound sizzled with far less intensity this time. The rest of the booze he drank.

His work done, Marcus extinguished the lantern and crawled into bed. He traced his finger over the black stitching, thinking of the man who'd cut him open: gaunt, sallow-skinned, with narrow eyes and lustrous black hair falling below his shoulders. Apparently, he'd claimed to have sailed across the Far Ocean on a merchant galleon. Marcus had no idea how much of the man's story was true, but one thing was for sure: his skill with a blade had been no bluff.

The blade itself had been a tanto, its cutting edge black with oil and its handle sheathed in an ivory carapace gaudy as a piece of costume jewellery. The knife, like its wielder, was honed steel beneath a tacky façade. Marcus wished he'd taken it, but there'd been no time for keepsakes with his radial artery spouting blood onto the thirsty hardpan.

The setting sun had cast an orange haze over everything, morphing Marcus' switchblade into a tongue of flame. Plumes of dust crested in the wake of every scraped bootheel. A grizzled man with baked bean teeth and a stringy grey beard took bets, pooling his money in a round hatbox covered in peeling yellow paper.

The foreign man drew his tanto from his scabbard and held it out with both hands. The hem of his kimono flapped in the breeze, adding to his look of storied otherworldliness. Marcus had to admit, it was a pretty good act. He was sorry he hadn't thought of it first.

The crowd solidified into a ring around them, the grizzled bookie closed his hatbox, and the fight began. Marcus and the foreign man stepped toward one another, the foreign man with his blade extended, Marcus with his switchblade dangling nonchalantly at his side. He let his opponent set the terms of the fight, studying his cautious approach and his stony face and the rigid outcrop of his arms. Eventually the foreign man attacked. Marcus sidestepped the first swing and darted back from the second. He thrust his switchblade forward, hoping for an easy hit while the foreigner was off balance. But his opponent was too quick. The tanto struck the switchblade half an inch above the hilt, the force of the blow nearly knocking it from Marcus' fingers. Marcus slipped back, his casual posture replaced by a predatory near-crouch.

The two men paused, facing each other with their blades drawn and ready. They circled one another, their feet in perfect rhythm as they danced the knife fighter's two-step. Marcus slashed, jabbed, feinted, lunged, even switched blade hands behind his back with a conjurer's sly grace, but nothing could touch the strange foreign man with the almond eyes and improbable backstory. Frustration made Marcus hasty, and when he reached out with a fierce jab that fell a few inches short, the foreign man struck.

He cut backwards, finishing a phony upwards stroke with its perfect twin in reverse. The blade's hooked tip scraped across Marcus' forearm, splitting the sleeve of his chambray shirt from elbow to cuff. Marcus screamed. Instinct threw him backwards and saved his life, for the foreign man's next swipe would have taken his head off otherwise. He fell to one knee with his knife held out and his injured arm bracing his fall.

If one of the men had asked Marcus after the fight, he would have claimed to have taken up the handful of dirt by accident, his fingers working in pure mindless reflex. But in truth, Marcus had trained his lower mind well, and it knew what it was doing the second his fingertips touched ground. It closed his hand around the dirt and swung his arm backwards as he stood to better hide its new payload. It tilted the knife in his other hand until the flat of the blade caught the light of the setting sun, drawing the foreign man's attention. It brought the blade up in a ham fisted strike the foreign man could easily dodge. It saw this, glowering through the red-tinged lenses of its hungry eyes, and it waited until the perfect moment before tossing the dirt into the foreign man's face.

The man recoiled. His hands flew to his eyes as he staggered backwards. Seizing his moment, Marcus plunged his knife into the foreign man's exposed belly again and again. He continued to stab as the man fell, kept stabbing when the man dropped his tanto and reached up, palms out, begging him to stop. He stabbed until the man was dead and the ache in his flayed arm made him woozy. He stumbled over to the man with the hatbox.

"My fee," Marcus said. Blood dribbled from the tips of his fingers. He pressed his injured arm against his stomach to stem the flow. The hatbox man shoved a stack of bills into Marcus' outstretched hand. Marcus tucked them away without bothering to check the count. He noted the hungry glance several bystanders cast his way as he passed them by, carrion sizing up a meal.

Marcus took a room on the second floor of a local tavern. He cut away the remnants of his tattered sleeve and observed his injury: a gruesome canyon as long as his forearm and an inch deep. The foreign man had nicked a vein, but he hadn't julienned it as Marcus had feared. Marcus drew a roll of gauze from his rucksack and wrapped it tight around his arm, stopping only when the roll was empty. He fastened the bandage in place with a pair of safety pins, tucked a chair beneath the doorknob of his room, and let himself out the window.

Climbing was tough with one arm, but Marcus had always been agile. The walk was harder, in its way, and a stitch dug into his side before long. He was exhausted, angry, and dizzy with blood loss, but his instincts screamed at him to flee. He hadn't liked the way those men had looked at him. They knew he was hurt, possibly dying, and that he'd earned more in five minutes than they would in a month.

The hostler had retired for the night and it took Marcus five minutes of tapping on his front window to wake him. His legs grew weak and rubbery and he almost keeled over when the hostler's face appeared in the window.

"What you want?" he spat. "I get up 'fore dawn tomorrow and I don't much like bein' roused."

"I apologize," Marcus said, in a tone that suggested he did anything but. "But I am in a bit of a situation." He thrust his injured arm through the door. The first traces of blood had begun to soak through the gauze. The hostler recoiled. "Jesus."

"I've got a chore for you. The bad news is you must do it. The good news is it pays very well. You have me over a barrel, yes?"

The hostler didn't look like he had anyone over a barrel. His lower jaw quivered. "What's the job?"

Marcus' smile flashed in the dark. "Easier than you think."

The hostler rode Marcus to a sleepy, nameless village ninety minutes to the southwest.

The village had a single boarding house crammed with closet-sized rooms that stank of mothballs, but Marcus' chamber had a corn-oil lamp, and in his particular circumstance, its feeble light had been worth more than all the space in the Middle Wastes. He left the room long enough to buy the bottle of rotgut from a bow-legged farmer, then settled into his task.

Now, patched and out of immediate danger, Marcus stared up at the ceiling. Its plaster surface bulged with water damage. A dull itch nested in the crevices between his stitches, begging him to scratch. He closed his eyes. The room spun. He let himself succumb to drunkenness, convinced that, for the time being, he was safe. Still, he kept his knife close. Doing so was not an unusual precaution. He couldn't remember the last time he'd slept without its reassuring weight resting inches from his hand.

Fear niggled at Marcus, but pursuit by opportunistic thugs was not its cause. Nor was he concerned about his cut, per se, although that came closer to the truth. What he really feared was what the cut represented. Weakness. Mortality. The fact that he was getting old. Not that old—his skin remained smooth as ironed silk, and his hair was as of yet unblemished by so much as a single strand of grey—but age was a relative term in his line of business. He was fast, but there were other fast men out there, too. Other wounds would come. Worse ones. Soon the day would arrive where he could fight no longer, and if his debt remained unsettled when it did …

He thought of *pandilleros* kicking in Emilio's door, the children crying in confusion as their father is dragged into the bedroom. Of his mother, a fat knuckled hand yanking her head back by the hair while its twin raked a rusty barber's razor across her neck. Of the empty-eyed *asesinos* with their claw hammers and clubs, and the paths of ruin they would leave across Marcus' half-remembered life. All horrible visions, all painfully possible.

Selena. She'd been his one shot at salvation, the diamond big and bright enough to buy his freedom. But the so-called diamond was only a hunk of glass, and it had cracked. Even if she lived, he didn't think she'd be anything like she was.

An ache sank its fangs into Marcus' arm. *If this is the pain drunk, I can't imagine it sober.* On top of everything else, it seemed he might have to take a break from fighting until his arm healed. At least his short tenure with Selena had brought a decent windfall. That should buy him a little time. But only a little. That was the thing with time. No matter how much you spent on it, you could never buy all of it that you needed.

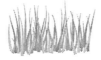

"What's the matter, kid? Why aren't you eating?"

A metal tray straddled Selena's waist. On it sat a plate containing a greyish pork chop, three finger potatoes boiled in their skins, and a mass of greenish-yellow slurry. Selena prodded the mass with her fork, digging a small cavern into its side. She pulled her fork free. The cavern collapsed with a flatulent splat.

"Not hungry," Selena said.

"You should eat whether you're hungry or not." Molly placed her hands on her hips. "You have to keep your strength up."

"What is this exactly?" Selena asked, pointing to the slurry.

"It's cabbage."

Selena gave the mass another prod. "When?"

"I'm sorry?"

"When was it cabbage?"

"It's cabbage now. Picked from the clinic's air garden yesterday morning. Plenty of vitamins in there."

Selena scooped up a bit of cabbage. Strings of it dangled from her fork. She tilted her wrist and the cabbage soughed off the tines, landing with a splat on the plate. "Once, maybe. Has it been boiling since you picked it?"

Molly made an exasperated sigh and moved to take the tray away. Selena held it in place and began to eat. Molly watched her chew, incredulous.

"You know, for someone who's so quiet, you're a hell of a handful."

Selena chewed, swallowed, shrugged.

"Act smug as you like. Your dressing's due for a change and I'm gonna spend this evening cleaning every last inch of your cut. You'll be wailing like a baby by the end of it, I'm sure."

Selena ate her meal without further comment while Molly tidied a nearby table. When Selena had finished, Molly took the tray and brought it into the kitchen. She returned, massaging a dollop of disinfecting gel into her palms.

"How's the head?"

"It's fine, I guess."

"Any pain?"

"A little." If Selena said none, Molly would know she was lying.

"Any itching or heat?"

"Not really."

"Let's take a look at the damage, shall we?" Molly worked her fingernails under the gauze. Selena's skin felt dry and tacky where the adhesive touched it. Molly scrubbed the area with a damp washcloth, using a dab of rubbing alcohol only where water and elbow grease wouldn't do. She soaked a cotton ball with antiseptic and began cleaning the wound.

"Can I see?" Selena asked.

"See what?"

"My ear."

Molly paused. She tugged at the hem of her skirt, smoothing out a pleat with her index finger. "I'm not sure you should, Selena. I don't want you to get discouraged. It's still healing, and apt to look a whole hell of a lot better once the scabs are gone and your hair's grown back."

"I don't care. I want to see."

"Alright. If you're sure." Molly opened a drawer to the right of the sink and removed a hand mirror in a blue plastic frame. She held it at waist height, the reflective side pointed inward at her belly. "Just remember that it'll get better, okay?"

"Sure."

Molly turned the mirror outward. Selena took it and held it out in front of her.

The first thing she noticed was not her ruined ear, but the pallor of her skin and the heavy purple bags hanging below her eyes. *My god, I really* have *been sick.*

In a strange way, her ear seemed less of an issue. It ended abruptly in a crusty red plateau half a centimetre above her ear canal. A gutter of scabbed flesh ran from her temple to the back of her head. Blond stubble covered the right side of her skull where Molly had shaved it. Selena scratched the inflamed edge of her gash gingerly, stopping only when her fingernail nicked a scab. She winced at the pain, rode it out, and returned the mirror. "Thanks."

"No problem," Molly replied, applying a fresh bandage. "Not so bad, eh?"

"I guess not."

"Gives you character."

Selena rubbed her bandaged ear. "I'm not sure character is something I need. Or want."

"Well kid, want it or not, you got it."

Molly left the room. A few minutes later the clop of horse hooves drew Selena's attention, and she tossed a casual glance at the road. Her eyes narrowed to dagger points.

She recognized the rider at once. He was a hard man to miss, both in size and from the canyon of scar tissue twisting its way up his cheek. He wore an outsized pistol in a holster at the small of his back, a rifle slung over his shoulder, and a truncheon dangling from a rawhide strap at his wrist.

Selena sank down and with one hand eased the window open half an inch. She bent over her footlocker, pain sloshing against her injured skull. She grabbed the edges of the locker and held them tight until the sensation abated, then began quickly and quietly gathering all of her meager possessions into her leather knapsack—save for the bowie knife, which she tucked into her belt. Bernard knocked on the front door, a hollow sound that carried far down the empty street. Molly answered.

"Can I help you with something?"

"Could be that you can, ma'am. I'm here on official business."

"Awful long way from Fallowfield, aren't you? I didn't think you had any jurisdiction beyond your borders."

"Special circumstances."

"Not to be rude, but I'm not sure how our law boys'd feel about all this. Maybe you should talk to them."

"I don't want to step on anyone's toes, ma'am. Like I said, this is a special case. I'm looking for a girl of about eighteen years old. Blond hair probably cut short."

"I see."

Selena winced at the sudden stiffness in Molly's voice. Apart from everything else, Molly had been good to her. She didn't like the idea of sneaking away, knowing it would solidify her guilt in Molly's mind. But what choice did she have?

"She might be going by the name of Selena Flood, though it's possible she's adopted a new pseudonym by now."

"A pseudonym? Why all the secrecy? What's she done?"

"She robbed a merchant name a McCulloch off the northern road. Put a bullet through his guard and stole one of his wagons. McCulloch got a shot off on her, but she got away."

"M-murder?" Molly stammered. Selena gritted her teeth. *Big talk from the likes of you, you prune-faced thug.*

"You seem anxious, ma'am. You got a patient matching her description?"

"I, well, I mean, it's hard to say …"

Selena slipped her knapsack's strap over her shoulder and tiptoed to the infirmary door. Beyond the doorway ran a narrow hall. A left turn would bring her to the front entrance, a storage room, a small lobby, and the clinic where Molly conducted minor surgeries. A right turn would bring her to Molly's office, the kitchen, and a steel door leading to the back of the building. Selena turned right and opened the door.

A Shepherd stood in the doorway, gun trained on Selena's chest. A smug smile smeared across his goony face.

"Best put that knife down, girl."

"Not before you put down your gun."

The Shepherd snorted a laugh. "Why would I wanna do that?"

Selena did her best to outsmug the Shepherd with her own smile. "Because I'm not alone, remember?"

Her eyes darted over the man's shoulder. The Shepherd, not quite fooled, still shifted his attention for half an instant. Long enough for Selena to slam the door. The Shepherd dove forward, blocking the door's swing with his body. He grunted as the steel collided with his shoulder. His gun arm kinked upward, barrel pointing to the ceiling. Selena jabbed her knife into his ribs and the gun discharged, its slug sending chiplets of plaster raining onto the floor. Selena traced the blade along the Shepherd's ribcage until it snagged on his sternum. The Shepherd wheezed, blanched, collapsed. Selena shoved her way past him and out the door, pausing long enough to snap up his gun.

A flood of yellow locust washed over the countryside, its high water mark ending just a few feet before the building's foundation. Seedlings of the bitter plant poked up through the gravel like the fingers of a greedy child, one that had eaten its fill but still cried for more. Selena ran two buildings down, found the stone protrusion that housed a building's cellar door, and ducked down against it, plotting her next move. Sturgis lay on the northern trade route, which meant there was really only one road in and out of town, and it was flat and level enough to spot a runner at a considerable distance. The yellow locust covered everything for miles, and it was as good a place as any to lose somebody—but it was a good place to get lost in, too. She could hide in a building, but she had no idea which ones were occupied, and couldn't trust anyone in town to keep her secret. What she needed was speed. If she could get out of town fast enough, put some distance between her and Bernard, she might be able to lose them between here and the neighbouring town. But the only way she could do that was with a horse and a head start. She didn't know if she could get both, but figured she might as well start with the one.

Footsteps crunched frantically toward her. Selena slinked lower against the abutment, and released her breath in a long, rolling gasp as they started to fade. She peered around the building, keeping hidden as best as she could. The stable was across the road and north, its roof just visible. It wasn't far, but how the hell was she supposed to cross the road? The street was a jumble of merchants pausing on their trek between Fallowfield and the northern cities, swapping stories and buying lunch from carts and hashing out side deals under the table.

But they had better things to look at than her, didn't they?

Fighting her deepest atavistic impulses, Selena tucked the pistol and her knife into her waistband and stepped into view. She walked slowly, each step a conscious one, each gesture deliberate. Her every pore screamed. Sweat dampened her armpits. She shoved her hands in her pockets to keep them from shaking.

Mercifully, the stables were empty but for the horses. Saddles hung from nails on the wall. Selena grabbed one at random and went into the nearest occupied stall. She had a bit of experience with horses from her summers in the Outer Baronies, but the horses she knew were docile palfreys bred for leisure. Farm horses had a different temperament, and Selena approached hers warily. The horse stepped sideways, sensing her anxiety. She forced herself to take slow, deep breaths.

"Come on now, girl. Take it easy,"

Someone rushed into the stable. Selena whirled, drew her knife, and dove at her assailant. Molly threw up her hands, emitting a single choked yelp. The blade halted inches from her face. They stood frozen for a moment, the raised knife a steel fence between them. Selena lowered it.

"Shit," she muttered.

"Did you do it?" Molly asked, her voice little more than a whisper.

"Kill someone? Yeah, I guess I did."

"One of them jumped you at the back door. Was it him?"

Selena nodded. "But he wasn't the first."

Molly bristled. Selena could tell she'd been hoping for a proclamation of innocence, maybe a story of having spurned a Shepherd and suffered their wrath, making the lie of her murderous past all the more egregious. Real life was seldom so one-sided.

"I can tell you that I didn't have much of a choice, I was under attack. It's true, but I don't know if it makes a whole lot of difference, to be honest."

"Neither do I." Molly swallowed. Her fingers flitted about her like flies, landing on her dress and shirt to make tiny pointless adjustments. "I should go."

"Now? That guy is still out there. And he could have others with him. Come back to the clinic. I'll set you up in a safe spot, bandage your face maybe."

Selena shook her head. "I don't want to risk more talk. The townspeople have seen me. They're going to know I'm not from here. Word might get back. They won't be so disorganized next time. Here." Selena searched through her knapsack and removed her stash of Standard notes.

"What are you doing?"

"I'm buying a horse." Selena counted out several large notes and handed them to Molly.

"From me? I don't own a horse."

"Then give the money to the owner of this one."

"I—"

"Is it not enough? I have more. I'm not trying to rob anyone. But I've got to get out of here."

"Keep your money. Take the horse in the corner stall, back there."

A piebald mare munched oats contentedly from a metal bin. "Who does she belong to?"

"Who knows? She's the one who brought you into town. If she's anyone's she's yours, I guess."

Working quickly, Selena and Molly saddled the horse. Selena mounted.

"You're still not better, you know," Molly said. "A graze can be pretty serious business."

"It'll be a hell of a lot worse if they set half a dozen Shepherds on me."

"They'll be looking for you on the road, too. Here you've got some protection, at least."

Selena shook her head. Molly massaged her temples. After a moment, she led a freshly brushed and fed horse from the stalls and climbed on bareback.

"What are you doing?"

"If you stick to the road, sooner or later the Shepherds'll run you down. There's a safer route, and I'm gonna show you where it is. Come on."

They rode side by side down the highway, keeping at a low gallop both to avoid attracting attention and to allow Molly to explain the path to Selena.

"There's a hidden path that a couple of goat herders used to take. What you do is find the spot and walk your horse into the grass. You'll feel these stones with your feet every few steps. Follow them about a hundred yards and you'll come to a small gravel clearing where some scrub grass grows. One of the only places to graze within miles. There's a dried-up riverbed nearby. It should be far enough from the road that you can ride safely without being seen. Follow the riverbed south and you'll make your way to Fallowfield. Go north and you'll hit one main road or another. Those'll take you all the way to the Prairie Republic, you have a mind to go that far. Do whatever you need to do to get safe, but first get through the grass and out of sight. I'll keep riding south to Berkshire. If anyone stops me I can say I'm on a supply run."

"Thank you," Selena said. "For everything."

"I don't even know why I'm doing this. I find out you're some sort of a ... a killer, and I'm offering to squirrel you away from the Sheps. You've made things around this place real complicated, kid. You know that?"

Selena shrugged. Her face betrayed a small smile. "It happens."

"You did what you had to do. Whatever it was. That's what I'm going to tell myself." She looked over her shoulder. "I don't like how those boys went about things."

"That makes two of us."

It was a nervous quarter mile. Selena glanced constantly over her shoulder, wondering when the Shepherds would ride up on her, cudgels in hand, or else waiting for the sound of a gunshot as they pursued. Rushing air pricked the corners of her eyes and filled her mouth with the sour, oily taste of yellow locust. Dust plumed behind her in a rooster tail, obscuring the town at her back.

Molly brought her horse to a halt at what appeared to be an arbitrary stretch of grass. She pointed down at the dirt, where a few old bits of broken pavement formed an interlocking pattern.

"This is the spot. See? Just—"

The bullet tore through Molly's throat, spraying a foam of blood and bone across Selena's face and shoulder. Her horse reared at the sound. Selena wrapped her arms around its neck, hands slipping from the reins. A second shot missed her by inches. The horse was not so lucky. It let out a screech as the bullet bored a hole through its skull. Another jet of blood geysered across Selena's face. The horse, still mid-rear, toppled. Its skull hit the hardpan with a sickening thud.

Selena rolled away from the equine corpse and skittered to her feet. Bernard galloped toward her. He raised a rifle to his shoulder and trained its barrel on Selena's chest. She sprang over the horse's body and dove headfirst into the locust.

Fronds clawed her face, their greasy residue burning. Selena hurdled through the locust like a swimmer through swamp muck, legs kicking, arms paddling desperately. She dodged at the expectation of bullets that never came. Instead, she heard Bernard dismount. His bootheels scuffed against the pebbly hardpan as he approached the bodies.

"Damn shame, takin' a life," he called. "Of a horse, I mean. Your bitch buddy here, that's another story." A zip, and the steady trickle of liquid. "Goodnight, sweet bitch. And rivers of piss lay you to thy rest. That's Shakespeare. You ever heard a Shakespeare? Grunts like us, we ain't supposed to know the name. Behind the Last War's smoky veil and all that shit. But I hear you Seraphim still read some of that old stuff. That true?"

Selena bit her knuckles. Bernard was trying to goad her out of hiding, that much was obvious. She wouldn't rise to his bait. But the pressure of her anger was building inside her, and it took more and more strength to hold it in.

"If you think I'm wading through that shit to get you, kid, you're mistaken. I don't intend to dirty my boots for the likes of you. Best just come out now and spare us both a hassle."

Fat fucking chance.

"Yeah, I know. You're thinking to yourself, 'this old prick has a prayer,' right? What sort of moron leaves perfectly good cover to chat with the asshole who just shot at her seconds ago? I know I wouldn't do it. But then again, the asshole in question doesn't have my brother in the palm of his hand."

Selena squeezed a stalk of locust hard enough to rend its innards to slimy pulp.

"Don't like that, huh? Well, you're really not gonna like this. Our esteemed Mayor has been chatting with a fellow called Eric Fontaine. Name mean anything to you? No? He's an under-Cardinal of Information for a little country called New Canaan. Oh, sorry, I meant Cardinal. He just scored a nice juicy promotion, I hear. Good for him."

Selena bit down harder. The copper stink of blood filled her mouth. *Fontaine.* The word twisted like a key and the gates flew open. Aldo Delduca's execution and the conquest of Niagara. She recalled his condescending smile, the veiled criticisms spat like poison darts at her parents, the sincere pleasure he took in watching five hundred people boiled alive, satisfaction evident in the prim pile of his hands in his lap and the upturn of his jaw. And another memory, forgotten until now:

a sly glance to the rows behind him, at Andrew and Emily Flood. *It was him,* Selena realised. *He knew about mom and dad and the Republic. Or he suspected enough to spring the trap. Either way, it was him.* Iron hands wrung Selena's insides. She clutched her belly. Her struggle not to scream commingled with a struggle not to vomit.

"He was very interested to hear about the two of you," Bernard drawled. He seemed to savor every word, each syllable a pinch of salt on Selena's open wound. "So interested he wanted to come way out here personally to check it out. We certainly don't want to disappoint the guy, so we got a whattayacall ultimatum for you. Here's the deal. Come out here and hand over whatever it is you got that The Mayor wants so bad, and we'll let you and your little brother go on your way. We'll even set you up with a nice horse to make up for the one I just shot. That's fair, right? I'm sure ol' Eric'll be a little down about missing the two of you—he's got some funny stories to tell you about your mom and dad—but we can tell him you slipped away. It'll be our secret.

"What do you say? Coming out? No? That's okay, you don't need to decide right now. You have five days to meet us back in Fallowfield. After that Eric and friends'll be here, and if they have to track that stick down themselves they won't be very happy. They'll probably have some cross words for your brother about it. Or maybe they'll just have a cross."

Bernard's horse trotted off. Selena lay where she was for a long time, until she was sure Bernard was too far away to hear her. Then she screamed. A formless, ululating wail that carried over the poison fields. The yellow locust listened with indifference, its silent swaying unchanged. She pounded the dirt, yanked stalks of locust up from the roots, gnashed her teeth, but her anger and hurt seemed only to build. The Mayor had played his trump card, and there wasn't a damn thing she could do about it. Her choices were abandon her brother to die alone or go to him and die together—the spiel about letting her and Simon go was pure bullshit. Data sticks could be copied, and whatever favor The Mayor sought from New Canaan, he would only get it if she and Simon were taken out of play entirely.

She knew what the right choice was. The cold blade of logic

demanded amputation. If she fled, the world lost Simon. If she stayed, it lost the Republic of California. What was one life balanced against an entire nation, the last beacon shining against New Canaan's darkness unending? She needed to reach the Republic, to secure their future and seek what vengeance—and what redemption—she could later. *You have to be strong. For Simon, for the Republic of California.*

Only she couldn't do it. If abandoning your only brother was being strong, then she'd just as soon be weak. Leaving her parents had only been possible because the choice had been taken from her— by the time the news of their crucifixion reached her, they were past saving. The same might be said for Simon, but the circumstances were different. She could go to him and spare him the added misery of dying alone and afraid—he'd still be afraid, but at least he wouldn't be alone. Perhaps Selena could even goad the Shepherds into killing them both quickly. It would be a mercy indeed compared to what New Canaan had in store for them.

Selena struggled to her feet. The data stick in her pocket seemed to weigh a thousand pounds. She took it from her pocket and observed it. It glared up at her, stoic, accusatory. She curled her fingers around it to block it from sight. So much trouble over such a small thing. But people had died for far less.

She trudged through the grass. Locust filled her vision, thick as toxic fog. Fronds probed her eyes, her lips, her nose. Selena didn't bother to bat them away. Let the locust have her. There were worse ways to die.

The locust parted, revealing a sweep of road landmarked by her dead horse. And by Molly, her throat blooming with petals of destroyed flesh, her face still wet with Bernard's piss. Molly, who'd sewn Selena tattered ear and fought off her infection when Selena was too weak to do it alone. Who'd helped her when turning her in would have been easier, safer, smarter. Who'd died choking on blood because she defended a woman she barely knew. Selena was not short on enemies. Her list ran long: the Archbishop, Eric Fontaine, The Mayor of Fallowfield, a dozen anonymous Templars, every Bishop and Cardinal in New Canaan. And now Bernard. So many wrongs unrighted, so many blood debts unpaid.

And now it seemed most of them would stay that way, though perhaps, if she played her cards right, she could at least kill Bernard.

It was good to have goals.

Selena pulled her cleanest cloth from her knapsack and, wetting it with water from her canteen, washed Molly's face. When the skin was clear and glistening, she shut Molly's eyes, straightened her legs, and knotted the cloth around her ruined neck, hiding the wound from sight. She had no tools to bury her—and even if she did, the woman deserved better than an eternity amongst the shitgrass. Her people would find her soon, and when they did, at least their last sight of her would be one with some dignity. It wasn't much, but it was the best Selena could offer.

"You deserve a lot better than this," she told Molly. "I'm sorry."

She set Molly's hands neatly on her lap and stepped back into the locust, tracing the stone markers as she'd been instructed. A few dozen steps brought her to a narrow clearing, a bubble of air in the yellow swamp. She'd found Molly's goat path. It ran like a half-healed scar in the Waste's colossal flank, its loose dirt furry with yellow locust sproutlings. To her left it wound north toward Denver and the outer townships. To the right, it ran south toward Fallowfield. She turned right, taking her first step on a long and friendless march to her brother and her fate.

Although perhaps it didn't need to be so friendless. New Canaan was coming west, and that affected everyone, not just her. They were coming as reinforcements, not conquerors, but that would make their arrival no less bloody. Anyone who stood against The Mayor stood against New Canaan too, and The Mayor was long on enemies. As if to prove this fact to a skeptical companion, Selena reached into her rucksack and pulled out the piece of paper the masked man had given Marcus. She read the words to herself, muttering them like some dread incantation. Like a curse.

The Mayor wanted her to come back to Fallowfield? No problem. She'd come back.

And hell would follow at her heels.

22: Fate Spares the Foolish

Simon lay in bed until the sun went down and the sky turned its usual nighttime shade of bruised purple-black. On the covers before him sat a tray of roast beef and mashed potatoes. He prodded the food with a sterling silver fork, immured by an invisible wall of nausea that left him unable to eat. Eventually he set the plate aside and crawled back beneath the covers, wishing for sleep and knowing it wouldn't come. His throat was parched, his nose red and chapped.

He needed a drink of water, and he told himself that was what he had in mind as he slipped out the door and tiptoed down the hallway. He maintained this belief as he descended the stairs, walking with his feet flush against the outer railing to keep the aged wood from creaking. It wasn't until he slid open the pantry door and dropped to his knees that he admitted to himself that water wasn't the goal, had never been the goal. His hands jumped and skittered through a forest of glassware—jugs of vinegar, vials of corn oil, jars of pickled beets and peach preserves and asparagus stalks suspended in brine—in search of a bottle of gin or brandy. They found one, a sleek column of clear glass, and closed hungrily around its neck.

Nearby, a door clicked shut. Hushed voices, incomprehensible with distance, whispered through the hall. His thirst forgotten, Simon crept toward the source of the sound.

He identified the first voice as belonging to The Mayor, though it lacked his usual glossy composure. It sounded rumpled and rushed.

"This is hardly the time and place, John. If you want to speak with me, you best come by tomorrow at a decent hour."

"I can't wait no longer! I can't sleep, I can't eat. Every time I look out a window I see faces lookin' back at me!"

Simon slipped into the dining room. The voices became clearer. He couldn't pin a name to the second one.

"For god's sake, calm yourself. Here, if we must do this then let's go somewhere more private. Come with me."

A pair of footsteps creaked up the stairs and toward The Mayor's office. Simon waited until they were a good ways ahead before following, each step a calculated maneuver: toe first, exploring for potential creaks or groans, then the ball of the foot, with the heel landing last, bracing his weight for the following step. The office door muffled their voices, but as Simon drew closer, he could make out most of what was said.

"I done all you told me! I told the girl about you, I got her to the barn, I told you all about the silo. And now all them people ..."

The farmer's word sank like a fishhook into Simon's brain. *Girl? What girl?*

"Please, John. There's no need for these histrionics."

"Don't call me absurd! You didn't have to plant no bomb!"

"Do you seriously think I bombed anyone?"

With a final silent step, Simon reached the door. He lowered himself gently to his knees and peered through the antique keyhole.

The man with The Mayor was in his fifties, dressed in farmer's garb. He looked deeply unwell. Pouches the color of bruised flesh hung from his eyes and his stubbly cheeks had a greyish pallor. He was a doughy man, but the weight hung on him loosely, giving him a slightly deflated look. He stood across from The Mayor's desk, one hand resting on its corner, as if he were unable to support his own weight. "Them chemicals weren't explosive. I've helped you spread Compound L over half these fields in my time."

"Perhaps they were manufacturing other things besides. Weapons. They've expressed rabid discontent, anything is possible."

The farmer's voice dropped to a whisper, but his words carried with magnified intensity through the still house. "I went to the silo. The one you blowed up. I could smell it in the soil, Mr. Mayor. I spread Compound L for these last fifteen years and I know what it smells like."

"John, I'm growing concerned. Paranoia is a serious illness. You're seeing demons dancing in shadows. You need help."

"Them farmers were makin' Compound L and you bombed them. That makes you a murderer."

"John—"

"And if Otto could make Compound L, then you didn't just kill him. How many a them migrants starve over the winter? How many can't eat 'cause we ain't able to grow enough in our fields? You're a stone murderer, ain't you, Mr. Mayor?"

"Conjecture. Conspiracy theories. Groundless accusations."

"This ain't no court of law! Them fancy words don't mean nothin'. I want to look in your eyes and hear the truth. The *real* truth."

"No one looks in my eyes," The Mayor growled.

John McCulloch thrust out his chin. "Then I heard everythin' I need to hear."

The Mayor moved fast, much faster than Simon expected, but the action took on the crystalline slowness of dreams. In a single fluid twist of hand and arm, The Mayor pulled open his drawer, drew a revolver, and fired. Two slugs took the farmer in the chest. He jerked like a marionette. The Mayor stood, his face even colder than his reflective lenses.

Simon fled. He'd seen enough. It took every ounce of restraint in him not to run full out, to hell with creaky boards.

He found himself back in his room, unsure precisely how he'd gotten there. His mind sputtered and strobed, absorbing the world in a series of jerks and flashes. *You're drunk,* he thought. *And here you thought you needed booze for that!*

Simon chuckled to himself, though it was a rough, parched, ugly sound bled dry of humor. He knew what had happened to Selena, knew it with the urgent, irrefutable understanding that comes in bad dreams, when you know the thing behind your back will devour you the moment you turn to face it, yet your head swivels helplessly all the same. It was an insane thought, he told himself. A dangerous thought. Yet it stood before him, silent and implacable.

He spat, his dry mouth producing little more than a stringy film of mucus.

Footsteps rattled the ancient plumbing. Simon scurried to the window. The drop from the sill was negligible, no more than ten feet onto spongy soil. But where would he run from there? Fleeing would seal his fate, prove he'd heard something he shouldn't have heard. Ignorance was the safer gamble. He crawled into bed, slapped his glasses from his face, ruffled his hair. The door opened. A figure stood in the doorway, dark save for twin points of shimmering reflected light where its eyes should be.

"Did I wake you?"

Simon injected sleep into his voice, blinking theatrically and fumbling for his glasses. He hoped The Mayor didn't notice that they weren't in their usual place on his nightstand. "No, I don't think so. I thought I heard a bang a second ago."

"Yes, that's why I came in. Nothing to worry about. I keep a pistol for my own protection, and it went off while I was cleaning it. Embarrassingly, I must admit I hadn't checked that it was loaded. Quite silly on my part, but sometimes fate spares the foolish. I injured only my floor and my pride."

"Oh, okay. Thanks for telling me."

"Not at all. Sleep well, Simon."

Simon laid his head against the pillow and stared up at the ceiling. *Funny for a gun you're cleaning to go off twice.* He closed his eyes, willing himself to sleep and knowing it wouldn't come.

Stupid. Stupid to think he could run, stupid to have trusted The Mayor, stupid to have wanted to stay here in the first place. Had he really thought Fallowfield might be safe? Had he really been so naïve? He was stupid, stupid, stupid, and now he was paying for it. Selena had seen clear through the deception, and it had caught even her. What chance did he have to escape?

But had it caught her? Simon's back went rigid. Sweat prickled his palms. Somewhere deep inside himself, Simon had accepted that Selena was dead, even if most of him couldn't yet deal with the fact. There was simply no logical reason why she would disappear for this long without contacting him, unless death stayed her tongue. But if The Mayor was the one hunting her, her absence made a lot more sense. Maybe she'd been driven into hiding. Maybe she'd tried to get messages to him but failed. Maybe she was badly injured somewhere and recuperating. If he could only find a way to reach her.

He lay awake until morning, the sun casting pallid light through a cataract of haze. He needed someone to talk to, and The Mayor had proven an unreliable confidante.

It was time to find another one.

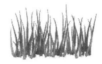

Selena trudged along a narrow band of pebbly earth. To her left ran a trail of broken pavement, its ridged and jagged slabs jutting outward like the vertebrae of some half-buried leviathan. To her right lay untold leagues of yellow locust. Stray stalks peeked up from the ruined road, proud as the flags of a conquering army. The right side of her face was in agony, broken flesh sizzling beneath her bandage. A corkscrew of misery twisted through her ear canal and into her brain, every step adding a quarter turn. She hoped that feeling wasn't the sign of her infection coming back. Molly got all her medicine from a single supplier in Dallam, and her stock of antibiotics had been worryingly low even before Selena arrived. All that remained were a few pills rattling in a tin in her pocket. She took one now, dry-swallowing it; her canteen had run out of water that morning.

In the distance, a city rose from the yellow grass, tall buildings of glass and steel. A few leaned drunkenly on their neighbors, others were semi-collapsed skeletons of fire-eaten metal. A fringe of mountains rose tantalizingly in the distance.

The streets were quieter than on her previous visit and she made her way through them easily, wandering up and down main roads until she found a street she recognized. From there she worked her way to the alley, one eye on its sloping windowed roof, and rapped her knuckles on the green utility door. After a moment, a heavy man stepped out. A caul of shadows fell from his face.

"*Saludos* once again, Selena. You've come for another fight, maybe?"

"Maybe. But it won't be happening here. I want to get in touch with Marcus. Can you get a message to him?"

"He could," said a voice from the hallway. "But there is a more direct route." Marcus' head appeared above Gustavo's shoulder. His smile glowed like a jack-o-lantern's.

Gustavo led Selena and Marcus to a tiny office on the building's second floor. It was lightly furnished and smelled of mildew, but it faced away from the collapsed building next door and so provided a better view of the street. Selena sat on a folding chair, Marcus on a corduroy armchair mottled with stains. His bony frame sank into its springs, forging a crevice that fit his shape precisely. Gustavo poured them each a glass of vodka. Selena sniffed hers and took a sip.

"Thanks."

Gustavo nodded. "I'll leave the two of you to your business. You know where to find me when you've finished."

"You are a generous host, Gustavo," said Marcus.

When Gustavo had left, Selena spoke. "How long have you been here?"

"It is good to see you too, Lena."

"Not good enough to stick around the hospital, though."

Marcus shifted in his seat, gaze drifting to the far corner of the room. "My work calls me, yes? How can I refuse?"

"You seem to be doing a pretty good job of it now."

"I have been, how you say, taken out of commission for the moment." Marcus rolled up his sleeve, revealing an angry red gash puckering from wrist to elbow. Black stitches held the wound shut, particles of blood and grit and dead skin congealed within the fibres.

"Jesus."

"He was there, I'm sure, but he did not intervene."

Selena touched the side of her face. Her gauze was coming loose. She ran her finger through the gap between the bandage and her cheek, tracing the ridge of tenderness beginning just below her temple. "Same here."

"It would appear that we chose a dangerous business, yes?"

"Yeah. Who'dve thought beating and killing people for a living might have negative consequences?"

"These are dark times, where brutes and killers cannot practice their art in peace."

Selena nodded sagely. She sniffed the contents of her glass, pulled back. Even the fumes were enough to get you loaded. She thought the liquid would make a better disinfectant than beverage—but gunshot wound or no, she needed a stiff drink. The first sip went down like napalm. She coughed her way through it, her face tucked into her forearm to block the worst of the spittle.

"An excellent vintage, yes?" asked Marcus.

"Of what, paint thinner?"

Marcus smiled. "You New Canaanites have no appreciation for strong liquor."

"Sure we do. We use it to power trucks." She looked up from her glass. "How'd you know I was from New Canaan?" There was a time being called out on her origins would've terrified her, but with the might of the Templar Knights already on her heels, the admission hardly seemed to matter.

"Your voice. You do not speak with the rhythms of the Waste."

"Thank god for small favors." *My voice. Damn.* How many others had seen through her little K City story before she'd even finished telling it? "How do you even know what a New Canaan accent sound like? Have you been?"

"I spent a few months in the southern Baronies. Though I am not intimately familiar with them."

"Well, you're about to be. That's why I'm here. The Mayor's been telling tales to one of the Cardinals there. My brother and I ... I guess you could call us persons of interest. I have something they want, and The Mayor wants to be the one to give it to them. I have three days before they arrive." *Or so Bernard tells me. It could be more. Or less. Or it could be they're here already.*

"A thrilling story. But I do not understand why you are telling me this."

"If I go back to Fallowfield alone, I'll die. You know that as well as I do. You promised to help me get my brother and I west. I'm calling in that promise."

"Our deal, I think, was that you would first earn me Standard."

"And I have. Plenty."

"Not enough to appease my debtors."

"The deal was supposed to be for two weeks, before you blindsided me. I fought with you for three, at least, and I won every time. You got your half of the bargain, I want mine."

"I do not see it this way. What you ask is suicide."

"No. Suicide would be sitting on your ass and doing nothing."

"Is this so? In this case, it sounds more appealing than I would have guessed."

"Does it? Think about it, Marcus. Your world is shrinking. Denver's gone unless you're hiding out here at Gustavo's. How many other impresarios have you pissed off?"

"There are always more towns."

"That still leaves you fighting for Standard. And it looks like those days might be drawing to a close." Her eyes fell to Marcus' sutured arm.

"A small thing. The hazards of the job, yes?"

"And how many more hazards can you afford? How long until your nest egg runs out? Then what'll you pay those gangsters back in Juarez, hmm? Then what'll happen to your family?"

Marcus frowned into his drink.

"I'm not asking you to fight a war, Marcus. I'm not even asking you to draw a blade. What I want is much simpler. And if it works, I promise you, you'll be able to pay your debts in Standard before the week is out."

"I have heard such talk before, Lena. But I suppose I can stand to hear more."

"You know the job you got offered back in that brothel? The one the masked man gave you?"

Marcus rolled his eyes. "I am disappointed, Lena. This job is foolishness. I will not take it."

"I know you won't," Selena said. "But I will."

Harvey Freamon leaned against the stone well, half-heartedly turning a crank. His lower back felt crimped and battered, a piece of sheet metal worked by an ungifted blacksmith into a useless shape. He dug the fingers of his free hand into the flesh above his tailbone, wishing for the thousandth time that Fallowfield's plumbing system extended south of the ramparts. But so little of value ever did.

He'd felt scared for a long time since he and Magnus and the boys took up their treasonous side project. Scared for himself, scared for his friends, scared for his wife and daughter and the unborn child floating in her swollen belly. The fear had been a constant companion, walking silently beside him from morning to night. Whenever he spotted the silo on Magnus' property, the fear would give him an affectionate pat on the shoulder, rub its grimy fingers over his back, whisper a few words of comfort into his ear. *They're coming for you. Shawna can barely feed the tyke as it is. What you think she's gonna eat when you're rottin' in the fields and she and Elaine are sent south?*

When the silo had blown, the fear died in the fallout, and for that Harvey could almost be grateful. Magnus had come to him that night, nearly weeping in impotent rage.

"They fucked us, Harvey! They did something to the mix!"

Harvey wasn't so sure. The chemicals they worked with seemed exotic and dangerous to him, and though Otto Hellmich inarguably had a knack for chemistry, he was nevertheless an untrained novice, fumbling forward on a path darkened by guesswork. And volatile compounds weren't the most forgiving things in the world. Any number of screw-ups could've caused that explosion.

In the wake of his fear came a sense of defeated fatalism. It wasn't good company, but he preferred it to the fear hands down. It didn't press on him, heave its chill breath in his ear, mutter threats. It just sat there, flabby and inert. Harvey could get used to that.

A bucket peeked above the lip of the well, its belly full of trembling water. Harvey locked the crank and poured the bucket into another container, slopping an infuriating amount of hard-won liquid onto the grass. He set the container on a small cart nearby and covered it with a lid. The ground had stolen enough of his labors, he didn't want it snatching up any more.

He unlocked the crank and let it spin as the bucket plopped into the water. His hand tightened around the handle, his shoulders bracing for another pass.

"Excuse me, are you Harvey Freamon?"

A boy stood on the other side of the well. He was well dressed, his dungarees and chambray shirt freshly pressed and free of dirt or wear, but dark circles raccooned his eyes—large and watery behind wire-rimmed spectacles—and his nose looked chafed and runny. He seemed familiar, but Harvey couldn't place him.

"I am. And who might you be, son?"

"My name's Simon. My sister worked for you a while ago. Her name's Selena."

Selena's little brother. The gears clicked into place.

"Your sister was a good woman, son." He winced inwardly. *Was. You damn fool, that ain't what the boy needs to hear.* "She does real good work 'round here. I was sorry to hear what happened, though I s'pose I don't know much about what that was. Have they heard anything new?"

"I …" Simon's mouth hung slack. He shut it with a clack and left, moving at a pace just shy of running.

"Hey, wait up there, son."

Simon paused. Harvey was surprised though as the boy turned it was clear his decision had nothing to do with the farmer's plea. He walked back to Harvey and stomped his foot, as if staking it to the earth.

"I just heard something new," he said.

The story the boy told was long and disjointed and scaffolded with supposition and rumor, but there was enough truth there for it to stand up unassisted, of that Harvey was sure. As he listened the look of curiosity and anger drained from his face. By the time Simon had finished telling him about his excursion into the silo and moved on to eavesdropping on The Mayor, he looked a like a statue of himself, rigid features displaying no perceivable emotion. *Christ, Magnus. You were right. I guess paranoia pays off sometimes.*

"John McCulloch," Harvey said.

"I guess so," said Simon. "I just heard John. It was his barn where … where it happened. He said The Mayor made him set the whole thing up. Just like he made me … you know, in the silo."

"That ain't on you, son," Harvey said. "You were scared and alone. That man used you, just like he used John McCulloch." *Though ol' John's got a lot more to answer for than you, kid. That bastard. No wonder he always seemed to have enough to eat. How long has he been in The Mayor's pocket?*

And how many others were in there with him?

"He said you were the ones who took Selena," Simon went on. "He said you did it for New Canaan. That you were probably making weapons or bombs, and wanted their help to take over Fallowfield."

"I don't know a damn thing 'bout New Canaan. New Confederacy's close as I've ever been to the place. But as for makin' bombs and guns and such, we wouldn't even know where to begin." *Though now I'm startin' to wish we did.*

"I know. It looked like fertilizer or something."

"Close enough for bureaucrats. It was Compound L."

Simon gave Harvey a quizzical look. "Then why did he want to bomb it?"

"Same reason the man does anything. Control."

A large figure clad in black rounded Harvey's farmhouse. Harvey narrowed his eyes. Bernard's slab-of-granite face regarded them without expression. His scarred cheek twitched. Harvey plastered on an enthusiastic smile.

"Say, you been doin' repairs around the farmholds, right? Fixin' up machines and such? You think you could rig up a way to haul this here well water without a crank?"

Simon inspected the crank, brow furrowed in scrutiny. He kept his gaze pointedly away from Bernard.

"I think I could manage it. But maybe it would be easier to just install a pump instead. That way you wouldn't have to empty all those buckets. I'll have to see if we have the parts. Otherwise we may need to talk to Denver."

Harvey gave Simon an approving smile. *The boy's quick. I s'pose by now he's learned he has to be.* "Bernard!" Harvey said, injecting his voice with every ounce of goodwill he could muster for that troll. "Simon here's gonna set me up with an automatic pump! How you like that?"

"He's a clever kid, alright." He put a hand on Simon's shoulder. It wasn't a forceful touch by the look of it, but Simon nearly buckled under its weight all the same. "Let's go check on those parts."

"I know where to find 'em."

"The Mayor thought it best if I kept an eye on you." His eyes jabbed Harvey like pins of frost. "This can be a dangerous place. Ain't that right, Harvey?"

"No doubt about it, Bernard. It's a sad fact, but there's savages everywhere. Even in a nice town like this."

"Say hi to that daughter a yours, Harvey," Bernard said, and led Simon back toward The Mayor's manor. Harvey watched them for a while, then unlocked the crank and set to dredging up another pail of water. Something needed to be done about The Mayor.

Harvey just wished he knew what.

23: A Plague Upon Us

Selena and Marcus stood at the crossroads. The cold nibbled Selena's fingers. She stuck her hands in her pockets and the chill focused on her ears instead. Marcus gave no sign of discomfort. He whistled a meandering tune, the notes hanging in the air for a moment before being snatched away by a sudden gust of wind.

"How long do we have to stand out here?" Selena asked.

"Until they arrive," said Marcus.

"And how long will that be?"

"Who can say? Watches are scarce in the Middle Wastes. Unless one hears the Fallowfield clock tower toll, one must measure time by the sun and stars. For such meetings, 'after moonrise' is as precise as men get. If we are doing this, then we must wait."

"So we wait then."

"If you insist, though to leave might perhaps be not such a bad idea. I admire your thinking, Lena, and your thirst for blood. But you waste your time here, I think."

"We'll see."

Selena rubbed her hands together and stuffed them back in her pockets. When she'd arrived in Fallowfield it had been difficult to imagine it ever being cold, the heat had been so ubiquitous and oppressive. But it retreated a little further every day, yielding minutes to either side of the season's clammy afternoons. Soon it would be driven out altogether, making room for winter, which would make room for spring. And if she wasn't in Visalia by then, the summer would be a dark one indeed for the Republic—and for her.

She heard the man approach before she saw him. He came through the yellow locust, his presence announced by a rhythmic crunching sound. He wore a dustcoat dyed black, its hem flapping around his ankles. A bandanna covered his face, but Selena could tell it was the same man who'd met Marcus in the brothel. His birthmark took on a pale cast in the moonlight.

"Who is this?" the man asked. His voice wore a crust of deliberate gruffness. Selena figured he was aiming for anonymity, but it made him sound faintly absurd, as if he were playing a troll in a children's puppet show.

"This is my associate," answered Marcus. "She will be attending our meeting alongside me."

"We agreed that you'd come alone."

"And there was no way to get a message to you otherwise. We must sometimes roll with the punches, yes?"

The man hesitated and, with an air of resignation, handed Selena and Marcus each a strip of cloth. "You're lucky I brought extras."

Selena held the cloth up to the moonlight. Loose bits of string hung from its frayed edges.

"What's this?"

"A blindfold."

"Is that really necessary?"

"Things have changed. We're not taking any chances."

Marcus tied the blindfold around his eyes and stuck out his hands. "Very well. Lead me."

The man with the bandanna motioned to Selena. "You too."

Sighing, Selena tied on her blindfold. A sliver of vision escaped from the bottom of the fabric. Selena felt fingers tug it into position and the sliver vanished. A callused hand took hers and led her down the road. After a while, the man told them to stop and helped them into the back of a wagon. The creak of axles replaced the shuffle of feet. Marcus whistled until the man told him to stop.

Selena tried to count the minutes they rode, but it was surprisingly difficult. After three or four counts to sixty, time blurred at its edges, minutes dissolving like sugar in water. All she knew was that they rode for a long time, probably at least an hour, before the axles ceased their creaking and the wagon jerked to a halt. Hands guided her from the wagon and steered her into a building. There was a flurry of motion behind her head and the blindfold came free.

They stood in a lodge of some kind, a long low building with walls of intercut logs. Timber roof beams crisscrossed the ceiling. Three men with bandannas covering their mouths faced Selena and Marcus. The first was the birthmarked man who'd greeted them. The second was older and broader of shoulder, his blue eyes staring balefully from beneath bushy grey eyebrows. The third stood farther back than the others, his form hidden in a loose flowing robe of spun wool. Unlike the other two, this man's face was entirely covered, the bottom half wrapped in a tartan bandanna, the top half shrouded by a crape of shadows hanging from the brim of a straw hat angled low. All three men held rifles, old and plain but serviceable by the looks of them. A fire burned in a stone hearth, dividing the men's cloaked faces into hemispheres of light and shadow.

"Gentlemen," said Marcus. "It is a pleasure to see you all. The parts of you I can see, anyhow."

"It pays to be careful," said the man who'd met them in the field. He dropped the artificial gruffness from his voice—or simply forgot to maintain it—and spoke plainly. "We still don't know for sure whose side you're on."

"I've never been one for sides. It is always so much more pleasant in the middle."

"The middle's gone," barked the old man. "It's us and them. We offered you a job. You takin' it or not?"

Marcus buffed his fingernails on his serape and studied their sheen. "I am not."

"But I am," said Selena.

The hostility vanished, replaced by snorts of incredulity.

"You a hired killer, girl?" The old man asked.

"Hired? No. A killer? I can be. I don't want your money. I want my brother back, and I can't go and get him without help. That's my price. Give me my brother's life and I'll take The Mayor's for you."

"That's not the deal we offered."

"No, but it's the deal you're getting. You want The Mayor gone, I want my brother back. I'll work with you to get what we both want, but I won't be your puppet. We fight together or not at all. And that means dropping the masks."

"I don't think so."

"Suit yourself. But you're breathing a lot of stale air for nothing, Magnus."

Selena grinned at the old man's shock. He and the man with the birthmark raised their rifles. Selena spared a quick glance over her shoulder, measuring the distance to the door. To her left, Marcus remained indifferent—perhaps even oblivious—to the guns. Selena matched his blasé stance. She'd laid her cards down, and the farmers needed to decide whether or not they wanted to play.

"Oh, please. Put your dicks away, you two. This lady ain't out to get us." The man in back pulled down his bandanna and tossed his straw hat aside. He'd been the only one whose identity Selena hadn't be sure of. The answer couldn't have been better, from her perspective.

"You don't know that," Magnus said through his bandanna.

"You think she's gonna sell us out to The Mayor? He'd gun her down before she got the chance." Harvey stepped between the gunmen and Selena. "The girl's got a point. We're in this, whether we wanna be or not. So let's drop the damn bandannas already and talk like adults."

With a snort of contempt, Magnus yanked his bandanna away. David Akros did the same, his young cheeks slightly red where the rough fabric had rubbed them.

"Good," Selena said. "Now we're getting somewhere. You wanted the Mayor dead bad enough to reach out to Marcus. You had to know that was a risk. What's he done to you?"

"We don't have to explain ourselves to you, girl."

"It's Compound L," answered Harvey.

"Tellin' tales outta school, Freamon," Magnus warned.

"She ain't the teacher, though, is she? Her brother did us a good turn. Least we can do is answer the girl's questions."

"What, you mean spyin' on us? Blowin' up my silo? Killin' Otto Hellmich and half a dozen good fieldhands besides? You call that a good turn?"

"None a that's on him, Magnus. We both know who to blame."

"Wait, wait, hold up," Selena raised her hands. "Who blew up?"

"Otto Hellmich," said Harvey. "He was workin' with us on a way to synthesize Compound L. Without it, we can't do nothin' unless The Mayor keeps us supplied, and he's happy to wring every last drop from us in return and let us starve through the winter. We lose a couple a good men each frost, and this summer was especially bad. My daughter's pregnant and I been watchin' her getting' skinnier instead a fatter. That ain't a pretty thing to see, 'specially for your own flesh and blood." Harvey paused, swallowed, continued. "Mayor knew as well as we did that if we could get Compound on our own, then we wouldn't need him as much as he needed us. So he had your brother plant a bomb."

"Simon wouldn't do that," Selena countered.

"He didn't know it was a bomb," Harvey explained. "For all he knew it was a radio transceiver. Mr. Mayor just wanted to do a little snoopin' to figure out who was responsible for your disappearance. He was so sad 'bout it at all."

"Yeah, it must've broken his heart," Selena said. And in a way, she supposed it had—since she'd had the data stick in her pocket at the time.

"Anyway, your brother's got sense enough to tell somethin' was up when the silo blew, and he pieced the rest together on his own."

"Where is he now?" Selena asked, struggling to keep her voice even.

"The Mayor's manor, I suppose."

Selena bit her lip to keep from shouting. She wanted to berate these cowards for abandoning a boy to the whims of that Machiavellian monster, but it occurred to her that she'd done much the same. Guilt sharpened its claws on her stomach lining.

"We didn't have no choice," Harvey said. "Bernard and the Sheps keep a hawk eye on the kid. The Mayor ain't about to just let him wander off for days on end."

Well, there goes that idea. For a moment, Selena thought one of the farmers might be able to sneak Simon away to safety. Now that didn't seem too likely. It would have to be Plan B, then.

"If we're doing this, we need to act fast. I have an idea that might work, but you're gonna have to be able to muster up some support, and do it quickly."

Magnus frowned. The lines bracketing his mouth grew darker than the mouth itself, which he pressed into a barely visible line. "You ain't our field general, girl. We rush into things, we're gonna end up like Otto."

"You don't have the luxury of time anymore. None of us do." Selena met each of their eyes in turn. "New Canaan is coming."

Magnus blew dismissively through loose lips. "What the hell you mean, New Canaan is coming? New Canaan ain't set one foot in the yellow locust in the fifty years they've been around. Why the hell would they start now?"

"Because they're ready now, that's why. They've taken Niagara, and now they're coming west. By the spring, they'll have the Republic of California."

"You're talking bullshit, kid. Half of us farmers are from the Outer Baronies. Why the hell you think we came out here in the first place? Cause New Canaan don't give a shit about the west."

"Things change, Magnus. I know that better than most people. Why do you think I'm out here in the first place?"

"Cause you're a drifter from the dead cities, probably. Some punk kid who talks a good yarn."

"Where would a drifter get this?" Selena asked, and took out the data stick.

At the sight of the New Canaan sigil, Magnus' face turned a cottage cheese white. His cheeks sagged as if the muscles beneath them all atrophied in an instant. When he spoke, it was with the husk of his former voice. "What the hell is on there?"

As best she could, Selena told him. By the time she finished, all three farmers were studying her with rapt attention. Even Marcus seemed fascinated. But of everyone, Magnus was the most affected. He seemed shrunken somehow, drained of his bluster and left flaccid by its absence.

"If all that's true," he wheezed, "then you've brought a plague upon us."

Selena shook her head. "The plague's in the wind. I'm carrying the cure. New Canaan wants the continent for itself. It has the east, and now it's coming west. The Mayor's in their pocket, and if he's in charge when they roll up, he's going to throw open the gates. And you know what happens when New Canaan conquers fresh territory."

"The Red Theatre." Magnus more mouthed the words than spoke them.

"So what?" asked David Akros. "Even if we get rid of The Mayor, that won't stop New Canaan. A hundred Fallowfields couldn't stand against them."

"No, but the Republic of California can. Only trouble is, they need my help to do it. And I need yours."

Magnus offered no reply. David studied the fire burning in the hearth. Finally, Harvey spoke.

"Okay, if you two ain't bitin', I will. What's this plan a yours, Selena?"

"It's pretty simple. First, we arrange a quick, full-on strike. Wrangle up your fieldhands, the other farmers, and any townsfolk you think might be on our side. Cast a wide net. We'll need as many people as possible. If you spread the word, how many will fight?"

"Selena," Harvey cautioned. "We ain't soldiers. I don't own a gun. I never even fired one. I'd say we could get maybe twenty rifles between the lot of us, and half a those are so old they'd as soon blow our own dicks off as shoot a Shep."

"How many will fight?"

"If we give the full story? I'd bet a couple hundred. But they'll come with pitchforks, not pistols."

"Then do it. Make the call tomorrow night, tell them we ride at dawn the next morning."

"Ain't you listening to Harvey?" growled Magnus. "The Sheps got us outgunned."

"That's why we need to outsmart them."

"There's a problem with your plan," David said. "We can't do a general call to arms and keep the details secret. Even if we hold back as much as possible, we're gonna have to give up the when and where eventually. We've already discovered that The Mayor had one mole. He's bound to have others. Probably dozens."

Selena cracked her knuckles. "That's what I'm counting on."

Part III: Blue Vole

24: There Are No Generals in Chess

Hands burst through the fabric of The Mayor's dream. He reared back, sensations of soft flesh and velvet light clinging to his skin like droplets of rain. The hands kept shaking. As he woke, The Mayor thrust his face into the crook of his elbow, eyes squinched tight. His free hand struck out with blind violence. The assailant grabbed The Mayor's wrist and placed his sunglasses in his grasping hand. Their effect on The Mayor was immediate and calming. He slipped them on and opened his eyes.

Bernard stood over him. Shadows crisscrossed his scarred cheek like threads of inky webbing. The Mayor sat up, drawing forth as much dignity as is possible for a man in pajamas.

"I assume this is urgent."

"Nothing we can't handle, but I figured you'd want to be in the know. We just got word from some of our ears. The farmers are rebelling. They plan to attack Fallowfield at dawn."

The Mayor furrowed his brow. "You can't be serious."

"Heard it from half a dozen different sources. All of 'em are telling the same story. Magnus Hill is calling every farmer and fieldhand to ride into town and put your head on a stick. Roy Karlsson swears on the cross that the old prick had a halberd and was wavin' it like some Harrier conqueror. I'd call the boy a mad fool but he ain't got the imagination for that."

"Well, that certainly sounds … dramatic." The Mayor swung his legs out of bed and began to dress. "How many men does he have with him?"

"Latest talk is around a hundred and fifty, but they're not armed for shit. Maybe half a dozen rifles between them that'll actually fire. A few have bow and arrows they don't know how to use. The ones with more sense got pitchforks, sharpened hoes, booze bombs. Nothing with any range. Twenty Sheps with rifles on the wall could hold 'em off 'til winter if they needed to. They might've had a shot if they'd taken us by surprise, but they didn't."

"I doubt that rabble would pose any real threat if we invited them into my living room. Still, we best take no chances. If they entrench themselves they may prove an annoyance to trade." *And paint a less than flattering picture of my capabilities for Fontaine and his Templars.* "Find every man in Fallowfield with two hands and a heartbeat and deputize him. I want the ramparts thick with bodies. We'll let Magnus and his cronies break themselves on our wall, and once they're sufficiently bloodied we'll ride out and end them."

The Mayor reached for his jacket. Bernard grabbed his shoulder and lassoed a leather strap around his arm. Something cold and heavy thumped against his side. Bernard reached around him and buckled the strap, pulling the weight taut against his ribs. Looking down, The Mayor saw the butt of an automatic pistol rising from a leather holster.

"I've no need of a manservant, Bernard. I can dress myself."

"I gave you one gun already and you stuck it in a drawer. You should be carrying at all times."

The Mayor sighed. "Very well. I suppose one should be armed if one is to step onto a battlefield."

"Respectfully, sir, you aren't going near the wall."

The Mayor levelled his quicksilver gaze on Bernard. "Is it you who commands me?"

"The only chance those fools got is if one of them with a working rifle gets a lucky shot and takes your head off. I don't intend to give 'em the opportunity. If the general goes, the war is over. It's like chess."

"There are no generals in chess. Only kings."

"Well, here there's Mayors. Come on."

Bernard escorted The Mayor to his office.

"Go wake Simon if he hasn't woken already and bring him here. I don't want the boy wandering off into danger."

"Yes, sir."

The Mayor stood at his office window and waited. His cheeks pulled back in a grin so wide it was painful, a lupine flash of hungry teeth shining as brightly as the mirrored lenses floating above them.

Harvey walked north along the cobbled road, his shoulders thrust back to look—and feel—as soldierly as possible. In truth, he felt less like the vanguard of a conquering army and more like a refugee, fleeing with his ragged countrymen from some blight or famine. Behind him marched—well, plodded, really—a hundred farmers and fieldhands dressed in muddy shirts and torn dungarees and armed with whatever junk he and Magnus could dredge up from their barns. Hoes, pitchforks, axes dull from chopping firewood, lengths of ash and poplar, rusty pipes, spears fashioned from kitchen knives affixed to branches with lengths of twine. A Juarezian migrant had scrounged up a longbow from god knows where, and old man Felton wielded a shotgun that was out of date when the Last War was still a hundred years distant, but their only real ranged weapons were a pile of fist-sized rocks and bottles of grain alcohol stuffed with oily rags.

At the head of the troops rode Magnus astride an aged palfrey. Where he'd managed to get a halberd Harvey had no idea, but it lent him the air of a field general, albeit a tin pot one. He raised the weapon as Fallowfield's walls came into view: a band of dirt and stone ten feet high, a ditch dug into the ground before it. Shepherds studded the ramparts like living parapets, a rifle slung over each of their shoulders. *Now there's an army,* Harvey thought sadly. *We ain't but a bunch of puppies goin' up against a wolf pack.*

"Alright men," Magnus growled. "Today's the day we stop getting' pushed around. Today's the day we tell those city folk that they ain't gonna suck our blood no longer. That we ain't gonna starve while they stuff themselves on our hard work. That we ain't gonna shiver through winter in tents and run-down cottages while they roast their butts on a nice warm fire. Today's the day we show The Mayor and his cronies who this city really belongs to. Are you with me?"

A roar from the crowd. *They're really with him,* Harvey thought with wonder. *Them poor dumb fools.*

A group of the stronger fieldhands wheeled half a dozen wagons loaded down with sandbags and rocks. They heaved them as close to the wall as they dared, ducking beneath the first shots as the Shepherds opened fire. When they were about fifty feet away, they turned their long ends parallel to the wall. Fresh fieldhands hacked the wheels to kindling, mooring the wagons where they stood.

Bullets splintered wood and sent up geysers of dirt. A few found their marks, spilling fieldhands and farmers onto the bloody road, but most of the invaders gained safety behind the wagons, where they began lighting the rotgut bottles and hurling them over the ramparts. One bottle struck a Shepherd in the head and set his upper body alight, eliciting cheers from the farmers. When flames danced along the wall, the farmers tried their first charge.

Only a handful even reached the moat. The rest were either cut down or turned back by a hail of rifle fire. The Shepherds moved with quiet precision, taking time to aim and follow through each shot. Others stomped out the flames. Bodies littered the road, the fields. The few farmers who reached the wall hacked fruitlessly at the gate, axes thudding against solid oak. The Shepherds leaned over their parapets and picked them off one by one. Bottles and rocks pelted the wall, causing a nuisance but doing not real damage. The old farmer with the shotgun ran out to give cover fire. There was a muffled bang and his face evaporated into a bloody mist. The gun had backfired. The Juarezian fieldhand quilled the wall with arrows until a sharpshooting Shepherd put a bullet in his eye. A stalky farmer went for the bow and a Shepherd blew his head off. After that, it just lay there, useless but oddly tantalizing.

Harvey watched the scene from behind the wagon, lobbing rocks with a fury he feigned but didn't truly feel. Fear muted his other emotions, covered them like a blanket of new-fallen snow. Above him the sun had barely crested the horizon, its wan light draping shadows over the road as if hoping to hide the ugly scene from view. The bottles kept flying, but the fieldhands looked nervous, and the second charge fell back almost immediately after the Shepherds opened fire.

We came on too fast, Harvey realised, a numb terror caking like rime to the lining of his stomach. The fieldhands' blood was up, adrenaline driving them forward with the single-minded intensity of a gored bull. But the town was well-fortified and the Shepherds well-armed, and in their defiant charge all they'd managed was to bloody their own noses before landing so much as a single punch. If the farmers lost their nerve, fell back before Selena had a chance to do her thing, then they were all as good as dead. Retreat was nothing but slow suicide. They had to win this today, this morning, this *hour*, or they all might as well fall on their pitchforks and save the Sheps the trouble.

With trembling hands, Harvey touched the stem of a bottle to one of the torches until the rag caught and stepped clear of the wagon's cover. Magnus grabbed his bicep. He'd dismounted from his horse as soon as the fighting started. Farm horses were loyal beasts, but skittish and unused to gunfire.

"What're you doin', Harvey? Get back behind here."

Harvey shook his head. "These fools need a bigger fool to lead 'em. And I might be the biggest damn fool there is, buyin' into this plan." Pulling free of Magnus' grip, Harvey hurled the bottle. It twirled through the air, a glittering glass comet trailing a tail of flame, and smashed right in front of a Shepherd, who rolled clear of the shrapnel. It did no damage, but at least it spoiled the man's shot.

You best hurry, girl.

25: The Red Theatre

The earth was pebbly and barren and red with blood. It had drunk a thousand gallons of it over the years, so much that it had taken on a crimson blush even when dry. A buzzing copper smell rose from the baptised dirt. Simon could feel the tendrils of its odor curl around him like seaweed, ensnaring him.

He stood at the bottom of a great amphitheatre. A smear of faces filled the stands, their features strangely liquid. Sneers overfilled their flowing mouths, dribbling onto robes of formless black. Occasionally a face would coalesce within the slurry, a flash of Bernard, Harvey Freamon, John McCulloch. But mostly the horde remained anonymous, its hostile mirth radiating from it like heat from a fever victim's forehead.

Simon hunted for an exit, a fissure in the ring of stone that defined the amphitheatre's bottom. He saw one from the corner of his eye, a portal of light leading out to … Simon didn't know. He had no idea where he was or how he'd gotten here, but he knew he wanted to leave more than anything. So he ran.

The audience seemed disappointed in this decision. Jeers rained on him like arrows, the words physical things battering his face, his chest, his arms. The air, soupy, clung to him, making every step a struggle. The portal inched closer. Simon clawed through the murky air. He could see a silhouetted figure in the hallway running towards him with equal urgency. It was him. Stunned, Simon reached out the portal, felt the cold, implacable touch of its membrane. Not a doorway at all. A mirror. Simon glanced left and saw its twin. Two giant mirrored eyes peered at him. They rose, unearthing a nose, a mouth, a sloping, almost feminine chin.

The Mayor stood, monstrous, behemoth, his coat the night sky, his hands big as cities.

"Only one way out," he tittered, and pointed a colossal finger behind Simon.

The pit was full of crosses. Thousands of them, millions. Figures hung from their wooden planks, writhing, howling. He saw his parents among the thicket of wood and pain and bodies, their faces wrinkly and drooping like deflated balloons. He knew where he was now, and knowing was like holding a ball of razors in his hands—the Red Theatre, Jericho's chief execution grounds. It had grown monstrously since he'd last seen it, spreading outward like a sore on a syphilitic cheek.

Simon stood beneath his parents, their candle wax faces running down their shirts. He reached up to help them, to bear them away from this awful place, but the crosses were much too tall.

"Not that one," A voice said. Sad, familiar. Simon turned.

Selena dangled from the tallest crucifix in the field. Her head hung slack to one side, its right half oozing like a great burst carbuncle. She fixed her remaining eye on him.

"There's room next to me," she said, and lolled her head toward a vacant cross.

"No," Simon said. "I don't want to!"

Great hands seized his shoulders and pulled him aloft. Simon wriggled, helpless as a bug in amber. The hands bore him toward the crucifix, shaking him.

He woke with a muffled cry. Pale green eyes peered down at him from a sombre, mutilated face. Bernard cocked a thumb over his shoulder.

"To the office, princess."

"Now?" Simon rubbed his eyes to get the sleep out of them and also to avoid looking at Bernard. He glanced out the window at the night sky. "Why?"

"Because I said so, that's why."

Simon slipped his glasses onto his face, curious but not terribly bothered. He was used to being watched. The Mayor, citing concerns for Simon's safety, had assigned him a personal contingent of Shepherds, who studied his every move and followed closely at his heels whenever he left the manor. He slid out of bed and followed the big Shepherd down the empty corridor.

The Mayor sat at his desk, which was covered by a large-scale map of Fallowfield and the surrounding region. Stones, coins, and other objects littered its surface. Though obviously assembled in haste, there appeared to be some logic to their placement, with darker-coloured bits clustered on the fields south of town and the light-coloured pieces forming a ring around the city ramparts.

"What's going on? What's this?" Simon motioned to the map.

"Ah, Simon. I'm sorry to say that some of our farmers have resorted to violence to make their displeasure known. Magnus Hill has some of them up in a stink, and is trying, quite in vain, to break through our gates and ransack the town."

"Are we ... at war?"

The Mayor let out a laugh. "The word gives our opponent far too much credit. A few disgruntled farmers beat their pitchforks on our city walls. Our Shepherds have them outnumbered and outgunned. Soon they'll tire and we'll ride out and send them packing."

"Oh."

"You should stay in the manor just to be on the safe side, but there's really no need to worry. Why don't you go paint? Bernard and I have matters well under control."

"O ... okay, sure."

The Mayor flicked his fingers in a small shooing gesture. Simon went into his annex. One of the Shepherds closed the door. Simon sat on the stool, hands folded in his lap. He thought about what the attack on Fallowfield might mean. Could The Mayor have been telling the truth about the farmers? Simon wondered if he'd made a terrible mistake in confiding in Harvey. The man had seemed honest enough—but so had The Mayor. And there was John McCulloch's confession to consider, and the way The Mayor had shot him dead. It was all too confusing.

Sweeping the tumultuous thoughts from his mind as best he could, Simon began mixing pigments on his palette. A sense of calm washed over him as he touched brush to canvas. A confidence that eluded him in every other station of life swelled in his chest, replacing the weak and hollow feeling with something sturdy and tough.

Simon made fast, aggressive strokes with his brush. Paint flashed and whirled and bled, leaping from the canvas in bursts of red and black and silver. It was unlike anything he'd ever done in style and tone. Hours passed like minutes, and soon it was full morning and the painting was complete.

Stepping back, Simon regarded his canvas. It wasn't beautiful, per se. But it was masterful. He would never paint a better one. Setting his brush in a cup of water, Simon turned his head, watched the play of birds out the window. A trail of smoke wound skyward from the Shepherds' barracks. Simon blinked, expecting the image to vanish, but it didn't. The smoke kept coming, pulsing like misty black blood from a split artery. As Simon watched it uncoil, a volley of gunshots rent the air, louder and closer than the others. The conversation in the office grew heated and frantic.

"What the hell is that? What's on fire?"

"Is it the manor?"

"It looks like the barracks."

The Mayor cut through the babble with a word.

"Listen. We need to contain this immediately. It could be a couple of yahoos climbed the wall, or maybe someone inside has decided to throw their lot in with the farmers. In either case, the house is old and the grass is dry. Fire spreads. Half of you build a breakfire, make sure the manor stays clear. The other half, find whoever's responsible and make an example of them. Get to it."

"All of us, sir?" asked one of the Shepherds.

"Yes, all of you. The absolute maximum. You're familiar with the concept, I trust."

"But sir," sputtered another Shepherd. "Shouldn't a few of us stay back to—"

"Keep me safe? I'm not a frightened woman. I'm armed. And how safe can you keep me if the damn place burns down? This manor is built of three-hundred-year-old timber. It'll roast like so many matchsticks. Now do as I say."

The Shepherds tromped out the room, the cacophony fading as they marched down the hallway. Except some remained, it seemed, for The Mayor continued talking,

"I said all of you."

"It's a mistake." Bernard's voice rumbled through the door. "They're trying to lure us out."

"You give these bumpkins too much credit. Some hothead farmer climbed our walls and thinks he has a shot at glory. And if we do nothing, he may. We can't defend this house. It's not a castle. A single well-placed torch could burn it down. Rout them now and they'll no longer be a threat."

"Fair enough. But hold a few men back here, as a precaution."

"To do what? Massage my feet and fix me coffee? They're of more use keeping the grounds in check."

"I don't know about that."

"This conversation is over. Go lead your men, Bernard. If you move swiftly you can take care of the matter and be back here before you've even had the chance to adequately fret."

Bernard left, too, though his stride was slower than the others' had been, more measured. The Mayor sighed. Simon slipped into the office.

"Is everything okay?"

"Certainly, Simon. These farmers are wily creatures, but they're no match for the strength and discipline of our Shepherds. You've absolutely no need to worry. The fighting will be over by lunchtime."

The Mayor's confidence seemed genuine. The Shepherds were soldiers, after all, and the farmers were just farmers. They probably didn't stand much of a chance.

Simon wasn't sure whether that comforted him or not.

26: Technique

The apartment hadn't changed. Selena lay on her bed, arms crossed over her belly, and studied the kidney-shaped stain bulging from the plaster ceiling. She'd come the night before almost as a kind of joke—or perhaps more accurately a moment of quiet reflection, a nod to days past—and had found to her shock that her key still worked in the door. Even stranger, all her stuff was still here. Why hadn't the innkeeper gotten rid of it by now? Was someone still paying rent? And how long would it have continued to stay here if she died this morning? Or, for that matter, if she didn't? Would her things remain indefinitely, the debris of her turbulent trip west floating forever in this still little pocket of space? The thought disturbed her in a way she had trouble articulating—that something so transient could be more permanent than she was.

The first gunshots warbled through the apartment window, tinny with distance. Magnus would be leading his charge against the southern wall. It was time.

Selena slid off the bed. Something under her feet made a crumpling sound. She reached down and picked up a piece of paper. Swirls of graphite described a mountain range, shaded canyons brightening to peaks of negative space. A path wound through the center of the landscape, and on it, two figures walked hand in hand toward the distant background. Selena folded the paper neatly and tucked it in her knapsack. As she did, her hand brushed against the pistol wrapped in a hank of terry cloth. She picked it up and peered into the sliver of bore visible through the cloth, shadows flowing down its chamber. It seemed to carry on forever, a tiny sinkhole worming into darkness.

Outside, the streets felt strange and empty, dredged of the bustle and noise of a typical day. Carts stood unattended, stores shuttered midday, and the absence of merchants allowed the smaller sounds to creep through unimpeded: the creak of signs swinging on iron chains, the groan of the boardwalk as it flexed in the heat of the morning sun, the rustle of dead leaves and litter in the wind. The few people Selena saw seemed cowed by the silence, for they didn't speak and moved quietly. But the stillness was broken on occasion by bursts of shouting and gunfire. There would be no fighting circle in Green Plaza today. A different sort of fighting had taken hold of the town. There would be no submissions or tapping out here. This fight was to the death.

Selena moved toward the noise of battle, but stopped short of its source, instead taking shelter behind a clapboard barn. From around the corner she could spy The Mayor's manor and, a short distance past it, the Shepherds' barracks. She knelt in the barn's slanting shadow. Her thigh muscles soon grew hot and lactic. She shifted her weight, careful to keep tucked within the curtain of darkness falling from the barn roof's overhang. Soon a lone figure emerged from a nearby clutch of forest, a lit Molotov cocktail in his gloved hands. He hurled the flaming bottle through the barracks window and darted back behind the curtain of trees, long black hair fanning behind him.

While Magnus and Harvey had rattled sabres among the farmers and fieldhands, David Akros had taken a dozen of the men they trusted most, armed them with rifles—using up nearly their entire supply—and led them into town under cover of darkness. They camped in the forests overnight as the walls of Fallowfield fortified around them, waiting for the right moment. And it seemed that moment had come.

South of the wall, Harvey and Magnus were playing their part, and now David was playing his. Soon it would be Selena's turn. She wiped a sheen of palm sweat onto the haunches of her jeans and waited for her cue.

A single curl of smoke wisped out the barracks chimney and disappeared on a current of air. A wriggling line followed it, bending in the wind like a child's streamer. The line thickened, darkened. A second line followed out the window, and soon a thunderhead of smoke brooded over the barracks. *Not long now.*

As if reading Selena's mind, a swarm of Shepherds buzzed out of the manor and charged the barracks. They outnumbered the farmers by an easy four to one, each with a high calibre rifle hugged to his chest. They fanned out, forming a wave of muscle and flesh and steel that washed over the field. *Well, at least we've got the element of surprise.*

The lead Shepherd gave a cry and the corps dropped to the ground as one. The move was eerily prescient, as the first shots came from the forest half a second later.

Shit, Selena thought. *Never mind.*

The field erupted in gunfire. The Shepherds crawled forward on their elbows, shooting at the trees. The trees fired back, and occasionally a Shepherd would let out a cry and stop moving, but their advance was inexorable. Soon they'd take the woods, and the farmers' advantage would be nullified.

Selena slinked around the barn and made her way toward the back of the manor, keeping clear of the Shepherds and the guerillas and the crossfire between them. She tried her best to look the part of a fleeing refugee, shoulders curled up, gun stowed inconspicuously in her knapsack.

It was a short dash to the manor's back doors, no more than seven hundred feet or so, but it seemed to stretch on for ages, a Zeno's paradox of static steps that failed to culminate in a trajectory. She forced herself forward, and after an indeterminate period reached the manor's bulbous shadow. The rear door was locked and reinforced with iron crossbeams, but the windows were only glass and they broke easily.

Selena used her elbow, shielded with the stiff cotton of her poncho, and swept away the jagged remnants with the flat of her bowie knife. She tucked her knife into its new makeshift scabbard—a hank of rumpled leather from an old saddle, crudely sewn together and looped with strips of rawhide—and hoisted herself inside.

She stepped down into the dining room where she'd first met The Mayor, the table overlong, the walls festooned with fading portraits. The sounds of the battle grew muddy and indistinct. The manor was the center of this conflict, in a way, yet it felt removed from it, set back along the axis of some unperceivable dimension. Selena moved cautiously through near-silent corridors. She found the staircase and headed toward it.

A fist materialized from a doorway and crashed into her chest. Selena flew backwards, arms propellering, and landed on her side. She reached for her pistol and realized with a twinge of frustrated anguish that she'd never unwrapped it or even removed it from her bag. Her hand found the bowie knife instead. She unsheathed it and lunged. Bernard swatted the blow aside. Selena's grip was unpracticed and poor and the knife flew from her fingers. In its absence, her fists fell into old habits, rising in a boxer's stance. Bernard smiled wanly, his scarred cheek amplifying the effect. He raised his fists to mimic hers.

"They sent you, huh? Funny, I thought it'd be Marcus. Him I'da shot."

Bernard's stance swivelled slightly, and she noticed the antique Magnum slung in a holster at the small of his back. Her fingers danced in their loosened fists. *Get the gun,* she thought. *Hit him quick and hard and get the gun before he realizes he's underestimated you. He wants a fight so bad, give him one.*

"But not me? Why's he so special?"

"Cause he knows how to use a knife, for one. But you're a fists kinda girl, right? And good, from what I hear. You even thumped my boy Kaeric. I wanna know how that's possible."

"I did a lot more than thump him. I slit his asshole throat, ear to ear."

"I suppo—"

She charged as he was replying. An old trick, but it worked. Her left hook connected before his guard was fully up, rattling his teeth. A jet of blood-flecked spittle sprayed from his lips. She followed with a cross but he was prepared this time and the blow glanced off his forearm. Selena went with it, letting her arm drop and scythe around him. Her fingers brushed the holster of his gun, looped under the handle. *Big,* she thought triumphantly, *but slow.*

Bernard's hand snapped down, cocked, and shot forward. His open palm hit her sternum, launching her backward. She landed on the balls of her feet, fists raised, ribs aching from the strike.

Fuck me, Selena thought. *Not slow.*

Selena came in low, arms pistoning at Bernard's midriff. Bernard tucked his elbows and took the punishment, showing no signs of discomfort beyond a few huffs. He swatted her back, a clumsy move but quick, so quick. No boxer, then. She didn't think this one had ever learned the craft. In his case, she figured it'd never made a difference. When you were big and tough and fast, technique usually didn't matter—until, of course, it did. Selena prayed that would be the case today.

Bernard threw a cross. Selena blocked it, but the blow vibrated up to her shoulder. She tucked inward and let the quicker blows that followed bounce off her forearms. Bernard's breath grew labored. Seizing the moment, Selena rushed him. He shoved her back, but not before a right cross split his chin. It was a powerful punch and should have broken his jaw, but his whole face was like concrete.

Blood reddened the gaps between Bernard's teeth. He smiled savagely, spat a blotch of crimson ichor onto the carpet, and continued circling. Selena tried a second charge, but he was expecting her and parried the worst of her punches. His long arms gave him an advantage in range, and he capitalized on it with a haymaker to her ribs. Selena felt the blow ripple upward and set her injured skull ringing. She needed to keep her head well protected if she was to have even half a chance.

Selena came in low, blitzed Bernard's stomach, and slotted an uppercut neatly through his folded arms. His head snapped back violently. He took two lurching steps backward, stumbled, and fell to one knee. Selena rushed forward, hoping to snatch his gun away and end this farce, but Bernard managed to find his feet and pirouette aside.

Bernard's gaze squared on Selena, who tightened her stance to better protect her right ear. Sweat soaked her bandage, making it ripple and sag. Beneath it, her tender skin itched madly. The pulse of blood in her ears felt inordinately loud, the steady beat of drums in the jungle.

Selena closed in, launching jabs and crosses. Bernard huffed, his great chest rising and falling, his inhalations quick and ragged. *He's winded,* Selena thought. *He's tough but he's old, and it's starting to show. I can wear him down.* She thought of the gun, calculating how best to approach, what could serve as a distraction. Her eyes dropped from Bernard's fists, missing the millisecond windup as he brought his left shoulder up and around in a fierce hook.

Agony, high and howling, tore through Selena. Thought evaporated into a mist of pain, and her body caromed into the carpet. Her backpack flew off her shoulders and landed beside her, one strap tangled around her wrist.

Too big, she thought to herself, more disgusted than afraid. *Too fast.* She felt betrayed by the old stories, David and Goliath and all that, the tales she'd sneered at as a cynical teenager yet prayed to in her silent way all the same. *Technique. It was supposed to be all about technique.*

Bernard gave Selena the appraising look of a tradesman untangling a knotty and atypical problem. "You're good, kid, but you got a lot to learn and no time to learn it."

"Still, pretty risky," Selena said. She felt bizarre conversing with the huge humorless man, but couldn't seem to help herself.

"Nah. If you'd showed more pep than I'd counted on I woulda brought in my backup."

He pulled the Magnum from its holster. It was too much gun for the task, but also one of the only pistols that wouldn't look absurd and toyish in his hands—which, Selena assumed, was why he chose it.

"Always have backup. Another lesson someone shoulda taught you sooner."

"I'm worth more alive," Selena said. The words clung to her lips, bilious and syrupy—they came much too close to begging for her taste—but she managed to spit them out. Bernard shook his head.

"No, dead's how he wants you. I've heard him say it to half a dozen guys by now. Dead, not alive, but I've got to bring him the body and everything you got on you. It's an odd request."

Selena tried to rise to a crouch but Bernard waved her down with a shake of the gun.

"I suspect you aren't in the mood to tell me why?" Bernard asked, bending the sentence into a question.

"You wanna know so damn bad? Fine. You used to be a Templar, didn't you?"

Bernard flashed a sarcastic grin. "Gee, how'd you guess?"

Because you're just that big an asshole. "I'm getting better at picking out accents. You ever heard of the Diocese of Plague?"

"Course I have. What's your point?"

"My mom and dad got some of their intel. They gave it to me to sneak out of the country. Everything you need to know about their biggest weapon."

"I got plenty of weapons already, thanks."

"Not one worth nearly as much as mine. You know how badly New Canaan wants this thing back? They're marching halfway across the damn continent for it, right? Well, The Republic wants it even more. They promised my folks a hundred thousand Standard for it. And that was just for a copy. You could sell this puppy in every state from here to *la Republique du Quebec.*"

"That so?" Indifference, heavy as a stone wall. But was there something else hiding behind it? A flicker of desire, maybe?

"It's yours, if you want it. All you need to do is help me and my brother get out of here."

Bernard snorted. "Or I can kill you. Three guesses which one's easier."

"You kill me and all you'll get is a lump of plastic. This thing's encrypted, and only I know the code."

"I bet I could get it from your brother quick enough. A few broken fingers usually do the trick."

Selena laughed. She was surprised how easily the sound escaped her lips. "You think *Simon* knows? I can barely trust that kid enough to tell him the time."

Selena could see Bernard's mind working behind his stone mask. Was he thinking of the money? Or maybe just the glory of outsmarting her, getting the code and delivering the payload to his boss? Selena didn't much care either way. The important thing was that he was listening.

"Look, you want to see it?"

Bernard let out a snort of incredulity. "You think I'm stupid?"

"Please. It's in my front pocket. You think I could fit a weapon in here?" She motioned to her jeans. The denim hugged her hip. It was true; she could barely fit a pocket knife in there, let alone a gun.

Selena reached into her left pocket. She moved slowly, almost casually, channeling Marcus' poise. As she dug out the data stick, her right slipped subtly behind her, creeping into her knapsack and closing around the pistol. Her finger wormed its way through the cloth and into the trigger guard. She removed the data stick and held it up to Bernard. He stared at the object, his aim drifting off mark by a hair.

"Damn, kid. You weren't kidding."

"I don't kid," Selena said. Then she whipped her arm around and fired.

The bullets shot up through the knapsack and into Bernard's abdomen with a buzzy hornet sound. Bernard grunted. He fired back but Selena was already rolling and the bullets found only the floor. They tore up the carpet and sent splinters of hardwood gusting into the air.

Blood cascaded over Bernard's fingers, which he pressed to his punctured abdomen. His other hand held the gun, and he took aim with it single-armed. Selena leveled her pistol, still wrapped in terry cloth, at Bernard's head. The cloth hid the sight and obscured the barrel and she could only aim generally, but she feared a chest shot wouldn't kill him. The bullet grazed his uninjured cheek. Bernard shot back, his gun a dragon's roar to her mosquito whine, and the chunk of doorframe over her shoulder exploded. Selena ran at him, zigzagging to foil his aim. She dropped low, jabbed the barrel under his armpit, and fired.

Bernard juddered like a machine with a broken motor. The Magnum slipped from his fingers. He took two steps and fell to his knees. Blood poured from his side, his belly, his mouth. His cheeks turned the ashen white of a virgin canvas marred with two terrible slashes, one fresh and ragged and sodden with crimson pigment, the other old and gnarled and black. He collapsed.

Selena grabbed the Magnum, flicked on the safety, and tucked it in her bag. She watched Bernard's huge body twitch, the last of him spoiling one of The Mayor's many Turkish carpets.

"Fuck technique," she said, her voice hoarse.

She stripped the cloth from her pistol and took a firing stance, waiting for the flood of Shepherds to cascade over the railings and through the doors to drown her. None came. She adjusted the knapsack's weight on her back and climbed the stairs, wincing absurdly at each creak—if they didn't hear the gunshots, a creaky floorboard wasn't about to tip them off. Her bandages, grimy with sweat and windblown dirt, had come loose in the fight. They hung from her chin like a waddle. She tore them free and tossed them away. Her injured ear sizzled. The pain buzzing through the right side of her skull was so strong and constant it was almost audible, a cicada of misery nesting in her temple. She clenched her jaw until the buzzing subsided and began climbing the stairs.

27: Three Is a Good Number

Simon sat in front of his easel, pretending to paint. He thought about Jericho and New Canaan, about the crystalline shards of fear that had jabbed him a thousand times since he'd left. Somehow, that sharper terror had been less unpleasant than the fear he felt now, which was limp and brown as gutter slush in a city winter. On his journey with Selena, he'd feared a lot of things: starvation, robbery, pursuit by New Canaan's Templars, cannibals, goblins, the slurry of a thousand tales and fables bubbling up from his subconscious after nightfall. They were things that could happen—or that he convinced himself could happen in the valley of time between dusk and dawn—but with Selena beside him, they seemed surmountable. Now, sitting on his wooden stool in the center of a crumbling city, the culmination of his fears seemed inevitable. And if what he feared was inevitable, then the fear served no purpose. It just sat there in his belly like a broken battery, leaking its caustic fluid.

A flurry of bangs rattled the house. Simon dropped his brush. He slid from the stool and ran into the office where The Mayor had been studying his map. He could tell The Mayor had heard it too, for he wore an odd expectant look on his face.

"I think those came from inside."

"A simple trick of acoustics, my boy. Often sounds from the field or even the town proper can play strange tricks on us here, particularly on still days. But all the same, I should perhaps take a look."

The map of Fallowfield crinkled beneath his fingers as his pushed himself upright. He stepped toward the door and set one mirrored eye to the antique keyhole.

"As I suspected," he said. "No one the—"

The last word stopped as if severed by a cleaver. The Mayor pulled his gun from its holster, its barrel trembling.

"Go in the office, Simon. There may be a confrontation and I don't want you to see it."

"But—"

"There's no need to be afraid, but please heed my words. Whatever happens, whatever you hear in this office, stay in your annex and do not come out until I say so. Understood?"

"I—"

"Understood?" The Mayor repeated, more sharply.

Gulping, Simon nodded.

After barely surviving Bernard's ambush, Selena treaded with exceeding caution. Every step was weighed and considered, every doorway studied, every creak and shift of the house analysed for source and intention. She found it hard to believe that Bernard would be the only Shepherd left in the manor, yet the persistent silence told her otherwise. It seemed David and his men were still holding them off, though for how much longer? The sound of gunshots rattled through the walls. Had they gotten louder, swelling in volume as the Shepherds converged on the manor? There was no way to tell; the hall was windowless, its corridors silent save for the battle noises intruding from outside. She'd best do this quickly, or there was a good chance she wouldn't get to do it at all.

Selena recited the directions in her head, counting steps like rosary beads one after another: up the stairs, right at the top, around the bend, end of the hall. She rounded the corner in a single swift turn, pistol cradled in both hands, its barrel slicing the air. The hallway was empty. At its end stood a door, much like the others yet imbued with eldritch power, a portent thrumming its message in an alien tongue. How many Shepherds stood behind it? Surely they were expecting her, or at least someone, to be heading their way. Even with the battle roaring outside, the Magnum's thunderous discharge would have carried up here. Part of her expected to be gunned down before she reached the door, high caliber bullets tearing through the hardwood. She reached the door and listened. Silence hummed on its other side. Her eyes traced the contours of the oak door's grain, as if the room's contents were printed in its undulations.

For an uncountable moment, she balanced on the edge of the doorway's precipice, pivoting between retreat and advance, delay and a headlong rush forward. The door watched her in stone-faced silence. She could stand here forever, she realized, and learn nothing more than she already knew. Forward was death, more likely than not, but to go backward was to relinquish Simon to The Mayor. It was an ugly way to think about her brother, as a prize to be won or forfeited, but she couldn't shake the thought free any more than she could leave Simon behind.

With a final breath, Selena kicked the door open.

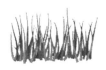

The Mayor licked his upper lip, noting the salty film that covered it. His normally steady hands shook. Behind him, he could hear Simon delaying his walk to the annex, shuffling his feet and nervously fumbling with the drawers of The Mayor's desk. He was about to give another verbal nudge when the boy disappeared into the annex of his own accord. *Thank god for small favors.*

He crouched lower and took another glance through the keyhole. Selena Flood was walking straight toward him. Her right ear was a bloody stump. She held a pistol out vaguely in front of her.

Months of fruitless searching, and she was walking right into his arms. Of course, she was walking into Simon's as well. If the boy so much as glimpsed her, handling him would become a lot more challenging. Doable, certainly, but unpleasant. *Better to have his trust than his ire, at least until Fontaine gets here.*

He would have to ruin her face. From there he could claim she was an anonymous farm girl who'd somehow clawed her way past the Shepherds. Simon wasn't about to inspect a corpse too closely. He'd take The Mayor at his word.

The Mayor grinned, immensely pleased with himself. In a stroke, he could take for himself what his army of Shepherds had failed to deliver. He tucked himself against the wall, rested pistol's barrel against his cheek, and waited.

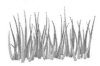

Selena's foot struck the door just below the handle. The door swung inward, a shower of splinters raining from the place where the latch scraped the jamb. Selena let the momentum of her kick carry her inside, pistol drawn, pupils wrenched wide as possible, drinking in everything.

The room was empty, her gun trained on bare space above an ornate mahogany desk.

A revolver laid a cold round kiss on her wounded temple. The Mayor's smile enveloped his face. Selena could see her distorted reflection in his aviator sunglasses, all eyes and nose and bulging forehead. The gun's gaping bore ground painfully into her temple.

"So long, you little bitch."

A roar and a flash tore open the world. Selena fell backwards, caught herself on the doorframe, and realized with a blink of wonder that she was still alive. Another gunshot sounded, this one dull and muffled in her ringing ears, a cough in a crowded theatre. The Mayor jerked back. A red hole opened in his satin blazer, puckering three inches above a similar one. Two shots had hit him, though Selena hadn't heard the first one at all; the roar of The Mayor's gun had overwhelmed it completely, though all he'd managed to do was punch a hole in his chestnut wainscoting.

The Mayor dropped to one knee. His glasses flew from his face, revealing a pair of milky blue eyes staring off in incompatible directions. The left trained its cold gaze on Selena while the right glared stupidly at the wall. He scrambled for his glasses ineffectually, flailing his gun at Selena and firing wildly. Bullets rushed past her on all sides, one passing close enough by her left ear that she heard the buzz of its jet trail. She pushed The Mayor over and kicked the pistol from his hand. It skittered under a table.

Across the room, Simon stood behind The Mayor's desk, both hands wrapped around the butt of a revolver. Rivulets of sweat ran into his eyes. He blinked them away, his arms so stiff they could've been mounted on a tripod. A hitching moan issued from his throat like the clicking of an exotic insect.

"I, I saw you," he managed. "I peeked through the doorway and I saw you. And he had a gun and he, he was gonna ..."

The clicks came again, telegraphing his speech in dots and dashes.

Cordite singed Selena's throat. She coughed it away, crossing the room to Simon, who kept his gun up as if warning her to stay back. For a moment, she thought he might shoot her, not out of anger but out of blind panicking reflex.

"I know," Selena said. "Thanks."

Simon's mouth flapped but made no sound. Selena put a hand on his and gently lowered the gun. Simon threw his arms around her, squeezing with surprising strength. Selena hugged him back. They stood that way for a moment, an eye of calm amidst the chaos howling around them.

"How," Simon said. It seemed to be all he could get out. He swallowed, gathered saliva, tried again. "Where ... what happened to your ear?!"

"Soon," Selena answered, rubbing his shoulder and gently loosening his grip. "We'll talk about everything soon. Right now, we need to get out of here."

A wailing siren rent the air. The Mayor's bloody hand curled around a small rectangular device. His fingers went slack, as if pressing the button had drained the last of his strength. He let out a wheezy, rattling breath and lay still.

A clamber of boots trampled back into the building as the Shepherds flooded toward the source of the sound. Selena levelled her pistol and stepped forward, ready to fight her way out. If they ducked into one of the bedrooms, they might make it through an initial search. From there—

Simon touched Selena's wrist.

"Not that way. Come on."

He led her into the annex, where a canvas stood on a plywood easel. On the canvas was The Mayor as seen through the eyes of a biblical prophet, proud and scowling and rendered in brushstrokes harsh and bright as tongues of flame. They filled the canvas with swoops and twists and whirls, a vortex of crimson and ocher and charcoal black coalescing into a single hellish, chiasmic figure, a ghoul haunting the ragged gulleys on the outer fringes of the universe. His eyes, twin blobs of quicksilver, gazed at Selena.

"Neither the time nor place, I know, but this is really good, Simon. Has he seen this?"

"I don't think so. I guess now he never will. Come on!" He ran to the back corner of the room and threw open the window. Beyond it, a wrought iron trellis crisscrossed its way to the ground. Threads of ivy wove through the bars. Selena grabbed the trellis and tugged to test its sturdiness. The metal was rough but strong, the bolts firmly fastened to the building's frame.

"Go," Simon said, and ran back to the office.

"Simon, what are you doing? We have to leave!"

"Go on, I'm coming. I just need to get something." He darted through the door and disappeared beneath The Mayor's desk, returning a moment later with a black case hanging by a strap from his shoulder. He stuffed the gun in the waistband of his pants and grabbed the trellis.

Selena followed Simon down. She climbed with one hand, her other gripping the butt of her pistol. The siren kept screaming, its voice hysterical and needle sharp.

By the time they reached the ground her wounded ear was buzzing and her palm was coated with rust. She wiped the hand on her poncho, ignored the pain and ran for the forest. Her heart was an overheating boiler stoked with a surplus of adrenaline. She looked to her left and the boiler misfired.

A phalanx of armed men charged at her, truncheons ticking furiously back and forth. Sunlight turned their Shepherd pins the blinding white of lit magnesium. There were eight of them, each heading straight for her and Simon.

"Simon! Down!" she screamed, and threw herself at the grass. Her chin struck the dirt hard, sending shockwaves of pain through her injured ear. Warmth trickled down the side of her face. *Great. The fucking thing's split again.*

A fog of bullets rolled over them. Selena squinted through her pistol sights, squaring each target before she fired. The Shepherds took on a magnified clarity. She could see the gape and pucker of their pores, trace each hair to its follicle, chart each mole and freckle with the mathematic fidelity of an astronomer mapping stars. One Shepherd fell, then another, each an eternity apart. She was dimly aware of Simon on the ground beside her, but whether he'd dropped on her command or after taking a slug to the chest she had no idea. She sighted a third Shepherd, fired, and cursed as the bullet only grazed his side. They were approaching too fast. A bullet burrowed into the earth beside her right leg, spraying her with bits of grass and dirt. Another exploded six feet in front of her face, sending up a geyser of debris. She could hear the chorus of their labored breathing, feel their trampling approach like buried thunder. *One more. Let me get three. Three is a good number.* She squinted through the dust, locked the front sight on a red-haired man's chest—

The Shepherds jerked and screamed as if struck by a plague of palsy. Blood spurted from dozens of fresh orifices. A few charged and died and a few fled and died and the rest just stood there and died, the whole group cleaved neatly as a crop of rapeseed beneath her sickle. Selena stared at the carnage with stupid wonder, turned, and saw the farmers, their faces masked with bandannas, breaking through the trees. They descended upon the Shepherds, put rifles to their heads, and fired. Hands grabbed Selena under the armpits and hoisted her upright. She turned and saw Harvey Freamon's chestnut eyes staring out from above a blue tartan cloth. He held a high calibre rifle in one bloodstained hand—a Shepherd's gun, by the look of it.

"All right, Selena?" he said, his forehead lined with worry. He reached out to her ear. She smacked his hand away.

"Simon! Is Simon okay?!"

"He's fine, girl. It's you I'm worried about."

"Me?" Selena touched her face. Her fingers came back wet with blood. The world clenched down, a howling darkness swirling about its edges. The disc of light and color that encompassed the world shrank, its edges dissolving. Selena took two steps backward and tumbled over the side.

28: A World Left to Conquer

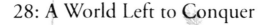

Selena's eyes opened. Starched sheets crinkled beneath her as she stretched, working kinks out of stiff muscles. Something held her left arm in place. She turned and saw Simon sitting beside her, clutching her hand in both of his. Selena reached over with her free hand and brushed a lock of hair from his forehead.

"Simon," she said.

"Selena," he mouthed, his breath hitching. "I thought you'd die. I thought you'd showed up after all those weeks just to die. I ..." His sentence crumbled into sobs. Selena pulled him in close, her arms wrapping around his narrow shoulders. He'd gotten thinner since she'd last seen him, the nascent flesh he'd gained in Fallowfield once more wasting away.

"Hey," she said. "Hey."

"It's all been so unfair!" he wailed. "Everything that's happened! Why should this be any different?"

"It is, though," Selena answered, her palm tracing circles on Simon's back. "That's the important thing. It *is* different."

Someone knocked on the door. It was only then that Selena took in her surroundings. She was on a lumpy mattress suspended from the floor by a plain metal frame. To her right was a metal trolley stacked with salves and gauze and polished steel implements. To her left stood a nightstand and a chair on which Simon sat, and beyond that a couple of cupboards. A hospital room, by the looks of it, albeit a very small one. Three paces at most separated the foot of her bed from the door, where the knock gently repeated itself. Moans and coughs and the brisk chatter of orderlies carried through the thin walls. Clinics were crowded places after a battle; Selena was surprised she had a room to herself, even one this size.

"God, I'm so sick of hospitals," she muttered. "Come in!" Her voice turned hoarse and pained when raised above a whisper.

Marcus and Harvey crowded into the tiny room. Neither man was particularly big, but the space was small enough to feel cramped with their presence. Marcus looked deeply uncomfortable, clutching his elbows with opposite hands and chewing the corners of his mouth. Harvey, by contrast, beamed, brown eyes glittering with something like paternal pride.

"Well hell, girl, you're harder to kill than the locust, I think."

"But not half so pretty," Selena added, pawing gingerly at her bandage. The pain had receded, leaving behind it a pervasive itch that clung to her skin in a greasy film.

"I'm happy to see ya, all the same. You too, son."

Simon mumbled thanks, doing his best to hide his tear-stained cheeks.

"What'd I miss?" Selena asked.

"The Sheps had us pinned. We couldn't even've retreated without losin' half our men. Then we heard some siren and they all went runnin' back to the manor. A few fieldhands hopped the wall and opened the gates for us and we stormed inside, pickin' up whatever the Sheps had left behind. Got ourselves some a their extra rifles." He paused, his brown eyes brimming as they met Selena's. "You saved us, girl."

"I guess that makes us even."

"It ain't just that. None a us would've had the stones to go against The Mayor. Not straight up like you did. The man had a hold over this town. I think that's gone."

"So you mean—"

Harvey, sensing her question, shook his head. "No, he's still holdin' court, far as we can tell. He's hurt bad, though. Half the Sheps who rode in on that siren a his have up and defected. I s'pose with Bernard dead and The Mayor shot to hell, they don't see much of a future for their profession. We figure the rest'll cave altogether the second he stops breathin', but who knows? Maybe them that stayed are plannin' a last stand in his honor."

"What are you doing with the defectors?"

"We treat 'em kindly enough. They hand over their weapons and they're free to go on their merry way. Some've joined up with us, helpin' out with repairs and such. We don't give 'em guns and we don't let 'em guard the manor, though we do let 'em wander free nearby. That way the others still inside can see they'll get a fair shake with us."

Selena nodded approvingly. "So where does that leave us?"

"That there's the question, ain't it? Magnus and David are debatin' 'bout it now. Magnus wants to burn the damn thing down. David's tryin' to talk them boys into coming out peacefully."

"And what do you think?"

"Magnus is all bluster, same as usual. He ain't any more into bloodshed than the rest of us. If we gave in, he'd badger us out of it, actin' as if the damn thing was our idea all along. David's way is better, but I don't s'pect it'll gain much ground. That Mayor's stubborn as a stone mule."

"So what, then? Kick your way in?"

"That'd be awful messy. They're still a bunch a tough nuts. I'd as soon wait 'em out. Magnus already cut off the water pipes. They gonna get real thirsty real quick."

"Good. I wouldn't mind seein' that bastard crawl out on his hands and knees."

"I don't blame you. But all the same, I think you'd best be on your way."

Selena puzzled over Harvey's comment. *That was a quick switch.*

From surrogate daughter to tossed-aside drifter in under a minute. "Am I that big a hassle?"

"It ain't that." Harvey scratched the back of his head. "It's just, The Mayor ain't the only thing we have to worry about."

Selena's face went a stony grey. In the heat of the battle, she'd forgotten about the very thing that had spurred it on in the first place. New Canaan was coming. Selena grabbed Harvey's wrist, her fingers leaving divots in his ruddy flesh.

"Come with us. Gather your family and the other farmers. We'll leave this morning. Now."

Moving gently but firmly, Harvey pried Selena's grip free. He shook his head. "Can't do it, girl. This is our land. We've sweated over it, bled over it, fought for it. None a these boys are gonna leave that behind."

"But you'll be in danger."

"Maybe so. But if you don't get gone with that stick a yours, we gonna be in danger no matter where we go. If New Canaan's really comin',' then we all in it up to our necks. Sounds as though you the only one can dig us out again."

"But even if we high tail it west, we won't make it to New Washington before New Canaan makes it here."

"Well, when they show up they might find we shitkickers got more fight to us than they suspect. 'Sides, they gonna be busy enough trackin' you down. Might be they'll let us alone for the time bein'." The confidence in Harvey's voice suggested he really believed this, though his eyes said otherwise.

Selena gave a hesitant nod. "In that case, I guess we'd better go."

Marcus coughed into a closed fist. His usual composure was nowhere to be seen. He shifted from foot to foot, rubbing his bicep with one hand. "I do not wish to be heartless, but there is still the matter of my payment."

"Sorry, son," said Harvey. "The merchants all bolted the second they caught wind a trouble. They and their money'll be half a day in the wind by now. 'Less you wanna take rapeseed instead a Standard, I'm afraid you're outta luck."

"No," corrected Selena. "His luck's just coming in."

Selena's pronouncement was met by a barrage of puzzled and skeptical looks. Even Marcus seemed doubtful, though he twirled his hand, motioning for her to continue.

"I can get you the money you need. Follow me."

Simon put a hand to her chest, preventing her from sitting up. "Wait." He turned to Harvey and Marcus. "Could we have a minute?"

"I wouldn't take more than that, kid. You're livin' on borrowed time."

The two men stepped into the hall, leaving Selena and Simon in the tiny room. Simon undid the clasps on the briefcase he'd taken with him and removed a slim rectangle of brushed metal.

"Is that a lightbook? Where did you even get that?"

"The Mayor had it. I think he wanted it to read what was on the data stick."

He uncoiled the cord on the light book's charger and tilted its solar disk into the sun. Its green-checkered face glinted as it drank in sunlight. Simon plugged in the cord and the computer beeped to life. He held out his hand.

"Can I have the stick?"

Selena fished the data stick from her pocket. She held it in her palm, flexing the muscles in her hand around its blunted contours. Giving it up, even to her brother, took a great deal of effort. She watched as he connected the stick to the computer port. The computer emitted a satisfied beep. Simon scrolled through the stick's contents: folders full of coordinates and schematics and transcribed bits of conversation. One folder stood out from the rest, in that it held only a single text file. Simon opened it, filling the screen with the opening slide of a ninety-eight-page report entitled *Blue Vole*.

"Blue Vole?" Simon asked.

"Never heard of it," said Selena. "Some sort of new weapon, maybe? Or a piece of equipment?"

The pages scrolled downward, line upon line of technical jargon. It wasn't until they reached the first imbedded image that Selena began to realize what Blue Vole might be. The picture showed a cross-section of a herbaceous plant with a narrow stalk. Blue leaves jabbed like rapier blades from its tip, and its roots unspooled in tangles across the bottom of the page. Despite its cobalt cast, the grass seemed far too familiar. The roof of Selena's mouth grew tacky and dry. She swallowed a ball of gluey saliva.

"It's yellow locust. Only worse."

Simon scrolled down farther, and now coherent phrases burst through the blather: *Virulence increased 9.76-fold from prototype – extended growing season – advanced root system fragmentation eliminates possibility of manual removal – resistance to compounds L, O, Q.*

Selena shut the screen and yanked the data stick from the port.

"Why?" Simon cried. "Why would New Canaan make something like that?"

"The same reason they—or whoever—did it last time."

Simon's eyes swallowed his face. "Break it, Selena. You have to break it. They can't make more of this stuff. It'll kill everyone."

"Not everyone," she said, pocketing the stick. "Just the people they want it to."

"Selena!"

"You think this is the only copy? They'll have a dozen backups of this thing. We break this one and all we do is put ourselves in the dark."

Simon touched his fingertips together. "What are you going to do with it?"

"What mom and dad asked me to do. Bring it to the Republic. Give it to Hoster Telaine."

"But what good will it do? It won't stop New Canaan from making the stuff."

Selena ran her thumb over the stick's plastic chassis. "Maybe it will. Mom and dad told me the Republic needed this to survive. The Blue Vole must be the reason. Maybe that file also has a way to stop it."

"You think so?"

"Why would New Canaan make a weapon it couldn't control? The Archbishop's evil, but he's not suicidal. He'll want a world left to conquer once he's done with the Republic."

Selena stood. Her vision browned out and a wave of dizziness swept her backward. She clenched her teeth and braced and eventually the feeling passed. Simon tugged at her shirtsleeve.

"Where are you going?"

"To get Marcus his money."

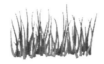

Green Plaza had never been so empty. The few people wandering its boardwalks did so with glazed, sleepwalker's expressions, feet scuffing along in half-hearted strides, hands loose at their sides. There was no banter, no cry of vendors from carts or market stalls, no drunks braying donkey laughter as they tumbled out tavern doors. The farmers weren't foreign conquerors, and so the city lacked the grisly pandemonium common to most sacked towns. No buildings burned, no looters plundered, no women lay raped and battered in alleyways, no townsfolk hung from lampposts or rotted in gutters. It was probably the most peaceful invasion in recorded history, and for that, Selena was grateful. But in place of the terror and chaos drifted a soft-spoken awkwardness. Selena felt it churning in her guts, a sense that the ground had shifted in a fundamental way and no one, including her, quite knew the right way to stand any longer.

Selena crossed the square to the eastern road and stood before Fallowfield Bank and Trust. It was an impressive structure, at least by Fallowfield standards. Two stories of red brick atop a limestone foundation, it was the only building in town—apart from the jail-cum-courthouse—not made from wood. This, combined with its stout walls and barred windows, gave it an imposing stature.

"I dunno how I feel 'bout this," Harvey said.

"Little late for cold feet, Harvey." Selena knocked on the door. Built from solid iron, it rattled in its jamb and left Selena's knuckles smarting.

A strip of metal in the door slid aside, revealing a pair of bulging eyes. They regarded Selena as if she were something a dog had chewed up and spat half-digested onto the stoop.

"Go away!" shouted a high, reedy voice beyond the door. The viewing strip clacked shut. "We're closed up."

"It's okay," Selena said. "You're safe."

"In *here* I am."

"The fighting's over. You can come out now."

"You a Shep?"

"No, I'm not a Shepherd."

"Guess it wouldn't matter even if you were. Captain himself told me to close up shop and not open until I got his say so."

"Captain?"

"Of the Sheps," explained Harvey. "Big ugly fella, name a Bernard."

"You aren't gonna hear from him any time soon, I'm afraid. He's dead, and the Shepherds are disbanded."

"I ain't openin' up for no Harriers, you can bet your ass on that. You just wait 'til The Mayor hears about this."

This poor asshole's gonna have a real rude awakening when he steps out of there. Unless he starves to death first "What's a Harrier?"

No response. Harvey rolled his eyes and banged on the door with the butt of his fist.

"For God sakes, Kyle, open up. You can't live in there forever."

" ... Harvey?" The viewing slot opened again, the bulging eyes less hostile, more searching. "Harvey, that you?"

Selena stepped aside, allowing Harvey to take her place in front of the viewing slot.

"It sure as hell ain't the Archbishop a New Canaan."

"I got my orders, Harvey. I can't open the door."

"There's been some changes. The Mayor ain't Mayor no more."

"What?! Then who is?"

Harvey opened his mouth, closed it. He looked as if he was only just now considering the question. "I guess we'll have to wait an' find out. But you gonna get awful hungry if you stay in there 'til we do. Now how's about you open the door, huh?"

There was a pause, during which Selena assumed Kyle had either stopped listening or left to get a rifle. But soon, a deadbolt slid home, tumblers rattled, and the door swung open, revealing a stoop-backed kid with greasy hair, a constellation of pimples aglow on his sallow cheeks. He couldn't have been more than a few years older than Selena. He wore a smartly tailored suit that only emphasized his strange dimensions, arms too long, legs bowed inward. *This guy runs a bank?*

"Where's Mr. Peters?" Harvey asked.

"He left town in an armored caravan. They all did, once they heard there was trouble. Not me though, I came to work, just like I always do. Then the Captain told me to shutter the place, though I reckon he's not the Captain no more, is he?"

"Fraid not."

If this bothered Kyle, he gave no sign. He led Selena and Harvey into a musty room divided lengthwise by a long, marble-topped counter. Checkerboards of light lay atop threadbare carpets, their arabesque patterns sun-bleached and pale. Behind the counter ran a matrix of locked metal boxes, each festooned with a tiny placard bearing a number in faux-gold print.

"Mr. Peters didn't want me to be doin' no big business without him, but if you wanna talk about another loan or somethin', I guess I could do that."

"Actually, we want to make a withdrawal," Selena said. "But not from Harvey's account. From The Mayor's."

Kyle's tongue circled his lips. He glanced from Selena to Harvey, wiping his hands on the front of his pants. Selena stared back impassively, Harvey with an apologetic twitch of the shoulders.

"You got a letter of authorization?"

"We do not, but I would be happy to sign for you." Marcus slipped from the shadows by the doorway, switchblade glinting in his hand.

"In red ink, yes?"

Harvey clutched his forehead. "You were supposed to wait outside."

"You can't do this!" Kyle cried. "The Sheps'll get you 'fore you leave Green Plaza."

"Damn you, Kyle, are you really that big a fool?! There ain't no Shepherds comin' for him or anyone else! They're gone! The Mayor's gone! Put that through your thick skull and get the girl her goddamn money!" Harvey's voice boomed in the closed space. The effect on Kyle was withering. He folded into himself, thin arms curling against his chest, and slinked away, keys rattling in his trembling fingers. He opened half a dozen of the metal drawers and pulled out stacks of currency—mostly Standard, though there were Juarez pesos and New Confederacy notes, even a slim pile of dollars from the Republic of California.

"Mr. Peters took the vault keys with him. All I got's the small stuff. You want more you best come back when he's here and shake him down. I'd like to see how that goes!"

Selena thumbed through one of the piles. The smallest denomination was twenty Standard, though several piles were of hundreds. *This is the small stuff? What kind of grift was The Mayor running on this town?* She waved Marcus forward, who swept the bills into a burlap sack. Harvey looked ill. He swallowed, a wet audible sound that filled the silent room.

"That's just The Mayor's accounts, yeah?"

Sulking, Kyle nodded.

"That's good. You don't gotta hand out any money to anyone else, okay? We'll get some men on the door. They won't be Shepherds, but they'll keep you safe. And don't you fret about Mr. Peters. We'll sort it out with him. No one gonna blame you for nothin'. Understood?"

Harvey clapped Kyle on the shoulder. Kyle wriggled free of his touch, hands stuffed into the pockets of his suit. He studied the underside of the counter.

"We should go," Selena said.

The door slammed shut behind them, tumblers clattering. Marcus danced along the cobbles, his bag swinging and pirouetting like a potbellied partner in a lunatic's ballet. Harvey shuffled along behind him.

"Well," Selena said. "That felt like shit, huh?"

Harvey pursed his lips. "That damn fool. Why'd he listen to me, huh? Who am I, to tell him his business? But he did it. Pulled out them keys and handed over every last Standard."

"It feels wrong," Selena admitted. "But there are no clean coups, Harvey. Hands always get dirty. You and Magnus and David kept this one cleaner than it had any right to be. You should be proud of that."

Harvey kicked a stone. It struck the edge of the boardwalk and skittered beneath an abandoned cart. "This wasn't our coup, kid. We were just a couple punk kids playin' at army. It was you who did it. Without you, we'da never had the guts."

"Should I be proud of that, or ashamed?"

Harvey shrugged. "I s'pose we'll see, in time."

Selena looked at Harvey. She considered his easy rapport with his fieldhands, recalled how he'd stuck up for her and Simon in their clandestine meeting a few days earlier, noted the way Kyle had deferred to him.

Fallowfield was short a Mayor. They'd need to pick a new one, and fast. Magnus was sure to offer his services, and there would be other old hands who felt their time to have a say was long past due. They'd hack it out one way or another, and if they were really bent on change they'd put it to a vote. Selena didn't know this place or its people well enough to guess what the outcome of that might be.

But she knew who she'd vote for.

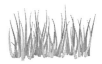

Simon sat in the back of the wagon, knees drawn up to his chest. The relief on his face when he saw Selena was palpable; it dribbled off him like sweat. He scooted aside, making room for Selena in the straw-stuffed bag that comprised their only seat. Marcus vaulted in after her, landing with the hushed effortlessness of a pouncing cat. He shoved his face into the burlap bag and breathed deeply, reeling like a man drunk on ether.

"Is there a finer smell than this in heaven and earth, children? I would guess not." He spun the bag shut and stuffed it into his rucksack.

"Okay, you've got what you're after. Now it's your turn to live up to our bargain."

"Did you ever doubt me, Lena? We go west. But first I must make a little stop."

"No stops. You said the west coast."

"It is a long journey, yes? It cannot be done in a single night. And this errand will not take us out of our way." Marcus patted his rucksack. "Once my debts are paid, I will not rest until you and your brother set your bare feet in the waters of the Far Ocean."

"Past the mountains will do just fine."

The driver climbed onto his perch and set the wagon rolling. Selena watched as Fallowfield rolled past her, its boardwalks and timber houses and cobblestones sliding from view. The ramparts came next, still manned by men in cambric shirts with rifles clutched to their chests. They nodded to Selena as she passed. Next came the fields, acre upon acre of fecund farmland, a mosaic of green and russet and gold. They seemed to stretch on forever, but soon enough the yellow locust closed its jaws around them and Selena saw what forever truly looked like. Sickly yellow-grey stalks touched every horizon, an expanse so vast it seemed poised to jump up and swallow the sky itself. The endless miles scrubbed Fallowfield from her memory, left its image faded and blurred. Its bountiful harvests and green hills felt like something she'd read about in a book once, a land pivoting on the chiasmic ridge between history and myth. Selena looked at Simon, staring back in the direction from which they'd come. She touched his arm, stirring him from his thoughts.

"Do you miss it?" she asked.

Simon paused, thinking. "A little bit. But what good does it do?"

"None," she answered. "None at all." She put an arm around his shoulder and squeezed. Simon, shocked, squeezed back willingly.

Some miles later, Selena realized that her question had been vague, and she couldn't say whether Simon had been referring to Fallowfield or New Canaan. She turned to ask him, but found him curled up on his straw cushion, eyes shut, breathing low and even. Best not to wake him, she figured.

In the end, it didn't much matter either way.

EPILOGUE: A Circle of Thorns

The man who called himself The Mayor of Fallowfield gripped the edge of his desk, a rictus of silent fury stapled to his face. Sitting was agony—he wanted nothing more than to collapse prostrate on the floor and whimper—but he forced himself to remain upright. A leader should maintain a certain decorum at all times.

His Shepherds stood around him in a nervous semi-circle, watching, saying nothing. A few studied the carpet, paying particular attention to the red stains by the door. Others glanced out the window, contemplating a final charge against the men besieging them, or perhaps calculating the best way to give themselves up. The Mayor didn't blame them for thinking such thoughts.

That wasn't true. He blamed every damn one of them to hell and back.

His chest itched where clumsy black stitches held his punctured skin together—his Shepherds were competent field medics, professional and effective under pressure, but they lacked finesse. Still, they'd drawn two bullets from his chest and closed up the wounds with remarkable efficiency, working even as he punched and clawed and screamed for his sunglasses, eyes shut tight enough to burst blood vessels. Eventually someone set them on his face, a greater relief than when the last bullet came free. He studied the bullets now, lined up on his desk all blunted and bloody. Not a pretty sight, but they took his mind off the damn itching.

Twelve days. Twelve days drinking from toilet cisterns and eating clumsily-prepared root vegetables and counting his miseries by candlelight. They'd siphoned what water they could from the pipes before that pustule Magnus shut off his water, but that was little enough. Soon they'd be dry, and thirst cut much quicker than hunger. Half the Sheps would turn before the week was out, and the rest would follow close behind. He should give up, spare himself and his men the unpleasantness of a prolonged siege. But he still had one straw to cling to, and he could not pry his fingers from it no matter how absurd a lifeline it had begun to seem.

New Canaan was coming.

They were later than expected, much later. The Mayor's radio entreaties had summoned only silence robed in a little static. Eventually some cretinous farmer had remembered to kill the electricity, and now he could make no more. Despite these setbacks, The Mayor knew they would come. They had to. A leak of the data from the Blue Vole project—even the slightest possibility of one—would be a full-on catastrophe for the state. News of it would resonate across Jericho. The Archbishop would have no choice but to act, lest all his plans tumble down on top of him.

And when they got here and discovered that the Floods were gone, and the data stick along with them?

Well, The Mayor had bluffed his way out of execution once before. Perhaps he could manage again.

Able to resist no longer, The Mayor scratched at his stitches. The sewn flesh burned, but more worrying to The Mayor was the way his rib sang a high hollow note of pain at the touch. It was an ugly hurt, much like an abscessed tooth. Not a pleasant simile, especially when one's internal organs lay in close proximity to the affected area. He opened his mouth to speak, let out a noise like a rusty hinge swinging shut, cleared his throat, and tried again.

"Where's McCuthers?"

"Sir?" asked a young Shepherd, his lineless face covered in blond stubble. *Who's this one?* The Mayor wondered. *I don't even know all their names any more. Bernard was the one who kept track of all the names.* Spit flooded The Mayor's mouth, its taste coppery and sour. He swallowed.

"McCuthers. Get him for me, please. I'd like him to take another glance at his handiwork." The Mayor motioned to his injured chest. *A good man, McCuthers. Quick hands.*

"He's, er … he's gone, sir."

"Gone?" *A defector? That no good bastard. I always hated him.* "Popped out for a pint at the Rye and Sickle, has he? I was unaware that there were many places to go at the present juncture. I should explore my options more carefully."

"No, I mean *gone* gone, sir. Dead. He got shot in the battle. It was Gervais who stitched you up."

Who the hell is Gervais? The Mayor scratched the skin beneath his hairline. His fingers came away hot and drenched. His forehead felt like a rock in a Gilead sauna. *Fever. Well, if I must die, I'd prefer to do so at the hands of the highest form of life available. In this case, I suppose even bacteria outstrips those oafs camped outside my door.*

The Mayor sank into his chair, his hands hanging over the armrests like so much wet laundry. He figured he should tell one of the Shepherds to check his medical stores for aspirin, but couldn't convince his mouth to undertake such an arduous task. *Finished,* he thought. *Just another sad little corpse scarcely fit to feed the yellow locust.* That's the best his beleaguered body could hope for. There was no way Magnus was going to bury him in town.

A vibration rose through the floor, setting the building's ancient foundations to creaking and rattling the windows in their panes. *A bomb? No, too sustained and too even. A piece of machinery, most likely.* The Mayor sucked his teeth. What nefarious siege engine did the farmers possess that was big enough to shake the earth?

The Shepherds seemed to be asking themselves similar questions.

They crowded the window in an effort to see beyond the rolling hills. A quiver of excitement worked through The Mayor's fingers. He pushed himself upright, biting back a cry as the skin around his stitches stretched. A few Shepherds looked back at him, surprised. They cleared a path as he hobbled to the window. The glass felt good and cool against his forehead.

From the manor's vantage point atop Shepherd's Hill, The Mayor could just see beyond the city ramparts. His window looked east, where the locust conquered a thousand miles of broken farmland. There was nothing that way but stalks of poison grass. At least, not on most days. Today something else made its way through the plains. Something with a belly full of thunder and size enough to set the locust trembling. The Mayor waited, hands pressed to the glass, and saw a standard rise from the sickly fields, a great blue banner borne on a long steel pole. Emblazoned on the blue field was a symbol that once made The Mayor gnash his teeth, but that now set a balm upon his vision like the resurrection it was supposed to represent.

On the blue field sat a white cross surrounded by a circle of thorns. New Canaan had arrived.

Acknowledgements

The process of writing *Yellow Locust* began in autumn 2008, when a striking image flashed through my mind on my way home from class at the University of New Brunswick: a brother and sister alone in a sea of yellow grass, picking through the scraps of a city that had died long before. It concluded nearly ten years later, as I reviewed final proofs with my infant daughter on my lap, while her older sister asked—for the fourteenth time—if I was done yet, so she could sit at the computer and type.

Clearly, a lot happened to me in the interim. I'd like to express my heartfelt thanks to the many people who have helped me during that long stretch of years.

To my classmates at York University and UNB, whose friendship and gentle yet unflinching criticism helped hone my strengths as a writer and whittle away the worst of my excesses: Claire Kelly, Sean Patrick Nolan, Luke Gobert, Mike Doyle, Benjamin Griffin, April Ripley, Corinna Chong, Jeremy Whiston, Chris Button, Nick Faeita, Robert Ross, and Matthew Heiti. To the professors at both schools, whose support and guidance encouraged me to continue writing: Richard Teleky, Priscila Uppal, Shyam Selvadurai, Ray Robertson, Ross Leckie, and Mark Jarman, whose discussions inevitably spilled over from the classroom into the grad house bar, where they became even more fascinating, if slightly less coherent. To my employers, former and current, at the CHILD Studies program and the Bruyère Research Institute, who took a chance on a young English major venturing out into an unfamiliar field: Nicole Letourneau, Simone Dahrouge, and Clare Liddy.

Thank you to my agent, Alec Shane, whose edits and insight have enriched this novel by an incalculable degree. Thanks also to Georgia McBride, Jennifer Million, Tara Creel, and the rest of the Month 9 Books team. Having strangers believe enough in your work to shoulder the massive burden of getting it published is a great honor, and I appreciate it immensely.

Thank you to my family: my mom and dads , my sister Madeline, and my grandparents, extended family, and in-laws. All of you have helped me in more ways than I could name.

Lastly, thanks most of all to my wife, Chantal, who tolerated my almost pathological secrecy about my writing and waited patiently for several years until *Yellow Locust* was finally ready for fresh eyes.

Justin Joschko

Justin Joschko is an author from Niagara Falls, Ontario. His writing has appeared in newspapers and literary journals across Canada. *Yellow Locust* is his first novel. He currently lives in Ottawa with his wife and two children.

OTHER MONTH9BOOKS TITLES YOU MIGHT LIKE

STANLEY AND HAZEL
THE SPONSORED

Find more books like this at http://www.Month9Books.com

Connect with Month9Books online:
Facebook: www.Facebook.com/Month9Books
Twitter: https://twitter.com/Month9Books
You Tube: www.youtube.com/user/Month9Books
Blog: www.month9booksblog.com

"Stanley & Hazel has spooky thrills, snappy dialogue, and rich historical detail. It makes for a swell read and one that fans of Libba Bray's Diviners won't want to put down!
- NEW YORK TIMES BESTSELLING AUTHOR JESSICA DAY GEORGE
STANLEY & HAZEL
A dark discovery.
A forbidden relationship.
A dangerous path.
BY JO SCHAFFER

THE
SPONSORED

DON'T BREAK THE RULES.
DON'T FOLLOW YOUR HEART.
DON'T GET CAUGHT.

CAROLINE T. PATTI

CPSIA information can be obtained
at www.ICGtesting.com
Printed in the USA
FFOW03n0524240418
46319965-47881FF